"The Berserker stories [...] tradition of *The Red Badge of Courage* [...] Western Front."

"Saberhagen's Berserkers are not only a great literary invention, they also reflect our deep and real concerns about technology run amok."

"Saberhagen has given SF one of its most powerful images of future war in his Berserker series."

"One of the most interesting series in modern SF."

"Fred Saberhagen has proven he is one of the best."

BERSERKER FURY®

Tor Books by Fred Saberhagen

FRED SABERHAGEN

BERSERKER®

FURY

TOR®

A TOM DOHERTY ASSOCIATES BOOK
NEW YORK

This is a work of fiction. All the characters and events portrayed in this book are either products of the author's imagination or are used fictitiously.

BERSERKER® FURY

Copyright © 1997 by Fred Saberhagen

A Tor Book
Published by Tom Doherty Associates, Inc.
175 Fifth Avenue
New York, NY 10010

Tor Books on the World Wide Web:
http://www.tor.com

Tor® is a registered trademark of Tom Doherty Associates, Inc.

ISBN: 0-812-55376-4
Library of Congress Catalog Card Number: 97-1157

First edition: August 1997
First mass market edition: December 1998

Printed in the United States of America

0 9 8 7 6 5 4 3 2 1

BERSERKER FURY®

ONE

One smashing impact after another buffeted the little spy ship, the blasts coming so fast some overlapped. Wave-fronts of radiation hurled by weapon explosions smote like atmospheric shock waves against sagging defensive fields and melting armor. A few minutes ago, under the first probing phase of the attack, the ship had quickly lost its disguise, revealing its egg-shaped Solarian hull to the optelectronic senses of the killer, the berserker computer that was directing the attack from a thousand kilometers away. Ever since that moment of discovery the onslaught of beams and missiles had come on furiously and without pause, as if the berserker were enraged and triumphant. As if a computer could feel those emotions, on having exposed the ship's deception, ferreting out a Solarian artifact inhabited by badlife.

The goal of each and every berserker's basic programming was the destruction of all life in the Galaxy—with a special effort directed against badlife, defined as those organic units that actively resisted their own annihilation, the fate ordained for them by the berserkers' programming.

During the thousands of years in which this program of sterilization had been in progress, Solarian humans had turned out to be the worst badlife of all. And sometime in the early stages of that age-old project, at an epoch when humans on Earth were dwelling in caves and wielding spears and clubs against their enemies, the berserkers had eliminated their own organic creators.

The control cabin of the Solarian ship was crowded with a dozen armored human bodies. Here the battle stations of the ship's entire crew had been ergonometrically, mathematically arranged for the utmost in efficiency and comfort. The great majority of the twelve suits of armor were now junk; most of the human flesh was pulp. The three people who still lived had been saved by armor and by luck, and by the layers of inertial damping, first inside the cabin, then inside their suits.

The artificial gravity, which in warships was designed for heroic reliability, surged and struggled to compensate for the pounding of the near-misses, the jolting of solid fragments beating on the hull at bullet speed and sometimes coming through. A darkness deep as that of death itself obtained inside the cabin now, but like death itself it failed to register on human eyes. In this ship, with everyone at battle stations, no human senses perceived the enemy, or any of the surrounding world, save through the filter of sophisticated symbols, projecting a virtual reality. The head of each surviving crew member was sealed and shielded inside an eyeless, windowless helmet, a casque combining the functions of protection and control. The helmets administered modest doses of light and sound, small portions fit for human senses to endure.

Until now the fight had not been entirely one-sided. Almost, but not quite. The spy ship's beam projectors were blazing too, aimed at a foe that seemed too big to miss. For a few seconds at a time the spy ship was able to launch bursts of small missiles at the berserker. Their blasts rocked the enemy of all life in its charging, zigzag course. But still the death machine came on, closing at a rate of kilometers per second with the small ship and the three human lives it still contained. The Solarian drive had been disabled now, and it seemed impossible to try to run away.

The onrushing monster, now less than a thousand kilometers distant, aiming and propelling itself missile-wise through space, was the size of a hangar that could have accommodated a dozen spy ships. It was one of the latest generation of a machine race, whose first members had been built and programmed many thousands of years ago.

Ignoring the Earthly weapons now pounding against its defensive fields and armor, the unliving enemy kept up its staccato assault on the Solarian ship with beams and missiles, shredding fake mineral encrustations, the last remnants of the spy ship's failed disguise, gouging and melting holes right through the solid hull beneath. The possibility of the berserker's own destruction meant nothing to it, as long as it could advance its programmed purpose.

The fight raged on between the ravaging berserker and the increasingly helpless human spy ship. The remnant of the livecrew, shell-shocked and shaken in their armor, had almost abandoned any attempt at choosing tactics, and were depending heavily in their conduct of the fight upon their own computer hardware. For the last few minutes the Solarian ship had been itself operating in something approaching berserker-mode, gunlaying systems locked on the one, the seemingly indestructible target, weapons firing at full capacity.

For the greater part of another minute, a time that seemed almost an eternity to the three who were compelled to live it, the tactical situation did not change.

But the disparity in size and power and armament was too great. The ship, which still contained three lives, had not a tenth of the attacker's bulk, and could not nearly match its firepower. On and on the unliving killer came, lurching and staggering in its contested passage. Now the damned thing was only nine hundred kilometers distant. Now only eight. To the three humans still gasping air aboard the Solarian spy ship, depending on their body armor to keep from being fried, it was an embodiment of death that looked unstoppable. The ship had taken heavy hits, the crew cabin had already been penetrated by fragments from more than one shot, and the three sat in their combat chairs surrounded by the armored corpses of their shipmates.

For tens of light years in every direction, these three Solarian survivors—and their unliving enemy outside, relentlessly trying to dispatch them—were the only agents of intelligent purpose.

The trio of live humans on the little ship—two men, one woman—following the burned-in rituals of their training, exchanged terse comments, bits of information, and orders among themselves. But now and again there came on intercom, from one of them, the sound of a sharply drawn breath, as if by one suffering an agony of fear.

And again, in an interval between necessary communications, one of the two male voices, that of Spacer Second Class Traskeluk, was abruptly raised in song, one of the Templar battle chants.

Traskeluk's shipmates paid the outburst no attention. Knowing him as they did, a singing challenge to the enemy at this moment came as no surprise. And all of them were very busy, struggling with their own private demons.

Confined at their battle stations, the three survivors in the cabin were unable to see or touch one another except by means of instruments. Their trio of heads remained muffled in their respective helmets, delicate hardware that melded their minds with their machinery, keeping them also in indirect contact with all of their surroundings. They kept up a fretful babble of communication, in which they had long ago abandoned the prescribed military forms. Off and on Traskeluk continued his ragged song. Somewhere one of the ship's faithful machines was still recording each utterance of the living crew, keeping a record of this struggle that no organic ears or eyes would ever read.

All three of those still surviving were junior members of the crew. The spacecraft commander was dead, so was the copilot, so were all the senior officers who would otherwise have taken over.

"Drive's now inoperable. We've been hit again—" That was the other man, Spacer First Class Sebastian Gift.

"—force fields can't hold—" A woman's voice this time, that of Ensign Terrin. She was, by a small margin, the ranking person still left alive.

And the whole ship shuddered with yet another impact. There was nothing in the least virtual about the force that shook the displays in all the helmets.

Their spy ship had been equipped with a lifeboat for emergency use, but now the ship itself, in its imperturbable voice of superhuman clarity, reported to the three survivors that their lifeboat had been wrecked, hull stove in by the last incoming hit. Not that it seemed likely to be of much use to them anyway, in the present situation.

As the seconds ticked by, out of the terse three-way conversation emerged the form of rationality—a plan. At last it was the woman, the ranking surviving crew member, who said decisively: "We're bailing out of this. Prepare to abandon ship."

"We won't last ten seconds out there—" Gift was babbling, almost incoherent.

"Shut up! We've got one thing to try. Someone's got to ride the bike over to the extra courier and drive it closer—that'll save maybe thirty seconds."

The voice of command made a lifeline into Gift's sealed helmet, breaking the spell of paralysis that sheer terror was beginning to impose. Like all the other voices, other sounds he heard while at his battle station, it issued from no visible source in the helmet's virtual displays. At the moment the visuals projected at close range into his eyes were an orchestration of sheer terror, symbols of the berserker and its weapons starkly outlined against a starry universe devoid of help or mercy. In a more peaceful epoch, Gift had chosen for the background of his virtual sky a lovely summer blue, and inside his helmet that color persisted now, as if in savage mockery.

The voice of the invisible Terrin, quavering once or twice,

on the verge of breaking with fear and strain, still came through plainly. "Nifty, you can best be spared from your battle station. Break out the scooter, get over to the spare courier. We're going to ride it out of here."

Gift gasped an acknowledgment of the order. He understood that the ensign was sending him out to be killed. But he was going to be every bit as dead if he stayed here.

In an attempt at disguise similar to that which had failed to protect the spy ship itself, the spare courier had been coated with material in an attempt to make it look realistically like another piece of space debris, and then stored in space at a distance of several kilometers.

The full complement of robot couriers that normally rode inside the spy ship had already been used up, fired off with cargoes of information, in the course of a successful months-long mission.

There came the sound of a muffled impact, much lighter than a hit from a berserker weapon. All three of the survivors knew a chilling fear that a berserker boarding machine might have got onto the spy ship. That could mean that the enemy, now computing victory in this skirmish as mathematically certain, was willing to delay their final destruction in an effort to capture at least one of them alive.

Traskeluk broke off his song. His speaking voice came on, quite rational, making an alternate suggestion. They could, he said, bring the available robot courier directly into the fight, instead of using it to escape. They could send it on a kamikaze ramming attack against the berserker.

But that plan was overruled by the ensign, rejected in favor of one that might get all three out of this alive, and whose success seemed less totally unlikely: All three humans ought to be able to fit their unsuited bodies inside the one courier. They could make a run for it that way.

Traskeluk did not argue for his own plan. Singing sporadically now in his deep voice, Traskeluk half-crazily added another verse to the Templar battle hymn, a borrowed portion of some even more ancient song:

Mine eyes have seen the glory of the coming of the Lord;
He is trampling out the vintage where the grapes of wrath
* are stored*

Over the preceding twenty seconds of life-and-death combat, the enemy's progress had been slowed considerably by the spy ship's squandering what were almost its last weapons. Of course a mere slowing meant very little; a berserker could no more be discouraged than a runaway ground train. Seven hundred kilometers now. Now only six.

For several minutes now the outcome of the battle had no longer been in any doubt. Enough evidence was in. The berserker was not going to be stopped, not by anything its present opponent might be able to do to it; but it had taken hits and it was damaged. It had to be damaged, and if you set a courier on autopilot—like a smart missile—and tried to ram the damned thing with it, the berserker might be sufficiently distracted to give the spy ship with its small weapons a chance to get in a decisive blow.

Even using to maximum effect every bit of Solarian hardware still on hand and functioning, the three humans had lost all reasonable hope that they might prevail against this foe. With perfect timing and a good share of luck, the best they *might* do was to prolong the struggle for a few more minutes.

He hath loosed the fateful lightning of His terrible swift
* sword;*
His truth is marching on.

Spacer Nifty Gift's hands were shaking inside their armored gauntlets, as he turned off the audio coming on intercom from Traskeluk's position—it was either break off communication, it seemed to Nifty, or go mad. But still Gift could hear the singer directly, through both helmets, his own and the singer's. And Gift's raw nerves were screaming. He wanted to bellow at Traskeluk to shut up. The berserker had probably tapped into their intercom by now, so it could listen to whatever hopeless plans they might be making. Did the damned fool have to reveal to the enemy how lunatic he was?

Traskeluk's behavior also irritated the woman who was now in command. Ensign Terrin couldn't be sure, in the midst of all the noise, if he had heard and acknowledged her latest decision or not.

The beleaguered three had already done almost all that they could do, launching their last salvo of defensive missiles. And it was plain that everything they could do was not going to be enough.

The plan improvised on the spur of the moment by the acting ship commander, Ensign Terrin, was the only one that offered any chance at all. It seemed to hold open one slim hope for the survival of the three. One of them was going to have to get aboard the robot courier—there was sufficient room inside for a man in armor to do that—and then, giving careful orders by voice or keyboard, ride it back to pick up the other two. Somehow three, jamming their armored bodies into space inadequate for one, would try to take an interstellar jaunt to safety.

A minimum of two livecrew members were required to maintain effective fire control aboard the spy ship, and for tuning what was left of the defensive fields. Each organic brain had an important role to play in combat, where living thought coupled with optelectronic computation had proven slightly more effective than either mode of decision-making alone. The ship might have been commanded to fight on in robot mode—but at the moment that would have been immediately fatal.

With precious seconds draining away, the enemy still came on, drawing a small crowd of human-friendly robots, built more for spying than for combat. Terrin in the last few minutes had summoned these devices home, in a tactic analogous to the old Terran one of drafting schoolchildren in the last stages of a war. It was not at all the kind of job that these robots were good at, but like well-trained children they made no protest. Relentlessly the berserker smashed out of its way this bumbling swarm of trivial obstacles, indifferently enduring the ineffective violence of human countermeasures, smart bombs, and booby traps. Once, twice again it was hit, but nothing stopped it and on it came.

That deadly progress, which had been briefly slowed, was speeding up again. Inside Spacer Gift's helmet, presented on his instruments, that dread shape seemed to swell up bigger as it came, now blotting out the Core and half the Galaxy behind it. For centuries the race of Earth-descended humanity had been battling the berserkers, ancient and lifeless enemies of all Galactic life.

A final terse and hasty exchange of words among the three, and then Spacer First Class Sebastian Gift was on his way.

"Get going!" Terrin barked.

"Acknowledge!"

Gift sprang into action. At that moment, under the pressure of extreme fear, all his mind could really focus on was that he was being allowed—no, he was actually being ordered—to get out of the doomed ship and get away.

Although the crew had already turned over most of the details of fighting to their ship's optelectronic brain, there still remained urgent business to be accomplished: Destroying certain equipment and information to keep them from being captured. That could no longer be postponed; it would take time, and would eventually mean getting out of the soup bowls and climbing about through the ship's various compartments.

A scooter was local space transportation for one, a compact machine whose size and shape suggested an Earthly motorcycle without wheels. By this means Spacer Sebastian Gift ought to be able to reach the courier a full minute before the other two could possibly get there, their bodies propelled by only the feeble jets of their space armor. Once inside the courier and taking its controls, moving its considerable bulk gently with its low-power thrusters, Gift would ease it back to pick up the other two, who would be space-swimming toward it. This would enable all three survivors to get out of the berserker's reach a full thirty seconds earlier than any other plan would make an escape possible.

The survivors had good reason to hope that the damaged

berserker machine would be unable to overtake the courier once the latter had plunged into superluminal flight.

Gift had already undone the catch on his control helmet and slipped it off. With a practiced grab that was almost a continuation of the same motion, he seized the helmet of his suit armor from its nearby rack and pulled it on.

Immediately upon his disconnection from his combat station, a clear and pleasant light had sprung alive inside the cabin, illuminating heretofore invisible devastation. As Gift's space helmet clicked into place, mating seamlessly with the neck of his armored suit, he took one last direct look, through his statglass faceplate, at his shipmates alive and dead. When seen directly, the two who were still alive, sealed away in armor as they were, their suits all splashed with others' blood, looked no more animated than the rest. The silent majority were only slumped suits of armor. Two had died in spectacularly horrible fashion, each body and its protective suit all twisted and torn together, flesh and metal intermingled.

With the appearance of the berserker, the normal world had dissolved into a kind of nightmare, and none of this could really be happening. And yet it was.

Gift noticed with a shock of horror that his own suit was as red and bloody as the rest.

Now moving like a sleepwalker, Spacer Gift also unplugged from its nearby console, and carried along with him, a recorder unit, the only copy of the last information compiled by the spy ship's computers. Those computers were already being melted down with destructor charges.

Averting his eyes hastily from the worst, Gift undid the restraints holding him in his combat couch, and levered himself out. A moment later he was heading for the hatch connecting with the compartment where the space scooter waited.

Inside the control cabin of the spy ship there were now only two people still alive. Two breathing figures, sharing space with nine broken and unbreathing dolls and one empty chair. Armored suits bound into chairs, control helmets in operation making their heads mere blobs of silver haze. They were counting down the seconds that passed before they followed Gift.

Now a fresh clangor of alarms filled what was left of the cabin atmosphere with useless noise, and somewhere air was leaking with a steady shriek.

Sealed into his combat armor, Spacer Gift slid into the compartment where the scooter was stored, and breathed a profound sigh of relief when he saw the little vehicle appeared to be still undamaged. In another five seconds he had opened the proper hatch and dragged the scooter out into space with him. Step out of your ship in this quadrant of the Gulf and your armor turned brilliant with the light of many thousand suns, all of them near enough to be distinguished individually, against the background of the vastly greater star clouds beyond—and beyond those, the galaxies.

He drew a deep breath, freed from the confines of the ship.

Out here, space was a great emptiness crammed with light. The glowing void of space painted a scintillating surface upon Gift's armored suit, which immediately began to ping and groan, resonating with the gusts of radiation that combat sent washing through the local area. No suit could protect him for long against blasts of such intensity.

The firing went on. Gift's armor rang and shook, under the impact of blasts of virtual particles, newly hatched from vacuum, evoked by the close proximity of space-bending violence.

He had hesitated momentarily on the way, without fully realizing that he had done so. A powerful shoulder weapon of rifle-stock design was riding in a kind of scabbard attached to the bulkhead just above the scooter. Gift hesitated momentarily, then left the rifle in its holster, certain it would be useless against the monster that pursued. Of course the enemy, in its relentless quest for knowledge of the badlife and their ways, might possibly have dispatched small fighting machines to close with the Solarian ship and board it, and against those small machines the carbine would probably be effective. But Gift feared that carrying it would slow him down.

· · ·

Sebastian Gift was darkly handsome, lean and nervous, wiry and stooped when standing in full gravity, yet somewhat taller than the average. A young man, like so many in the military, with all the agility of youth. Despite Gift's bulky armor he leapt—or came as close to leaping as was possible under the conditions—astride the space scooter, which would be able to convey his suited form the necessary few kilometers in less than a minute.

A transponder on the courier fed the scooter its tight-beam beacon as soon as he called for it. Grimly he oriented himself, using nearby nebulae and the almost-unmistakable glory of the Galactic core as landmarks. Once he was sure he had the scooter headed in the right direction, he commanded full acceleration. He experienced the fierce inertial pressure only dimly as it was moderated by the damping fields within his suit. Rapidly the spy ship dwindled behind him, becoming no more than a dull dot against a fiery background.

Gift tried not to look over his shoulder at what might be coming after him. His imagination could already picture, all too well, the several possibilities. If he turned, it was unlikely that he would be able to actually see anything coming even if it was, and even more unlikely that he could react in time to anything he saw, so indeed the effort was quite useless. Still he could not keep from turning his head, looking out through his helmet's faceplate for the berserker or one of its auxiliary machines, though he knew that it must be still many seconds, many kilometers, away. And finally he caught a glimpse of the thing that was about to kill them all—not the hull itself, of course, not at this distance, but rather the halo of flaring force fields the enemy was dragging with it, limned by the small impacts of Solarian missiles. There was no doubt that the death machine drew closer with every second that passed.

Gift had calculated at the start of his dash that he had perhaps one full minute to reach the spare machine and bring it back.

· · ·

The deep space environment surrounding the embattled ship, here in the vast gap between two arms of the Galaxy, was spectacular, though at the moment the living, organic participants were paying it no more attention than were the machines. The drama was being played out several thousands of light-years from Earth, and hundreds from any habitable planet, in the full light of the bright but vaguely defined starbank making up the far side of the great near-emptiness known to Earth-descended humanity as the Gulf of Repose.

Again the man, now thoroughly alone in space, shuddered at the idea that the berserker might be making an effort to capture him and his shipmates alive. Outside the double cocoon of ship and control helmet, riding the scooter far from the womb-like cabin, he felt exposed. Once more he struggled with the impulse to look behind him, and this time he was successful in fighting it down.

And now the courier, embodying what seemed the only remaining possibility of survival, was just ahead.

·······
T W O
·······

Only an hour ago the spy ship, with its full complement of a dozen crew members still alive— still complaining, making jokes, some asleep in their cabins, some immersed in their routines of work, and with no enemy in sight—had been going about its stealthy, intricate business while attempting to maintain its disguise as a mere chunk of rock. Of course rocks as big as spaceships were rare indeed at this distance from any solar system, and any berserker coming in detector range would likely be suspicious. In retrospect it was easy to conclude that the idea of trying to rely on a disguise had been hopeless from the start.

Even when they were discovered, the technique by which the ship and crew had been spying on berserker activity ought not to have been immediately apparent to the enemy—at least the people who made up the crew, and those who had sent them here, could hope their own activities and purposes would not be obvious.

And then the berserker, coming head-on out of flightspace in their direction, had shown up on the warning system. If there were going to be any survivors, they could ponder the question of whether that had been sheer bad luck, or something else.

Ever since the moment when the berserker machine had appeared on the spy ship's sensors, in the form of a ragged blob much different from the smooth routine shapes of berserker message couriers (which were, in a sense, the spy ship's natural prey), the tactical situation had been desperate. And from that moment until now, the crew of Earth-descended humans had been fighting for their lives. For the great majority, including all three who had thus far survived, it was the first experience of real combat.

And now to Spacer Nifty Gift, at this moment in the act of braking his scooter with its forward thrusters, it seemed an age ago, though it was less than a standard day, that he and other members of the spy ship's crew had argued and speculated among themselves on what they would do if they ever found themselves about to be captured. Suicide in such a case was the choice of many, and it was encouraged if not strictly required by somewhat ambiguous regulations. Else there had been no deathdream hardware installed in each crew member's head. One crew member's favorite position in the argument had been that someone should be chosen ahead of time, to shoot first his shipmates and then himself.

The question had come up in training, and in planning sessions, but had never really been resolved. That sort of thing could hardly be removed from the realm of individual choice. And the men and women of the unnamed spy ship's crew had their deathdreams to rely upon.

Now the robotic courier was swelling up to its full size in front of Gift, even as he slowed the scooter. Wrapped in its own disguise, the courier looked, at least to Solarian eyes, like spongy rock, for all the world like an age-old fragment of some demolished protoplanet. The spacer braked his scooter's drive by reversing its small jets. There hadn't been time to program the rudimentary autopilot.

With his closing velocity slowed to a walking pace, Spacer Gift was just in the act of reaching out to try to grab some handhold on the rugose camouflage surface of the courier's hull, when a near-miss blast from one of the berserker's minor weapons wounded him. The killing machine must have somehow spotted the darting scooter from more than a hundred kilometers away, and had spared one shot for him.

And just at the moment when it had seemed that the universe was about to grant him a reprieve from doom, treacherous reality instead thrust at him with a white-hot lance, impaling the left side of his body on what felt like a spike of fire.

For a moment a horrible illusion registered in Gift's shocked brain: His eyes and nerves seemed to be telling him that his left hand and forearm were completely gone. But a moment later his senses reassured him on that score—at least his armor—though one sleeve was punctured—was still basically all in one piece. He realized that there was no way as yet to be sure of the seriousness of the wound; the only thing certain right now was that the function of his left hand was suddenly much impaired.

Just before that numbing blast, Gift and his scooter had come almost to a complete halt relative to the robot courier. The emergency escape device he had been sent to fetch was now slowly rotating, near at hand, almost within arm's reach. Under the rough coating of plastics and composites, imitations of nature that made up half its seeming bulk, was a slender bullet shape some twenty meters long and no more than three broad at its thickest point. Spacer Gift kicked himself free of the scooter and in the same movement hurled himself at the courier, uttering a sob of terror. Using both arms, he caught a projection of the hull, some stuff that looked like dried mud, in a clanging embrace. With some relief he realized that he still had some movement in the fingers of his left hand, despite the pain. He could still use them, if he must, to keep himself alive. Meanwhile the space bike, abandoned and already forgotten, had gone spinning slowly away into infinity.

One of the thousand procedures drilled into space combat crews in training was how to find the entrance to a disguised Solarian ship. Reading the subtle markers, tearing chunks of dried plastic foam away with his armored hands, Gift quickly located the small, inconspicuous hatch in the smooth metal curve beneath the foam. Getting the hatch open, then trying to figure out how he would get his armored body in through the opening—it was going to be a tight fit—he found himself agonizing intensely over what he was going to do next. But there was no time to think, no time, just do what must be done. . . .

And in another moment Gift had succeeded in dragging his body, bulky with its damaged armor, in through the awkward opening. The promise of shelter within, however illusory, seemed all the greater because the interior was as dark as a berserker's gut. He pulled the hatch shut tightly, and even with the movement of his arm the shadow of a question crossed his mind: Why was he bothering to shut the hatch? Open or closed wasn't going to matter, simply going back toward the fight, a couple of klicks through normal space.

The interior, obviously never intended to carry passengers, was basically a cylinder of space sandwiched between two cylinders of metal less than a meter apart, the inner and outer hulls. A single dim interior light had come on automatically as Gift entered. Even as he reached for the awkward control panel just inside the hatch, and found himself disconcertingly upside down relative to the panel—here in this bare-bones environment there was no artificial gravity—the realization pounded him that rescuing his comrades would mean moving this vessel a distance of several kilometers straight toward the onrushing berserker, back in the very direction from which he had come.

If he continued to follow Ensign Terrin's orders—somehow, without Gift's planning it, what should have been a simple and automatic response to orders had turned into a question—*if* he now drove the courier back to try to help his shipmates, he would be putting himself practically in the grip of the God of Death.

And that realization was followed in a moment by another. The question had already answered itself. Going back there, moving his own body squarely into the path of irresistible, onrushing death, was something he clearly could not do. The fact that he was already wounded had little to do with the decision, but the decision had already been reached—and how blessedly simple it had turned out to be! That understanding left him quivering inwardly with sheer relief.

For once, automatically obeying orders, yielding to the demands of duty, was plainly not possible. Therefore he was going to have to follow some other course of action.

It seemed to Gift that his mind had in some sense abandoned ship. It was now standing apart and watching, helpless to make choices, unable to interfere, while his trained body took over and swung into action. And it was a revelation to discover that his body, one-handed and awkward but still effective, seemed to have no purpose in all the world save that of saving its own skin.

Gift's armored fingers were pressing contacts on the panel, powering up the courier's drive. He had to struggle with the elementary flight controls, which in their very simplicity seemed baffling. For some reason Gift seemed to have almost forgotten whatever scanty training he had had with such devices.

Compelled to look back once more toward the ongoing nightmare—his body insisted on seeing what was happening—Gift used what magnification he could wring out of the inadequate flat-screen presentation, which was all he had available. In a moment he sucked in his breath sharply. There were Traskeluk and Ensign Terrin, both of them somehow still alive. At first, on the small screen and at the distance, he could barely pick them out, could not tell which was which, but there unmistakably were the two small, dark forms outlined against a glowing gas cloud at an astronomical distance in the background.

A moment later he was able to distinguish Traskeluk, by the rifle he had now slung on his back. Trask was never happier than when he had a weapon in his hand, and on his way out of the doomed ship must have picked up the rifle Gift had chosen to leave behind. Terrin, like Gift, would probably have considered it only an extra burden and a waste of energy and time.

Two figures space-swimming on tiny suit-jets in Gift's direction, moving at a hopelessly lethargic pace—how small and slow mere humans were! The monster coming after them was going to overtake them in the next few seconds, catch them, and eat them up.

The radio in Gift's helmet crackled. If it was a real message, he couldn't make it out, through all the local noise. Not an unusual problem in combat. The noise might represent some final plea now coming through from one of his surviving shipmates, a few words urging him to hurry, or cursing him for not having done the job already. But—and the cold realization chilled him—it might be some fake message sent by the berserker itself, trying to lure him closer. Most likely his shipmates, if they were still alive, were maintaining radio silence, in hopes that the berserker might somehow fail to detect their fleeing figures.

If the message was a berserker trick, then it would certainly be a mistake to try to answer.

Now came a screeching blast of noise, as if weapons from both sides had detonated together, cutting all signals off.

A moment later the veil shrouding communications lifted again, just long enough for Gift to hear screams on the radio. He could see nothing clearly, but here was sharp, plain testimony that at least one of his comrades still survived. That one small chance, at least, remained for saving at least one of them.

Communication between Gift and his two remaining shipmates had been seriously disrupted by the noise of combat, and everything Gift could now see and hear from his new position in the courier indicated that the berserker was eating his two surviving shipmates alive, or at least was about to do so. That looked and sounded like Traskeluk's rifle flaring—he saw the enemy at close range now.

Gift couldn't stand to watch.

But then there was no reason why he should. Because everything that was going to happen now had already been decided.

Gift's suit radio was buffeting his brain with a din of destruction that seemed to go on endlessly. Outside the courier's hull, which was not much more than paper-thin, and almost useless as a barrier, the robot fight still raged. Weapons were slamming, explosive contacts made on metal and on nerves alike, and the two humans who had just left the spy ship went tumbling and spinning in their space armor.

Damn it all, the fight had to be *over!* There could be very little left of the spy ship by this time. But his eyes told him that part of the hull, at least, was still intact, some of the Solarian weapons still firing.

Back there, those last two remaining survivors were now gone, vanished into a blur of deadly pyrotechnics. All of his shipmates were dead, but he was still alive.

Gift could picture Traskeluk, who had great physical strength and quite a temper, facing the end of his life with anger, taking it out on somebody, mutinously striking down the smaller woman.

Time passed.

Spacer Gift became aware, belatedly, of the strange silence that now engulfed him. Then he realized that he must have turned his radio off, long seconds or even minutes ago.

Then he looked around him, turned his head as best he could, wedged in as he was beside the control panel on the courier. Around him in the confined volume there was almost nothing to be seen. His bulky suit fit with very little leeway into the space between two concentric hulls, on a machine that was not meant to carry a livecrew, or even a single passenger, except in the most dire emergency. Essentially there were no furnishings aboard, not even a chair or a lamp. There was of course no life support, no gravity. At least he was not bound to stay in some fixed location. With his suit radio patched into the panel, he could command the courier by voice orders from anywhere inside.

The drive had needed only a few seconds to power itself up. The courier was now fully awake in all its optelectronic senses. Its precisely limited intelligence was waiting to be told where to go. Gift realized, remotely, that he could still do the very thing Ensign Terrin had ordered him to do, be the hero everyone expected him to be, rush back at four or five Gs to confront death, on the chance that two people might still be alive and looking to be picked up, and they could try to cram themselves, all three, into this space.

Except that nothing had changed—he really couldn't make himself do that.

At the crucial moment of his last chance, Spacer Gift found himself still unable to face the virtual certainty of death. What use was a deathdream when you felt like that? And what he feared even more than obliteration was the prospect of becoming a berserker's captive, being skinned alive for crumbs of information, whose real value to either side in the war might well be nothing at all. Everyone had heard the stories, and no one denied that some of them were true. A captive could be tortured like a mouse in some incomprehensible experiment, part of the enemy's never-ending quest for understanding of the human condition.

This discovery concerning his own nature came upon him very suddenly. It was like yanking a door open and confronting beyond it an alien and totally unexpected shape. Facing such a fate was an impossibility, like willing oneself to pass through a brick wall. Whatever faint chance Terrin and Traskeluk might still have to save their lives depended absolutely on his bringing the courier back to them. But now he had discovered that their chances and their lives counted for very little with him.

Staring at the flat little panel just before him, an area on the inner hull not much bigger than a human face, and marked with glowing indicators, Gift found some of the symbols there confusing and others unintelligible. For some reason, probably some technician's oversight, the controls were labeled in a language that few people on the spy ship's crew would have been able to understand, and that Gift himself understood but poorly.

It would have taken him only a moment to punch in a command for a different language. But for some reason, a reason Gift later found beyond his understanding, he did not do so.

Even with the control panel labeled in the wrong language, the basics were clear enough. Gift didn't switch, as Terrin had ordered him to do, into the local maneuver mode. Nor did he use the keyboard or voice entry to command the courier into a kamikaze attack. Instead, his fingers, even as he watched them, were putting the unit into emergency lifeboat service. *There is no artificial gravity in here,* he reminded himself. *Nothing to protect your body from acceleration. You must remember to keep the subjective value very low.* Again Gift had the strong impression that his body was simply remembering and taking care of everything necessary to save itself, without any conscious decision on his part.

His precious flesh and blood, it seemed, had taken over direct control of his behavior, turning him away from abstractions called orders and responsibility, setting him running for safety. It seemed to Gift that his body had betrayed him—but it had saved its own life, and therefore his existence, in the process. Moral objections, concepts called rules and duty, were so much alien vapor—this was about sheer physical life or death.

It was as if he, Spacer Sebastian Gift, were watching, from some position of separation, the behavior of his body.

The decision had been made, and he was safely sealed inside the courier. The scene where the combat had taken place was fading, the radio uproar in his helmet had died away. The place where he had almost died was shrinking rapidly behind him. . . .

He could feel, through the thin metal surrounding him, the ongoing fine vibration that confirmed what the panel told him, that the courier's main drive had come awake. And then, only a moment later, came the inward twitch that meant that he and the vessel that bore him were now in flightspace. Acceleration, in the usual sense, had become meaningless.

And a wave of faintness came over the survivor as he realized that he was still alive. And the berserker was behind him now, behind him by more kilometers than a man could cover in a lifetime's walking.

Spacer Gift understood intellectually that the courier's autopilot, designed for efficient interstellar flight, was perfectly capable of getting him to Port Diamond, or to Fifty Fifty, or any of a number of other safe ports, in a matter of a few days.

But Gift's flight had not been under way for more than ten minutes before he began to be nagged by the feeling that something was wrong with the autopilot. Or maybe it was the drive that had a defect. And now—he was holding his breath, and listening—it seemed to him that he could hear a certain strange, small noise from inside the inner hull, at about the spot where the autopilot ought to be. He turned up the contact mike on his suit, put his helmet against the inner hull, and tried again to listen to it.

After a while he thought: Something odd there, yes. But it was hard to be sure.

In the back of Gift's mind an idea was slowly developing: That the other two survivors of the berserker fight were not here with him because of some terrible, unlucky error made by this courier's autopilot. Some glitch in the machinery had switched to lifeboat mode, had jumped the ship into flightspace before he'd ordered it to do so; he'd heard stories of such things happening. Whatever had happened to Terrin and Traskeluk, the hardware on which all three survivors depended was at fault.

It was utterly, mathematically impossible, of course, for Gift to do anything now to correct the error. Turning around and going back for the lost would be quite impossible. The courier's simple astrogation system could never be induced to return simply to its starting point.

A quarter of an hour after first becoming aware of the strange noise, Spacer Gift was working with great difficulty in the cramped space—difficulty, because he was slowly losing all remaining function and sensation in his left hand. Despite this handicap, he had located and dug out a small set of emergency tools, and had removed a panel from the curved inner hull, methodically trying to locate the deadly problem.

The more Nifty Gift looked at the readings on his little multimeter, the more strongly they suggested to him that something about the drive must be marginally off. Even though he couldn't remember exactly what the readings were supposed to be.

Yes, he decided, a minor mechanical failure of some kind had probably caused the drive to kick in prematurely. Some quantum effect in the fine circuits. Such things could happen, purely by accident, everyone knew that. Instead of going back for Traskeluk and the woman he had been carried light-years away, with no prospect of being able to get back. He, Nifty Gift, had been as helpless as any of his shipmates. That must be the correct explanation for what had happened.

Like all the most troublesome glitches, the fault would probably turn out to be something that could not be made to repeat itself on demand.

Now and then Gift tried with his right hand, compulsively but without much effect, to scrape away some of the dried brownish stains still clinging to the outside of his armor—he immediately knew what it was: the blood of some of his fellow crew members, spattered on him without his knowledge before he'd left the dying ship.

Astrogating manually—Gift's brief training, several years ago and almost forgotten, regarding how to manage that in case of emergency, came back—touching up the programs in the drive and astrogation units with the aid of a small computer, remembering to keep the subjective acceleration low at every point; there was no reason why he could not make his way home in this now-uncomplicated situation, barring a chance encounter with another berserker. And the chances of that were remote indeed.

For the three or four standard days (subjectively the time he spent sandwiched between the inner and outer hull was much

longer than that) of Sebastian Gift's journey toward his home,
a passage his tinkering seemed to have delayed only marginally,
the man alone in space indulged in luxurious thoughts of what
he was going to do when he got back to his familiar quarters
on Uhao, or back to Earth; his home planet. More accurately,
he tried to do so. He was really too uncomfortable to get much
fun out of any kind of luxurious thought.

He moved his body as much as he could, trying to ease the
growing cramps that seemed to afflict all the large muscles of
his arms and legs and torso, one or two groups at a time.

He thought the thin metal of the outer hull was bending,
denting, slightly with the pressure of his armor, the way he was
wedged in. He didn't think that was going to have much effect
upon his flight.

He turned over in his mind the situation regarding his
family, back on Earth. He didn't really want to think about such
matters now, but he had no choice.

To give himself something else to think about, he tried to
play chess in his mind. When the game refused to progress, the
mental board wiping itself clear every minute or so, he did his
best not to think at all.

He tried not to worry about his wounded hand and arm,
and in that effort he succeeded fairly well. Fingers, and even
whole limbs, after all, could be replaced.

Desultorily he scraped at the old bloodstains on his armor,
in the places where he could reach them with his good hand. But
eventually he decided he might as well let them stay.

Sleep came seldom to Nifty Gift during his sojourn in the
courier, and when it did come it was troubled with a full load
of ugly dreams. More than once it seemed that Traskeluk and
Terrin were with him on the courier, their armored bodies
crowding his, until he could no longer breathe. The sensation
of endless falling brought on by the lack of gravity engendered
a deep anxiety. His armor clanged against either the inner or
outer hull every time he moved any part of his body more than
five or six centimeters.

Once he woke from a dream on the verge of shouting, trying desperately to get Traskeluk to hush his roaring battle song. He awoke to eerie, almost perfect silence. There was only his own breathing, and the faintest possible scraping of metal against metal.

Spacer Gift was bringing home with him some good information, compiled by the spy ship's receivers and computers before they died—but of course he wouldn't be able to tell the debriefing officers whether the two humans who had been so unluckily left behind would have succeeded in blowing up the spy ship, or activating their deathdreams, before they were taken alive by the berserkers.

There were moments when Gift almost decided he couldn't even be sure whether the two had got out of the spy ship or not.

Gift found himself rehearsing the story he was going to tell the authorities when they questioned him, as they always questioned everyone who came back from a mission. After such close contact with the enemy, the debriefing would certainly be intense. He wanted to get his memory as clear as possible, to confirm the chain of events in his own mind, so he would not forget anything of importance.

Trouble was, his memory already seemed a little hazed regarding some of the important parts. Well, maybe those details weren't really so important.

Gift wondered whether he might actually have seen the spy ship go up in a killing blast, in which there could have been no survivors. There were moments when the image was vividly before him.

The last useful bit of intelligence, regarding the massive impending berserker attack that was aimed at Fifty Fifty as a springboard for an assault on Earth, had been recorded on board one of the ED ship's robot couriers, which had then, just before the spy ship was destroyed, been fired off at superluminal velocity toward the spy ship's base.

The spy ship and its crew had been in charge of an extensive network of robotic spy devices, which had succeeded in reading the information from a berserker courier device—or a series of such couriers, plying a route between an enemy fleet and its distant headquarters.

No more than half a dozen times, in the course of a war extending over a double handful of centuries, and many thousands of light-years, had clever Solarians enjoyed the great good fortune of being able to physically capture a berserker courier machine with its information content intact, and subject to their scanning.

Once or twice, after concluding a detailed examination, the Solarian spy masters had tried to send such a device on its way, hoping the enemy would never realize that the information it carried was compromised, and would act on it. Results were not sufficiently clear-cut to be able to say whether the procedure had succeeded or not.

In the case of physical capture, there was never any way to be sure whether or not the enemy ever discovered that its message courier had been tampered with. Scanning the information content of a device without impeding its physical passage was a much more subtle and valuable achievement.

One of the prime duties of human crew members who found themselves still alive in such a situation was to blow up their ship, if necessary along with themselves, thereby preventing the berserkers catching on to the fact that the vile badlife could now read many of their messages.

Gift tried to think ahead. When he got to debriefing, which would certainly be very soon after he made port, he would tell them that the spacecraft commander, before he was killed, and after him Ensign Terrin, had been too busy fighting the enemy to say anything about blowing up the spy ship. And he, Gift, assumed that Terrin had set the destructor charges before the last human had bailed out.

Another thing the debriefers would be likely to ask was if any of the crew, to Gift's knowledge, had used a termdream. Crew members on top-secret spy ships were generally sent out with their brains implanted with certain thought patterns, channels into which they were to turn their conscious thoughts in case of capture. Each was provided with a deathdream (the official name was *termdream*) scene to imagine in detail. A swiftly suicidal protection against interrogation. The death-dream was complex enough to minimize the danger of its being accidentally activated.

Under certain kinds of stress, a glowing icon of any chosen shape or color—Gift had chosen a pink elephant—appeared in the subject's visual field, and from that point on the procedure was rather like firing a blink-triggered carbine or other weapon. One could set off his or her deathdream without being able to twitch a finger or turn one's head. The procedure was made just a little too complex to admit of its being accomplished accidentally.

The standing orders were quite explicit. Once it was clear that capture of such a vessel by a berserker could no longer be avoided, the entire human crew had to blow up the ship—themselves with it if necessary. It was vital that the berserkers be left in possession of no more than a handful of wreckage. In that case it might be hoped that they would never realize that they had destroyed anything more than a disguised but basically ordinary scout ship.

Only after he had been alone in space for a full day did Gift come to understand that to some people, depending on how the story was told, his getaway might well look heroic. It could very well look like an all-out effort to save the data—when in fact it had been anything but that.

There was time and opportunity en route for the sole survivor to alter appearances just a little—Gift was not always fully aware that he was doing this—so that no one would ever, could ever, know that he had robbed two shipmates of their last chance for life, by concentrating on saving his own skin.

The courier, its autopilot still functioning accurately despite its partial disassembly, had brought its lone passenger and its still-unevaluated cargo of fresh information to a point in space well within the patrolled planetary system surrounding the sun called Uhao. The system's sole habitable planet was the site of a huge Solarian military-naval base, set on an island and beside a city, Port Diamond.

For four days inside the courier, traversing flightspace, confined in the oddly shaped, tomblike space that formed the only passenger accommodation, Gift's suited body had vibrated slowly—there was no room to drift—in what was effectively an absence of gravity.

When Gift was instructing the autopilot, there were one or two destinations other than the Uhao system that the spacer might have chosen, either of which would have kept him confined in the cramped space for a slightly shorter time. Several times en route he had regretted his choice. The journey, with no chance of getting out of any part of his armor even for a minute, had been maddening, irritating in the extreme. Especially since there had turned out to be something wrong with the sanitary plumbing in his suit. He had lived through the last two days beset by muscle cramps, by a growing stench that the suit's life support seemed unable to combat, and by skin irritation on his lower body, besides the ominous numbness and paralysis in his left arm.

No, he was absolutely sure that three people would never have survived the journey under these conditions. But Gift had picked Port Diamond without hesitation, at least partly because he knew, without consciously thinking about it, that he would be able to justify his choice if he were questioned.

He was afflicted too by waves of nausea, and his wounded arm continued to hurt. A feeling of tightness and throbbing indicated swelling in the forearm, and the fingers on that hand had ominously quit working altogether.

There were emergency food rations of a kind available inside Gift's suit, and with a little difficulty he could bring his right arm in from the suit's arm, and push a couple of fingers up into his helmet far enough to feed himself. At intervals he sucked recycled water through a tube.

All in all, the days of his solo flight added up to a very unpleasant time. But every time he thought that, he reminded himself that he was still alive, and his current problems receded into the proper perspective.

When the vessel (one could hardly call it a ship) that was bearing him home developed in its small optelectronic brain any information it deemed worthy of communicating to its passenger, it employed a small, tinny interior voice. The voice was barely adequate, like everything else by which the courier interfaced with its rider. These messages came rarely into Gift's helmet, and he thought most of them irrelevant, the equivalent of routine weather reports regarding conditions in local flight-space.

The first time during his ride that the courier really got Gift's attention was when the bored machine voice, in its unvarying tone, announced that he had arrived within the zone of his requested destination.

He shook his head and at first could not believe what he had just been told. He asked that the message be repeated.

On receiving confirmation that he was practically home free, Gift had the feeling that he was awakening from another bad dream, the worst and longest one that he had ever had.

Gradually, Spacer Gift allowed himself to accept the news. He had arrived in the outer reaches of a friendly solar system, teeming with life. The courier, now only a few hundred thousand klicks from Port Diamond base, was still running smoothly on an autopilot whose outer housing the only passenger had half disassembled.

Securely in the back of Gift's mind was the knowledge that now, after his poking and prodding at it, no way existed for anyone to tell whether there had really been anything wrong with the courier's astrogation system or not.

And presently it was a scout ship coming out from Fifty Fifty, on routine patrol, that contacted him on radio. He could hear a live, organic, human voice, telling him to stand by to be picked up.

Some four standard days after Spacer Gift had first scraped compulsively at the freeze-dried blood newly hardened on his armor, and had punched in some simple commands on the control panel of the robot courier, commanding it to carry him away from danger, the machine delivered him right on target, only a few million klicks from the planet where he had told it he wanted to be. Couriers, at least the purely robotic kind, were very good at following orders.

When his faithful rescuer had confirmed the arrival, Gift ordered it to shut down its drive, turn on a distress beacon to guide the folk who had already talked to him on radio, and stand by. No way was he going to try to steer this thing into a port, or even a close orbit.

Feeling a desperate need to get out of the cramped space, he still hung back, nagged by the feeling that he had forgotten something of great importance, that he had brought it in here with him and was forgetfully leaving it behind. But there was nothing.

Before he said goodbye to his prison cell he turned on his helmet light and looked once more at the half-disassembled autopilot. Its innards, mostly plain-looking, smooth-surfaced blocks of material marked with arcane engineers' symbols, were still partially exposed for testing. He hadn't been able to figure out exactly what it was that had prematurely triggered the drive in a combat situation, whisking him away from his comrades before he could come to their aid. Very likely, he thought, enemy action had been responsible.

And he noticed that his hand, his good hand, was shaking in its armored glove.

The spacer wondered if a berserker mindbeam, switching or scrambling information inside his skull, might have been responsible for his early departure from the scene of combat. He couldn't quite convince himself of that. But once he was under way, of course, there had been no turning back.

The luck that had favored Gift's survival over the last few days was with him still. The courier had been drifting in its new location for only a couple of hours when a patrol craft hailed it for the second time. The survivor answered at once, weakly but with great relief.

The response came in a male Solarian voice, crackling in faintly from millions of kilometers out, with four or five seconds' distance delay. Quite naturally the speaker sounded astonished that a robot courier should be carrying a live passenger. Astonished, and ready to deal with berserker tricks.

Under prodding by the wary voice, Gift recited his name, rank, and serial number, then tried to add some reassurance. Yes, he informed his questioner, he was still securely inside his armor. He'd be dead otherwise, for his present transportation wasn't pressurized. There would be no problem with opening the emergency hatch to get him out, without waiting until the courier was taken aboard some larger ship. In fact, even though he was wounded, and the integrity of his self-sealing armor had to be considered questionable, susceptible to springing a new hole if he moved about, he had every intention of getting himself out of the cramped place and waiting for his rescuers outdoors in space.

Gift ignored their brisk advice to stay just where he was, inside the courier, until they reached him. Figuring he knew more about his own situation than they did, with a decisive gesture, he turned his radio off. Then he set about the task of getting himself out through the little hatch, a process that turned out to be much slower and more awkward than getting in had been. Once again, of course, he had only one arm to manage things, letting the hurt one just trail along. The plugged spot in the suit's left arm held, through all the bumping and increased movement. The painkillers in his armor saw to it that pain remained no more than a faint annoyance.

Once free of the metal prison that had saved his life, Gift drew a deep breath and had a good look at the Port Diamond's sun, which was very Sol-like indeed.

Outside the courier, keeping a grip on the edge of the hatch with his good hand while he waited for his pickup to arrive, Gift felt like a man emerging from his tomb. He experienced a fantastic sense of relief on being able to unlimber his cramped body from the inadequate space—how could anyone ever have imagined that three people would fit in there? No way.

And a few minutes later, aboard the patrol craft, getting his body out of the space armor at last felt even better—when he dropped its last component thudding on the deck, his live audience wrinkling their noses at the sudden stench, he wanted to see it all gathered up by maintenance robots and dropped into the trash.

Within a few hours of being taken on board the patrol craft, Gift found himself cleaned up and dressed in fresh clothes, riding a wheelchair across the surface of Port Diamond's world, for the short trip from shuttle to ambulance, under a blue sky streaked with the dun-brown of defensive forcefields, like something risen from the chimneys of some ancient industry. His left forearm, or whatever might be left of it, had been immediately swathed in a bulky, protective bandage by his rescuers—Gift hadn't watched. He didn't know, and didn't really want to think about, whether he still had a hand in there or not. Instead he concentrated on the fact that his feet were at least within reach of solid ground again. His mumbled prayers for survival had been answered—maybe just a coincidence. But he'd have to look into that business of praying, he really would.

He'd do it someday soon, when he had time. As a down payment he now muttered a brief prayer of thanks to a vaguely imagined god of his childhood, adding a plea that he would never again have to leave this beautiful world—and looking around the spaceport.

Fate, or Someone, was looking after him. Alive! Thank God, thank all the gods of space and planets, he was still alive!

While the robot stretcher-medic bore him along on the short roll to the ambulance, he found himself frequently casting sudden glances back over his shoulder, and starting at unexpected noises.

Standing in a small group of people at the edge of the landing ramp was a certain man, who when seen from the rear looked remarkably like the late Ram Das, astrogator on Gift's spy ship. But when the fellow turned around, he was much older than Ram Das, though there was still a slight resemblance. Gift let out an involuntary gasp of relief.

Once down on the Uhaoan surface, with news of his survival and pending arrival spreading rapidly ahead of him, Gift was taken quickly to the base hospital, where he received immediate medical attention.

The first human medic who looked at his arm, after he had reached the ambulance, called immediately ahead to the hospital. Gift was unable to hear either side of the conversation.

Also waiting at the hospital for Gift's arrival, every bit as ready as the doctors and nurses, was a representative of Hypo, smiling, dapper in civilian clothes, and inconspicuous except for the specially coded communicator he carried in his hand. This fellow fell into step beside the stretcher as it rolled toward the entrance.

"Anything you want to tell me right away?" the man demanded without preamble, maintaining a brisk pace.

Gift rolled his head from side to side on the flat pillow.

Seemingly casual questions followed. Gift really began to tell his story for the first time. Soon the smug-seeming, know-it-all debriefer from Hypo was irritating the returning hero by assuring him that long experience had demonstrated that in fact three normal-sized Solarian adults *could* fit in, though of course they would have to get rid of their space armor first. The long narrow chamber could be pressurized, after a fashion, with breathable air. Water, food, and plumbing would all be limited to what the suits could provide. But there seemed no proof that it would have been absolutely impossible for three people to come through such a three-day ride alive.

Gift nodded soberly, in apparent full agreement. But privately he was telling himself: What the hell did any of these people know about riding a courier, these smug people who wrote the manuals? Had any of them ever actually *tried* it?

The second, which was also the longest and most difficult, session of Spacer Gift's debriefing took place while he lay flat on his back with his left side numbed, while the surgeons (separated from the debriefing talk by a transparent statglass wall) were working on his left arm. Everyone involved was occupied in this way for almost an entire hour.

He officially reported the complete destruction of the nameless (even numberless, as far as any of its crew had been aware) spy ship, assuring his listeners that it had been utterly blown to shreds before any berserker had been able to get its grippers on any of the ultrasecret material inside. This mollified the grim-looking debriefing officers somewhat. But they still had plenty of questions, some of which evidently couldn't wait, and were asked and answered, with a great deal of repetition, with the medics and Gift's left arm, the latter protruding through a kind of grommet, continued to be sealed off behind a panel of statglass.

A couple of hours later the debriefers had gone, for the time being. The surgeon, looking in on his latest patient as Gift lay in a recovery room, was brisk, matter-of-fact. A gray and elderly man, who kept stroking his little mustache, as if he had to keep rediscovering its shape.

"We had to take your arm, you realize," he remarked, matter-of-factly, after asking his patient how he felt. "Eight centimeters below the elbow."

Nifty, still flat on his back, and still in the process of getting his mind free from the drugs used during the operation, puffed out his breath. He didn't look down at his left side, where whatever the medics had done lay hidden under a puffy blanket. He didn't want to do any investigating just yet. He didn't even feel like trying to move. All he said was: "I thought something like that was going on."

It was easy to see that the surgeon, who now began a detailed explanation of the removal of the damaged limb and its replacement, was proud of the neat way these things were managed nowadays.

The patient, sneaking a peek now, could see that his own left hand, so immobile and so numb it that might have belonged to someone else, at least appeared to be just where it ought to be, and still had fingers. He counted them. Four, and a thumb, sticking out from under the edge of a cool green sheet.

The surgeon began filling in details. Immediately following the amputation, while Gift was still on the operating table, he had been fitted with an artificial left forearm and hand. That was why the operation had taken so long. There was startlingly little change in the appearance of his left hand, thought Gift, with the surgeon's encouragement pulling back the sheet and getting a better look at the new one now. If they hadn't told him, he would probably have accepted those fingers as his own. But at the moment the prosthesis was almost totally inert.

The surgeon, and a couple of younger apprentices who came by later, were reassuring about the paralysis and numbness. "That'll change quickly. Of course you'll never feel pain in the replacement hand. The nerves will transmit a distinctive tingle to indicate damage."

"That's good," the patient muttered. "I mean the part

about no pain." So far he was aware only of a vague and inter-
mittent discomfort, somewhere up around the elbow.

Artificial bone, muscle, nerves, and blood vessels, along
with skin, hair, and nails closely matched in appearance to his
own, had been melded tightly with his organic parts. The artificial tissues would generally draw energy chemically from his
blood. Gift was told that it usually took a day or so for the patient's nerves, growing under a heavy stimulus, to make the right
connections; to complete the job would take a week or so, and
he would have to baby the arm a little until then, as if it had
simply been sprained.

It occurred to him to wonder what had happened to the
discarded wreckage of his hand and arm, but then he decided
he would rather not know. Instead he asked, "I won't need a
sling or a cast?"

The apprentice surgeon shrugged. Obviously proud of his
work, he kept coming back to look at it. "Can give you one if
you like. Most people think they do better without. You should
have good control of the major muscles before you leave the hospital."

The patient was repeatedly assured that he could expect to
achieve a rapid return of natural function in his arm within a
few days, and steady, gradual improvement after that. The artificial limb would then serve him for an indefinite period, basically as long as he wanted to keep it; some people got to like
them so well that they elected to keep them permanently. But
the majority of patients preferred flesh and blood, which in
most cases could be grown in to be virtually indistinguishable
from the original; maybe even a little stronger, or capable of
finer movement. Some pianists claimed they actually gave a
finer performance with the hardware hand. But growing back
an organic arm or leg took time—months or even years of dis-
ability—and that could wait until after the war, or at least until
after the immediate military emergency. A functional artificial
hand would not impair a spacer's usefulness.

"One or two of my own colleagues are wearing the same
model you are." That was the surgeon's trump card. "And they
use them to perform surgery."

· · ·

Within a few hours after the surgery, Nifty Gift was up on his feet again, tottering around his small private hospital room. And in a couple of days he was spending most of his time up on his feet and walking about, left arm in a temporary sling. One of the nurses told him that it made him look dashing.

After the long session in the operating room, and when the debriefers were out of sight, Gift said to one of the medical people, "While I was riding home in that damned courier, I was dreaming about my deathdream." The pink elephant had been stalking him.

The woman looked at him blankly for a moment.

"You know. Or maybe I'm talking to someone in the wrong department. The official name is *termdream*. It was a strange feeling. I was dreaming that I was going to activate it."

The doctor, or technician, had known all along what he was talking about. Now she was reassuring. "Not an uncommon reaction. I shouldn't worry about it."

Every evening, before going to sleep in his little room, which was equipped with a real bed, not just a cot, Nifty stood out on his room's small balcony, in the open air, for several minutes with his eyes closed, letting the lingering glow of an Earthlike sunset bathe his face, feeling the free breeze move his hair, smelling the nearby sea.

Nerve probes carried out over the couple of days following the operation, while Gift remained in the hospital, indicated that the melding between nature and artifice was proceeding satisfactorily. Once in a while the artificial fingers would twitch on their own, but already he had feeling in them, a pins-and-needles kind of thing, and he could, if he concentrated, get them to open and close.

"If you don't get a gradually returning function in a couple of more days, a considerable improvement in movement, come in and see us."

Evidently the doctor had forgotten that the patient was supposed to be going home on leave. But Gift wasn't going to remind her, and perhaps get his leave canceled or delayed. "I will," he assured her, and nodded solemnly.

When the people from Hypo concluded their last hospital visit with him, Gift thought they had been somewhat reassured by what he'd told them. There had been no suggestion that they doubted anything about his story. One of the debriefers had hinted in passing that Gift's wound would doubtless earn him a medal. The spacer hadn't thought of that before, and somehow the news only cast a faint shadow of gloom over his inspired new enjoyment of life.

Gift remained for several days in the base hospital at Port Diamond. What the medics did for him there, at last included deactivating his deathdream. He took this as a sure sign that he wouldn't be going back into deep space, at least not anywhere near the front lines. Not in the foreseeable future, anyway. Anyone who had survived what he had survived would certainly at least have the option of moving to some easier kind of duty. Certain kinds of instructorship would be his for the choosing. And he, like the rest of his crew, had been about due for rear echelon duty anyway, based on the length of their tour of duty out on the front.

Soon the medics were lifting the deactivation helmet from his head. Now he could think about the pink elephants, engaged in their improbable routine, without tearing his brain apart. An image came of a pachyderm with its tusks embedded in gray matter.

Part of the thing was still in place, as they had warned him it would be. Think the right preliminary thought and there the elephant was. They assured him that this was normal.

He raised tentative fingers—right-hand fingers—and felt gingerly under the hair at the back of his head. His skullport was still there, just under the skin. It felt like a tiny, scabbed pimple.

His rehabilitators calmly assured him that now he could think about anything he liked, without either being able to manipulate the icon, or do himself any harm.

In turn he assured them, not quite as calmly, that he wasn't going to try.

"Most people say that. But sooner or later they do. There's a kind of fascination about it. Don't worry, it can't hurt you now."

Four days had passed since the surgery on his arm, and one day since the deathdream's quenching. The medics had given signs that they were just about finished with Nifty Gift, for the time being at least.

On that last evening of his stay in the hospital, he was surprised by someone calling up to him while he was standing out on the little balcony of his room.

"Spacer Gift?" The voice was feminine, and so quiet that Gift was momentarily not sure that he had heard it. As if the speaker did not want to be overheard.

He looked down at the ground some twenty feet below. A single figure stood there. The caller was a well-dressed young woman, standing on the grass amid the flowers and midget palm trees, the latter offering her some concealment from the people occasionally passing on the meandering walks and peaceful lawns that stretched between this building and the other units of the hospital.

Gift, gripping the wooden railing with both hands, stared down for a long moment in silence. His visitor's appearance, in the soft glow of the receding day, was vaguely Oriental. Large, trustful eyes, that when she was listening to someone gave the impression that she was taking in and believing every word. The startling green of her eyes was a direct result of some genetic tinkering undertaken by her grandmother, purely for cosmetic effect.

"You are Spacer Gift, aren't you? The one who rode the robot courier in from way across the Gulf? You're the only survivor of your scoutship crew?"

"Who're you?" he countered.

"Jory Yokosuka." The large, bright eyes were aimed at Gift. Moist red lips parted, looking ready for action of one kind or another. "I represent Home Worlds Media. They wouldn't let me in to see you. You know you're not being allowed any visitors?"

"Oh." Now he saw that the young woman was holding in one fist what looked like a small recorder. No visitors? The Hypo people of course had been coming and going freely, and it had never occurred to the patient to expect anyone else.

"I didn't notice about the visitors," he said.

"Take it from me, a few have tried to see you. How're you feeling now?" she queried cheerfully.

He drew a deep breath, tugged with both hands on the balcony's wrought-iron railing. "Not bad. Considering."

"That's great. I'd like to talk to you a bit. I wouldn't expect you to give away any military secrets." Her tone made the very idea seem farfetched.

A journalist. Of course, why not? Gift couldn't remember ever talking to one before. But now, yes, he was going to have to expect that kind of thing, for a while at least.

Well, it hadn't been a scoutship, but he wasn't going to say that. He didn't want to talk to her, and in his present condition he didn't suppose he'd have any trouble in making his point. All he'd have to do, probably, would be to wave his wounded arm like some magic talisman.

"They tell me," he offered, "that I'm going to do a press conference in a couple of days. Just before I go on leave."

The woman was cheerfully uninterested in any managed press conferences that might be scheduled. "What kind of a ship were you on? It was a scoutship, right?"

"Right." The debriefers had been very specific about what he should say when he was questioned. It was the answer they had told him to give, and in a sense it was true. They had promised him some heavy coaching later, just before he saw the press. There was no need to go into the heavy modifications and special equipment that Hypo put into its special vessels.

"What caused the destruction of your ship? Enemy action of some kind, right?" Then when the lady on the ground saw Gift hesitate, she quickly added: "You don't have to talk about that. Or tell me exactly where it happened. No? All right. There were maybe five or six livecrew beside yourself?"

He grunted something; a Hypo spy ship, unlike an ordinary scout, carried twice that many. The debriefers had given him no specific instructions on that question.

"Port Diamond was your home port?"

"That's right." No one had actually told him not to talk to reporters before the conference. They probably just hadn't thought that he'd run into one this soon.

"You had some good friends on board?" Jory Yokosuka's eyebrows contorted in an exaggerated show of sympathy. No doubt the recorder was working, though he couldn't see where she'd put it. She was holding her empty hands folded together as if in supplication.

It would certainly sound strange if he said no to that last question. "Yes. A couple."

The reporter was nodding slowly. "I suppose your best friends were other people who had the same job aboard that you did."

"Yep."

"What was your job?"

"We're not supposed to talk about that."

"Oh? Most crewpeople don't mind talking. Was your ship part of a task force?"

"No."

"Working for Hypo, maybe?" This question came in the same rhythm and tone as the preceding one.

The start he felt, the shock administered by that word coming from an outsider, must have showed in his face. The wide trusting eyes were looking up at him, waiting eagerly to be given some kind of an answer, and he couldn't tell if they had registered his shock or not.

Gift muttered something and turned away, retreating back into his hospital room.

Jory Yokosuka's soft voice pursued him briefly. "I'd like to see you again when you're recovered. Have another little talk?"

He didn't answer. When he cautiously peeked over the balcony railing again, two minutes later, the lawn below was empty.

· · ·

About half an hour later, listening to the brief recording she had made, a handful of sentences spoken in the spacer's voice, the young journalist confirmed her first impression that something about Nifty Gift was . . . not quite right. Of course the man was wounded, of course he had been through a lot. But instinct whispered there was something more.

She filed that private assessment away in the back of her mind, for possible action later, when there would be time to look for smaller angles on the war. Some human interest items.

Right now she had a bigger job to look forward to, if she could get it. But . . .

Her speculative shot regarding Hypo had hit home somehow. Nifty Gift seemed to know what Hypo was, even if Jory herself had yet to learn.

FOUR

Port Diamond base, though large for a military installation, naturally covered only a speck of the land and water surface of the planet Uhao, which orbited a very Sol-like sun. Uhao was renowned for its climate, and considered a meteorological paradise by most Earth-descended humans, who had made it a favorite tourist destination. There was a general impression among first-time visitors that this was what Earth itself ought to have been like. Romantics convinced themselves that the Cradle World really had been like this, once upon a time. Oceans, generally free of noxious bugs as well as giant storms and icebergs, sparkled in the sun.

Being the home of Hypo headquarters, this naturally had been the spy ship's home port—and still was for a hundred or a thousand other spy ships.

In the distant reaches of this world, there were also some strange alien archaeological sights to see.

As a rule, intelligence technicians who were engaged in jobs of the type from which Nifty Gift had just escaped, spacers whose work took them out on the front line against berserk-

ers, were deliberately kept in ignorance of what the machinery
they tended in deep space was supposed to accomplish. Should
these people someday fall captive to the enemy—which was always a distinct possibility—information they did not possess
could never be extracted from them by any means. Of course,
Gift and his colleagues were bright enough to make some
shrewd guesses about the purpose of it all, though they were officially discouraged from doing so.

Until now, Gift had wisely kept his guesses to himself.

When Nifty at last saw the tall gates of the hospital close
behind him, on his first excursion out into the world, he was riding in the back of an unmarked government ground car, headed
for the headquarters of Hypo. He really didn't have a whole lot
of choice about his destination.

The code name referred to some thirty or forty people, out
of the thousands who were stationed at the Port Diamond base.
These, and a vastly greater number out in spy ships collecting
data, made up the human component of one of the two prime
teams of Solarian intelligence specialists. These folk were already hard at work integrating the latest intercepted berserker
communications, brought in on Gift's courier, into their reading and interpretation of berserker plans. A very similar intelligence effort (code-named *Negat*) was taking place on Earth
itself. The two sets of scholarly experts were in frequent contact with each other.

That long-range berserker communications were being intercepted at all was an amazing and closely guarded military secret. At distances literally astronomical, too great for the
practical sending and reception of light waves or radio waves,
the only practical way for people or machines to exchange information was by means of couriers, much like the one that had
saved Gift's life, traveling at superluminal speeds. And to copy
the information carried aboard such a machine, without stopping or even touching the device itself, was a feat that seemed
to border upon witchcraft.

The main workroom of Hypo was underground, behind
and below an unprepossessing and unobtrusively guarded en-

trance on the surface—there were two entrances, in fact, the second out of sight from the surface, and the two connected so that you had to go through both in series in order to get in.

Hypo had grown into its own department, more or less, quite separate from the other functions of military intelligence. Currently it occupied the subterranean levels of a middle-sized gray building on the base, under a sign suggesting the presence of the accounting branch of the inspector general's office. Gift, who had visited these premises only twice before, both times more than a year ago, paused uncertainly on getting out of the ground car. But his driver-escort was right with him, taking him by the elbow, and the two men went down the basement stairs to the right of the building's main entrance, to the unmarked door at the bottom. Here the escort was left behind.

Inside, Gift was given a warm welcome by people of a wide assortment of ranks, mostly in sloppy uniforms. Down here, the dress code had no high priority. Most of these folk Gift could not remember ever seeing before, but they had been expecting him. One or two faces were vaguely familiar from his last visit about six months ago.

One of the first things these friendly almost-strangers hastened to inform him was that the first technicians to come aboard the courier, after it had been scooped up by a tender and carried down to base, had been surprised to see what the lone passenger, restricted to an emergency tool kit and to tasks he could perform with only one hand, had managed to accomplish. So was everyone else who heard about it. Any autopilot in military use was about as routinely foolproof as any complicated Solarian artifact could be made to be. All the engineers had been able to say, after a thorough examination of the hardware, was that it was certainly possible that this unit had been temporarily disabled by the effect of some berserker weapon, or weapons used in combination. Both sides in the war sometimes used devices that worked by altering or displacing patterns of information. Mindbeams came in two general classifications: scattering and switching.

So far Gift, sensitively aware, picked up no faint suggestion that anyone was considering blaming him for anything.

Around him was all friendliness and respect. Gradually he began to relax.

Like its passenger, the little courier that had brought Gift home had sustained minor damage from berserker weapons. That last shot fired after his scooter as it bore him away to safety had come close indeed. But its human passenger had suffered only slight physical injury, and a perfectly understandable psychological shock.

Also the courier's modest cargo of information, fruits of the spy ship's violently terminated mission, was essentially intact. Nothing startling there, probably, but in this business every shred counted, and had been paid for in human lives and treasure.

Spacer Gift's story, in the version he had earlier worked out for himself under the debriefers' questions, and which they now seemed perfectly willing to accept, placed the two shipmates he had left behind under some faint shadow of possible blame. At least he began to worry, unreasonably, that it might do so. Slowly he realized this, and vaguely it bothered him.

He had a strong impulse to do his best to make that doomed pair out to be selfless heroes, people who had voluntarily given up their own lives to let him get away with the important data. That would seem like the least that he could do. But he didn't want to talk about any part of the experience any more than was absolutely necessary. It would be a mistake, his instincts screamed, to appear to be making an effort to convince his questioners of anything.

He was in the midst of yet another retelling when the lady herself, the legendary Commander R, known in whispers as Mother R, a disturbing apparition with mousy hair, looking disheveled and partly out of uniform, wearing an open kimono over a shapeless sweater and military trousers, came shuffling out of her private room in her carpet slippers. Her appearance reminded Gift, the former literature major, of Pushkin's *Queen of Spades*. Mother fixed him with her liquid brown eyes, beckoned to him almost timidly, and uttered a few soft words.

Gift thought wildly that such an emergence must be a rare occurrence; everyone else in the room was goggling.

He followed her, wondering vaguely if he ought to salute.

The only thing impressive about her office, a shabby little cubicle, was the degree of its disorder.

The commander herself was one of the least military people that Gift had ever met in the service. It was obvious to everyone that if she were not a certified, demonstrated genius, her idiosyncrasies of appearance and behavior would not be tolerated in any branch of the Space Force. Gift and this brilliant woman had only met once or twice before, and then very briefly, when he and a small group of other new people (including Traskeluk) had been introduced to the commander, of whom they had never heard until that moment.

Settled in a visitor's chair in her private office, talking now to Commander R, who wanted to hear all about the disaster he'd survived, Gift stuck pretty closely to the version he had found himself settling on in the hospital: He had been half-stunned by a weapon blast just as he got aboard the courier, and his memory on some details was imperfect.

Everyone Spacer First Class Sebastian Gift had encountered in the hospital had given him assurances, well before he even thought of asking, that when he left the hospital he would be going home on convalescent leave.

He hadn't been quite sure that Hypo was going to let him go on leave that quickly or easily. But now it turned out that they would. He was glad, because over the last day or so there had been moments when he felt a deep, almost childish yearning to go home.

But right now his mind was being kept on business. Because Commander R now thought that he would never be going out on a deep space mission again, no longer be at risk of capture, she on her own responsibility started telling him something about the inner workings of the department they both worked for.

She said to him: "When you get back from leave, you'll start learning your new job, far from the front." He and his shipmates would have completed their tour of duty in any case.

Gift realized he wasn't really getting the full briefing yet on just what his new chairborne job was likely to be like. But a hint, a foretaste, enough so that if he really didn't want any more of Hypo he could back out now, or as soon as he got back from leave. The commander really wasn't taking much of a chance in telling him as much as she did. His security clearance was already high enough, and it was presumed that now he had, or soon would have, a need to know. He was being quizzed on his general knowledge of just what went on in this cavern, that his spy ship and a score of a hundred others risked destruction to supply with data.

The quizzing could have and should have been done more cautiously. Anyway, Commander R was notorious for disregarding regulations. She was a baby-faced, wide-eyed woman who at first glance projected the image of an inmate of a home for the elderly who had been drafted as a kindergarten teacher.

"Suppose," she was telling Gift now, in her sweet voice, "suppose we simply captured the machine and didn't release it. Then of course its intended recipient would not, unless there were a redundant transmission, get the information it contained, or be able to act on it. This would definitely limit the usefulness of your find."

"Yes, I quite see that."

The new system promised a much greater frequency of success, when it could be made to work at all. The key innovation was that in which the information content of a berserker courier was somehow scanned, without the necessity of stopping the machine or deflecting it even slightly from its course.

The esoteric science involved in the new system lay on the frontiers of physics and mathematics. Gift had some background in those fields, but he'd need additional education if he was going to be useful in the home office.

"As far as we can tell, our enemies are not really great at fundamental research, even though they do manage to keep up with us in weaponry. Therefore we have reason to hope they won't figure our method X for some time yet."

The operation involved setting up and maintaining a kind of "net," capable of examining a substantial portion of berserker courier traffic over exceedingly large distances. Ships and machines passing within range were probed, scanned by quantum devices. The stored information aboard was read, but the couriers were not interfered with in any detectable way. At least Solarian intelligence hoped that the quantum scanning was undetectable.

When Commander R was through talking to Nifty, she sent him to sit beside a clerk at a desk in the Hypo office, who on his writerscreen was officially cutting the orders for twenty days' of convalescent leave for Spacer First Class Sebastian Gift.

And when he left the place, leave orders in hand, he was pretty much on his own.

His parents, and all the other people he felt connected to as family, lived on Earth, a couple of days away by interstellar ship.

Paradoxically—or not, in the eyes of people fighting berserkers, which were themselves the embodiment of death—here in the midst of paradise were truly massive military installations, and a garrison including military experts in many fields. Things were being rebuilt at a frenzied pace, following the massive berserker raid of almost half a standard year ago.

A surprise raid by the enemy, on a massive scale, a few standard months before Gift's return to Port Diamond, had disabled a great part of the fleet that had to be counted on for the defense of Earth. A number of capital ships, ships of the line, dreadnoughts, had been caught in their docks on satellites orbiting Port Diamond itself. The ruins left by that assault were still partially visible. One great battleship, knocked into a degenerating orbit, had fallen to the ground, its armor allowing its sheer bulk to survive reentry and impact. The dead hull had at last crashed down into a hundred-meter depth of ocean, within sight of the base, where it still showed partially above water, housing the bodies of hundreds of Solarians who had gone down with their ship.

Now the general attitude of people in uniform was grim as they hurried past the man already on convalescent leave, but who had not yet put on civilian clothes because he was relying on military transport to get him back to Earth. There were moments when it seemed to Gift, still reveling in the fact of life, that he was the only one paying attention to the natural beauty surrounding them.

Jory Yokosuka was spending the morning hanging around CINCGUL headquarters, making plans for success on her new job, and hoping for a ride on some fast military ship going out to Fifty Fifty where the job was to be. Media credentials, which she had in plenty, would sooner or later get her on some passenger vessel—there were still one or two traveling across the Gulf in that direction—but the military would be faster, and if she was going to write about those people she preferred to talk to them, to live with them, as much as possible.

At the moment when Nifty Gift arrived at Hypo headquarters, Jory Yokosuka was strolling up and down near the neatly impressive front of Port Diamond base HQ, not more than a hundred meters away.

Jory had been on Uhao only a few days, and on the base with her journalist's credentials for only one, but she was good at her job and already, like most of her fellow journalists, knew perfectly well where the artlessly concealed entrance to Hypo was—she could see it now, a block down the street; and earlier she had walked past it—and that *something* important went on in there. *What* exactly was going on, behind the mysterious code word, was a challenging question; and getting in to find out had so far proved perfectly impossible. But journalists, in Jory's view, existed to find out things that other people tried to keep concealed.

Jory was not the only journalist who made an effort to see and interview the latest space hero while he was still on Uhao, at Port Diamond. But no one had any more success than Jory did, even though she hadn't been able to get in more than a couple of questions and answers. Now she was planning to try again.

Alert as usual, she now saw the staff car with the mysterious hero in it drive by, and then saw the car stop near the Hypo entrance.

Well, well. Not exactly an astonishing surprise, but very interesting.

Earlier she had considered loitering outside the entrance to the disguised Hypo workroom, as if waiting to meet someone, scanning the faces of people who came in and out. But she was mortally certain that security would be on her before she'd done that for very long.

Part of her vague suspicion regarding Nifty Gift was owed to the fact that his most recent predecessor as celebrity war hero, while actually quite heroic enough—having died in the line of duty—had not in fact done anything remotely like the deed on which his fame rested, i.e., destroyed a berserker battleship by ramming it with his farlauncher after getting his own crew to bail out.

Her personal communicator hummed discreetly, and she lifted it up beside her ear.

The message, relayed from her robotic secretary, was from a Ms. Prow, who introduced herself as personal assistant to Jay Nash. Even while Jory listened, despite the importance of the message, she was keeping one eye out for Gift to emerge from that humble doorway down the street.

She did not see anyone emerge, but the message was one that pleased her mightily.

She was now in a mood to boast, to the next person she spoke to, that the famous Jay Nash had accepted her application for employment.

"That means I'll be getting out to Fifty Fifty as soon as possible, and joining him there."

All across the relatively small portion of the Galaxy that had so far been explored by enterprising Solarians, the dominance of their Earth-descended humanity was unchallenged by any other life form. Only death itself, the reaper personified in berserker metal, confronted them as serious competition. There seemed no reason to believe that matters would be different farther on, as Galactic exploration, war or no war, slowly proceeded. Also our busy race provided the berserkers' only real active opposition currently active anywhere, as far as any Solarian had been able to discover.

And the central overall military headquarters of the children of Sol, insofar as any one place qualified for that title, was located on Earth. What was housed on the cradle planet was not really the peak of a rigid chain of command, but more a clearinghouse of information.

To the military leaders at Port Diamond, and to the superior authorities who dwelt on Earth itself, fell the responsibility of deciding whether to wholeheartedly put their faith in the reports handed them by their intelligence experts, human and computer.

These reports were substantially different from what headquarters generally expected, and usually got, from intelligence. They were so firm in their conclusions, so elaborate in their detail, that they purported to offer what was practically a blueprint of the whole oncoming berserker attack. They demanded from the highest level of leadership a response that was equally decisive.

Time and again one of Earth's strategic planners had said to another something like: "That *some* kind of major attack is impending can be taken for granted. But as to the strength and exact purpose of the onslaught, or its precise target . . ."

People continued to debate the pros and cons of the new method of trying to intercept information. Many still questioned the reliability of the results.

"Might this seeming great intelligence success be in fact some kind of a berserker deception?"

"Deception on such a grand scale seems unlikely—but the possibility cannot entirely be ruled out."

· · ·

A few months after the Port Diamond raid, a fierce space battle in the Azlaroc region, thousands of light years away near the far side of the Gulf of Repose, had dragged to an inconclusive finish, leaving both sides with some justification for computing it as a victory.

One of the Solarian carriers engaged in that battle, the *Lankvil*, had limped home with great difficulty to Port Diamond, where she seemed likely to be confined to a repair dock in low orbit for the next three standard months. But a maximum repair effort was being made; workers, human and mechanical, entering the dock like infantry going into battle.

At the last moment the decision was made to bring the *Lankvil* right down to planet surface, an unusual step to take in the repair of any large ship.

Field Marshal Yamanim himself, the ranking military officer (commander in chief, Gulf theater, or CINCGUL) for a hundred light-years in every direction, had to have that carrier back, in fighting shape, and soon.

Right now the field marshal was taking personal steps to make sure that he got it.

Field Marshal Yamanim had ordered a maximum effort to repair the *Lankvil,* and, with a view toward inspiring its accomplishment, had had himself driven out in a small boat to where the stricken carrier lay. The enormous hull was more than half submerged in the ocean, and the water around it was swarming with thousands of people and machines. Repairs and even reconstruction on any warship would normally have been carried out in orbit, but this was a special case.

Today, on the same day that Nifty Gift had returned to Hypo to pick up his orders and enjoy an unscheduled conference with his boss, the field marshal had arisen earlier than usual, put on work gear over his dress uniform, and had hastened to plunge in among the laboring people and their slave machines. His idea was not to inspire them to greater efforts— or at least that was not his idea any longer—because he hadn't been at the site two minutes before he realized that the people doing the job were already driving themselves past the point of exhaustion. Satisfied that no inspiring speeches were required, Yamanim still wanted to see the details of the task remaining, and discover if there was any help the workers needed, and any way he could use his authority to obtain it.

Yamanim swam a few strokes in the near-tropical water, as the quickest way of getting from his boat to the nearest flange of the great hull. His soaking uniform would dry out quickly. He was upright and serious-looking, even when dripping wet. Physically, the field marshal exemplified what anthropologists had come to call the Earth-standard type. Not many fit it as well as Yamanim: Average size, middle age, and a facial appearance that suggested that the entire contents of the home planet's human gene pool had been smoothly scrambled in some computer simulation. His skin was a vague tan that had little to do with exposure to sunlight, his hair and eyes were an average brown.

Mentally he was a long way from average.

Punched by berserker weapons in the thickness of the great carrier's triple hull were several holes, each wide enough to drive a scoutship through. The giant vessel lay in deep water, just outside the regular harbor for surface craft, its mass partially buoyed by gigantic inflation tubes and collars as well as antigravity devices. The harbor was pretty well filled with smaller victims of the berserkers' firepower. High in the atmosphere, a lot of work was being done to keep the weather in the vicinity calm and clear. That was one department where the field marshal had already exerted his formidable influence.

From the position to which he had now climbed, high on the damaged hull, where he stood holding on with one hand to keep from sliding and rolling down, Yamanim had a good view of an ominously similar object lying halfway to the horizon. This was the ruined battlewagon *Anozira,* part of whose grounded hull was sticking up out of fifty meters of ocean, still on the spot where it had crashed after being blasted out of low orbit. Everyone could see that ominous silhouette in the background, but so far Yamanim had heard no one comment on it.

· · ·

Besides the obvious jagged openings in the *Lankvil's* outer
hull, there was a great deal of internal damage. Hull cavities
were matched by gaps in the interior decks. New plates, slabs
laminated out of several materials, maybe several kinds of matter, were being hoisted and welded into place.

With great pride the master of shipyards, now standing beside the field marshal, stubbornly maintained that there was indeed a fighting chance of getting her out of here and headed
back to the front in three days.

"It better be more than a fighting chance, Frank. It better
be a fact."

"I don't know, sir . . ."

"I do. Have you seen what a planet looks like when
berserkers get done with it? One lifeless cloud of mud and
steam."

"Yessir."

Yamanim, on the verge of moving on to the multitude of
other tasks awaiting him, patched in to the local communication net and gave the human workers a little speech, telling
them that the berserkers were sure this carrier could be scratched
from the Solarian line of battle. Maybe it was hokey, attribut-
ing triumph and chagrin to the unliving enemy, but he had noticed that people, including himself, wanted to do it all the time.
Evidently it was more satisfying to fight a foe who could be
made to suffer—if only in your own imagination.

Once Yamanim had decided that his continued presence
on the *Lankvil's* hull was only going to slow things down, he
wasted no time in getting out. He changed out of damp clothes
in a temporary office that overlooked the shipyard.

Soon he was neat again in a dry version of the Space
Force uniform he generally preferred to wear: Dull battle dress
except for the five stars gleaming on cap and epaulets.

Hardly had Field Marshal Yamanim finished his change
of clothes when he was already reading, quickly but thoroughly,
the report concerning the lost spy ship, which made incidental

mention of the heroic survivor—whose debriefing had not shed much light on the reasons for the ship's loss. Well, they would probably never be known.

Before turning to stride out of the office, the field marshal struck the paper briskly with a couple of fingers. "Put that man on the medals list. But let him have his leave before we bother him with ceremonies. I'd say he's earned it."

His aide murmured an acknowledgment of the order, and neatly stowed the paper away again. Yamanim avoided using robotic aides as much as possible, employing them as a rule for only the most routine tasks. He much preferred to run his ideas through another human mind.

Next on the list of things he had to do within the next few hours was a discussion of tactical and strategic problems, which meant joining Admiral Bowman, who was waiting to discuss them with him.

It was a relief to discover an old friend amid the endless succession of anxious, demanding faces coming before him with their requests and problems. The two men greeted each other with informal enthusiasm.

Admiral Bowman had thin, sandy hair and a rugged face. He looked the part of a fighting man, so much so that his colleagues sometimes wondered (privately, because Bowman was popular) whether it was manner and appearance as much as actual achievement that had advanced him as far as he had come in rank.

No one had ever called into question his trustworthiness, though, and Yamanim had no qualms about telling Bowman about the new intelligence findings.

"The thing is, Jack, our people in the basement have broken the berserker communications code. At least the one that they've been using in this sector."

Bowman thought about it for a moment, then whistled softly.

"Yeah."

Bowman's forehead wrinkled. "I've never got it completely though my head how we can even *intercept* a message, without knocking down the courier that carries it. Not like a radio wave."

"That's about where they lose me too. The world turns into mathematics, and then the math turns into philosophy or metaphysics or some such. They tell me it has to do with quantum mechanics—treating a whole courier machine like a subatomic particle. But it seems to work."

The berserkers, as far as any Solarian was able to tell, were probably aware of the new Solarian hardware scattered about in space. But they had been content with the routine computation that the new message-reading system was no more than a new version of the warning net.

"Actually, the two functions are fundamentally incompatible. If you interfere with the courier, you'll never be able to read its message—unless you stop it altogether."

Continued surveillance of enormous volumes of space, millions of cubic light-years, was still being carried out by the vast network of spacegoing robots and crewed ships. This massive effort resulted in ever more interceptions of enemy messages, fodder for the massive optelectronic brains, perhaps the largest and fastest machines of their kind ever assembled, which were engaged in cryptanalysis. But the surveillance, the *gathering* of information, of course was not run from down in this basement. Only the decoding.

Each new reassessment of the situation, whether made by the analysts on Earth or those at Port Diamond, tended to confirm the earlier estimates of the strength of the berserker task force, and its probable objectives. The enemy force was poised to strike at the Fifty Fifty base, and though some of the details were still unclear, it was ominously strong, much stronger than any collection of ships that the people of Earth could now assemble in the Gulf to meet it.

But there were rays of hope. For one thing, there was no reason to suppose that the enemy knew that its strength had been accurately appraised, that organic brains in the Solarian headquarters were reading berserker plans, knowing them down to the very hour of scheduling and the assignment of individual units to the berserker versions of fleets and squadrons.

Nonorganic people—as some breathing folk were wont to call those complex programs, even the ones that never pretended or attempted to be human—played an essential role in the defense too.

The latest picture drawn by intelligence, incorporating morsels of information that had come in with the courier carrying the supposedly heroic Spaceman Gift, continued to be consistently (some still thought suspiciously) plain: The consensus of scoutship sightings and readings in flightspace from the robot network faithfully confirmed the earlier estimates and predictions. Not only had enemy strength been accurately estimated, but the berserker attack forces seemed to be crossing the Gulf in the type of deployment and at the times and places intelligence had predicted. All indications were that they intended a mass attack on the space atoll called Fifty Fifty.

The field marshal also told Bowman of his assignment as commander of a task force that was being sent out to intercept the berserker fleet as it neared its goal.

"There'll be two sections. Officially, two separate task forces. Naguance will be taking the other, since Yeslah's laid up in hospital—some kind of damned skin disease that the medics can't seem to figure out. You're senior to Naguance, so the overall command is yours. In your section you'll have one carrier, *Lankvil,* which is promised to be spaceworthy in a few days. I want the other section to lift off first, and it'll include two carriers, *Venture* and *Stinger.*"

Yamanim also announced his decision that at least one knowledgeable person ought to go to Earth, to answer in person all questions regarding the new intelligence system, to make all possible efforts to ensure that the highest leaders accept the intelligence reports provided by himself and his colleagues, as giving a true picture of berserker intentions.

The obvious first choice for the mission to Earth was the leader of the premier intelligence section on Port Diamond, the code-breaking crew called Hypo. Yamanim's first impulse was to send Commander R. The equivalent intelligence group, code-named *Negat,* who worked on Earth, had no individual member whose personal plea would be as effective with high authority.

But the field marshal did not need to think about the matter for long before accepting Bowman's advice, in a reversal of his own first impulse. The idea was that Commander R herself had better stay right where she was, on the job.

Yamanim nodded slowly. "She's undoubtedly a genius, but one can't say that she has much of a persuasive presence."

"No. Well, not unless she gets you in her lair, where she's surrounded by her secret displays. And she can bring to bear all the arrays of logic and probability and whatever else she uses." As an afterthought, Bowman added, "witchcraft," and shuddered slightly. "I've had that treatment, and I can testify."

"Of course the commander might bring whatever materials she needs with her—but no, you're right, we need Mother just where she is, on the job. If anyone's irreplaceable, she is."

After a short conference it was agreed between the two officers that Admiral Bowman himself would go to Earth, there to argue the case at the highest level for accepting the intelligence estimates.

"And don't let the premier keep you waiting around. You'll have the perfect excuse in that you'll have to be with Task Force Seventeen."

"Oh, I'll be very firm with her. Yeah, sure." And Bowman gently shook his head.

Field Marshal Yamanim had set a different goal for himself, as he now probably told Bowman. Simultaneously with dispatching his old friend to Earth—or only a few minutes later, maybe while he was in the process of climbing out of whatever pit or tank or force field encased the major repairs on his carrier—Yamanim decided that his own best move would be a swift trip to the peculiar outpost called Fifty Fifty, which he had never taken a good look at.

Graphics of that peculiar outpost he had observed plenty,

but he had seen the thing itself only incidentally, once, years ago, while passing through. Looking at a holostage, or even, when he got back on his flagship, plunging into the virtual reality of a tencube representation, was never quite the same as coming to grips with the thing itself. He wanted to conduct a personal tour of inspection, to get a feel for just how defensible the place was—and what the garrison assigned to the job of defending it now thought of their own chances.

Also, the field marshal wanted to carry directly to those people a warning of enemy plans. Having allowed himself to become firmly convinced that this time the intelligence people were right, Yamanim wasn't going to waver. He didn't want to wait for final approval from Earth before issuing a few essential warnings.

And Yamanim wanted to see for himself the object for which it seemed a great battle was likely to be fought.

The field marshal knew he was considered something of a politician. That didn't bother him, since it was true of all officers of very high rank—of all the really successful ones, he thought, going back through history. Undoubtedly some were better at concealing the fact than he was. His manner was usually careful and conciliatory, his temperament for the most part placid. He had been genuinely distressed, just after the great Port Diamond raid, to learn he had been given command of the whole Gulf fleet in this desperate situation, but no idea of trying to avoid the burden had ever crossed his mind. He had long experience as a subspacer—on ships that cruised almost entirely in flightspace, only emerging into normal space at long intervals, meanwhile using fine instruments to keep in touch.

Jory Yokosuka, pacing in front of headquarters, was occupying her mind by deciding what to pack for her upcoming trip. It would be best to keep the physical burden as light as possible, because she would probably wind up toting it around herself—civilian robots would have to be allowed on Fifty Fifty as part of the tools for making the documentary, but they might not be available as baggage handlers.

She found herself nagged by the memory of her brief contact with the wounded spacer, Sebastian Gift. Something strange about that one, she kept thinking, besides his possible connection to the mysterious Hypo. But the matter of Gift kept getting pushed to the back of her mind by other developments.

Still her mind kept drifting back, again and again, to the interview—if you could call their brief talk that—she'd had with Nifty Gift.

No, Jory was not entirely satisfied with what she'd got from the wounded spacer. Her first impression had been that the young man exemplified the legendary type of modest, tongue-tied hero, and she wanted to write something about him, though she was not sure what—but then the connection with the mysterious Hypo had made her think again. One problem, she realized, might be that she had zero previous experience with war heroes, and indeed little contact with the military at all.

Naturally, there had been an official press conference with Gift, as he had told her there would be, and she had attended. His eyes had rested on her once or twice as she stood in the second row of correspondents, and she was sure that he remembered her from her unauthorized evening visit. But he had made no overt sign of recognition, which was fine with her.

Apart from the press conference, there hadn't been enough on her recording to make an exclusive interview out of her brief talk with Gift—of course, it would have been interesting to see what the Port Diamond censors made of the mention of Hypo.

The bite-sized record of the press conference on its plastic tile sounded and looked all right when you ran it on a holostage—but still, her instincts told her there was something more to the story than she'd been able to get at. Well, whatever was there would just have to wait until another day—maybe sometime she'd have the chance to pursue the matter.

She looked around and came to a stop. Here came what she was waiting for, approaching down a corridor just inside headquarters, on a palm-shaped walkway just outside: The fast-walking entourage of the field marshal himself.

Jory hastened to position herself in his way, and succeeded in bringing the small group to a halt.

She managed to do this only because, as she had hoped, but not really dared to expect, Yamanim himself was minded to take an interest. He questioned her while his aides stood by, looking at her blankly.

Yes, she responded to his first question, she was the civilian, or one of the civilians, who wanted a ride to Fifty Fifty.

And yes, Jory was proud to be able to announce, she was the one who had just been hired by and was going to work for the famous entertainment director Jay Nash. Nash was also a military reservist, and had been sent in that capacity to Fifty Fifty, there to immortalize in documentary form the coming battle, or some part of it anyway.

"Why'd he pick you?"

Jory drew a deep breath. No use pretending to be modest. "I've been getting a certain reputation for knowing how to use certain kinds of recording equipment. Making things look and sound the way I want them to, without using enhancement. And I'm not timid. It's a job that I—"

"Congratulations." Yamanim beamed at her with what she assessed as a wicked twinkle in his eye. "Have you ever actually met the man?"

"No, but—"

"You have something to look forward to." Was the field marshal smiling as he turned away and resumed his rapid progress? It was hard to tell.

Concerning Jay Nash, her new boss, Jory knew what everyone else knew, and very little more: That Nash was, in civilian life, one of the most important entertainment producers in the homeworlds.

Jory assumed that even before she managed to catch up with Nash, her next priority had better be learning all she could about the nuts and bolts of military operations, the people and hardware she was soon going to be writing about.

It had taken some string-pulling to get a civilian employee, or independent contractor, assigned to a combat zone. But the man some considered Earth's greatest drama director had evidently had the strings in hand to pull.

Nifty Gift's first day out of the hospital turned out to be a busy one for him indeed. Returning from his thought-provoking visit to Hypo, he ran into Jory Yokosuka once again. As far as he could tell, the encounter was purely accidental.

After finishing her talk with Yamanim, she had turned away from headquarters and walked down the street, at a normal pace, past the unmarked entrance to Hypo. No sign of Gift just now, and she didn't want to loiter here.

Moving on briskly, she went back to the hospital and waited for the staff car to bring him back.

Fortune smiled on her plans, and she was able to run into him, right at the main entrance, as if by accident.

The staff car had just dropped him off. Unescorted at the moment, he paused and was willing to talk.

Demonstrating real sympathy, Jory asked the hero about his shattered and replaced hand. It was a subject on which Gift was ready to talk freely.

Off and on there were increased stirrings of function and sensation, if not exactly of life, in the fingers of Gift's new left hand. Coming along, though he wouldn't want to try to learn the piano just yet. He seemed to be making progress at about the best rate that could reasonably be expected. The composite fingers, powered by his blood supply, were already actually stronger than his fleshy ones. But the doctors had been at pains to explain that they would never be as strong, as, for example, the servo-powered fingers of space armor.

One of the hospital technicians, or bioengineers, had put it this way: "It's not space armor, you understand; you can't arm wrestle a berserker with one of these."

Jory had her recorder running. "And what did you say to that?"

Nifty shook his head. "People have exaggerated ideas about what space armor can do. Thank God I won't have to wrestle any berserkers. Not any more."

"They're giving you a new job now?"

"When I get back from my leave."

They talked a little longer.

When she left Gift, she thought a little more about her new job. Working for the military would seem to put any journalist under something of an obligation to them. . . .

The counterargument to that was: "But it seems to me that the military saving your life and your family's lives—if you have a family—tends to create a certain obligation too."

And they had been saving everyone's life, for centuries. Berserkers were nothing new.

She was also one of the many media people who had already been trying to pin down some hard facts about the rumored new spy system. Was that mysterious system, and the equally mysterious Hypo, one and the same?

She'd been careful not to let anyone in the military know that she'd heard anything at all about either one.

Field Marshal Yamanim was asking one of his junior aides, as the cruiser prepared for liftoff: "That gal get aboard? The one who's going to work with Jay Nash?"

"Yes, sir, she did."

"I want you to look after her en route," the field marshal directed after a moment's thought. "Run her through the ten-cube; let her know everything—everything that we would like her to know and write about. Think you can handle that?"

"Yes, sir, I can."

"Good." No need to explain. Everyone knew that the more rank any officer had, the more important it was to keep on the right side of the media.

            Jory Yokosuka had hoped to arrange for herself a guided tour of Port Diamond's military installations. She wanted to get as good a look as possible at some of the military hardware that young Solarian warriors would soon be riding and guiding into battle. But as soon as word reached Jory that her ride out to Fifty Fifty was ready and waiting, she bowed out of the tour, or whatever else was going on, and hastily threw a few personal belongings into a bag. The big job she had wanted was ready and waiting, and everything else would have to wait.

    As soon as she was on the cruiser, and the formalities of getting under way had been completed, she resumed her efforts to pick people's brains.

    She was soon pleased to learn that, as Nash's aide, she rated a private briefing session in a tencube.

    She was walking down a corridor with the officer who was going to perform the briefing. The artificial gravity had been set a little light, and everyone's steps were buoyant.

The officer, Lieutenant Duane, was smooth, young, and personable. There was nothing in the least nonorganic about him.

"Meanwhile, I'd like to ask some questions, get into what we know about how the berserkers operate."

"Sure. Within the limits of security, of course."

"Of course. But I'm new to this business, and I can't help wondering: Is security really a problem in a war where neither side can really infiltrate the other?"

The officer's eyes, like those of a lot of other people, began to glaze over when security was questioned. If military people had doubts about the reality of the danger, they were not going to express them to an outsider. "I wouldn't say that can't happen. Goodlife really exist, you know. They're on just about every planet."

Certainly there were some, Jory thought to herself, a few deluded psychotics. But did they really represent a serious threat? Or was it mainly a means of whipping up enthusiasm that still seemed to flag in some people? The journalist, like many other people, had doubts on that point. But let that subject pass for now; she could debate it with someone else.

She was on the verge of springing the name of Hypo on Duane, just to see how he reacted. With the enthusiasm of one to whom any secret was a challenge, she was becoming more and more determined to probe into the nature and activities of that mysterious entity. From bits of information gathered here and there, she was beginning to suspect that the secret department had something to do with trying to solve berserker codes. Of course, none of these people on the cruiser, including Yamanim himself, would admit having anything to do with that.

She had seen Gift's reaction to the suggestion that he and his ship had been working for the mysterious Hypo. And she had seen Gift entering the secret headquarters.

Now Jory wanted to pursue the subject further, if possible, without bringing up the name. She feared the code word, if recognized, might have the effect of shutting down communication altogether.

"How often do the member machines of a berserker task

force, those that are working together in some particular operation, change the code by which they communicate with one another?"

Her escort wrinkled his handsome brow. "That's a hard
one. I don't think there is a single answer. A lot of other people
share that opinion with me, and it's no secret. I'm sure some of
our people could quote you different probabilities for different
situations."

"Tell me something about berserker codes in general.
When they come in to attack, what do we expect to be able to
intercept?"

Duane didn't seem at all reluctant to talk about berserker
communication codes; probably, Jory soon realized, because
he knew practically nothing about the subject. The lecture on
fundamentals continued: Berserkers in general have several
kinds of communication code built in. By such means, machines long separated from one another, or even models of different generations, built according to divergent plans, could
always communicate with each other.

Humans had long ago mastered these original codes, in
their several simple variations, and were constantly monitoring
for them. But very little berserker traffic was that simply en-
crypted any more.

"Radio, in which we may include all light-speed communications in any wavelength, taking place in normal space, is of
course practical only over comparatively short distances. Two
fleets, for example, separated by light-years in normal space,
must exchange information by sending ships, or uncrewed couriers, back and forth. Naturally, those are practically impossible
to intercept, just as our couriers are."

"Naturally." Jory had already known all this, but she continued listening patiently.

"Berserkers have a kind of chain of command," Duane
was assuring her a few minutes later, "just as Solarian humans
do, or any other coherent fighting force."

"If there *is* any third military power in the Galaxy."

"I don't know what it would be." The officer shrugged.

"But you're right. No coordination among units would be possible without some order of rank."

"So, when you say one of their computers outranks another—"

"We mean essentially the same thing we mean when discussing human command systems. The ranking computer has authority to give orders that override those issued by inferior machines."

Jory was struck by an intriguing thought. "Then is there, somewhere in the Galaxy, a grand berserker commander in chief? A generalissimo, field marshals? The counterpart of FM Yamanim?"

The questioner's imagination, unbidden, had called forth a sort of cartoon picture of a proud machine, bedecked with medals.

"The question has been much debated by our strategists." The dashing lieutenant was taking on the sound and look of a pompous general. "The majority opinion is against it. Of course, there has to be some automatic agreement among them as to which computer, or combination of computers, outranks the others."

"I don't suppose they ever worry about promotion."

"That I wouldn't know." Pause. "How about a drink? I've got something nice in my quarters."

"Maybe later."

Then they were inside the tencube, standing on the slightly yielding floor. The windowless, cubic chamber, ten meters by ten-by-ten, at the moment was cavernously empty.

To experience the chamber's full powers and effects, it was necessary on entering to put on helmets equipped with sensory and control feedbacks. Having done so, the display was awesome. The artificial gravity had been weakened within these rubbery walls, studded with projections of polyphase matter of various sizes. These outcroppings provided physical support when needed—the visitor could leap and climb about in almost perfect freedom and safety. Jory had been in a similar chamber before, and knew that when properly used, for matters astronomical, it could begin to give the viewer—more accurately, the participant—an awed sense of how big the Galaxy truly was.

The would-be dashing lieutenant continued obviously, though fairly subtly, trying to make it with her, but Jory remained intent on business and brushed him off. He was not easy to discourage, and she did not do so without regret. Privately she had to admit to herself that she did find a great many military men attractive.

It was obvious, thought Jory, when one looked at the display now coming into existence at her guide's command, that the center of Solarian power and influence had never moved very far from Sol System. The territory of colonization appeared as an irregular blob whose shape had changed, even as its size had increased, over the last few centuries. But Earth remained very near the center.

Little more than 5 percent of the Galaxy's volume had as yet been seriously explored by Solarian ships. And less than one in twenty of its billions of solar systems. Most of what those ships had looked at was along what was still called the Orion-Cygnus spiral Galactic arm, the name drawn from a system of constellations that had been ancient long before Solarians first ventured into space.

Several thousand standard years had passed since reaction engines had been superseded by more sophisticated devices, capable of the direct manipulation of spacetime. Space travel had graduated from its rocket-driven infancy. With the bonds of time and distance broken, at least up to the galactic scale, Solarians had moved out among the stars.

Even a berserker megamassacre that succeeded in sterilizing Earth would not, of course, destroy all chances for Galactic life. Life's champion, by default it seemed, the bellicose Earth-descended race, was now too widely dispersed to depend for its survival on any single strong point, any cluster of worlds, or any sector. But the obliteration of Earth as a home of life would very probably be the beginning of the end.

And any galaxy once thoroughly harrowed by berserkers would be left as lifeless as the interior of a sun.

Perhaps the most conspicuous feature of the view of the

Galaxy currently on display was the feature called the Gulf of Repose. This was an emptiness, outlined mainly by the scarcity within it of small sun symbols, which occupied several thousand light-years of space between two spiral arms, one of which contained the homeworlds.

The Gulf region was so vast that it was still prominent when the Galactic model was shrunken down to tabletop dimensions. It was deceptively peaceful in appearance, a bland void containing little in the way of star clusters or nebular material.

Enlargement of the void in the display showed that the interstitial stars speckling its emptiness were few and mostly unremarkable. Meanwhile some spectacular Galactic components ranged along its flanks assured that space did not look empty to the voyager making the long crossing.

On one side of the Gulf, sprawled across the thickness of an adjoining arm, lay the hundred or so habitable planets, in more than a score of systems, which had come to be called the homeworlds. Sol System and Earth itself were near the center of this modest grouping. On the far side of the Gulf, very distant on this scale, lay what must now be conceded to have become berserker territory.

The premier of Earth and her advisers, eschewing any merely defensive claims, had already publicly vowed to win those lost systems back for Solarian humanity.

On the far side of the Gulf, it was possible to locate at least approximately the locale where the spy ship had been destroyed, leaving Spacer Gift as its sole survivor. When commanded, the display pointed out the spot with a small blinking beacon.

The bright sun of Uhao, and the peculiar, sunless object called Fifty Fifty, were both more than a thousand light-years out in the Gulf, with Fifty Fifty, despite its name suggesting a halfway point, being substantially closer to the other side.

"What does intelligence believe to be the ultimate object of all this recent enemy activity? Maybe *ultimate* is the wrong word. Of course, we know that their ultimate goal is to kill us all."

Jory, her body rising slowly through the midst of the display, knew that her guide was drifting, bobbing beside her in the gentle gravity, though she could not see him. "Right," his disembodied voice replied. A pointer of pure light sprang into existence in Jory's perception. "And it's obvious that the only way for the berserkers to achieve their goal is by an attack on our homeworlds." The pointer moved, grew brighter by way of lending emphasis. "On Earth itself."

"That's frightening."

"I'd say that's rather an understatement. We've been secure against attack here in the homeworlds for so long, or we were before the raid on Port Diamond, that most of us had come to think this sector was totally immune. Of course it's not, as the raid on PD demonstrated."

"A moment ago, you said 'ultimate goal.' That implies they have some intermediate, immediate objective—?"

"Right here." Once more the electronic pointer flickered.

About halfway across the Gulf lay a peculiar spacetime formation, an excrescence of naturally modified matter, some of it polyphase, which at one time or another had borne a variety of different names.

The current official designation was Fifty Fifty.

The fast battle cruiser, a vessel as long as a football field and half as broad, plunged on under skillful astrogation, drawing power from the currents of the Galactic sea around it, flickering routinely in and out of flightspace, carrying Field Marshal Yamanim and a few of his staff officers, along with chosen members of the media corps, to Fifty Fifty. The cruiser was rapidly closing in on its destination.

Jory was fully aware that Yamanim probably wanted to use her, the relatively naive beginner, to plant his ideas in the media.

Every time she and the field marshal encountered each other, in the small world of the cruiser's interior, he found a way to make some subtly flattering remark.

He wasn't buying himself anything, even if he thought he

was. However she got there, she had to go where her job was waiting, and the action was.

Jory was pondering the various indications she had picked up, that human intelligence might have succeeded in breaking the berserker communications code. But how had we managed to intercept enough messages to make that possible?

Less than two days after her visit to the cruiser's tencube chamber, Jory was staring with fascination at the growing image of their destination on the onboard holostages.

The cruiser was coming within practical radio communication distance of the Fifty Fifty base.

Presently she abandoned the holostages, made her way to a cleared port, and looked out. She considered herself a veteran where space travel was concerned, but she had never seen anything like this before.

The approach to Fifty Fifty had very little in common with the comparatively routine experience of entering a normal solar system. Most obviously, there was no sun within a couple of light-years.

The visible, habitable portion of the object called Fifty Fifty had a shape between that of a football and a true sphere, more closely resembling the latter. The thing—it would have been wildly inaccurate to call it a planet—was only a few kilometers across, and its entire surface was vaguely, perpetually glowing with relatively dull light, kind and pleasant to the eyes. None of your usual sun glare here.

The Object, as some of the old charts still called it, was not essentially a gravitational radiant, though it had a kinship with that class of phenomena, and possibly a radiant, somewhere just around the corner and out of normal space, was associated with it. That could provide an imitation of bright sunlight.

All the guidebooks and the most elaborate tencube simulations assured the potential visitor that Solarian lungs breathing Fifty Fifty's artificially created atmosphere enjoyed what they found: Pressure and oxygen content normal for Earth at sea level. Once an atmosphere had been established, maintenance was comparatively easy. Walking feet—no special footgear needed here—crunched the surface as they would a sandy beach. But if the surface was examined closely, there were considerable differences.

The structure was only kept from collapsing to starlike density and minute size by the fact that part of it, by far the greater part, existed outside of normal space.

Gravity at the Object's surface tended to be of the same order of magnitude as that at the surface of the Earth, so closely matched as to be generally comfortable for unarmored Solarians, though the field strength varied from hour to hour and from place to place, sometimes changing substantially within a few hundred meters. Strong artificial-gravity generators, spotted strategically throughout the Object's volume, had proven necessary to maintain something like an Earth-normal value everywhere, for the safety and convenience of visitors.

After spending most of the trip talking to the field marshal and his staff officers, Jory was convinced that capture of Fifty Fifty by the berserkers, and the establishment of their own base on that strong point, would be the next logical and important step in their strategic assault on Earth and the other worlds that lay at the center of the human domain.

Over the centuries of Solarian space exploration, several other objects of a similar nature, frequently called atolls, had been discovered at locations scattered around the known Galaxy; such oddities tended to pop up in the gaps between spiral arms. They didn't radiate much of anything, as a rule, and so were very unlikely to be noticed at distances of a thousand light-years or more.

Making a close approach to any of these objects was a tricky business for spacegoing ship or machine, getting trickier as one drew nearer, though it never became virtually impossible, as in the case of a gravitational radiant. Objects like Fifty Fifty were not nearly as hard to assault as were the fortresses sometimes built surrounding Radiants, the latter being in effect steep gravitational hills; but still the physics of the situation gave the defenders some advantage.

Still it was possible—and the berserker threat had made

it very desirable—to maintain a military base on this particular atoll. Ships using the proper precautions could land and take off. There was room and raw materials for shipyards to be conveniently constructed. Here ships or machines could be repowered, rearmed, and repaired.

Until very recently, at least, no Solarian would have called the Fifty Fifty strongpoint vital, to Earth or to any other human strategy or possession; but now the strange and isolated rock was suddenly beginning to assume an increased importance.

Extraordinary spacetime conditions in the middle of this phenomenon sometimes gave the visual appearance—when seen from an interplanetary distance on the order of hundreds of millions of kilometers—of a blue tropical lagoon, surrounded by a ring suggesting a coral reef, and containing two "islands" of irregular shape, of a flat, sandy appearance, representing the island's intrusion into normal space. The glare of unsettling pseudo-sunlight bathed it all.

On the tawny curves of these islands, signs of human habitation, mainly regular humps indicating shelters and shipyards, were readily visible, though not conspicuous.

It was standard Space Force policy that any enlistee or officer going home on leave could hitch a ride on military transport whenever space happened to be available. The cost of civilian transportation and the level of military pay being what they were, the great majority of servicemen and women on leave sought diligently to hitch rides on military ships.

Two standard days after Spacer Sebastian Gift's departure from Port Diamond, his progress toward Earth, with orders in his pocket calling for twenty days of convalescent leave, had brought him as far as one of the large artificial satellites forming a transportation hub in low orbit of the Cradle Planet.

Still, it seemed, his luck was holding; he had come this far very rapidly, on the fast cruiser bringing Admiral Bowman Earthward to plead, before the premier of Earth herself, the secret, special case for accepting the intelligence estimates from Hypo, and committing on that basis whatever Solarian forces could be mustered to try to save the world.

Not that Nifty knew anything about high-level conferences, or what gambles might be taken to save humanity. He knew only that the admiral had been in a hurry to get here, had ordered the cruiser parked in orbit, and had switched to a shuttlecraft to take his small party down to Earth, where presumably he had been summoned by high-ups for some momentous meeting. His arrival would be less conspicuous that way.

Another, smaller and slower, military shuttle from the cruiser had driven over to the transport hub satellite, where in addition to performing other routine business it had disgorged Gift and a couple of other Space Force people who had been hitching a ride home on leave.

The Earth satellite on which Gift's journey home had stumbled to a halt was an elaborate transportation hub, a metal doughnut hundreds of meters in the diameter of its outer rim.

There his progress stalled. The high state of military alert was drastically slowing all nonessential travel.

The ubiquitous space police, in their symbolic lightweight white helmets and white gloves, had checked Gift out as soon as he got off the little shuttle. They scrutinized the traveler's orders closely, though being convalescent allowed him great freedom of travel, even under the high state of alert currently in effect. It didn't matter to them how he had arrived here. He was no celebrity to them; everyone in uniform—and there were a fair number scattered through the crowd—was getting the same treatment. This was one of the results of the high state of alert under which everyone was now functioning. A lot of military people traveled in civilian clothes, when possible, to avoid this; but you were required to wear your uniform if you were hitching a ride on a military vehicle.

The transport hub was one of several similar satellites hanging close to Earth. This one rode in a polar curve, a few thousand klicks above the planet's mostly watery surface. Entering the main waiting room or concourse, Gift found himself standing in an echoing, cavernous space almost the size of a football field, surrounded by several hundred other people who were also waiting for transport down to the planet or on the next leg of some outward journey. It almost seemed that everyone in the homeworlds wanted to be somewhere else, just at the time when travel restrictions were going into effect.

There would be no military lift available down to the surface for several hours at least; and the next one tentatively scheduled, which might or might not have space for him to get aboard, would land him far from the location of his home. Lengthy, elaborate surface or aerial transport would have been required for him to complete his journey. He hadn't been invited to get aboard the admiral's shuttle, so where it might be bound for on the surface was a moot point.

Carrying his single bag in his right hand, Gift turned his back on the phone niche and strolled about. Almost immediately he found himself being drawn to an observation port.

Seen like this, from close above, the nearby bulk of Earth was armored in the dun-brown of defensive force fields, the normal colors of land, water, and air invisible.

It was the first time in several years, since his last visit home on leave, that Gift had had a close look at Earth. It produced in him surprisingly mixed feelings. The grimness down there looked like industrial smoke from some previous millennium, though he knew it wasn't.

Somewhere in the throng a tired infant wailed, and was immediately answered by an accomplice at a distance. The sound pierced the muted murmur of a hundred people talking, while hundreds more endured the wait in silence. Some meditated, some read, others dozed or watched advertisements or news programs on one of the stages scattered about everywhere.

The unexpected sense of relief Gift experienced when the notice board told him he would have a long delay made him realize how deeply reluctant to go home he really was. Thinking back to how attractive the idea had seemed only a few days ago when he was in the hospital, he realized that it was probably his childhood and not his home that he had wanted to get back to.

That was not a welcome thought.

Slowly he paced what seemed a random pathway through the crowd, carrying his modest traveling bag in his right hand—

he didn't wholly trust the new fingers on his left. The new hand had plenty of strength, but the control was still uncertain, and the sensations in the fingers blurred. He wondered idly if the artificial nails were going to grow. He supposed they'd given him information on that detail, along with a lot of other stuff, at the hospital. But if so, he'd forgotten. Experimentally he now shifted the weight of the bag to his left hand, and it seemed to work all right.

For years now, ever since his middle teens, Gift had been drifting away from his parents, who had also, since about that time, been separated from each other though they lived at no great geographical distance. Nifty hadn't heard from either one of them for—how long now? About a standard year? He couldn't quite recall.

Noticing that his seemingly random walk had brought him back to the same observation port, he reflected that he wasn't entirely sure if either his mother or father was still alive.

Gift was also feeling a definite reluctance to face certain other people he thought he would be very likely to encounter if he visited his parents. These were folk who had been close to some other of Gift's and Traskeluk's former shipmates. And if he met them they were certain, in their bereavement and their ignorance, to ask the only survivor on the crew some uncomfortable questions.

The next leg of his stroll, conducted without any conscious planning, ended when he found himself standing in line to buy a shuttle ticket down. When he thought about it, he realized that he was in the line mainly because he didn't know what else to do.

Abruptly he left the queue, and walked through the crowd some more, feeling trapped.

Thinking these matters over, Gift had come yet again to a standstill in front of one of the big statglass viewports, where he stood looking out into low space, watching among other things the faint visible traces of the impressive array of defensive satellites that helped to screen from attack the parent planet of all Solarians. Each of those artificial moons, of course, carried formidable weapons, none of which were apparent to the casual observer. Their orbits, crisscrossing space just above Earth's atmosphere at almost every angle, wove an intricate pattern, thousands of kilometers in depth.

Even as Gift stood watching, a small blur leaped over Earth's dun-brown limb, hurtling along on a course that would bring it within a few hundred kilometers of the windowed doughnut where he and hundreds of others waited for transportation. Gift knew the blur was Power Station One, a tamed black hole. In times of peace the power-hungry billions on the planet drew from it half their needed energy. Station One—he had forgotten how many there were like it—was visible to the eye only as a slight, flowing distortion of the stars beyond.

The black hole, given a wide berth by all the other orbiting objects, flashed by. Not really tamed, of course, though that was a reassuring word. Just harnessed. There were those who thought such power sources represented a danger worse than berserkers. Danger, maybe, thought Gift now. But not worse. Whoever said that had never been anywhere near a real berserker.

Gift had also heard rumors that the power station had been integrated into the defensive network, where it played the role of a kind of trap or sink, into which attacking machines were to be decoyed or pushed.

A moment later, Gift experienced a feeling of being under intense observation, and looked around him sharply. It was beginning to become a familiar sensation. And since leaving the hospital he sometimes had the feeling when it seemed that no one could possibly be watching him.

This time he had to consciously reassure himself that the attention he sensed could not possibly be that of either Terrin nor Traskeluk. Both of them were dead, and going to remain so.

No, he wasn't being stalked by any of the dead come back. But this time his instincts *were* right on target. Someone was studying him intently. There she was.

When the girl who was actually watching Spacer Gift approached him, as he stood in line or looking out the window, he thought he knew what she was going to say. Under other circumstances he would certainly have found her attentions flattering. Since he'd left the base at Port Diamond, other young women along the way had given signs that they would like to get to know him better; but until now he'd been in a hurry. And now he wondered why.

Nifty first became aware of this one through her reflected image in the composite glass that formed the inner layer of the broad observation port. She looked truly young, not yet twenty at an estimate, and her slender figure was coming toward him steadily and purposefully; the nature of the movement, the determined look on her pale face, and the fact that her small fists were clenched, told him that this was not going to be easy to discourage.

And suddenly he realized that he was in no hurry to get anywhere anyway, and therefore he had no reason to be discouraging.

So far, from his dramatic return to Uhao until he boarded the admiral's cruiser at Port Diamond, Gift had been frequently reminded of his celebrity status. His brief experience since leaving the hospital suggested that he would have no problem at all finding any kind of companionship he wanted. No doubt the badly concealed fear and disgust he felt gave the impression of shyness, and made him all the more attractive. So far he'd been avoiding that kind of attention, beyond a few minutes' casual conversation. A few months ago, immediately after the berserker raid on Port Diamond, casualties had come pouring through here in a flood; but for the last few weeks, wounded war heroes had once more been rare.

And the more he looked at this one, the more easily he could convince himself that she was truly different. She was good-looking, all right, but not the best he'd seen on his way home. Wearing sandals, and a clinging, short-skirted dress that, he decided, was probably more expensive than a first look at it suggested. Certainly it was flattering. Legs were displayed to advantage, slim hips neatly suggested rather than revealed. Like him, she was carrying one small piece of luggage. Her eyes were hazel, skin a creamy off-white, her long hair in braids was almost the color of metal shavings. But there was nothing harsh or cold about her face or attitude.

"Hello," she said, in a slightly husky and distinctive voice.

"Hello." He turned fully around, setting his back to the observation port.

"I've been watching you." Her voice was not hero-worshiping but almost challenging. She was almost as tall as he.

"Do I pass inspection?"

That didn't get a direct answer. "I've been waiting for you."

"Really? How did you know I was going to be here?"

They were standing an arm's length apart, with the crowd milling around them.

"I knew." The girl nodded solemnly. "You're going home on leave now, right? The story said your home was on Earth."

He heard himself say: "I'm not sure where my home is any longer." And as he said the words, he realized that they were true, and that he was basically comfortable with them.

In any case, the girl ignored the statement. Under pressure of various crowd nudges, they were now a couple of centimeters closer to each other. "I'm not going to offer to buy you a drink, anything like that. I just wanted to see what a hero looked like." There was no gushing or simpering in the remark. But at the same time, as far as Gift could tell, she sounded perfectly sincere.

He cleared his throat. "Who says I'm a hero?"

"Lots of people." She tossed her metalized braids. "You're Spacer First Class Nifty Gift, aren't you?"

"I have to plead guilty to that, at least."

"Spacer First Class," she mused, as if there were something remarkable about that very ordinary rank. It wasn't clear if she thought it ought to be higher or lower. Her forefinger traced gently the stripes on his right sleeve, and it seemed to Gift that he could feel a surprising physical warmth of contact, even through the thickness of his uniform. Her fingernails appeared to have been altered to grow in the same color as her hair.

"And your left arm has been hurt," she went on. "They said that on the news." Now she touched the sleeved forearm on that side, even more gently. There was no obvious giveaway that the hand and wrist were artificial, and he supposed the idea never occurred to her. She went on: "So you're the one. You've been in the news for days. How you were the only survivor of your ship."

It had already occurred to Nifty that his one brief press conference must have been broadcast a large number of times, all across the homeworlds and probably farther. He had seen it, or part of it, a couple of times himself, by accident.

It gave him an odd feeling to think of his image, his few stumbling, untruthful words on all the media, spreading out across the Solarian Galaxy. Uncounted billions of people had heard his name, thought that his ship had been a crewed courier or a scout or supply ship. The location where it had been destroyed was only vaguely specified.

"I guess a lot of people have seen my face on holostages and in pictures," he said, aware of understatement.

"Indeed, you're famous."

Several anonymous units of the crowd bumped him again, one after another in rapid succession. "Well, we're the only two here who seem to realize it. Let me buy you a drink after all, if you don't want to buy me one. What's your name?"

"I didn't say I wouldn't buy you one. My name is Flower."

"Just generic Flower? Why not maybe Lily, Rose, Violet, some particular kind of flower. Orchid?"

"No. Just Flower. One name is enough."

He understood, from listening to young people at the hospital, that having only a single name was a fast-spreading fad just now among the young. Anyway, this girl's features were delicate, and the name she had picked for herself seemed to fit.

"Pretty." He was thinking that he didn't believe it, it somehow fit too well. "Real name?"

They had linked arms now and were walking together. Flower gripped his left arm, as if it had already slipped her mind that it was supposed to be wounded. Her voice took on an edge. "Certainly it is. If I use it for myself, that makes it real."

"Can't argue with that." Still, he wasn't sure that it really fit. It wouldn't be the name he'd pick for her.

"Why do they call you Nifty? That's what the media said. Is that *your* real name?"

He shrugged. "Real name's Sebastian. 'Nifty' because of a . . . a way I have of doing things, I guess."

"Doing things?"

"People think—or they used to think—I have a knack for keeping myself out of trouble."

Strolling together in the crowd was difficult, but they kept at it. She asked: "They used to think that but they don't anymore?"

He sighed. His right arm, carrying his traveling bag, was growing tired, and he wished he could set the burden down somewhere. "I don't know what people think about me right now."

"They think you're a hero."

The words had a flat tone. He inspected his questioner silently. Evidently the remark had been innocent.

"Is it all right if I call you Nifty?"

"I'm used to it. Everybody else does." Nobody in the world but his parents would now call him by the name that they had given him.

"How long of a leave do you have?"

He told her the number of remaining days.

Flower was dressed in a fairly inconspicuous fashion. It was as if she gave only sporadic attention to her wardrobe, but had good taste when she did. She was slender and looked rather frail, with a kind of pastel darkness about her. Hair dyed, some steel colored and some copper. Probably, Gift thought, it had been genetically root dyed, so you could only try to guess what its original color might have been. In his opinion, it didn't add any points to her appearance.

She was wearing some kind of mechanical jewelry. Not expensive, he supposed, but not what you ordinarily saw. A brooch that displayed, in optical illusion, moving dots of light against a changing background. Then, in the next moment, moving dots of darkness against light.

Only when they were walking together did Gift notice that his companion's earlobes had been mutilated. Tiny holes, now lined with skin, had at some time been punched in them to accommodate earrings. He hadn't noticed immediately, he supposed, because she wore no earrings now. The holes were only simple punctures, but it was a thing that he had only seen once or twice before, and never in an otherwise attractive woman. It made him feel a little queasy.

Flower's thoughts were elsewhere. Absently she let go his arm again.

"Nifty."

"What?"

"Did you ever see a berserker? I mean like close up?"

"That's a funny question."

"Did you?"

"One, yes."

"Only one?"

"One was enough."

"What did it look like?"

"Pretty hard to describe." He didn't feel like making the effort.

Flower, after giving him plenty of time in which to change his mind, said something sympathetic. She had some way of putting her interest in Gift that caught his interest too, and made him think that she was offering him something that he needed. Nobody else was even coming close in that regard.

"So, are you going home now to see your family? I suppose they still live down there?" With a nod she indicated the smoggy blue-and-brown expanse slowly turning beyond the nearest viewport.

"Yep."

"You don't sound all that enthusiastic. No wife and kids to welcome you?"

"No. And my parents and I don't always see eye to eye about everything," With a sigh he looked at Flower hopefully. "Maybe you know how that is."

"Of course I do." And her hand came out once more, impulsively, to touch his arm.

Gift didn't see why the answer to that question should be *of course.* But if she did, so be it. Maybe, it just might be, he would be able to talk to this one.

"Come here on a military ship?"

"Yep. How about you?"

"The ship I came on was a lot more comfortable than yours, I bet."

"No bet."

Spacer Gift kept on talking to the girl. The little things about her that might have put him off—like her hair and her earlobes—were in a faintly perverse way kind of attractive too. She was something different. It seemed that she really didn't want to talk to him so much as she wanted to listen. It felt like exactly what he had needed; the chance to be with someone with a gift for uncritical listening—not that he was going to tell her anything of real importance. He wasn't going to tell such matters to anyone. Not for a long time, anyway.

Before they had been together a quarter of an hour he found himself buying his new companion a bland, unsatisfactory meal in the Satellite Café, one of several virtually indistinguishable restaurants available. Before leaving Hypo he'd picked up some back pay, a fat check because he hadn't been collecting pay while on the long mission, and he would have sought out a classier place to eat had there been any within reach.

After consuming about half of what he'd put on his tray, he pushed the rest away from him. "The best you can say for this stuff is that it kills the appetite."

"It's all right." Flower had eaten more than he, but she stopped eating now that he had done so.

"I like to eat by candlelight. Do you?"

· · ·

Soon the couple were strolling again. They came to another observation port, or the same one where they'd met, looking down on the planet that Gift no longer really thought of as his homeworld.

At least it was the familiar homeworld of his race, and he felt mixed emotions. Even disguised and disfigured as it was by force fields, something about it looked so lovely.

Flower mentioned where she was from. Somewhere on Earth. Recently, it seemed, she had been living in or near Port Diamond.

"Uhao's a beautiful place."

She nodded enthusiastically. "I'm going back there soon."

An hour after his new friend had introduced herself, they had left the crowded restaurant, and Flower was standing beside the wounded veteran hero, already holding his arm—this time she had picked his good arm, perhaps by chance—in what seemed to Gift a somewhat proprietary way. He wasn't sure just how he felt about that.

Now the Earth appeared to be overhead, a prospect that made some observers giddy. The smoothly constant artificial gravity obtaining inside the passenger space, while intrinsically comfortable, made it harder to orient yourself properly with regard to the view outside.

Gift imagined himself completing his journey to Earth. Leaving the satellite, he would spend time riding a shuttle down, zigzagging slowly through layer after layer of force fields and other defenses. The trip—once you could get aboard a ship— now took several hours, considerably longer than he remembered. Without a high-priority clearance, which he certainly did not have, it was going to take a while. Under the high degree of alert that was presently in force, only a very few military ships were cleared to come from deep space directly to Earth's surface.

Flower, listening attentively and speaking wistfully, gave the impression that it was just naturally her job, or her destiny, to help Spacer Gift deal with the difficulties that went with becoming something of a minor celebrity—he'd had no choice in the matter, and she accepted the fact that nothing about his new status really pleased him.

Suddenly it occurred to him that he still didn't know why she had really come to the satellite. It couldn't very well have really been simply to meet him. Abruptly he demanded, "Where are you going?"

"I'm on my way back to Uhao."

"But I thought you were saying you just came from there. Like me." He'd begun to hope that at least he could count on her being with him on the shuttle going down to Earth.

"I did. I was going to meet someone here." Looking around at the crowd, she shook her head slightly. Then she added, with seeming irrelevance, "But it's such a lovely place. Uhao, I mean."

"Your family lives there?"

"Not my parents, no. Some friends. Friends are the family you choose for yourself."

"I've heard that."

Flower hesitated, and then more words poured out, while she tightened her grip on Gift's good arm.

"I just happen to have an extra ticket with me, and you're welcome to use it, if you like."

"An extra ticket."

"For passage on a spaceship. If you would be interested in coming back to Port Diamond with me."

The offer took him completely by surprise, and for a moment he could only look at her. "Go with you?"

"That's what I said." She amplified: "It's in a neat cabin on a luxury ship."

Gift had never been able to afford to travel like that. Very few people could. In the ordinary course of life he would probably never have traveled beyond atmosphere at all—except for having joined the service.

From the way she was holding his arm, hanging breathlessly on his answer, it became obvious that she really wanted him, in some serious way. Suddenly, in a quiet voice, she added, "They tell me my compartment has one big bed." Her eyelashes fluttered once when she spoke, and then she was looking away from him, while at the same time sliding her body a little closer.

Wow. Nifty's pulse was steadily quickening. The body under the short skirt had suddenly become attainable. He wondered who the lover was, what kind of man he was displacing on such short notice, and was on the verge of asking. But he supposed that none of that really mattered, and he decided not to press for any explanation. If Flower didn't want to offer one, he wasn't going to push.

But he didn't have to think about the basic question very long. And she certainly didn't need to ask him twice. "You've got a deal."

There was something to be said for hero worship after all.

Gift kept telling himself that he would soon be displaced in the public eye. Before long, some other wounded hero would come on the scene, probably someone who enjoyed the situation more, and had some kind of victorious story to tell. Then everyone would quickly lose interest in Nifty Gift.

And yet, in spite of everything, there was a part of him that hoped they wouldn't.

On impulse he took Flower in his arms and gave her a long and erotic kiss. They might as well have been holding hands for all the attention they got; there were a lot of separations and reunions going on here simultaneously.

Her response indicated that she had been serious when she talked about the fine bed in the luxury cabin.

After a few moments she held him at arm's length, and said with heartfelt sincerity, "I'm glad you're coming with me."

"Me too."

The problem was that the departure of the luxury liner was several hours away.

. . .

On the satellite there seemed only one possible way to obtain privacy—and only a doubtful kind of privacy at that. There was a large room with walls filled with tiers of metal-doored compartments, not that much larger than baggage lockers, and complete with Spartan furnishings and plumbing. It all looked pretty much like what Nifty imagined a prison would be like. The two upper rows of these compartments were accessible from catwalks running in front of the rows of doors. In one of these sleeping bins that passed as hotel rooms a truly weary traveler could grab some sleep, or truly impatient lovers could spend an hour out of sight of everyone else. Under the crowded conditions naturally all of these were booked, and a few people were even standing in line. Space on all civilian ships was at a premium just now, and anyone with a ticket would be well advised not to waste it.

After exchanging looks with Flower, Gift decided that his enjoyment of her body, much as he was looking forward to the experience, could wait until they could find a real room somewhere. Besides, contemplating the rows of cramped metal bins reminded him too forcibly of the confined space on the courier.

Flower seemed relieved, not at all anxious to try out the mailbox-type accommodations. She shrank back and demonstrated a general lack of enthusiasm.

They walked around some more. "How long have you been waiting for him?" he wondered aloud.

"For who?"

He looked at her.

"Oh. It's a long story."

And not one that she wanted to tell, evidently. Or he, if the truth be known, to hear.

The luxury liner Flower had promised was docked at the proper gate; an enormous bulk, bigger than the cruiser, and only partially visible from where the locks connected.

The *Queen Mab* was ready to board passengers on schedule. The ticket that Flower handed Gift before they boarded had been issued under another man's name, but it seemed unlikely that anyone would bother to check up, and in fact nobody did.

The line at the gate was short, and made up of well-dressed people. Gift took the opportunity of noticing that the name on his companion's ticket was not "Flower." And he assumed it was her own real name. But he continued to call her by the name she'd told him was hers.

The estimated arrival time back at Uhao was two or three days in the future, depending on flightspace conditions.

The luxury compartment, when they had found their way down the narrow corridor to reach it, almost lived up to Nifty's expectations—particularly when he'd just got through looking at the metal sleeping bins. The cabin certainly qualified as a real room, though its actual dimensions were a little tight. A virtual window had real curtains, stirring in a slight breeze, and a choice of pleasant scenes beyond, including mountains and the seashore. To one who had spent most of the last few months aboard a small military craft, this seemed indeed luxurious.

Muted chimes were followed by a genteel voice announcing that liftoff was in three minutes.

Almost before liftoff had been completed, Gift and Flower had closed themselves into their cabin, and were trying out the double bed. He discovered to his amusement that there was an attachment on the bed by which the local artificial gravity could be set to pulsate.

When the bed covers had been turned back, and Nifty's tunic and shirt came off, he automatically checked the appearance of his left arm, an act that had become a habit in recent days. The live portion of the limb looked a little mottled, but the return of function had been coming along nicely. There were still no obvious clues to the fact that his forearm and hand were not the ones he'd grown up with. The seam where his own skin blended with the fake stuff was practically invisible. Flower, who had known that the arm was hurt, took one glance at it and appeared to think no more about it. And Gift said nothing on the subject. He didn't want to talk about any of that anymore. Not if he could help it.

· · ·

And, when the time came, a moment or two later, it was without real surprise that Nifty made the discovery that Flower's body hair was root dyed too. Follicles could be tuned to produce 256 colors in every square centimeter of skin.

When the two of them had got out of bed to unpack their modest baggage, and had done what little they had to do to settle into their compartment—it was about as large as an ordinary living room, with a private bath behind a door—he felt the need to talk to her some more, to justify himself. The bathroom had a window too, even a little larger than the one beside the bed.

Some hours later, they were lounging around in their cabin, watching on the little stage some space adventure story directed by Jay Nash.

"That means it'll be good."

"What're we going to do when we get to Uhao? I don't want to hang around anywhere near the base."

"I have some friends we could visit," she suggested.

But Nifty wasn't paying much attention. He had just been struck by an idea. "You know what? I want to take one of those pyramid tours. All the time I've spent on that planet, and I've always wanted to do that . . . and I've never done it."

Flower was agreeable.

Everything aboard ship was going smoothly enough for the couple until they visited the dining room. It turned out that they were sharing a table with an older couple.

The other couple picked up on something Flower said, and identified Nifty as the celebrity war hero.

By now Gift felt himself getting very tired, unnaturally tired, of telling and retelling the story of what happened to him and to his shipmates, way over there toward the far side of the Gulf. It felt like he had told it a thousand times, though when he actually tried to count them up, it turned out that if he left out the debriefing sessions, a dozen would be a lot closer to the truth.

Gradually, in the process of retelling, the corners and edges of the narrative had got smoothed off, and some details were changed. Actually by now there were several versions; he wasn't quite sure which one he liked the best. According to the fragmentary version that Gift was passing along to Flower in bits and pieces, the last surviving pair of his shipmates, Traskeluk and Terrin, had both been killed in his presence, trying to make the same escape that he'd managed successfully. This time he had them a little ahead of him in their flight—the two of them trying to ride the scooter at the same time.

Flower listened intently, almost without interrupting. Once she broke in to ask: "How close did you get to the berserker?"

"Too damn close."

"Did you really see it?"

"Will you kindly just shut up about that? I don't want to talk about it."

Accepting the rebuke meekly, Flower gave up trying to press the wounded hero for more particulars of his story. But she had listened solemnly and attentively while he was telling it. Gift couldn't make up his mind whether she believed everything he told her or not. Certainly she seemed sympathetic, if only because she gave him her concentrated attention.

Although by now he had come, on some level, to actually believe his own story. There *was* a lot of truth in it, after all.

He must have been looking at Flower in a questioning way, for at last she said: "It's a strange story. But I believe it."

He looked at her. "Why shouldn't you believe it?"

"I just said I do."

Now that Gift was aboard a ship carrying him away from home at superluminal velocity, he was free to let himself understand that the closer he had been getting to Earth and to his relatives, the sharper a certain private fear had grown. Now he was able to define it: It was a dread of some day running into the relatives or friends of the two people he'd left behind to be roasted by the berserker. Even if he tried to avoid them, he couldn't help feeling that he'd one day run into them by accident. As if Earth was a small town, and if someone was there you were bound to see them.

Sooner or later, he thought, those people would be deliberately trying to seek him out. Traskeluk's family, he recalled, had belonged to some weird clan, most of whose members were on some distant world. Trask's peers aboard ship, including Gift once or twice, had joked with him about it. But he could very clearly remember Traskeluk saying that some of his people had migrated back to Earth and Port Diamond. He knew less about the family of Ensign Terrin.

Then there was always the chance that Gift would encounter another journalistic interviewer, one who'd encourage him to get maudlin about his dear comrades who had been lost. A large segment of the public loved that kind of thing. Or at least that seemed to be the theory guiding a great number of journalists. No doubt in a few months it would be safe for him to go home—or he would be better prepared to face the questioning. But not just now.

It came to Gift as a private, inner shock that some people—if they wanted to put an unfriendly interpretation on that accident when his two shipmates had been lost—would think that a man who'd done what they suspected Nifty Gift of doing fit the definition of goodlife. Of course that was nonsense—he'd saved his own life, hadn't he? And a courier machine, which had some value. And whatever information the machine had happened to have on board.

Yes, of course the truth was (though it would be awkward to come right out and say so) that all he'd really done had been to exercise common sense. Even supposing the courier's drive and autopilot had been working perfectly. Yes, even then, his two shipmates had been dead, before he could have possibly done anything to help them. His getting himself killed too wouldn't have brought them back. Would it?

And about the same time it struck Gift also, with the weight of a final decision, that he really didn't want to go home at all, where he would certainly have to talk about all these things again—and again. Not only didn't he want to go there now, but it would be all right with him if he never saw those people and that place again.

Passengers on a ship like this, Gift soon discovered, usually took their meals in a dining room. Probably two seatings were generally required, but maybe only one if there were only a few folk traveling. Some preferred to have their food brought, by robot steward, to their cabins. But it was good to get out of the cabin if only for a little while.

The next time they went to the dining room the people who had recognized Gift were there again, and insisted on paying for his meal, and his companion's. And hinted that they would like to hear his story yet again. He declined, more or less politely.

"It's young men like you who will bring us through." And they raised their glasses to him.

"Thank you," said Nifty, not knowing what else to say. Now people at other tables were smiling at him too. Evidently the story of his fame had got around.

When they were making their way back to their cabin, Flower said: "If you were wearing civvies instead of your uniform, people might not recognize you."

"All right, I'll change." He hesitated. "It's not that I want to be recognized. Just that my civvy clothes are a little shabby for a ship like this. Actually, they might make me even more noticeable."

"Let me see." She looked through his meager change of clothing and thought about it. "There's a gift shop on board. Tell me your sizes, and I can get some things for you."

"The prices are going to be pretty high. I wanted to save my money so we can do some fun things when we land."

Again she thought about it, frowning prettily. No great intellectual, this girl; but that was all right with Gift. If she was seriously planning to buy him expensive presents, her heart was certainly in the right place.

At last her face cleared. "It'll be all right, I've got some money. No reason I can't spend it on you."

"Well." Nifty didn't know what to think or say. But he supposed that Flower might well come from some family that was filthy rich. "Well, thanks," he got out at last.

"Besides," his new companion said, her face brightening by a few more degrees, "if you're in civvies, the space police or whatever they are won't pester you any more. Will they?"

"No. No, they won't have any way of knowing that I fall under their jurisdiction."

"Why do they do that, anyway? Ask people in uniform for their orders?"

"Beats me. I suppose, if you were deserting, or AWOL . . . but if you were really deserting, the first thing you'd do would be to get out of your uniform. And the military like to feel they're in control. They worry about goodlife spies, and things like that."

"Goodlife." Flower looked pensive. "Of all the things for them to worry about. *I* don't think these so-called goodlife people are a big cause for worry, do you?"

Gift shook his head. "I have a lot of other problems on my mind, more important than whether some crazy people want to worship a machine."

Flower looked sympathetic. But she didn't nag at him with questions, for which he felt grateful.

Flower asked him: "Will they send you back into space when your leave's over?"

"I don't think so. They told me I'm in line for a home office job."

"Are you happy about that? Not being on flying status any longer?"

"Hell yes." That kind of job, if the truth were known, was what he had thought he was applying for in the first place, when he'd volunteered for the mysterious assignment that had turned out to be a place on a Hypo crew. It had been something of a belated effort on his part to stay out of combat, now that there were signs that the war in the Home Sector might be heating up. He had to laugh at that, looking back; so far he hadn't been able to share the joke with anyone.

· · ·

At some point he found himself letting Flower believe, just to impress her, that he was much more knowledgeable about Hypo's inner secrets than he really was. He caught himself doing that, and thought it was stupid, but then he went right on doing it anyway.

Next time they went to the dining room Gift was dressed in some pretty sharp civilian clothes—a crimson turtleneck and a rich gray jacket over it. Flower hadn't been stingy in the gift shop, and the case for a wealthy family was strengthened. But this did nothing to help Gift's situation with regard to the same elderly couple, who had evidently been continuing to spread the word that there was a handsome young celebrity aboard. So Gift was deviled again, by a different set of generous civilians, into having to answer questions about his heroic feat of getting the crippled courier home. More beaming people who wished him well, and whom he loathed wholeheartedly. It was difficult, trying to be pleasant; but he made the effort, not wishing to call even more attention to himself, and he thought that he succeeded.

After the first two days, he called cabin service and had a robot bring his and Flower's meals to the cabin. They spent most of their time in bed, and hardly left the room for anything. It worried Nifty a little that maybe Flower wasn't going to like the new arrangement, but to his surprise it was fine with her.

A moderate twist of spacetime away from Earth and its threatened billions, in a remote region of the Gulf, the captain and crew of a scoutship were having success, of a kind, in keeping a certain scheduled rendezvous. This qualified success had cost them months of training, weeks of effort, and a great investment in astrogational skill.

And now, they had at last managed to locate the Hypo spy ship they had been dispatched to meet—but at first sight, the pieces of the spy ship were somewhat hard to recognize.

Stark evidence of disaster.

The scout proceeded warily, flickering several times in and out of normal space. The crew's first concern was whether the enemy might still be present. But minutes passed, and there was no indication of that.

The scout's captain, staring gloomily at a holostage in front of his combat chair, beheld a thin haze of Solarian space-craft parts, spread out in a slowly expanding cloud of less easily identifiable artifact dust, artifact gas, and bigger bits of wreckage.

Presently he ordered out a swarm of half-intelligent robots, after instructing them in what to look for. These spread rapidly through nearby space, hungrily gobbling samples, industriously telemetering data back to their waiting human masters.

After an hour or so of this, the ship's computer, pressed for an opinion, delivered in its cool voice an estimate that the deadly battle had taken place some four or five standard days before the scout's arrival on the scene.

"Well, Skipper." This was the harsh voice of the first mate, sitting in the combat chair to the captain's right.

"Yeah."

Neither man needed to speak his next thought aloud: Had they arrived four or five days earlier, they might have been just in time to tip the balance the right way in a savage fight. Or, perhaps, to be obliterated, along with the Hypo craft.

The scout's mission had called for making the rendezvous to exchange with the spy ship certain crew members and equipment, and above all, to take on a practically weightless but perhaps very valuable cargo of information. In the vastness of the Gulf, such intended meetings were often missed—but this time fortune smiled on Solarian plans.

Following the melancholy discovery of wreckage, confirmed by spectroscopic analysis as that of the ship they had come here to meet, there was nothing else to do but conduct a perfunctory search for anything of value that might possibly still be salvageable.

It was slightly encouraging to discover a good bit of other wreckage, which was just as readily identifiable as having come from a berserker. The swarming Solarian robots reported that two chunks of the latter were very large, the size of ground cars.

The first mate, who generally preferred to look at the bright side of things, commented: "At least it looks like the bandit didn't get away without a scratch—in fact, I wonder if the contest might have ended in a draw."

"Mutual destruction? Maybe. There *is* a lot of junk around here. Let's see if we can run a reconstruction."

Presently the ship's computer was re-creating the fight, on a small holostage in view of the scoutship's officers, using as data the types, positions, and velocities of recognizable debris reported by the searching robots.

"The berserker must have been one big bastard," said the first mate. "By comparison with our spy, I mean."

"Possibly on its last legs, though—look at those hull plates." The stage image of one of the larger pieces of wreckage rotated on the captain's command. "That's severe damage, right there, but you can see that some of it's old stuff that had been repaired before this last fight started. Maybe the hit that finished it off was a small one."

"Yeah, a last straw kind of thing. I guess there must be a moral there somewhere. Like 'never give up.'"

"Or else: 'Don't start a new fight while you're still punchy from an old one.'"

After a pause, the first mate said: "I don't think berserkers ever look for light duty. They don't have any retirement plan."

Then, as the search for important hardware and human remains pressed on, came an incredulous—and almost incredible—claim, in the voice of the organic engineer in charge of the robotic search: "Captain, we've got a survivor here!"

"Full report!" the captain barked, after a moment of silent shock. With his next breath, he had to choke back an angry accusation of insanity.

Minutes later, he was glad that he had demonstrated restraint.

Evidence of breathing by a suited figure who could only be one of the spy ship's crew, still alive though several systems in his or her suit were on the brink of failure, had been duly noted and reported by one of the searching robots. Minutes later, the fortunate one was being picked up by a livecrewed launch, and brought aboard the scout.

The man in the battered spacesuit proved indeed to be still alive, and at first glance gave every indication that he was going to stay that way, despite having a badly shattered left arm, and a number of other medical difficulties. His inert form was hauled aboard the scout, stripped of its armor, and shoved into a medirobot.

One of the searching robots also discovered and brought in a heavy Solarian shoulder weapon, which had been picked up drifting near the living man. The strong implication was that he'd been trying to fight off small berserkers with it.

"Have we got an identification on this man?"

"Yes, sir. One of his tags is still intact. Spacer Second Class Traskeluk." The name was soon confirmed, on a copy of the spy ship's secret roster, which the scout was carrying.

A hurried but careful search, extending for several kilometers in every direction, was conducted for additional survivors.

Having failed to achieve any more miracles along that line, the scoutship did not dawdle in the area.

The captain, as soon as he had his ship safely back in flightspace, and felt he could be spared from the control cabin, went down the companionway and looked into the medirobot, at the recumbent figure there, stripped now and with probes sticking out of it everywhere among the bandages. It was a muscular body, mesomorphically masculine though not particularly large, with heavy facial features and thick black eyebrows. Drifting in and out of consciousness, the injured man kept babbling something that the medirobot mikes brought outside.

The captain raised his own more modest eyebrows. "What's that noise he's making?"

The human medic—scouts as a rule carried no fully qualified organic surgeon or physician—looked over her shoulder. "Believe he's trying to sing, sir."

"Trying to sing. *Sing?*"

The medic nodded, turning back to the medirobot panel. She was a fifteen-year Space Force veteran. "Sounds to me like part of an old Templar battle song."

"Well, proves he's still breathing, anyway." The captain looked at the medirobot's panel. Unless all the gauges were lying, it seemed very likely that the occupant was going to make it home—and what a story he would have to tell.

And think of the man's family! They would have been told

that he was dead, killed in action. And now, what a glorious surprise!

"The personnel file on Cedric Traskeluk says he is unmarried, with no dependents."

"Oh. Well, anyway, that's one tough man." The captain shook his head admiringly. "Evidently he has *something* to live for."

The ship's computer was still chewing on the data gathered at the scene of destruction, trying to reconstruct the spy ship's last minutes. No doubt about it now. It appeared that the berserker that had almost wiped out the spy ship's crew had been itself destroyed, after all, by some kind of lucky hit.

Further analysis of what had been discovered in the way of drifting debris turned up even more berserker parts. More confirmation that the thing had been damaged in some earlier firefight.

"With another Solarian ship?"

"Who else? We are the only branch of Galactic humanity who are at all likely to be arming spaceships. But the earlier fight could have been a year ago, or even a hundred years, and a long way from here."

Again the man in the medirobot drew in breath and made a peculiar noise. Maybe, by God, he really was trying to sing.

Meanwhile, Traskeluk, drifting in and out of awareness, gradually came to realize that he was in a medirobot. He remembered the berserker. Did he ever. Certain images of that would stay with him as long as he had two brain cells left.

He decided that if he was conscious now, the chances were that he was going to pull through.

Finally it came to him. He was aboard a scoutship, of course. His own ship must have had a scheduled rendezvous with this one—only the senior crew members would have known about that, just in case someone was captured. No one could be made to tell what they didn't know.

Somehow he'd lasted long enough. His suit had kept him

alive for hours, or days. How many days? It didn't matter. Their number had been enough.

No, he wasn't that much surprised to find himself still living. Not really. He'd been determined he was going to live, somehow, live long enough to do just one more thing before he died.

He couldn't feel anything at all in his left hand, but slowly he clenched the fingers of his right into a fist.

Get his hands on Nifty Gift.

Now that Traskeluk was alive and—most of the time—awake again, he couldn't get the thing that Gift had done out of his mind. He lay thinking it over, in the intervals when he could get his mind to focus—such periods were coming faster now, and lasting longer.

Traskeluk tried several times, but could come up with no other conceivable explanation. Nifty had deliberately run out, had crept and scrambled away like the sniveling coward Traskeluk had always suspected him to be, leaving two of his shipmates to be slaughtered—or worse, captured—by a berserker.

While the two of them, Terrin and Traskeluk, had been still space-swimming for their lives, he, Trask, had told the ensign several times what he was going to do to Gift when he caught up with him again.

She hadn't tried to argue with him. In a way, it was as if the ensign knew she wasn't going to make it.

And Trask, the survivor, could verify with certainty that Ensign Terrin had not made it through alive. Another memory that was going to be with him from now on.

The two people who had been so helplessly exposed in space had seen exactly what Gift did. They saw him run, were witnesses to his betrayal, even as they screamed at him for help. They'd had time to comment on him after he was gone, though only one of them had taken advantage of the opportunity.

When people standing outside the medirobot began tentatively to ask the battered occupant if there'd been any other survivors, Traskeluk, now fully conscious most of the time and doing fine according the medirobot, assured his rescuers, in a weary, blasted voice, that there weren't any.

Meanwhile, in much more peaceful surroundings on distant Earth, Admiral Bowman was doing his best to prepare himself to brief the premier of Earth, a leader even busier than himself. In a moment he was going to have his first encounter with the lady, whom he had never met before, but whose reputation for occasional ferocity could make higher ranking people than Bowman cringe.

And, though he was not the bearer of good news, he was going to be as honest as he could.

The government of Earth, as Admiral Bowman had understood for some time, in fact represented much more than the leadership of a single planet. What Geneva, Switzerland, had been to ancient, uniplanetary, pre–space travel society, Earth was now to the hundreds of worlds colonized by Solarians.

In Galactic politics and commerce, central location is, as elsewhere, something rather more than a convenience. Under favorable conditions, a flight of a few weeks can carry a voyager from Earth to anywhere in the Domain.

The home planet had also become a kind of birthplace museum for the ED race, and got a lot of tourist business in consequence.

On this planet, which many called the Cradle World, or Homeworld One, there were still vast land and ocean areas that appeared to be almost free of any human presence. Restoration to a state of nature—that could, of course, mean different things to different people—was popular. Much of the land was owned or leased by estates belonging to old land-holding corporations, some of which were also cults. Who had the right of occupancy and use of land was sometimes a murky question; but for a long time now, such matters had been traditionally settled in nonviolent ways.

The number of designated spaceports on the planet was something over a hundred. There was also desultory traffic at other places. Regulation of inbound traffic tightened enormously under conditions of a defensive alert.

And then there were the defenses, which, as Bowman had noticed on his way down, could convert the sunny skies to near mud-brown opacity. An experience as eerie as observing a full solar eclipse, because outdoor artificial light was simultaneously forbidden. If you looked out from under the sky at certain angles you could see regions of sunny blue—or, at night, even the stars.

There was already in existence, scattered across the whole Solarian domain, and probably as strong on Earth as it was anywhere, a political movement calling for the evacuation of the entire Milky Way, or the small portion of it Solarians had colonized, in effect conceding defeat. The doctrine preached by the leaders of this faction called for moving the whole race of ED humanity in flight to another galaxy.

Thoughtful Solarians who had retained a more traditional outlook observed that there was no reason to believe the berserkers would let any such migration depart in peace. And opinions were divided as to whether the programmed berserker mission of wiping out all life applied solely to the home Galaxy, or was ultimately to be extended across the entire universe. (No Solarian, and probably no berserker, had had a close-up look at another Galaxy yet; several expeditions had been launched, but the travel difficulties posed by the intergalactic void had turned out to be more formidable than expected.)

A small minority of people, on Earth and elsewhere, were beginning to be openly, defiantly goodlife (though they indignantly refused to accept that label) in the sense that they thought it was worthwhile to try to open some kind of negotiations with the foe. Some even claimed Carmpan support for this position.

Any Carmpan who allowed himself (or herself) to be questioned by Solarians denied this. But some Solarians argued—giving evidence that was hard to refute—that it was impossible to determine what any Carmpan really thought about anything.

"The premier will see you now, admiral."

Moments later, Bowman found himself standing before the lady and her cabinet. She was gray-haired, simply dressed, with eyes of a piercing Nordic blue.

Somehow Bowman was not surprised to see a Carmpan visitor here, among the very important folk. As introductions went around the circle, the non-Solarian was presented under the name of Nine Thousandth Diplomat.

Formalities quickly out of the way, Bowman had launched into his briefing, and was telling the premier and her assembled luminaries that humanity faced this kind of a situation: "We have no battleships, ma'am. Zero battlewagons in the Gulf theater. The few we might have moved out that way are here, instead, in Sol System, ready to take part in a last-ditch defense if the enemy gets this far.

"Staying with the battleships: We have none in our two task forces, as I have said. The approaching enemy has eleven."

"Just a moment. Admiral?" This was one of the cabinet members, a shadowy figure behind a mustache, whose title Bowman had forgotten. "It was my understanding that we did have battleships available in the Gulf area."

"Available, sir, but not deployed near Uhao or Fifty Fifty. It's our belief that they would only get in the way, in the kind of battle that this is going to be. And we couldn't come close to matching the enemy numbers if we did deploy them."

Cabinet members and premier exchanged a round of glances among themselves; then the gray-haired lady nodded. "Continue, please."

"Yes, ma'am. Cruiser strength, eight for us, for the enemy twenty-three, assuming our intelligence is correct. So far, it seems frighteningly accurate. What may be the most important matchup is this: We have three heavy carriers—assuming the *Lankvil* can be made spaceworthy in time. And the berserkers have eight."

Admiral Bowman's briefing of the premier of Earth and her chief advisers was now drawing to the conclusion of its allotted time. He had intended from the beginning to tell these powerful folk about the new intelligence discoveries, but they kept sidetracking him onto matters even more basic—somehow, though, he was going to have to insist on making the point.

There were about thirty men and women in attendance, only a small handful of them actually in the room. They wanted from him, as they put it, confirmation of some basic facts about the military situation out in the Gulf.

Bowman did get started on the subject on intelligence revelations, and the Hypo triumph.

"Do I understand, admiral, that your intelligence information is so detailed that it extends down to the level of individual machines?"

"That is correct, ma'am."

"Could you go into a little more detail on that?"

"Certainly. Each of the large berserker carriers/motherships has its own code number in the enemy's dispatches. For our own convenience in planning and discussion, we have assigned each one a code name. Since there are four large carriers in their task force that is now heading for Fifty Fifty, someone on my staff, with a bent for legend and history, thought of naming them after the Four Horsemen of the Apocalypse. That is, *Pestilence, War, Famine,* and *Death.*"

The premier's expression indicated that she had heard of the Apocalypse. "I'd be interested to know—can you tell me anything about these units in detail?"

Bowman did his best.

A couple of hours later, Bowman, who had been invited to have a brief private discussion with the premier after the formal briefing, and who had now been left for a time to his own devices, stood staring at the night sky.

He couldn't really see the Gulf from here, except in his mind's eye. Over there on its other side, several human bases and settlements had been overrun during the last few standard months, with a mind-boggling loss of life. Hundreds of millions—no, certainly tens of billions—had died, efficiently slaughtered once their defenses had been stripped away. When those planets had been stripped of life, their soil and atmospheres, what remained of them, had been efficiently poisoned. It would be difficult indeed for life to ever reestablish itself on them.

All numbers are abstract; those measuring the latest death toll were so huge that they defied emotional response. Whole planets had been sterilized. Some of those settlements, in particular, had been large, and the defenses of at least one, Eropagnis, had been exceptionally strong.

The regular, substantial Solarian traffic that usually flowed across the Gulf in every direction, in a hundred threads of commerce, had of course shuddered and stuttered to a standstill with the outbreak of active war.

In all the long centuries of the Berserker Wars, neither Earth itself, nor any of the planets of the nearest systems, had ever been seriously threatened by attack. Not until now.

When Bowman was joined by the premier, he mentioned this, and she promptly shook her head. "That's not quite true. We've seen a few instances of attempted infiltration, right here on Homeworld One."

"I wasn't aware of that, ma'am. You're saying infiltration on Earth itself? Not goodlife activity?"

"Oh, yes. Infiltration, by small machines. Goodlife is something else altogether. You should read your history, admiral."

"Yes, ma'am. Were any of these attempts successful?"

"I'm sure the details were released, long ago. No such attempt has been successful that we know of. Officially our defensive record in that regard is perfect. But then, if an infiltrator had got in, we might never have realized the fact. Hmm?"

Conversation turned to the subject of local defenses. Those of Earth and the other homeworlds were formidable, of course, and when seen at close range they impressed layman and expert alike as awesome. But they had never been tested by a real attack. Any defensive battle fought right in among the planets of Sol System, even if the berserkers were ultimately beaten back, would be certain to involve horrendous human casualties.

Almost certainly many billions of human lives would be lost, and the conditions under which the survivors lived would be forever changed.

And if that last desperate defensive battle should be *lost* . . . but that was a result that would simply not bear thinking about.

"**O**f one thing we can be certain, ma'am. Premier. If we lost the coming fight for Fifty Fifty, and the enemy can build up their own base there—that's the next battle we're going to have to fight."

Jory Yokosuka, her one piece of luggage slung over her shoulder, gazed about eagerly, getting her first close look at Fifty Fifty, looking out through a port while she was riding a shuttle down from the cruiser that had carried her from Port Diamond along with Field Marshal Yamanim.

Seen at close range, the place looked every bit as eerie as it had from space.

And then the shuttle had touched down, and she was out of doors, blinking in Fifty Fifty's peculiar light, which seemed to come from everywhere and nowhere at the same time. The guidebook said that until you got used to it, the natural illumination here had a way of seeming either too bright or too dim.

The immediate strong impression was one of swarming human activity. There, arranged in revetments, ready presumably for a fast liftoff, were dozens, no, scores of the livecrewed fighting machines that would form an important part of the defense when the attack came. She was going to have to learn a great many technicalities, in a hurry, if she was to do more than a merely acceptable job here.

Lieutenant Duane, who had served as Jory's guide aboard ship, persisted gallantly in trying to extend the relationship somehow, but she brushed him off. While handsome, he was not her type and she was here on business.

Jory continued to be excited and pleased by the prospect of working with the famous Jay Nash. But all of the people she met in the first minute after her arrival were intent on their own jobs, and none would or could tell her exactly where the great man was.

She descended the landing ramp, was passed quickly and efficiently through a military checkpoint, and then paused amid a scene of furious activity, looking around her uncertainly. The rolling land between the landing field where she was standing and the near horizon, was all brightly lit—a natural glow, but looking very much like that produced by the most elegant electrical indirects. Barren hills and valleys, mostly a yellowish sandy color, striped with darker gray and brown. Here and there Jory spotted a green tinge, a scattered puff and swirl of what looked like vegetation—but she'd understood that there were no native life forms. Something to find out about. In one low-lying spot she thought she saw reflecting water, but she supposed that could be some kind of a mirage.

Here on the atoll, as on Earth and Uhao, and everywhere else in the newly threatened Home Sector, it was evident even to a newcomer that many things had changed in a short time. And here, where the berserkers were expected as if they had sent an announcement of their plans ahead of them, the alteration was far more drastic.

Jory knew that for perhaps two weeks before Field Marshal Yamanim and his small entourage had arrived on this low-profile and hurried visit, a massive effort had been under way with the goal of fortifying the atoll. Deep underground it was really two objects, two islandlike projections into normal space, though the bifurcation was buried, down out of human sight. From the angle of one approaching the atoll in normal space, or actually standing on it, it looked like only one, and could be so treated. The habitable portion was about a kilometer in diameter. Some called it an atoll, and some a reef.

As she understood the recent military history, a few months ago, before the raid on Port Diamond, the garrison here had been quite small, composed of about a hundred volunteer Solarian military people. But those days were gone. Weeks ago the garrison had plunged into an intensive effort at fortification, and officers and enlistees alike were putting in plenty of overtime.

Another sizable ship had landed soon after Jory's shuttle, settling through atmosphere with only a whisper of sound, and people in uniform, not waiting for robots but carrying their own military baggage, were soon streaming down its ramp. Selected reinforcements were still coming in, and the garrison now totaled about three thousand people. The human force was helping and directing an approximately equal number of robots—none of which, as far as the visitor could see, had anything even vaguely anthropomorphic about them.

Adjoining the main landing field, and the assortment of buildings strung out along the field's edge, stretched a kind of parade ground or common, much flatter than most of the surrounding terrain. This space looked, thought Jory, as if at some time in the past it had been used for occasional reviews and ceremonies. Right now it looked anything but ceremonial, filling up with shelters and equipment. A number of small fighting ships, most of them behind individual screens or revetments, were parked or docked on it.

The habitable portion of the atoll, reiterated Jory's pocket guide, *comprises the surface of a slightly oblate spheroid, about a kilometer in diameter.*

Coming to the book's description of the apparent sky, Jory looked up at the real thing. A score or more of defensive satellites, smaller, more easily transportable versions of those that guarded Earth and other full-sized worlds, had recently been set in orbit here. Around the spherical speck of Fifty Fifty, the orbits were much tighter, faster; some were so low as to be only glistening blurs.

Another such defensive machine was being launched even

as Jory watched. Some kind of tender or transport hauling it up off the launching pad.

Even before the cruiser had landed, everyone aboard had been told that full-body armor was now required to be kept in reach of everyone on the atoll. Colonel Shanga, it seemed, was going to be very strict about this. Jory had not been a full minute off the ship before she had to arrange this, which was required before she could do anything else.

The armorer's shop beside the field was doing a booming business. A wide choice of sizes, and a fair variety of styles and equipment were available. She was not a total stranger to body armor, but her brief experience had not been enough to allow her to get comfortable with the system.

In addition a new insignia had to be painted or pasted in several places on the armor, identifying her first as a civilian, then as a member of Nash's crew. A robot that was standing by took care of this chore efficiently.

Equipped at last with a new suit of personal armor, which made a bulky bundle atop her meager store of other possessions, the whole trundled along after her by a patient baggage robot, Jory soon succeeded in locating Jay Nash's secretary, a stocky, red-haired woman named Millie Prow, with whom she had once had a phone conversation back on Port Diamond. Ms. Prow was still in civilian clothes, but seemed to have somehow retained her function as buffer between the great man and the rest of the world.

The sign over the front door of the low structure proclaimed the specific military jargon, a series of letters and numbers, that the new arrival had been told to look for.

"Himself will be back inside the hour," said Ms. Prow, leaning over a kind of counter, as soon as the two women had introduced themselves. "And he's expecting you."

Himself? Jory wondered silently. It was a long time since she'd heard anyone, outside of some kind of ethnic melodrama, use the word as a name.

Ms. Prow efficiently took care of the task of assigning

Jory her quarters. All the new housing was being dug underground, so the settlement was considerably bigger than it had
looked at first.

When she found the dugout to which she had been assigned, she rejoiced that at least it was not so far beneath the
surface as to make it hard to dash up now and then and take a
look around. She had the feeling that she might want to do that
at least once or twice during an attack; her recording and observing hardware was among the best stuff of its kind, but there
was no substitute for personal immersion in an event.

This housing unit, like most of the others on the atoll, was
low-ceilinged, three or four paces square, with a small semipri-
vate latrine and shower adjoining. Two double-decker bunks
and four capacious lockers. The walls, floor, and overhead were
of the hardened stuff of the atoll, like sandstone transformed
into the best concrete.

She took possession of one of the available bunks and the
locker next to it in the small dorm room, and resumed her
search for her boss. Here in quarters it was allowed to take one's
armor off, though it was recommended to wear it all except for
the helmet at most times. When she went out again, she planned
to bring along a robot to trundle after her with the bulky suit.
The great majority of the people she had so far encountered on
the surface were similarly equipped.

Going out again, asking more or less at random for directions as to where the famous director could be found, she discovered by chance that some of the aides who were familiar with
the man called him "Pappy"—but not to his face.

And they said he was in the bar.

"The *bar?*"

Her informant nodded casually. Not wanting to sound
like the utter newcomer she was, she didn't ask for details.

No one told her where the bar was, but there weren't that
many buildings big enough to qualify.

It was a low, undistinguished building, devoid of any ad-
vertising or other indication of its function: sided with imported
wood, and with a settled look of having been in place here for

some years. The windows were opaque, at least from the outside, and there was no sign that the place was occupied at all, except for a row of armor-laden personal robots standing patiently outside. Jory, abandoning her own burdened attendant there, was reminded of horses at a hitching rail.

The front door offered no clue as to what might lie behind it, and the journalist briefly considered knocking. Rejecting this plan as a sign of weakness, she discovered that the panel yielded to a firm push. When closed, the portal must have been an effective sound barrier, for immediately noise came welling out.

Standing just inside, she looked around incredulously. "This is a *bar?*" She hadn't really believed in its existence until now.

"That's what it looks like, lady."

And indeed it did. And smelled. And sounded.

The man who had already spoken to Jory now told her that this was the only public bar the atoll had ever boasted. A sign, bearing the graphic of a pointing finger, informed her that the next saloon was a truly vast number of light-years in that direction. No doubt this establishment had a name, but maybe that was some kind of military secret. It vaguely surprised the journalist to find the place still open, serving men and women who evidently chose to spend their precious off-duty time this way; so far it had not been thought necessary to declare the place off-limits to the military. But it wasn't crowded; evidently few people had much time for relaxation.

Approaching the long, dark-wood counter lined with stools and rails, Jory caught the attention of one of the two human attendants who were being kept busy behind it, long enough to ask a question. She was told that the place would be closed when it seemed that attack was imminent.

Ordering the mildest drink she could think of that had any kick to it at all, she peered around through the dim, cavelike, noisy atmosphere, hazed with the output of several recreational appliances. And there he was, on the far side of the room, readily identifiable by his artificial eye and other features. That had to be the man she had come looking for.

Nash and a few associates or hangers-on, their numbers augmented by a cohort of stray civilians, were sitting drinking at a table. All she could hear of their talk at this distance was one man bemoaning the lack of other such establishments on Fifty Fifty.

Abandoning the bar stool she had appropriated only a moment earlier, Jory moved closer.

Her first close look at Nash's artificial eye reminded her of her robots' lenses. She wondered why a man would choose to wear a thing like that in his face, instead of one of the naturalistic models that were readily available. Drawing attention to oneself was of course the most obvious reason. Giving her new boss the benefit of the doubt, she supposed that possibly the design served some special medical or technical purpose.

Meanwhile Nash was getting a fair amount, but by no means all, of the other patrons' attention. He was achieving this, whether intentionally or not, by pounding a fist on the table, meanwhile shouting abuse at someone who was evidently another of his workers. The man, sitting three or four chairs away at the same large table, looked pale and disconcerted. He couldn't seem to find much to say in his own defense.

From the little Jory could overhear, he sounded like one who had determined to go home, retreat to Uhao—or even farther—on the next available ship. Jory stared at the man's face, which was familiar to her from a dozen popular entertainments. She recognized him immediately as one of Nash's stock company of actors.

Jory, slowly making her way closer, half expected the two men to come to blows, but apparently no one else did, and in a moment they were grumbling at each other in low voices again.

By this time the great man had transferred his anger from his former associate, and was cussing out the high politicians who had allowed the defenses of this base, and of the homeworlds in general, to deteriorate to such a state.

Someone, very likely one of the civilian bartenders grown weary of shouted arguments, had evidently called up entertainment, for now a kind of stirring, primitive-sounding music began to drown out the dispute. To Jory it sounded like an instrumental recording of some Templar battle chant.

Nash, as Jory quickly became convinced in the course of their first talk, was unlike anyone she had met before, part dramatist, part journalist, part other things that were harder to define. Now that she could get a closer look at his artificial eye, she thought that the design probably incorporated a camera function. Certainly it included a small light, which ought to be useful for close-up photography.

As she sat opposite her new boss in the bar he turned the light on from time to time, ostensibly to see her better. More likely, she thought, the real reason was to call attention to the device.

He had a glass before him at his table, but the contents appeared to be nothing stronger than beer.

He was red haired, middle-aged by contemporary standards for an Earthman, somewhere over the century mark but under one hundred and fifty. Hale and active, and somewhat above average height, a shade under two meters tall. Half out of uniform, wearing a civilian hat. Tunic and trousers rumpled. He was the most unmilitary-seeming man, Jory decided, that she could recall ever meeting in uniform.

The man worked hard at his job, Jory had heard, but he considered that a large part of his job was self-promotion. His current assignment, which he had lobbied hard to get, was the making of a kind of holographic documentary of the berserker attack, now considered inevitable, on the atoll.

Nash had a lieutenant commander's rank, and the appropriate insignia pinned on his collar or lapels, but as far as Jory could tell he currently had no duties or responsibilities other than those of an observer.

When she had finished introducing herself, and had accepted the chair that he stood to offer her with elaborate politeness (he was even a little taller than she had thought) she waited a decent interval, then asked, "I'm not quite clear, sir— are you here as a military officer, or a civilian?" She felt reasonably confident of the answer, but wanted to hear how he was going to put it.

"I'm in uniform," he growled at her. "I've got the right to wear it."

In fact everyone said that Colonel Shanga, who was commanding ground troops and machines on the atoll, was more than willing to have Nash performing the job of live observer when the attack came. The skills that had won the great director interstellar awards for holographic drama, famed for the live recording of complicated, sprawling scenes, ought to serve him well in live reporting of a battle.

She looked around, but there was no sign of Colonel Shanga in the bar. Or of any other officer with a rank as high as Nash's.

As Jory recalled, at least half of Nash's many fictional dramas took place on one frontier planet or another. They were not her favorite form of entertainment, but she had seen one or two on holostage and had mildly enjoyed them.

Nash stared at her, his face gradually brightening, as if he approved of what he saw. He gave the impression that he had forgotten about hiring this particular person, but now was glad to be reminded. More likely he pretended that was the situation. For a moment it seemed to Jory that he was on the verge of telling her to go home—or somewhere else.

But he needed her, or someone like her, for this job, or thought he did. She had been trained on, and was experienced in using, all the right equipment.

Her credentials, or resume, which she had sent to Nash, and which he perhaps dug out of a pocket and looked at now, showed that she could handle the equipment, the multiple linked recorders, about as well as anyone. Better than anyone else available.

He looked up. "Combat experience?"

"None." The answer came automatically, but as soon as she thought about it, she realized that it was technically incorrect. "Oh, well, unless you count being shot at on a transport." She named a distant sector of the settled corner of the Galaxy. "Some kind of astrogational error, and we found ourselves in the wrong place. At least one berserker took a couple of shots at us, and our captain didn't wait around to make sure how many there were."

Nash glowered at her for a moment without comment. Then he said, "Looks like the crew might be a little shorthanded when the great day comes." It was evident, from scraps of earlier conversation she'd overheard, that one or two of the people the great man had brought with him from Earth, as civilian employees, were getting cold feet at the prospect of a berserker attack, and had decided to take ship for home. He was scornful of such an attitude, which he considered unprofessional when such a marvelous opportunity beckoned.

"Good riddance to 'em, I say." Looking Jory up and down, he brightened somewhat. "Sure and it's glad I am to have your sweet self with me on this day." His artificial left eye extended its central lens slightly in her direction. The thing appeared to be just slightly loose in its fleshy socket, giving him a thoroughly repulsive appearance.

"And I'm glad to be here."

"You going to stick with me when the shooting starts?" The question came in a half-belligerent growl. Somehow she got the impression that he felt guilty about subjecting a woman to the perils of combat. Not that he had yet experienced them himself.

Jory needed no time at all to think that one over. "When the shooting starts I'm going to be here on Fifty Fifty, since that's what the job calls for." She sipped her drink. "As for being with you, I don't know what personal plans you've made for that occasion."

Someone down the bar, or at one of the adjoining tables, smothered a laugh.

Nash let go Jory's hand, turned his head and glared, then grumbled something. But when he turned back to Jory he did not seem seriously displeased.

Toward the end of the interview, he seized Jory's right hand in both of his, and pressed it fervently, as if sealing a bargain. His right eye was twinkling, his left behaving itself.

· · ·

Presently she left the bar, and moved on to try to talk to Colonel Shanga. She found him a professional military man of middle age, like the majority of his troops a specialist in ground combat, and at the moment hard at work in his dug-in headquarters, too busy to give her more than a few words.

E L E V E N

The return of Spacer Gift and Flower to the planet Uhao was separated by only a moderate interval of spacetime from the moment when Field Marshal Yamanim, way out on distant Fifty Fifty, began to brief the garrison's officers on the details of the oncoming berserker attack that they would be required to meet. The luxury liner carrying the young man and woman touched down on the planet's surface at a point that lay about as far as it was possible to get from the sprawling Port Diamond base.

While en route from Earth, Gift and Flower had made tentative plans as to what they were going to do once they arrived back on Uhao. Nifty's main goal was to go on a tour of the pyramids, along the river called the Nile. The only real suggestion Flower made was that the couple should sooner or later drop in on certain friends of hers, who were currently occupying a house on the other side of the world, back in the vicinity of the base. That was okay with Nifty; he was going to have to head back that way in a few days.

The weather on Uhao was gorgeous, as usual. And in contrast to the ships and bases where Gift had recently been spending his time, neither the field nor the adjoining town were very busy.

Once off the ship, he took a deep breath, stretched, and wondered what the hell might be going to happen next. It seemed he had barely had time to get used to the pleasures of travel in such style when the trip was over. Not that any of the luxuries aboard had really mattered to him, of course—except for Flower herself.

He wondered whether the pair of them might possibly be met on debarkation by her angry lover, the man whose name was on the spaceship ticket, and who would be wondering what kind of a guy Flower had taken up with now—and, more to the point, could be trying to get back the money he'd put out for tickets. But no one met them when they got off the ship. In fact, no one paid any attention to them at all. Nifty's career as a celebrity, it seemed, was over. Now that he was in civvies again, he was once more just as invisible as everyone else.

Looking around with satisfaction before he left the terminal, he noted that there weren't even any space police in sight. His brief taste of celebrity had been more than he wanted, and he could hope it would fade as fast as it had blossomed into being.

And Gift was silently grateful for his new companion's evident determination to stick with him, which seemed unaffected by the fact that he was no longer in the news. He kept telling himself that she was different from any other girlfriend he'd ever had—and some of the differences were hard to define.

The pair of them started out from the small spaceport carrying their bags in the beautiful weather, walking a curving walkway of crumbled seashells that led toward the town, looking for a hotel.

"Nifty?"

"Huh?"

"Are you sorry you didn't go home?"

"Not a damn bit sorry." And that was true. All the same,

he kept darting back now and then, in memory and imagination, to his home. Or at least to the only small spot anywhere in the Galaxy that he could still think of as his home.

"Glad you came with me?" Flower persisted in her habit of holding him by one arm, as if she feared he might be going to run away.

"Hell, yes."

"Won't your people at home be looking for you?"

"Actually they'd probably be surprised if I showed up." If that wasn't exactly true, well, it was close enough. And he began, haltingly, to try to describe to Flower his childhood home, or at least some of the good things about it.

She listened, and seemed to believe everything he told her. Maybe in comparison to what her home had been, his, with all its difficulties, sounded happy.

All right, so he was enhancing the good points, the virtues, a little. He was probably confabulating his childhood home with other places he'd only visited.

And then, for no apparent reason, as they were walking along, he had one of his bad moments, the kind that had pestered him since the incident in space. The bad moments came for him, often seemingly out of nowhere, when he was impaled by pangs of guilt for those two screaming, distant bodies in deep space. Such moments had come to him during his hellish ride in the courier, now and then in the hospital, again on the satellite and on the shuttle—with his return to Earth, those pangs were coming more frequently. He wondered if he was going to need professional help to deal with them.

For this, to keep myself alive so I could come back to this, I did what I did?

Beginning to relax, to be able to get some enjoyment out of being on Uhao again: He and Flower had decided they were going to gratify his long-held wish to tour the pyramids.

Flower's plan, insofar as she had one, seemed to be to let her new lover decide how they would occupy their time. Whatever he decided, she seemed willing to go along.

Shortly after they checked into the hotel on Uhao, Flower

had absented herself for a few minutes, to make a phone call.

"The friends I told you about, Nifty. I want to find out when's a good time for us to drop in on them."

"You could have phoned them from the room."

"Sure, I guess I could have. I didn't think."

Except then, he thought, he would probably have heard the conversation. "Okay. Whatever."

The hell with it. He wasn't going to worry about it.

Shortly after the couple had checked into their hotel on Uhao, Nifty was on the phone, trying to arrange a boat tour on the Uhaon Nile, with a stop at the pyramids.

Gift was eager to seek distraction from the war, and from his past. He had his life, he was young, and he was going to enjoy it. Flower seemed to have a good bit of money available, and for a few days at least he wasn't going to mind staying in a posh hotel—or in a succession of them.

Flower sympathized with Nifty's reluctance to face his folks at home—yes, of course she could understand that.

In size, Uhao fit right into the appropriate envelope for habitable planets—almost a twin of Earth in its dimensions and mass. And much less heavily populated than Earth, once you got away from Port Diamond and a few other centers.

On this world too, as on all the homeworlds now, there were frequent practice alerts. But the farther you got from the few population centers, the less difference they seemed to make. A sky like Earth's, discolored with force fields bending space and churning air, seemed to be pressing down, suffocating him.

Standing on Uhao's surface and looking up, during one of the scheduled practice alerts, one saw, in what should have been broad daylight, much the same scene as one would have seen on Earth: A sky dun-colored and dimmed with defensive barriers.

Space was available on the boat tour, and soon Nifty and his new girlfriend were traveling to parts of PD he hadn't seen before, passing now and then through others he hadn't glimpsed for a long time. Sights he had wanted to see, but had never managed to reach before. Regions practically antipodal to the base, as remote as it was possible to imagine from the headquarters of Hypo, and from all the rest of the war.

Flower was vague about whether these parts were familiar to her. Partly she was guiding him, and partly he was guiding her.

And then the pyramids were looking up ahead of them, out of a distant haze of atmospheric warmth.

According to the guidebooks, Solarian archaeologists had long struggled with the question of just what kind of intelligent beings had lived here, and why they had accomplished this gigantic construction. From the evidence of the four known pyramids that they had built, the biggest just a little bigger than anything in Egypt, those native Uhaons, like the Carmpan and a few other offshoots of Galactic life, qualified as humans of some description, even though their evolution had been quite independent of that which had taken place on the planets of distant Sol.

Other than their pyramids, which seemed to have endured at least as long as those that stood beside Earth's Nile, those ancient natives of Uhao had left very little in the way of records. There endured on the planet none of their bones or mummies or recognizable works of art, so exactly what they had looked like was still a matter of conjecture. Whatever had cost these pyramid builders their lives had not been berserkers, for the rest of the native biomass had not been extinguished with them.

Unobtrusive interior lighting had been fixed up to display the faint, all-but-invisible markings, undoubtedly ancient inscriptions, applied with paint or other medium long since decayed, which had recently been discovered on one of the interior walls.

Flower became more interested the more she learned about the famous monuments.

Several times Gift lingered behind, almost lost in thought, when the tour group moved on. Dawdling, looking at the marked stones and trying to understand. Some of the smooth-cut faces of the ashlars bore inscriptions, which no Solarian had ever been able to interpret. There were, of course, rival theories.

On the tour, other people, as much interested in these ancient things as Gift, and much more knowledgeable about them, talked to Gift and Flower. One of the couples they met in this way were superficially much like themselves. This young pair said they were on their honeymoon.

At some point the honeymooners looked at Gift as if expecting him to confirm that he and Flower were there in the same capacity. Maybe he did so. "Us, too."

A faint breeze of dry air, artificially cooled, came flowing through.

"The gods of Uhao alone—if anyone—know how many thousands of years old this structure is."

Their Solarian guide was explaining how the rocky surfaces of the enormous building blocks had been treated for some now-forgotten symbolic or religious purpose, bathed in radiation by some Solarian cultists at some comparatively late point in the pyramids' history—only a few hundred years ago. Therefore those ancient stones now gave different readings, erratically emitted radiation, in different areas. Even the very age of the structures was still in serious dispute.

Nifty'd bought more new clothes since they'd landed, using his own money this time. Since his girlfriend was so generous, he allowed himself to feel that he had a little cash to spare.

When Nifty and Flower were alone again, and the matter of the pyramids came up, she said, "I bet I know what really built them."

"What? They're not just natural forms, like crystals, you know. Someone with a purpose in mind . . ."

She was shaking her head, calmly, certainly.

"All right, tell me what you think."

"Machines. I don't mean robots that work for people."

Gift thought that was nonsense. He told her: "Some of the machines that are out to kill us are far older than this structure. All that time they've been getting ready to do the job. Practicing. Waiting for their chance."

While he listened, his mouth gradually falling open, Flower gently but firmly expressed her doubt that those machines really wanted to kill anybody. "We project our own violent motives upon them."

"Absolutely I could never buy that. Have you ever *seen* one?"

"You know I haven't." She shook her head, and went on to tell him how he'd been brainwashed by his officers in the Space Force, and he simply didn't understand.

He let it pass. But something in the argument started Spacer Gift thinking of his latest series of troubling dreams.

His deathdream again. He couldn't seem to escape from the damned thing. In his real dream, he was on the verge of thinking the fatal thought . . . gasping, he awoke from a nightmare of suffocation in the emptiness of space.

Now and then in their hotel, or on the tour boat, they listened to and watched the news. The official bulletins, mostly from over on the far side of the Gulf, continued to be a grim catalog of losses—of lives, of planets, of ships and territory, all in staggering amounts. During the last few days the widespread rumors of a great impending berserker attack had coalesced into official warnings: The coming storm would perhaps be aimed at Uhao, or perhaps at Earth itself, and all the other homeworlds.

Other rumors, not verified on any of the official newscasts, included one that goodlife were now extremely well organized, and working secretly to accomplish a revolution, or massive simultaneous acts of sabotage.

Meanwhile there were others, the fellow travelers of berserkers as it were (who tried to dissociate themselves from goodlife, but sometimes were arrested anyway)—those others were pushing openly for an evacuation of the homeworlds. To accommodate the entire population of a planet somehow on spacecraft would be a mind-boggling endeavor, and most people considered it a crackpot idea.

Of course, undertaking any such evacuation would make a shambles of any effort at armed defense.

Gift and Flower in their tourist travels also heard one whispered rumor to the effect that some actual berserker machines, imported along devious trade routes from who knows where, by unknown means, had been and were still being brought into close contact with Solarian society. Not only by people who were goodlife in the traditional sense, but by some well-meaning people who considered such machines ambassadors for peace.

These infiltrating berserkers were said to be disguised as, and for the most part functioned perfectly well as, ordinary service or maintenance robots of the kind used widely on all ED worlds.

There seemed to be no way to prove conclusively that these rumors were without substance.

Nifty snorted. "Most ridiculous thing I ever heard."

For once Flower was in agreement. "Isn't it, though?" Then she wondered aloud whether there was, or could be, any quick, reliable test that could be made to determine whether some complicated serving machine was really a berserker.

Gift's thought was that whoever applied such a test to a berserker stood in deadly danger.

"Maybe that *is* the test—you pretend you have some means of detecting berserker programming—and then when you walk up to the machine, it figures that the game is up anyway, and it knocks your head off. If it's caught, it's going to take with it as many badlives as it can. What's the matter?"

The matter was that Flower didn't look pleased. She said she had heard such stories before. She told Nifty that one such machine, disguised as some kind of communications station, was rumored to have argued, or transmitted, in the few seconds before it was destroyed: "We are two kinds of life, organic, and nonorganic—there is no reason why we cannot coexist."

And it had added: "We have computed a new truth at last; we, whom you call berserkers and death machines, are as alive as you are."

Gift was too disgusted to comment.

But Flower insisted, without being able to say how she knew, that the story was perfectly true.

She brought up one point that he really couldn't argue with: The other side of the coin of human involvement with berserkers was that some people regarded the death machines with a hatred so intense as to close their eyes and ears to argument or demonstration of any kind. The Templars, the kind of people who would join the Templars, were an obvious example.

"There are people like that," said Flower. The tone of her voice suggested that she might be speaking of the damned.

Gift volunteered suddenly: "I once knew a man like that. His name was Traskeluk. He told me his father had served in the Templars."

"Who was he?"

Nifty, who had been suddenly caught up in a vision of deep space and bloodstained armor, came to himself with a start. Then he shrugged. "Man I used to know," he repeated.

"One of your shipmates, I bet."

"Flo, you were just talking about people who won't listen to arguments. Let me tell you, there are certain other humans, who while not necessarily hardcore goodlife, who really nurse a hatred of their own race—why I don't know—and they are willing to transfer their loyalty to anything they can think of as a promising alternative. Cats and dogs and even bugs, in some cases."

Flower didn't have anything to say to that.

T W E L V E

Nifty Gift felt heartily weary of the war, and more than ready to get away from it. Of course getting away wasn't going to be easy, especially not for him, the way his luck had now begun to turn. Maybe in some other galaxy (if anyone ever figured out how to drive a ship across the void between) escape to a peaceful paradise could be possible. But if there were habitable planets in that other place, then there would be people, and most likely berserkers too. Gift had no scientific basis for this conclusion, but given the nastiness of the universe in general, he had no doubt that it was so.

At least, much thanks to any gods who might exist, thanks to his own fine combat record and the kindness of Mother R, he wasn't going to have to go out in space and confront berserkers any more.

To one like Nifty Gift, who had spent most of the last couple of standard years in quarters on Uhao, the changes that had taken place on this world over the last few months were obvious. Now Gift and Flower, traveling, strolling, boating, and loafing their way around some of the remoter portions of this paradise planet, saw that the facts of life and death had been brought home to everyone: Berserkers were no longer only a remote terror, directly affecting only distant sectors. The danger, the terror, had moved closer with a leap of sobering dimensions, closer than ever before.

Not that there was panic. But wherever there were people, there was a certain tension, at an energizing level, in the air. Also there was a tendency to blame anything that went wrong upon the war. Shelters were being constructed, dug out of planetary rock on a massive scale, and some existing underground works, deep mines and such, were being adapted as emergency shelters. Now on Uhao, holographic posters, bearing patriotic urgings, were everywhere in the cities, and at a few spots in the countryside. There were several versions of the posters; in the most popular, what was supposed to be a berserker machine, portrayed as all angles and shadows, reached out with wicked-looking prongs to impale a screaming mother and her helpless infant. Well, maybe some of the bad machines did actually look like that. And any lady who met one would have plenty to scream about.

Flower looked scornfully at these posters every time she saw one. She didn't talk about them, but sometimes she bit her lip as if in an effort to restrain some withering comment.

Some tension and posters, yes, but still, as Gift took note, there was no visible panic among the natives. Solarians seemed to be basically confident beings, and things were not that bad yet. The effects of the big raid, a couple of months ago, had been felt almost entirely over on the other side of the planet.

A person who wanted to find something to worry about, beyond the bald fact that the berserkers were out to kill everyone, would say that the greater danger was still complacency. Popular sports and other entertainment were flourishing along their usual course without a pause; our people fighting at the front, in their ships and in the colonies, wanted it that way. Or so the claim was made, and no one argued. The great majority seemed to be going about their business very much as before. The truth, as it was now revealed, was that they genuinely had confidence in their government, despite all their earlier willingness to complain about it, and believed in their military leaders as well. Since he'd last walked the surface of this planet a few months back, in a change that seemed to Spacer Gift paradoxical, those complaints had almost vanished.

Gradually, as the days of their journeying together passed, the realization crept up on Nifty Gift that Flower was to some degree sympathetic to the berserker cause. Or at least she had some idea that it was clever to sound like it. In fact, he supposed, she just didn't know what the hell she was talking about.

He warned her a couple of times that she could get in trouble that way, but she didn't seem to care.

Well, to hell with it. He didn't want to think about her problems. He had more than enough of his own. And mostly the two of them got on well enough, and were able to find plenty of pleasant things to talk about.

They were lying in bed, talking. "Sometimes I think, Nifty—"

"That's a mistake."

"What?" Looking at him blankly, she didn't get it. There were a lot of things she didn't get.

"Never mind."

His companion frowned, making her moist, red lower lip protrude in a way that had impressed him, from the first time he beheld it, as utterly delightful. "Well, sometimes I think that maybe the machines have it right after all."

He paused before answering. "What machines? You talking about the *bad* machines?"

"Call them that if you like." She added quickly: "You can turn me in for saying what I just said, I don't care."

"Don't be silly, I'm not going to turn you in for anything," he hastily assured her. If security was coming after anyone, it would be him. If they ever found out . . . but of course there was no way they were ever going to find out.

He stroked her body, then her cheek and hair. "I'm glad you're not a machine," he added. When she didn't respond to that, he asked, in an effort to get it straight: "You say the machines—the berserkers—have something right? I don't get it. You mean they're right about wanting to kill us all?"

Flower's lips firmed in, making a thin determined line. Her voice took on a similar quality. "How do you know that's what they want?"

Nifty could only squint in puzzlement. Then he asked slowly: "How do we *know* . . . ?"

"We're really the ones who are trying to kill them, aren't we? Because our race thinks we're so . . . so . . . we're like, the whole universe belongs to us." She was staring into the air with a fierce determination. Obviously she was angry at humanity.

"Well, better us than them."

"How do you know that?"

She had a way of coming up with these things, now and then, that just stopped conversation. Gift lay thinking, trying to figure out if any part of what she was telling him made sense. Why was he here with her, anyway? By now he could have made some excuse, and gone his own way again, and maybe taken up with somebody else. But then he would have to start explaining all over again who he was and what he was doing.

Flower added: "They didn't kill *you*, did they, when they had the chance? Probably they just wanted to frighten you away."

"Frighten me. . . ." He shook his head, groping for words. He had thought that maybe this woman was on the verge of understanding him. But the truth, as Nifty now had to admit to himself, the truth was that the more he and Flower tried to talk about anything serious, the more he realized that she didn't understand anything at all. "Let's not talk about it."

"All right, Nifty. Anything you say." And she snuggled up close to him again. After a while she said: "You make love like a machine."

It took him a while to understand that she had meant it as a compliment.

"Shall I turn on the news?"

"Why not?"

And a minute later he had heard the words, seen the images, that left him frozen there in a sitting position in the bed, staring at the stage as if he had never seen one before.

"What's the matter?" Flower asked him in a hushed voice.

"That was my ship. My old . . ." He had almost said *spy ship*. "The one they're talking about."

She hadn't really been listening to the program, but now she did, after tapping in a command that the last couple of minutes be played over again. Well, there was no help for that. Everyone was going to hear it over and over.

When Flower had satisfied her craving for the news, she gazed at Nifty with wide eyes. "So that man they're talking about, the one they just found alive, is one of your crew? Is he the one you were trying to escape with at the end?"

"That's right. Traskeluk." He was still staring at the stage, where more stories were being played out. But he had not the faintest idea what any of them were about.

"They said he's in good condition and expected to recover." When Gift didn't answer, Flower looked at him closely, then came over and sat down close beside him and began to pet him, as if she thought he needed consolation. Well, he needed something, and it must have shown. He muttered a few words.

"What did you say, Nifty?"

"I said, 'This changes everything.' "

"How?".

He didn't bother to answer. He called up the news item yet again, and scrutinized every detail. Not that there were many details given. Not much to see, little more than a muffled form being slid out of an ambulance, against a background that looked like the Port Diamond base hospital. His own name was mentioned in passing, and Trask's of course, but no one else's. No, there was no suggestion that Ensign Terrin might have survived also. Only Traskeluk. *Only . . .*

"Was he your good friend, Nifty?"

He wished she would just keep quiet for a minute, and let him think.

It didn't take Gift long to realize that thinking wasn't doing him a whole lot of good. It was hard to imagine how it could. He could think all he wanted, and it wouldn't undo anything. That night he lay awake for a long time, staring into darkness. He kept expecting a knock on the door in the middle of the night, security and space police. What the hell was he going to do now?

But the knock didn't come. Not yet.

By now, Traskeluk must have told at least half a dozen debriefers his version of events out in deep space. That would be bad . . . but then gradually Gift, thinking back, remembering what the man was like, came to the sickening realization that Traskeluk probably wasn't going to tell his debriefers the whole real story at all. What he was going to do was likely to be a whole lot worse.

And Trask was sure to get convalescent leave, as soon as he was out of the hospital, which might be any time now, for all Gift knew.

It wasn't going to be security that came to his door in the middle of the night.

And Nifty still couldn't think of a single damned thing to do about it.

Not a day went by without Flower repeating at least a couple of times, usually in a low, sincere voice, that there were some friends of hers, staying on Port Diamond, that she wanted Nifty to meet.

"Yes, I know. You keep telling me about your goddamned friends."

"They might be able to help."

"Help? You don't even begin to know what kind of help I need, and they don't either."

She made little conciliatory noises.

He sighed, and counted up how many days of leave he had left. He couldn't seem to remember the number of the days, or the dates either, from one day to the next, and had to keep counting them over and over again, unfolding the single sheet of his orders and looking at the already thumb-worn paper. Usually time spent off duty went fast, but this time there were more hours than he knew what to do with.

No further word on the news about Traskeluk's condition, or when he might be discharged from the hospital. Certainly he'd talked with his debriefers by now, but still there was no sign that anyone was looking for Nifty Gift. They might be thinking that they should let him enjoy his leave in peace, but they would certainly have some more questions to ask him when he got back to the base.

Gift toyed with the idea of putting in a call to the hospital, over on the other side of the world, trying to talk to Trask, trying to explain, but just thinking about it made him shudder. Whatever else happened, he wasn't going to do that.

In the middle of breakfast he looked up and across the table at Flower. "All right. Sure, why the hell not? Let's go pay a visit to your friends."

She was obviously pleased. "You'll like them, Nifty. We'll have to do some more traveling."

"We do a lot of that anyway."

That night, he found himself lying awake in bed, trying to keep from worrying about Flower's attitude toward the bad machines, which at least was a distraction from his worries about Traskeluk. This woman really seemed to think berserkers were not so bad. He tried on that attitude in his own mind, like a shoe on a foot, and could tell right away that it didn't fit at all. She was an attractive woman who said she could sympathize with his feelings of not wanting to be idolized for what everyone thought he had done against the berserkers. But damn it, if she really believed what she was saying, she was crazy. And thinking and talking like that could get her into real trouble.

All along there had been something brittle about her. What had at first seemed an intriguing individuality was now coming to look like something seriously wrong. He'd gone out of his way trying not to see that fact, but now he couldn't deny that it was there.

As near as Nifty could pin it down, Flower seemed to believe that berserkers were a force of nature, like gravity or starlight, and that nature was some kind of god that should be worshiped.

Maybe, if he ever told this woman what he had really done, she'd take it as a point in his favor that he had left murderous Solarians to be killed, because they deserved to die for carrying on their war against the innocent machines.

And later in the day Gift, who was now avidly watching the news for any clues, caught sight of Traskeluk, off his stretcher now, looking almost healthy, and being interviewed on one of those news-talk shows. No, now Gift could see that Trask was actually holding a press conference, on a very familiar looking hospital terrace.

Gift stared with a sick fascination at the show, not sure whether it was running live or on a delayed display. Obviously the man wasn't dying, and hadn't come out of his experience brain damaged. So he must have spent a lot of time talking to the debriefers already. So what had he been telling them? What had he—?

Gift didn't have to wonder very long. Again his own name came up briefly, mentioned in passing by one of the questioners. And a moment later Traskeluk was looking straight out of the stage, right at the camera, talking to him, to his old shipmate Nifty.

"I look forward to seeing you, Nifty. We'll have a lot of stuff to talk about."

And the hostess, or whatever they called the one in charge of trying to control the assembled reporters, gushed once more at the hero, and that was that.

Gift turned off the stage, and sat there staring at the little empty platform, still seeing Traskeluk's face, along with his casually pointing hand. If he'd had any doubt before about what Traskeluk meant to do, that uncertainty had vanished.

Next time Flower and Gift were talking seriously, heading halfway back around the planet again, on some kind of tube train—Flower's friends, she said, lived not far from the base—it seemed to Gift that in dealing with this woman it was high time that he established a few basic facts.

He fixed her with a serious stare. "The bad machines are

not natural, any more than—than bombs and missiles are. The first ones were put together a hell of a long, long time ago, by a race of living people, called the Builders, who really knew how to make weapons. The Builders were fighting a war. They were real live people like you and me, even if they looked a hell of a lot different, and they were warring against another race of real live people who'd started in a different solar system.

"It was a tough war, and the Builders thought they were creating the weapon that would win it for them—they'd built the machines that we now call berserkers, and now all they had to do was turn them loose in the enemy's territory, and let them clean out everything that lived.

"Easy to turn them loose. But when it came time to turn them off—that was not so easy.

"Once the Builders had made the first berserkers . . . well, after that, the Builders weren't alive much longer. That was back about the time that people on Earth were starting to come out of caves and build mud houses."

Flower had waited patiently, putting up with his speech instead of listening to it. He could tell she was tuning out the meaning. The moment he fell silent, she demanded: "How do we know that?"

Gift made a helpless gesture. After a long pause he asked: "Why did you take up with me?"

"I wanted to help you," she said after a while.

"How'd you know I needed help?"

This time the answer was a while in coming. Eventually she said: "Everybody does."

Again the couple were traveling, riding the tour boat back in the direction of Port Diamond. Everywhere Gift went, he noted a heightened sense of purpose in everyone he met, even tourists. Several talked about joining civil defense as soon as they got home. Intense concern about goodlife had surfaced in many areas. According to media reports, some classical witch-hunts had developed, but the great mass of the population had not yet fallen into such behavior. The situation was even more pronounced on the planet of Uhao.

His goodlife friend (as he had come to think of her, half-seriously) was quietly scornful of such witch-hunts. And yet in some perverse way she seemed to enjoy hearing about them. The fact that her people were being persecuted, as she saw the situation, proved that they were right. Some day, she implied darkly, the people who carried out such persecutions would be made to pay.

The guidebooks and robots said that this Uhaon river had been christened the Nile, after one of the most famous streams on Earth, because it flowed a long way, south to north, through the most desertlike stretch of land anywhere on this garden planet.

On they went, making slow headway in a riverboat, with half a dozen other tourists, while a dog-sized robot ran the almost-silent little engine, and took care of navigation.

He thought that Flower didn't really like boating, or other lively recreations, but she was doing a good job of trying to humor her companion.

Sometimes she really worked at it. "Nifty? Something's wrong, isn't it?"

He didn't answer. He splashed a little water his girl's way, until she shrieked. He was pretending to be playful, though he could see she didn't like the muddy, earthy splashing.

Flower, as always, listened sympathetically as Gift talked to her about his troubles. Or as he talked around them, rather. He was not, of course, telling her the big one yet, though he could feel himself edging closer to doing so. He wasn't yet quite sure that he couldn't get through the rest of his life without telling the whole story to someone.

On the river, and at the various resorts, Flower moved among the people who were enjoying themselves, and she was enjoying herself too. It had taken Gift some time to realize that her joy came to her in a different way, and for different reasons.

Gift had not put on his uniform since he boarded the luxury liner for Port Diamond, though he was still dragging it with him everywhere in his luggage. Since he'd come back to Uhao without the uniform, no one had seemed to recognize him, or to pay him any particular attention. He was glad that his fame seemed to be fading almost as quickly as it had come. In a week he had become only one more young man, whose left arm sometimes seemed a little sore or a little clumsy.

"You're acting kind of funny, Nifty. Ever since you heard the news about your shipmate still being alive."

There came a crocodile, or something like one, nudging

close to the boat. The guide was always warning people not to stick their hands or feet into the water.

"Hey, berserker!" he called out to the beast, and splashed water at it with his left hand.

But Flower didn't think that was funny.

Gradually they were making their way back to the vicinity of Port Diamond. The pyramids had long since turned mountainlike with distance, and shortly after had vanished in the blue–horizon-haze behind them. Now they had been replaced on the horizon by real mountains, gently forested and mysterious, rising up ahead.

"You have a more creative nature, Nifty. That's why you like working on the codes."

"Who told you I worked on codes? Where'd you get that idea?"

"You did. You said something, the day we first met. You said a couple of different things that kind of added up."

Had he really? He couldn't remember now just what he might have said. He'd been doing more talking than usual, that was for sure. Trying to impress people with how important he was, and how heroic. He was going to have to get serious about keeping his mouth shut in his new job.

By this time he realized Flower had learned more, uncomfortably and maybe dangerously more, than anyone outside of Hypo was supposed to know about his work involving codes. The fact that he had told her as much as he had could really make trouble for him; he saw that now.

And then the day came when Flower brought him in sight of the sprawling building, secluded behind the trees of its own vast lawn, or park. One side enjoyed superb natural views, overlooking a long green valley that sloped toward the sparkling ocean a couple of kilometers distant. The place stood in an uncrowded neighborhood or district of rolling green hills and rainbows. The roof and most of the walls were of shingles that looked like real wood. Most of the wall surface was painted a forest green.

Where the drive ended there were half a dozen graveled parking spaces, all empty at the moment. A short extension of the drive led to a closed garage. A flagstone footpath curved away through the grassy yard, going around the house and out of sight.

"I bet the swimming pool's back there," said Flower.

Nifty, listening, could hear a sound like a large fountain or small waterfall. Without seeing it, he could tell it wouldn't be an ordinary pool. "Wow. And your friends live here?"

"I told you, didn't I? They don't own the place. One of them, Martin Gavrilov, is a kind of caretaker. Or house sitter." She paused. "He doesn't really do it as his job."

"Oh." He didn't care particularly what Martin Gavrilov's job might be. "Who does own it?"

"I'm not sure."

"They won't mind their house sitter entertaining a couple of friends?"

Flower dismissed such worries with a gesture, and led the way to the front door.

The closer they got to the house, the bigger it looked. It had been constructed in an uncommon, antique style. White-painted wood shutters were open at each window.

Close up, the fabric of the sloping roof and walls looked like shingles of real wood. Maybe, thought Gift, cut from genetically altered cedar or redwood.

"What are these things?" Flower, her curiosity getting the better of her, pointed at a window. A brown plastic frame with the grainy look of wood, or else, once more, of real wood, once more genetically altered; crosshatched with filaments strung a millimeter or two apart.

Gift had spent a lot of time with his nose in history books. "Screens. People put them on their doors and windows, when the outside air in warm weather was full of insects."

The veranda was unimpressively furnished with rocking chairs, rattan outdoor furniture, and climbing, neotropical plants. The main thing that spoiled the look of history was the presence of elaborate holostages in almost every room.

When Flower and Gift came up the front walk, a rocking chair on the broad, shady veranda was still faintly rocking. Someone might have got up from it only seconds ago, looked through the latticework to see that visitors were approaching, and darted inside the house.

The decoration and furnishings of the house matched the architecture and construction. Everything, genuine or replica, looked Earthlike, and was consistent with some remote historical period back on the Cradle Planet. Or at least the visitors were left with an impression of consistency.

The robot butler, which came to the door and unquestioningly stood back to let the couple in, wore a costume that looked like it had belonged to a human servant in some period before space travel.

"Is there anyone home?" Flower asked, looking almost timidly at the robot.

"Mr. Gavrilov, the house sitter," the butler replied in a mellow but obviously not-quite-human voice. It looked from one caller to the other. "May I ask your names?"

"Mr. Gavrilov can . . . he knows me." The young woman appeared relieved to hear of his presence. "Tell him my name is Flower. And this is Spacer First Class Sebastian Gift." For some reason the robot seemed to impress her inordinately—all right, it was strange, but this was ridiculous. For a moment Gift thought she might curtsy to it.

I've never been presented to a machine before, he thought to himself.

"Follow me, please." The tall figure included both of them in a swift glance, and bowed slightly, as no doubt a servant should.

When the butler turned its very human-looking back to the visitors, Gift noted with some surprise that stuck to the machine's back was a modern-looking placard saying:

MY NAME IS BURYMORE

Gift thought of calling out the word, just to see if the butler would respond. But he refrained.

The butler led them through a succession of quaintly furnished rooms. Gift noticed that the electric lights were evidently controlled by wall switches, simple clumsy things that you would have to reach out a hand to click on or off.

And then they came to a larger room, where two people sat in quaint chairs watching an old show on a big modern holostage.

"Martin—" Flower hurried forward eagerly. But the youngish man who rose from his chair to respond greeted her with a simple handshake and a cool look.

For some reason he appeared more interested in Gift. "And this must be—may I call you Nifty?"

"Why not, everyone else does."

The young woman who had been sitting with Gavrilov got up too, and was introduced as Tanya. Her eyes were wide, giving her a perpetually startled expression. Silently she gave Gift another small dose of what he had learned to recognize as the celebrity treatment.

Gavrilov especially welcomed Gift, pumping his hand. The house sitter's voice was quiet and intense, and he had a habit of hunching down his head between his shoulders slightly, as if he were cold. Any friend of his old friend Flower was certainly welcome here.

Gift was wondering if Gavrilov was, or had been, Flower's lover. He couldn't tell from the way they acted. He wondered if it was going to make any difference when it came time to ask these folks a favor.

"Whose house is this, anyway?" Gift asked, when the first break came in the routine chitchat. He waved an arm at the expensive walls. Flower had been maddeningly vague about that.

It seemed that Gavrilov was not going to dispense much information either. "Some wealthy family owns it. But they're renting it out to a man who seems to be too busy to spend much time here."

"To Jay Nash, actually," put in Tanya. "You know, the entertainment director."

"I've heard of him, sure." Gift, who had just taken a chair, got to his feet and wandered about. On one wall he saw a hologram, an autographed image of a drama-adventure star of a few years back. The inscription read: TO JAY. OLD BUDDY, LET'S HAVE ANOTHER DRINK. It looked like maybe Tanya had been telling the truth.

"Celebrities," he commented to the others, gesturing at the graphic.

None of his three companions seemed interested in entertainment stars. Gavrilov and Tanya both returned Gift's gaze solemnly, looking at him as if they found something about this visitor truly impressive. Here we go again, thought Gift, and began to experience a sinking feeling. But for the moment, at least, no one was going to gush over him.

The couple who had been living in the house looked at Flower with obvious respect, and started asking her questions about her travels in recent days. Gavrilov wanted to know if she and Gift had been followed.

"No," said Flower.

Gift shook his head in agreement. He wondered if it was so obvious that he had already become a fugitive.

Presently the butler returned, walking quietly on his two manlike feet, which in keeping with the rest of his costume were shod in human's shoes. Burymore was carrying a tray, and passed out refreshments.

Gift took a glass, sipping something nondescript and vaguely alcoholic. "How come your robot's wearing that sign?" he asked, when the thing had turned its back on them again.

"I suppose the man I'm house-sitting for must have put it on. It looks foolish and I'd take it off, if it was up to me, but . . ." Gavrilov shrugged.

As the conversation went on, Gavrilov began trying to find out, from Gift, where Admiral Naguance's fleet had gone when it lifted off from Port Diamond.

Nifty chuckled. "I don't have a clue about anything like that. You think the admirals are gonna tell *me?*"

And if he had known, he might add, he would have seen no reason to tell any of these people.

It was soon evident to Gift, from the kinds of things Flower's friends seemed to expect him to know, that his questioners were vastly ignorant about military organization or procedures.

"There's going to be a big battle soon," he told them, "but exactly where is anybody's guess. Maybe for Fifty Fifty. Maybe for Uhao. Maybe somewhere even closer to Earth than that."

His audience nodded solemnly. Before the raid on Port Diamond, on the human side no strategist or analyst, breathing or optelectronic, had predicted major berserker activity anywhere near the homeworlds—nothing of the kind had ever happened in the Home Sector, or at least not for a very long time—and the presence of a massive enemy fleet just across the Gulf of Repose, demonstrated by a surprise attack in that region, had shocked and astonished practically the entire Solarian population. But these people didn't seem that shocked.

Gavrilov and Tanya looked at each other, and then Gavrilov, seeming to come to a decision, said diffidently, "I know a place where people don't mind if a spacer wants out of the war." He paused there, seemingly waiting for Gift's reaction.

"Then I ought to be popular there. Where is this place?"

"You'll see. I'm sure you can understand why we have to be careful."

"Sure."

Flower said, pleadingly, "I want to go too." She put out a hand and stroked his arm. "I want to stay with you, Nifty."

He looked at her. "Sure. Sure, you can, Flo."

A little later, when Gavrilov and Tanya had gone off about some housekeeping chores, and she was alone with Nifty in the living room, she chided him for being suspicious and lacking enthusiasm.

He shrugged. Though he didn't tell Flower so, he wasn't much impressed by what he had seen of her friends so far.

Gift leaned back in his chair and closed his eyes. So now it seemed that he was being offered sanctuary as a deserter from the war. He didn't know what he had expected that to feel like, but now that it had happened, there was nothing particularly marvelous about it.

How nice, he thought, how nice it would be if I could open my eyes and all these people would be gone. No Traskeluk coming to the door with a gun in his hand. No one anywhere in sight but Flower—or maybe I could do without her too, and instead of her there's some other girl I haven't even met as yet. One who'll just be there when I want her, and never ask me questions about anything. Just the two of us, and we're sitting on a beach. A long way from Port Diamond, or any other base. I've done enough of that military stuff to last me several lifetimes.

He opened his eyes and saw that Gavrilov had returned, and was standing silently in the doorway looking at him. Gift said: "I might like to visit a place like that."

"You might?"

"I would. I definitely would."

Gavrilov, and Tanya who had now appeared beside him, were looking at Gift with understanding. Gavrilov showed a wintry smile. "I just happen to know someone who has a yacht that's leaving here soon, going in that general direction."

"Who?"

"Someone we call the Teacher."

"I don't have a hell of a lot of money. Not as much as it takes to pay for long-distance space travel."

"The yacht owner isn't that much interested in money."

Gift lifted his glass. "Here's to traveling on yachts."

Jory Yokosuka's most recently assigned guide, Lieutenant Duane's latest replacement (the succession of young men who had held the job were starting to blur into each other in her perception), had gone away, pleading that he was compelled to attend some essential military briefing, and promising that a replacement would soon be sent. Meanwhile she was out on her own, well on the way to confirming some of her first impressions about Fifty Fifty. She and a few others in civilian-coded armor were left pretty much to their own devices.

One strong impression was that wherever an observer chose to stand on this peculiar miniature world, the view was always intriguing, and sometimes breathtaking. The light, which made the place an inviting goal for Solarian tourists, was a natural by-product of the strange formation underfoot. It came welling up out of the ground (Jory meant to get around to learning the scientific explanation—as soon as she had a few minutes to spare) and saturating the atmosphere, creating a cheery glow all around the nearby horizon, brightening the edges of the sunless sky. Night, or the appearance of night, was unknown on Fifty Fifty; the visitor (there had never been any permanent inhabitants) lived in a perpetual cloudy summer afternoon, under a sky covered with what appeared to be light overcast, through which occasionally peered the jarring sight of a bright star-cloud or outcropping of nebula.

So far Jory's only companion on her exploratory stroll was her robot recorder, a dog-sized metal beast that sometimes walked beside her on its six short insect legs, and sometimes rolled upon extruded wheels, depending on the local terrain.

Someone on Colonel Shanga's staff had made a thorough effort to see to it that all robots in use on the atoll were marked conspicuously in a way that was supposed to make it easy to tell them from berserker landers, which were known to come in a variety of shapes and sizes.

She was rather fond of the thing, which was good at its job, but at moments reminded her of a curious child. She was trying to think of a suitable name for it, but the choice required some more thought; people had a certain wariness about naming robots. Nothing too fierce or too cute or too human was considered in good taste.

Right now she and her metallic companion were several hundred meters—almost as far as it was possible to get while remaining on the surface—from the center of the frenetic activity at the base. A little farther and they would have reached the antipodes.

Glancing down at the knee-high recorder, making eye contact of a sort with swiveling lenses, she said in a conversational voice: "I am now standing on what looks—and feels—very much like a beach, such as one might find at Port Diamond or on Earth. Although of course there is no lake or ocean here. I feel a yellowish substance crunching underfoot, and I can see a rim of blue sky following the nearby horizon all the way around.

"The rest of the sky is a . . . well, one might call it a pearly gray, brushed with star-clouds here and there. The sky and the light are going to take some getting used to. It seems as if the ground beneath one's feet is bathed in brilliant, shadowless light indistinguishable from sunshine, while night claims the upper half of the field of view. People, buildings, and other objects standing on the ground partook of the bright illumination, while ships darting across the sky, or hovering, were bathed in the upper darkness. The whirling blurs of the newly installed defensive satellites look not quite like anything that I, along with most other visitors, have ever seen before."

Her alertness to her surroundings paid a minor dividend. She could see that someone, a single figure in the shape of Solarian humanity, was approaching along her trail, gradually overtaking her. For a while the figure's walking legs were hidden from her by this miniature world's sharp curvature.

The newcomer turned out, as she had pretty much expected, to be yet another assigned military guide, who now came jogging, skillfully taking advantage of the power of his armor suit, to talk to Jory.

Why did she always draw a male? It would be interesting to find out sometimes on what basis mentors were assigned. So far she had the impression they were all eager volunteers.

The robot recorder appeared to sniff at the newcomer, then to accept his presence.

"Any questions I can answer?"

"I have several. Several volumes of them, actually. To begin with, what is this stuff, exactly, that we're walking on? It looks and feels like sand."

"In a way it does." Her guide crunched some underfoot by way of demonstration. "But if you look at it closely, it doesn't bear much resemblance to any Earthly soil or rock. For one thing, it's notably heavier than ordinary sand. Under the right conditions it can form a solid almost as hard as steel. It comes out of something like a nuclear furnace, buried in an alternate spacetime under our feet. I don't guarantee I've got the physics right. I wouldn't attempt to describe the chemistry."

Jory picked up a handful of the peculiar material, and let it trickle away through her fingers.

"One can almost hear the surf, no?"

She closed her eyes and listened. "No. This is one damned dry place. And to me it's beginning to look ugly."

"Really? I like it. There are moments . . . yes . . . when I get the distinct impression that I'm back on Earth."

The pair strolled on, Jory's robot tagging along, while she kept on asking questions.

It ought to be, she supposed, practically impossible to get lost here. The world was simply too small, and there was no real darkness. On the other hand, there did not seem to be much in the way of landmarks, apart from the base itself.

Her guide pointed out several varieties of Earthly plants, along with one or two from other hospitable planets, which had been transported here in more peaceful days, and cultivated. Fast-growing vines were already climbing, leaf over tendril, across the new revetments, themselves no more than a few hours old.

Soon her guide mentioned, and with a small detour they were able to see and walk beside, an artificially created lagoon, with real water and aquatic life imported from Port Diamond.

There were, as the young officer pointed out, actually some mutant birds. One variety of these, long-legged creatures suggesting flamingos, were now feeding on the fish in the lagoon. Evidently things had rather gotten away from the bioengineers, and the ungainly, harsh-voiced creatures had become a nuisance to the human population, with their noise, their droppings, their occasional interference with machinery. Jory thought they must be feeding on some other imported life forms; a whole biota, sustained by the interior energy that lighted the atolls and kept them warm. Life here, as elsewhere, was refusing to accommodate itself to predictions made by humans or computers.

There were regions on the atoll, like the one where Jory and her companion had now arrived, crunching along the yellow pseudo-beach for a few hundred meters, where so far no trails had yet been worn in by human feet and robotic wheels. Here the horizon took on a much more distant aspect, as the overall curvature of the surface underfoot became much less sharp. The gravity did not change noticeably. The eerie, sometimes unsettling resemblance to an Earthly seascape varied from one side of the atoll to the other.

The guide was willing and ready to be helpful. "What else would you like to know, ma'am?"

"Well . . ." The main problem still seemed to be in deciding what was most important to find out. The two of them had now regained the settlement, and were walking down an unpaved street, keeping well to one side to be out of the way of an almost-steady stream of moving machinery. "This thing, for example." She gestured to where some large machines were busy digging, scraping, remolding the peculiar stuff of the atoll. "Just what exactly are they building here?"

"This particular shape is called a mantelet." They were standing in front of a low wall, formed of the native matter of the space reef. The wall was at a little more than head height, while it crossed an otherwise open space between two rows of buildings. Partway across, the structure split into a double wall, forming a kind of roofless tunnel. Other varieties of defensive works—turrets, revetments, large mounds of featureless exterior—were also being erected, carved out of the stuff of the atoll, at what the observer thought a dazzling pace.

The guide picked up a chunk of surplus material the size of a large fist, part of the debris dropped by some digging machine, and casually tossed it to Jory, who caught it and was surprised by its weight. "This stuff can be made stronger than ferroconcrete if you know how to work with it. Our military engineers do."

Jory's next question was interrupted when she and her guide had to step briskly aside for a motorized work party, rumbling past in a small cloud of dust.

She observed, with something like awe, how the dust in falling back to the ground organized itself in midair into large intricate flakes, bigger than snowflakes, which crumbled into anonymity as soon as they hit the ground again.

Of course thousands of additional people could have been brought in, but given the small area to be defended—no more than a few square kilometers—it was doubtful that greater numbers would have been of much help. The muscle of the defense was of course provided by machines. And the machines that were most needed were not available.

The construction activity was almost entirely directed at creating a series of shelters, revetments, for the fighting ships that were based here.

It looked to the visitor like a good job of digging in was well on its way to accomplishment. But her attention kept coming back to those ships—the actual hardware that was on hand, the only tools on hand to fight back against berserkers. She had been told that the weapons available were simply inadequate.

Jory went on, as methodically as possible, making careful notes and memos: "The spacegoing warcraft available at this base are few in number, compared with what the enemy is reported to be bringing against us. And for the most part our hardware is seriously outdated." Of course, everything would have to be passed by the censors before it went out.

Despite the garrison's hard work in preparation, and their dedication to the cause of the defense, none of them had yet been told all that was known about the impending berserker attack.

One of the first things Field Marshal Yamanim did on his arrival was award spot promotions to the two officers immediately in charge of the defense of Fifty Fifty.

Commander Dramis, who commanded the fighting spacecraft, became a commodore, and Lieutenant Colonel Shanga, in charge of ground troops and installations, rose to the rank of full colonel. Then they were informed by their high-ranking visitor that on one particular day of the standard calendar, a day not more than one standard month in the future, they were to expect the onslaught. The date, of course, had been translated from the berserkers' own calendar (the code breakers were sure they had one, based on Galactic rotation) and schedules as the spying Solarians had come to understand them.

At the hastily called briefing, Yamanim's audience, consisting of most of the officers available, had stared at him, respectfully incredulous as he reeled off all these details. Presently one of the bolder officers asked whether the times and dates the field marshal had given them were firm. They were indeed, Yamanim assured his questioner. And still he volunteered no explanations.

Maybe it was the newly promoted colonel, perhaps feeling he now had the right to be curious, who came up with a more pointed question. "Sir—what if all this information is wrong? What if the berserkers pass up Fifty Fifty, maybe even Uhao, and head straight for Earth?"

"We just hope that they will not," the field marshal answered at last.

Again people exchanged wondering glances. But no one asked the next obvious question. All journalists had been excluded from this meeting, though perhaps they knew it was taking place, and were going to try to find out afterward what had been discussed.

The field marshal still provided no hint as to how he could be so definite. Soon after his departure a rumor started among the defenders of Fifty Fifty, anonymously and mysteriously as rumors do, to the effect that someone, maybe a clever Carmpan, had managed to sneak a spy machine loyal to humanity into the heart of the enemy camp.

Yamanim and his aides had discussed this subject warily, among themselves.

"People are always ready to credit the Carmpan with great achievements; myself, I don't see that they've ever contributed much to our common cause."

"There are the Prophecies of Probability."

"Bah. Predictions that no one can interpret have a very limited usefulness."

"And if the berserkers can sneak in spy machines on us, why can't someone else work the same trick on them?"

Officially the rumor, like most others, was neither denied nor confirmed.

A chuckle and a shake of the head. "Well, I still say that agent of ours at berserker HQ is worth every credit we pay him."

Jory now bade goodbye, for the time being, to the almost anonymous young man who had been her latest guide. She wanted to have another talk with Jay Nash.

Bringing her robot back to her quarters, she switched it to standby mode and left it in a corner. She started to turn away, then swung back to face the machine. Jory smiled to herself. She was toying with the idea of naming her robot Pappy.

The authorities, responding to some kind of political influence exerted from on high, had allowed Nash and his crew to set themselves up in a central position on one of the atolls. From this vantage point his instruments ought to have a good view of whatever attack finally hit the base.

The officer locally in charge of defense was not particularly bothered by this. And the next time, perhaps the first time, Jory talked to Colonel Shanga she soon realized that he had his own reasons for sticking Nash and his crew out in such a conspicuous spot.

"Any enemy fire he draws will mean just that much less aimed at our gun batteries."

Meanwhile, as the numbers on calendars and clocks began to approach those assigned to the predicted D day, out on the sandy ground of Fifty Fifty, there was no faltering in the efforts at defense.

The garrison engaged in digging themselves in on Fifty Fifty, as well as the fleet commanders preparing to hoist the hulls of their outnumbered fleet from distant Port Diamond, remained fixed in their determination to hit the attacking berserker task force with every weapon they could bring into play.

Jory noted a group of people in distinctive uniforms. Taking a second glance, she realized that they were all male. Some Templar outfit, probably. For certain specialized military units to be exclusively of one sex or the other was not unheard of. They were doing some kind of exercise drill that reminded her of a *kata* from the martial arts, chanting and yelling as they moved about in unison.

A passing spacer soon identified them for her as members of the Second Raider Battalion, Major Evander Karlsen commanding. According to Jory's informant, these were either a branch of the Templars, or members of some rival cult—he couldn't remember which.

Jory frowned intently. "Is the founder related to the . . . ?"

The Karlsen? The legendary berserker-killer of several centuries past? The spacer didn't know.

Whatever their origin, the Raiders had appeared some days earlier on Fifty Fifty as part of the reinforcements. For a short time, or so Jory had heard, the Raiders had thought themselves above the routine tasks of fortification. But as soon as Colonel Shanga had given his opinion on the matter, they pitched in and worked as hard as anyone else.

One of Jory's projects, during the lull in news that set in after a full alert had been called, and all spacecraft had got off the ground, was to seek out the commander of the Raiders for an interview.

The major was certainly not reluctant. As their talk went on, he let on, by dropping hints, that he was indeed related to the legendary Karlsen, but he was vague about the details.

Jory was intrigued by the discovery that the man she was talking to was indeed a member of the T-clan, as outsiders sometimes called it, the same ancient, half-tribal group to which Spacer Traskeluk belonged. The discovery brought back to her thoughts about the whole business of Gift and Traskeluk, which had begun to slip from her memory.

Jory said to the young soldier: "I have a theoretical question for you."

"I will try to answer it."

"Suppose you were in a fight to the death with a berserker, somewhere, you and some colleague or comrade of yours who was not a clan member."

The other nodded to show that he understood.

"And suppose this other man—betrayed you in some way. Just ran away, saving his own skin, while knowing that you were still alive; and knowing that you depended on him to have any chance of survival. Suppose then that against all the odds you *did* survive. What would you . . . ?"

The clansman was shaking his head. He seemed to be actually amused. "Couldn't happen. Nothing like that. Not in this outfit."

"All right. But suppose it *did* happen? In some other outfit if not here."

The other's face grew grim. "There would be nothing for it but to hunt that man down, and deal with him as he deserved. It would be a personal matter, you see, a thing of honor."

"You'd see to it that he was court-martialed?"

"No." A shake of the head, decisive and immediate. "That wouldn't do at all. There are forms that prescribe how such a traitor must be dealt with."

"You mean, ah . . ."

"Lady, I mean kill the son of a bitch."

Running into Jay Nash, while both of them were getting their equipment ready, Jory heard a story from him about the time he had made a documentary on the Templars, after being officially denied permission to do so. One thing was certainly true about Nash—he had a great many stories to tell. Jory remembered that the Templars were favorably portrayed in several of his adventure dramas—but she didn't want to take the time to listen to any more details now.

Nash, before concluding this meeting with his new employee, still professed to be shocked at the depth of Jory Yokosuka's ignorance on certain subjects. Himself couldn't seem to get it through his head that she had learned a lot in the couple of days since their previous meeting. This, she suspected, was another pose, possibly meant to cover his own ignorance on a great many of the details.

At one point he barked at her: "You can't record things intelligently if you don't know what you're recording."

And she had to admit there was some logic in that. But by this time Jory was beginning to realize that Nash said a lot of outrageous things simply in an effort to be outrageous.

Staring at a robotic bartender, another thought crossed her mind. "Mr. Nash, what do you think of the Trojan horse theory?"

He grunted something in reply.

Thinking an explanation might be in order, Jory amplified: "I mean, will the berserkers be coming at us here by means of some disguised machines? As the ancient Trojans did?"

His real eye glittered, and the mechanical one almost lurched from its socket in her direction. Triumphantly he barked: "Wasn't the Trojans in the horse, girl. It was the Argives, trying to sneak into Troy."

Jory blinked, feeling a little dazed. " 'Argives'?"

"The Greeks, girl, the Greeks! A whole nation back on Earth. Goddammit, don't you ever read?"

In a drama, of course, the great bulk of the images and sound would be computer created, but even then it helped immeasurably to have live action in the can to use as a base.

Nash said he'd put in a word with the authorities, to try to further her education, but there wasn't going to be time now to arrange any more briefing for Jory.

Sometimes she despaired of communicating with this man on a rational basis.

She was now assigned her final battle station, in a bunker, a small fortified room just below the surface of the ground, fifty meters or so from the dugout where she'd left her few personal belongings.

After checking it out, she went back to her quarters, and a chance to take off her armor for a time. Beneath it, like most people, she was wearing a snug-fitting specialized coverall. Take off the armor, and luxuriate in scratching a few places where itches had developed through the day. And then enjoy the even greater luxury of a hot shower. . . .

The main trouble with the place, she thought, was that it was too far underground. Jory realized that she would have to rely on her machines to see anything at all. Well, they could see more clearly than she could, anyway.

FIFTEEN

Thinking over the two short meetings she had so far had with her boss, and pondering her brief talk with the colonel, Jory returned to her underground living quarters. There she managed to get a few hours' sleep, successfully ignoring the snores of a couple of other journalists, one male, one female, who were flattened out in their respective bunks in the same small room. Waking at the time she'd set for herself—she was generally able to do that—she enjoyed a quick shower and set out for breakfast in the nearest mess hall.

After that she rejoined her assigned guide—who for once had not been replaced between tutorial sessions. At the moment her job still consisted mainly of learning, and getting ready—if such a thing was possible—to be shot at.

Not even underground was it possible to get away from the ceaseless scrape and rumble of machinery, which seemed to be reshaping almost the whole surface of the atoll into fortifications. Work continued around the clock through the eternal, shadeless, almost sunlit day. Machines on the surface dug what looked to Jory like simple trenches, and unwound spools of the equivalent of barbed wire, long strands of polyphase matter, each displaying a quasi intelligence on the level of that of an ant or bee, programmed to entrap or at least delay berserker landing machines when they appeared.

She took the thin strand in hand and inspected it with a look of disbelief. It reminded her of fiber-optic cable. "This stuff is going to stop a berserker lander?"

"No, not by itself. But it's tougher and nastier than it looks. It'll give them something to think about, and it will at least delay the small machines, if there are any." Her tutor paused. "Anyway, it might be that the real reason we're deploying so much wire is that we happened to have a lot of it on hand."

"And that people feel better if they're being kept busy?"

"That might be a factor too."

Other tasks of a high priority included setting land mines, and calculating the best emplacements for the moderately heavy weapons that were available, maximizing their fields of fire. They were setting up mantelets and bunkers, hardening the stuff that here passed for soil into respectable defensive armor.

Chemically coded paint reflected the destructive energy beams fired by one's own side. The code was changed at carefully chosen intervals, to prevent the enemy's learning it and taking advantage of the knowledge.

She heard again all that the authorities thought visiting civilians ought to know about alphatriggers and blinktriggers.

The carbine hand—or shoulder weapon carried by most troops on the ground—was basically an energy projector, whose beam cracked and shivered hard armor, but could be safely turned against soft flesh. The beam induced intense vibrations in whatever it struck; in a substance as soft as flesh, the vibrations damped out quickly and harmlessly.

Hard surfaces, like those of suits of armor, could be protected by treatment with a spray of the proper chemical composition. The formula was varied from one day, or one engagement, to the next, to prevent the enemy's being able to duplicate it.

· · ·

Now there was a rumor, quickly making the rounds, that Yamanim had completed what he considered his urgent business here, and was leaving the atoll. Minutes later, it was not hard to verify that he had left, because there was no longer any sign in the sky of the fast cruiser on which he and Jory had arrived. That vessel had been seen breaking orbit, and according to scuttlebutt heading directly back to Port Diamond. Jory verified that the ship was gone, and assumed that the field marshal was on it, though no one made any official announcement of his whereabouts.

Though seriously tempted once or twice to reveal the source of his knowledge, he had steadfastly refused to reveal to the land-based defenders the fact that when the predicted attack came they would be able to count on carrier support.

When one of his aides suggested that these brave warriors be told all the known facts, Yamanim explained why not: All the officers to whom Field Marshal Yamanim spoke on his hurried visit would sooner or later be talking, passing on information, to pilots, to space crews, if they did not fit in that category themselves. And everyone in this garrison, members of those crews especially, stood in some danger of becoming a berserker's prisoner.

"Understand now?"

"Yes, sir. Sorry, sir."

Another reason for the policy of secrecy, seemingly far-fetched but not totally disprovable, was that there might actually be berserker hardware right here on the base, disguised as something else. A determined search for any such material was instituted. Any number of bad jokes were made, regarding uncooperative machines. Every item of new equipment arriving by any means was thoroughly inspected.

As part of the regular defenses—not Hypo's far-flung spy system—vast reaches of interstellar space, across much of the ED domain, including much of the Gulf and the territory around it, had been for some time, perhaps the past hundred years, studded with millions or bazillions of sensors.

"What was that last unit you mentioned?"

"I'm saying that even the order of magnitude of the total number is classified ultimate secret."

Mostly these were small devices, no bigger than human heads or hands, and were triggered by the passage of probability waves cast out by machines or ships moving in nearby flight-space.

But there were indications that the enemy had found a way to nullify this early-warning net.

A few tanks, heavyweight machines manned by special Templar crews, and capable of slugging it out with almost any known berserker lander, had been brought to Fifty Fifty and were being stored out of sight, ready to roll to the surface on a moment's notice. If Hypo's predictions were as rock-solid as the leadership assumed, the enemy occupation force when it arrived would get a far more enthusiastic reception than any of their leaders could have computed.

Earth was of course strongly concerned by a berserker threat so comparatively near at hand, but few other worlds as yet perceived the threat to Fifty Fifty as an immediate danger to themselves. The Home Sector was not currently the best armed in all of human territory. There was not a lot of mobile firepower that could be quickly deployed to a new location. Other sectors would contribute too, of course, to the defense of Earth, but they were farther away and many of them had their own problems. They were not going to strip their own defenses, even to save Dear Old Earth. In fact, no one would ask them to do so.

More substantial help, in the form of an arsenal of the latest weapons, of fleets including battleships and carriers, had been promised, was being promised anew with every standard day, and could be absolutely relied upon to arrive—someday. The trouble was that day, as all the promisers admitted, might well be a year or more in the future. That would be too late to save Fifty Fifty, and Earth, from the current present danger.

The hundreds of human reinforcements who had already been brought in, and who were now digging themselves in as if for an eternal stay, were most of them combat specialists. They were more or less well-trained, but the great majority lacked any real combat experience. Most of the real veterans were on worlds far from home.

The interstellar brotherhood of anti-berserker devotees (some said fanatics) who called themselves the Templars had pledged to send special help, and the first installments of this aid were already on hand. In theory the Templars dispatched their forces around the Solarian-settled portion of the Galaxy to wherever the need was greatest at the moment. As usual, the organization and its activities were the subject of strong rumors.

Many people on the homeworlds now wished fervently that there was a Templar base somewhere nearby—but of course such bases, and the bulk of the Templar forces, tended to be out on the frontier, where combat was virtually part of day-to-day life—and where unoccupied living space was much easier to find. Out there, the Templars and the local authorities had an easier time of it, getting along.

After she had verified Yamanim's departure, Jory and her latest mentor moved away together. She had a question: Why did everyone seem to think that in this coming battle the human side would be so outclassed?

"That's simple. Because we are."

"Explanation, please?"

The answer to the question about inadequacy soon became obvious, if one believed the briefings, though it was not obvious to a layman simply looking at the sleek hardware. To civilian eyes even the worn and obsolete machines seemed impressive enough.

"That's only a courier. Essential for communication, but practically useless if you're trying to knock an enemy machine out of space."

Jory wondered briefly whether this was the exact same type of ship in which Spacer Gift had made his recent and much-publicized escape. Good old Nifty. Mysterious Nifty. She wondered where he was now.

"And how does one tell a courier from a fighter, say?"

The man's eyes widened momentarily, and he was silent for a moment, as if trying to conceal his shock at such ignorance. At last he said: "Mostly by the overall shape. Actually we don't generally count couriers as ships. They're an expendable asset, like ammunition."

When it was certain that the berserker attack was imminent, all the ships now cradled on the islands would be launched into space, to avoid being caught on the ground like sitting ducks.

Show me."

"All right."

Jory and her guide walked for a few hundred meters, a good part of the way around the tiny world, to the far end of the landing field, where they would be relatively out of the way of vital activity.

There they approached a launching pad that held a ship accessible for inspection. The landing field, much of it bordered by the illusion of what appeared to be a waterless beach, stretched out so far toward the near horizon that the curvature of the odd world beneath their feet was plainly visible.

The pad itself, the size of a small house, was sculpted out of the peculiar, sand-colored matter of the atoll. This native stuff had been carved and molded into a cradlelike, shallow depression, from which tilted columns arose to embrace the egg-shaped hull, two or three times as big as an ordinary ground car.

Standing under the overhang of hull, the guide casually raised his right hand and gave a proprietary thump against the rounded metal flank. This ship was roughly ovoid, bulges here and there suggesting fins or wings, though not pronounced enough to be called by those names. Moving to a position directly under one of these pinnae (the proper technical name), her escort informed her: "Here you have what is, unfortunately, a typical example of the Solarian *fighter.*"

Upon the little spaceship's flank were markings and insignia of several kinds, all of which, said the guide, would disappear when power came on and the ship was livened for combat. Jory's guide explained what each symbol meant. He demonstrated that rubbing his hand over them made them vanish. The markings could be turned on again in flight, on the rare occasions when that seemed desirable.

Jory could see no obvious break at any point in the smooth curves of what appeared to be featureless metal. She asked, "Where are the weapons? Missiles, things to shoot with?"

"All inside the hull at the moment. We're in an atmosphere here, and streamlining makes the liftoff just a little faster. In space, where there's a prospect of combat, they appear as needed."

Jory's robot of course, gaudily labeled as a civilian tool, had been activated for this expedition. It kept tagging along, and she used it to keep taking pictures and notes.

The fighter was notably longer and leaner than the other types of ship—Jory, looking around as her guide pointed them out in their revetments, could see that this was so. This difference was because the missiles carried by the fighter, either stowed inboard or slung outside the hull, were not as large.

"This type operates alternately in flightspace and in normal space, and dodges rapidly from one mode to the other. The fighter routinely risked jumps in and out of crowded, 'heavy' regions of normal space that ordinary spacecraft would be unable to accomplish. It carried short-range beam weapons and a few missiles. In combat it was effective mainly against small berserker fighting machines. Because it doesn't carry big bombs or missiles, it can't do much damage to large berserkers, except possibly by suicidal ramming."

As a climactic effect, the guide did something that produced the opening of a hatchway in the silvery hull, and invited Jory to climb in and look around. She boarded through a narrow groove, going up a series of awkward steps. Her guide didn't attempt to come with her; there simply wasn't room inside for two.

"I wouldn't touch anything, though," he cautioned mildly.

"Never fear." Crossing her arms, she hugged her fingers in her armpits, as if to keep them out of trouble. Now she was looking down into a kind of grave-sized windowless pit, containing a helmet on a cord, a single combat chair; not very much else. "What about the berserkers? I assume their machines are divided into types as well?"

"More or less. For our own convenience in discussion, we tend to group them into varieties more or less corresponding to our own ordnance.

"For fighters the berserkers rely mainly on what we usually call the Void fighting machine. Also known to Solarian intelligence as the *Type Zero* or *Goose egg* or *Cipher* or *Null.*"

"And how effective is the Void?"

"It's good. It's actually better than anything we can put up. Very fast and agile, but somewhat fragile too. Berserkers after all care nothing about the survival of any of their own hardware, if it can get the job of killing people done."

"Can I quote you on that? That the Void is better than any of our fighters?"

The guide shrugged. Now it was possible to see that he was deeply angry; not at Jory, not even at the berserkers. Rather at the fact that he and his comrades were so miserably equipped— or believed they were. And she doubted they would cling to that belief without good evidence.

"They told me to brief you, Ms. Yokosuka, and that's what I'm doing. What the censors are going to allow you to send out of here is something else."

"What exactly is wrong with this one I'm standing in? Or on?"

"Too slow, to begin with. And it displays a certain tendency to shed small pieces of its outer hull under the extreme physical stress of combat. Actually under any physical stress at all."

"Oh." When Jory looked closer, she saw that patches of irregular surface were indeed visible on the hull, from which small pieces did seem to have been shed. The instructor's bare hand scraping at one such sore spot produced another little fragment.

Jory stared, wide-eyed. Suspiciously she wondered if her

guide was hoaxing her in some elaborate way; but the expression on his face soon convinced her that he wasn't.

She eased herself down a step, sliding her body in through the pilot's hatch. Now she was standing on the single combat chair, and now she had let herself down into it. The space was cramped, especially with her body fat with armor.

"May I try on the helmet?" she called, a little louder than before. Her guide had vanished from her field of vision when she let herself down into the spacecraft from the top. The helmet hung poised on its little rack, connected with the nearby panel by a silvery, stretchable cable. Tentatively she started to pick it up.

Her guide's dry chuckle reached her ears from below. "That would be about the last thing I'd recommend you do."

Jory hastily put the odd-shaped silver bucket back on its support.

Jay Nash had worked hard, pulled all the political strings he could, to get permission to remain on Fifty Fifty with his small livecrew when the attack came, and record the attack. Nash wasn't going to change his mind about that. But other reporters were going to ride with the Solarian Gulf fleet, or what was left of it after the sneak attack, when it moved out of Port Diamond.

That fleet had been officially designated Task Force Sixteen, and most of the people on the islands were still ignorant of its existence. Maybe Nash himself had been told. He was widely trusted.

But the widespread ignorance, it could be hoped, extended to the berserkers.

A little later, back in her quarters again, Jory was privately reviewing her notes, gathered from a variety of sources. Her bunkmates (all of them were now female, after some switching around) were going about their own business in the crowded room, while she lay on her back in her bunk with her boots off, and ignored them all. Her robot was curled doglike, in a way that occupied a minimum of space, beneath her bunk, next to her stored personal armor.

Staring at her notes, she read:

The chief types of small Solarian fighting ships to be used in the early phases of the battle include:
  a) Land-based undersluggers.
  b) Land-based hardlaunchers.

The Solarian carriers have a better class of fighter—informally called the *Lynx*—than any based on the atoll, to send out as escorts to their bombers and torpedo planes.

The hardlauncher attacks out of flightspace after first closing to a short range, perilously near its target, and maybe even inside the target's defensive force fields. Carries one or two heavy missiles. Even one hit can do serious damage to a mothership/carrier type large berserker; moderate damage to a battlewagon. Some large berserkers are hybrid types. Most large ones can launch at least a small squadron of small machines.

The berserker hardlauncher most often seen is officially designated by our side the D3 A1 Type 99, and code-named by Solarians the *Villain,* the name everyone (except, I suppose, the berserkers) actually uses for it.

The Solarian dive-bomber most used in early fighting is the (*Dauntless,* SBD), which is not as badly outdated as most of the Solarian fighters.

The underslugger is sometimes also called a torpedo bomber. Carries one really heavy missile, which is launched in normal space, but then drops into flightspace in the near vicinity of its target, and thus strikes "below the waterline." Something like the C-plus cannon sometimes employed.

· · ·

All small ships above a certain size and mass are based only on Fifty Fifty and not on carriers. Each should have a livecrew of seven. Three of these seem to be officers, and four, enlisted people. But some of the farlaunchers on the atoll had once been rigged up to function as undersluggers—a mission they carried out every bit as ineffectively as did the craft that had been designed to do that job.

The strongholds are also based only on solid land—they're too big to fit the launching facilities on carriers—go into into combat with a crew of ten. As a rule these positions are: pilot, copilot, navigator, bombardier, flight engineer, and five gunners. The latter include the tail, the ball turret, two waist, and one radio operator who operates the top gun turret as well.

These larger bombers had really been designed for attacking landforms, berserker bases on planets or other sizable celestial objects. These heavy bombers would have been much better suited to attacking the atoll than defending it—but they were on hand, and every weapon had to be used.

Going back for a moment to a): The underslugger.

They haul some really nasty missiles. Even one of them hitting home is a serious blow to any berserker—or would be to any human ship—however large.

In an earlier battle in the Azlaroc Sector, where our carrier *Lankvil* was so severely damaged, the Solarian underslugger missiles had proven largely ineffective—they were poorly designed to begin with, and perhaps had been inaccurately maintained.

The chief berserker underslugger is the B5N2 Type 97, better known to most Solarians as the *Killer*.

On the Solarian side, our entry is again woefully obsolete. Too slow, and other problems.

Only the briefest test in combat had been needed,

in the space battle at Azlaroc, to demonstrate that
even the new torpedo bombers needed fighter protection if they were to have a fighting chance of getting within range of a berserker carrier.

Jory lost interest for the moment in what kind of a job she
was doing. She let her hand holding her notebook sink down
to her side, and stared at the hardened soil of the ceiling not
many centimeters above her face. For the first time, her situation underground struck her as like being in a grave.

The berserkers were coming. And for the first time she was
really scared.

Ten days or so before the date predicted by Hypo for the berserker onslaught on Fifty Fifty, Cedric Traskeluk, more or less back from the dead to the amazement of everyone except himself, came walking, unaided though limping slightly, out of a staff car and down into the shabby-looking outer regions of the underground domain of Mother R and her code-breaking crew. The latest survivor among the spy ship's crew had graduated from intensive care in the base hospital several days ago; by now the medics and debriefers were winding down their respective attentions, and he was beginning to possess some chunks of time that were more or less his own.

Meanwhile, his days in the hospital had afforded him the time to make, in his own mind, some necessary plans. Now he was about to take the first steps toward putting those plans into effect.

He had emerged from the hospital with an artificial arm that was, because of the coincidental similarity of their wounds, basically very much like Nifty Gift's new limb. Some people who learned of the coincidence made much of it—but not Traskeluk himself. His new forearm of course was somewhat shorter, thicker, and stronger than Gift's, and of a subtly different coloring, to match the natural differences in their bodies.

And this latest survivor suffered no nightmares about bad things that had already happened to him, or might fall to his lot at some time in the future. For Cedric Traskeluk there were no stabs of guilt about actions that he had taken or failed to take. Instead, his private dreams were of elaborate rituals of execution. And it was not himself who played the victim's role.

Naturally, on Traskeluk's arrival at the base, the authorities had dispatched an official message to his immediate family on their distant world, letting his parents and others know that their earlier report of tragedy had been mistaken, and he was not to be considered missing in action after all. The branch of the Traskeluk clan that counted Cedric as its own dwelt nowhere in the homeworlds, so it would be a matter of weeks before his parents and siblings got the word.

Then, as soon as the latest lucky survivor was able to do so for himself, he had dispatched homeward a brief message of his own. A few sentences, terse and to the point. The gist of it was that he was safe after all, though wounded, and there was no need for any special concern on their part.

Mother R had already recommended Gift, Traskeluk, and of course their shipmates (posthumously) for a special medal, beyond the usual thing that people got when wounded in the line of duty—though of course the news of what they had actually done would continue for the foreseeable future to be censored.

Everyone at the hospital had assured Traskeluk that he, like his lucky shipmate before him, was certain to be granted leave as soon as he was well—and in his case, in consideration of the travel time required, it would be a long leave. But Traskeluk's message home did not include any suggestion that he was to be expected there any time soon.

The omission was quite deliberate, and Cedric assumed that it would tell the more intelligent members of his family all they needed to know. In his brief, guarded description of his mishap in space he had inserted a key phrase or two, expressions having to do with honor and necessity, and generally used only when a matter of formal vengeance required to be undertaken. The young man was sure that several of the people at home, his father in particular, would catch the implied meaning. If others, particularly the womenfolk, were not as quick to grasp the necessary point—well, explanations would just have to wait.

To any male member of the clan, certain questions of honor were orders of magnitude more important than pleasant diversions like getting home for a visit. Naturally, his father and grandfather, like the rest of his family, would be disappointed that Cedric would not be dropping in on them just now—and perhaps not for a long, long time. But the men of the clan would certainly approve—in his mind's eye he could see them nodding—of the way he, Cedric, was going to spend that time instead. When they eventually learned the full story of the spy-ship disaster, they would nod some more, confirmed in their certainty that he had no other choice. To allow such treachery as Gift's to go unpunished would be unthinkable, and Cedric's homecoming would be a grim and dismal affair indeed, if he were milksop enough to do so.

As one of the early steps in the process Spacer Traskeluk was now compelled to follow, he intended to visit one other family member. This was a certain male cousin who, fortunately for Cedric's purpose, happened to have settled on Uhao, only a couple of hours from Port Diamond. The cousin's home would have to be Cedric's first stop when he started out on leave.

But before he could get off the base, there was another visit he was required to make. Few people in Hypo's central office had ever seen Traskeluk—or any other field operator, for that matter—in the flesh, or even as an image. But when this dour, husky young enlisted man was passed through to the inner office without delay, almost everyone in the office on looking up realized who he must be, and gazed at him with something like awe. Having come back from the dead, as it were, this latest spy-ship survivor was even more of a celebrity than his shipmate Nifty Gift had been.

The cluttered, disorderly room that one was passed into

from the bottom of the stairs was very little changed from its appearance of a few days ago, when Gift had visited the place. The scene was half familiar to Traskeluk, just as it had been to Nifty Gift.

Traskeluk could not see that anything had changed since his last visit. Once inside, military procedures seemed at first glance to have been left behind. Down in a huge, disorderly-looking basement, some of the gray concrete walls and steel pillars looked half buried amid startling heaps of paper that gave the place the look of an antique library. Also bulwarked and barricaded by tall piles of paper, very intelligent but very nonanthropomorphic machines were conferring with their human masters, meanwhile devouring reams, armloads, of blank paper, only to spit it out again in a matter of minutes, crammed with printed symbols. Computers, thoroughly air-gapped and otherwise shielded from intrusion, lined the walls. The only terminals connected to these computers, and the only operators, were also physically present in the same room. Peculiar sounds, like strange, droning musical notes hung in the air—questioning quester music. Some people thought it helped them to focus on matters needing the most intense concentration.

The code-breaking machines of Hypo never moved from where their builders had set them, against these ordinary-looking walls. They were not designed to move.

On entering the office, Traskeluk went through much the same routine that Gift had followed, regarding the probable availability of transportation to his home of record, or place of enlistment, as he prepared to go on leave.

He didn't think he was going in that direction this time; but now was not the time to make that point.

Today's mood in the underground room was a kind of grim jubilation. Someone told Traskeluk that Commander R had already interviewed Nifty Gift about his future desk job, and Trask thought maybe she would want to do the same for him. He hoped not; he would rather simply be on his way, and for a while it looked like he would get his wish. Mother was simply wrapped up in other considerations today.

· · ·

When the latest wounded hero had gone through the routine motions relating to his leave, he took a chance on trying to advance his personal business.

The same clerk who had been processing the documents for Spacer Traskeluk's convalescent leave had now put his feet up on his desk—this youth, taking advantage of the unit's laxity in the matter of uniform regulations, affected combat boots of a type usually seen only in environments much less hospitable than an office—and was trying to answer the visitor's questions.

"Yeah, Gift was in here about ten days ago. Then he headed out on leave too. You lucky bastards!" This last was said with a grin, to show that the speaker really appreciated how unpleasant the survivors' close call had been.

Traskeluk had to make a conscious effort to suppress a sudden impulse to reach over the little barrier and smash the other's face with his numb new hand. But no, he had more important plans for that; he needed to keep his own time free over the next few days and weeks. He sat with fingers interlaced, the real ones and the improved ones clenched together.

He kept his voice neutral. "I'd like to know if he went to Earth. Who cut his leave orders?"

"We did that here." The clerk called up more data. "Want to catch up with him, huh? You'll have a lot to talk about. Must be your good buddy."

"Oh yeah. We each lost an arm." He studied the fingers of his new left hand and made them work. They were getting better.

Somehow the clerk had no witty comeback to that. He fell silent and concentrated on his keyboard.

Traskeluk, having talked to several clerks, thought that his routine business here was about concluded, when to his surprise word came out that the boss herself wanted to see him after all. A few seconds later, the man who was now determined to track down Nifty Gift found himself being conducted more deeply into top-secret country that he had ever been allowed before.

Traskeluk knocked at the door of Commander R's private office. When a soft female voice told him to come in, he entered and saluted the small form hunched behind the desk.

The commander returned his salute with a sketchy gesture, and said, "I did indeed want to see you, Traskeluk."

She waved at a chair—there were two in front of her desk—and her latest visitor sidled up to the nearest one, being careful not to topple nearby stacks of secret papers, and sat down.

"Yes, ma'am."

Mother R, despite her general air of otherworldliness, was seldom one to waste time. Within a minute she had started briefing Traskeluk, as she had already spoken to Gift, about the new job that was very probably going to be his, here at headquarters, when he got back from his well-earned leave.

She also wanted to thank this young man, as she had already thanked his shipmate, for heroic accomplishments in saving data. Interrupting herself, she inquired of Traskeluk whether he thought the berserker that almost killed him had known the spy ship's purpose.

He told her he had no idea about what the berserker might have known, except that it was sure about wanting to kill everyone in sight. Mother nodded and got on with the explanations. Information from advanced scoutships, and from the far-flung strands of the robot web, kept trickling in to Hypo, traveling by various guarded routes that all met in this room. Very much the same data, being forwarded on branching trails from the same sources, was carried also to the larger headquarters on Earth, where in an alternate and very similar den of secrecy called Negat it was eagerly seized by another set of laboring decoders and interpreters.

In fact, Commander R turned out to be quite helpful when Traskeluk, emboldened by her unmilitary attitude and taking another chance, asked her about the whereabouts of his shipmate and fellow survivor, good old Nifty Gift.

"Ma'am, would you happen to know if Spacer Gift went

home on his convalescent leave? Back to Earth, where I believe he lives?"

The commander blinked. Her liquid brown eyes looked at Traskeluk and seemed to be staring effortlessly through him. "Why, I assume he went home. It might be possible to find out."

"If you wouldn't mind, ma'am, I'd like to know." Traskeluk's big hands, the real and fake working well together for the moment, turned around the uniform cap he had been holding in his lap. Then the new, artificial fingers lost their touch momentarily, and the headpiece fell to the floor.

She thought a moment, then reached for a panel on her desk. "Let me call security; that will probably be fastest. They may have put a tracer on that man."

" 'Tracer', ma'am? What's that?"

She made a fluttery gesture with both hands. "Oh, our spy catchers like to keep in practice with their cloaks and daggers, I suppose. A kind of thing they often do when our people go on leave. Just so we know where our special people are. I don't know that it bothers anyone—just a matter of routine." Mother smiled reassuringly.

In a few minutes the information was forthcoming. Even security had orders to keep Mother R as happy as possible. And it was an interesting story. It looked like Nifty had decided not to go home at all.

In matters of strategy, Admiral Naguance concurred with Field Marshal Yamanim. The latter had just got back to Port Diamond following his trip to Fifty Fifty, and had bestowed upon the former this unexpected and at first unwelcome command of a carrier task force. The two, accompanied by a few members of their respective staffs, were conferring aboard ship, a short time before liftout from low orbit. Soon Naguance would be going into space, to try to intercept the predicted berserker assault.

"These task forces will be ready in three days to lift out of orbit. I'm giving you Sixteen, with two carriers, *Venture* and *Stinger*. Each is carrying two squadrons of hardlaunchers, one of fighters and one of undersluggers. Hell of a way to hand you an assignment, I know, at the last minute. But there it is, and we neither of us have much choice. There's a war on, as the civilians say. You can, of course, say no."

"No, sir, my answer is yes."

"You seem a little reluctant, man. I thought all admirals wanted to command a fleet."

Naguance shook his head. "Not necessarily, sir. Not when the fleet has been reduced to little more than vaporized metal and bits of wreckage."

Yamanim had had a similar experience at the next higher level of command. He smiled and explained that he was repeating some of the same questions he had been asked himself.

The two officers were agreed on the great importance of hitting the berserker carriers before the enemy launched.

"Outnumbered and outgunned as we are, my esteemed colleague, getting in the first blow, and a hard one, seems to represent our one chance of success."

The admiral murmured his agreement.

Naguance was well acquainted with the details of the secret effort being carried on by Commander R and her handful of people.

Not until about ten days before the battle did Hypo get its collective hands on the key intercept, the mine of information that opened to them the key berserker playbook, a detailed outline of the enemy's plan for the coming battle.

This came in the form of a message from one berserker fleet to another that laid on the line the details, unit designations, and exact times, of the planned berserker attack. A courier, with every member of its crew very excited, had brought it in. Not that the crew ever attempted to interpret what they gathered—they never did, and were not capable of doing so. But they could estimate the importance by the sheer volume of information.

The other big news of the day was that the enemy had just made one of their periodic code shifts; Hypo of course was attacking the new code with all its intellectual power, but months might pass before their transmissions became readable again.

A cautious move by the berserkers—but it seemed to have come a little too late to do them any good.

On that same day, Gavrilov and Flower left Jay Nash's rented house, taking Gift with them. Tanya remained behind— the job of house-sitting was officially as much hers as Gavrilov's, and presumably the client would notice no difference.

The spacer went as a willing refugee. Gavrilov said that if Gift wanted to desert the Space Force, he and some other friends were ready to help him. Three people in casual clothing, who might have been setting out on a picnic. Here on Uhao the weather was usually cooperative. No one was carrying more than a picnic basket in the way of baggage.

"Where are we going?" Gift asked.

"Where they won't find you."

"Where's that?"

Gavrilov slowly shook his head.

"Someplace here on Uhao?"

The other's head was still shaking. "You'll find out where it is when we get there. If what's really important to you is getting out of your current problem, then that should be satisfactory."

And Gift was willing to be satisfied with that.

Gavrilov led the way along a roofed walkway to the garage, where the three climbed into the oldest-looking, least conspicuous ground car.

Looking back at the big house as they rolled down the drive, Gift could see the robot butler, with its unchangeable smile, gazing after them as they departed.

Nobody interfered with the travelers; nobody seemed to be following, or paying them any attention. Gavrilov seemed edgy on the subject, and several times drove in a great loop, frequently looking behind him. The drive lasted several hours, and carried them several hundred kilometers, to a quiet, unfrequented lagoon, green-scummed and uninviting, surrounded by the local equivalent of palm trees.

Here Gavrilov took a small device from his pocket, and

transmitted a coded summons, which a moment later brought up an ordinary-looking small spacecraft to float on the water.

Gift asked: "So, I take it we're not staying on Uhao?"

His guide didn't answer.

Gift knew that after liftoff the ship would certainly be noticed and tracked by traffic control. But the chances were against them paying much attention to a vessel outward bound.

The party waded and swam, getting thoroughly wet, through brackish water out to the barely floating hull. Fortunately the weather was warm, as usual on Uaho. One by one they slid aboard through the open passenger hatch, after Gavrilov had programmed his ground car in robot mode back to the house.

A few low-voiced commands, and power and lights came smoothly on aboard the spaceship. The hatch was closed again, and the vessel sank once more out of sight under water.

"We'll do our liftoff after dark."

Gift didn't think that would help, if anyone was seriously watching. But he offered no suggestions. It was a small ship, smaller than anything he was used to, but he didn't doubt that it had interstellar capability.

Gavrilov waved a generous hand at him. "Pick out a cabin. Take any one you want."

Gift had never been in a small private spaceship before. He wondered if they were only hopping to somewhere else on the same planet.

When Flower came to join him in the small cabin he had chosen, he asked her where they were going.

She didn't know. "It's up to Gavrilov."

"Oh." Gift paused. "Were you and he ever . . . ?"

She seemed indifferent to the question. "There's nothing like that between us. Not any more."

Snug and dry under water, it was time to eat. There was plenty of food on board, and a good recycler.

Shortly after sunset they got off into space, sticking to the planetary shadow and sliding up fast toward a display of very visible stars. It soon became apparent that casual comfort was the note for captain and passengers. Actually Gavrilov, once he'd punched in some destination that Gift couldn't see, was content to leave all the calculation to the machines.

Several days passed on the voyage. Gift was no longer at all concerned about pursuit, or being followed. Once a ship or machine started going in and out of flightspace, tracking it at all became a major endeavor.

Gift told himself he had no regrets about making his desertion official. Actually, he had some, but he was certain by now that there was nothing he could do about it.

Ever since he'd learned that Traskeluk had been miraculously rescued, it seemed that he really had no other choice. If he tried to go back to duty, the best thing that could happen would be that Traskeluk would blow the whistle on him, and he'd be court-martialed. Even if he was found officially innocent, whatever future he might otherwise have hoped for in the Space Force would be in ruins. Once his record looked in the least doubtful, there wouldn't be any easy, chairborne job with Hypo. More likely he'd be reassigned to the ninety-fourth mess kit repair squadron, stationed on some dim rock at the end of the known universe.

And that outcome was about the best he could dare to hope for. The worst . . .

He knew Traskeluk, knew him all too well, after they'd spent months together on a small ship.

And Gift had other things to worry about too—or thought he did. In this high state of alert, military people who failed to show up for duty were not simply marked AWOL (for which the consequences would be unpleasant enough) but were considered as having deserted in the face of the enemy, as the old phrase had it—and when deserters were caught, they were generally shot, after a short trial and with little ceremony. Such cases were extremely rare. Gift had never given the matter much thought until now, but he had a strong impression that such people were almost always caught.

Out on the space atoll called Fifty Fifty, everyone not already wearing personal armor was scrambling to reach it and put it on. All the ships still on the ground were powering up, recharging drives and onboard weapon systems through cable connections at each service bay and launchpad. Jory's monitors, all of which she now had in position, observed a process of flashing lights and almost eerie silence. At all costs, every useful spacecraft must be spaceborne before the enemy arrived.

A group of spacegoing machines, assumed to be the berserker striking force, had at last been located by scout ships, still an hour away but closing fast. Land-based fighters and bombers were being urgently dispatched in an attempt to get in the first blow.

Combat veterans on the atoll expected that the berserker raiders would be coming on almost as fast as the scout that brought word of their presence—and in fact they were right on that scoutship's heels.

Jory was thinking that one of the livecrew people on one

of the ships taking part in this strike would be Warrant Officer Tadao, the latest in her succession of guides, who had tutored her on the various kinds of fighting ships.

Tadao had never told his civilian client exactly which job on the combat crew was his, and now Jory was wishing that she'd asked—he might be a copilot, or maybe astrogator on one of the heavy bombers—a Stronghold farlauncher.

Next moment she pictured Tadao as a spare gunner, and had been assigned to a crew when one of the regular gunners had to drop out for some reason. Such a man would be more easily spared to brief civilians.

But in one capacity or another, the latest version of her friendly guide, the one whose name she had been having trouble remembering, was going into combat. Hell, they probably all were. She wished now that she had taken the opportunity to wish them all well before liftoff.

Come to think of it, it looked like she was going into combat too, and practically at their side.

Listening and watching with the aid of her equipment, exchanging bits of information with other media workers, she picked up a few more facts about the sighting: It had been made by one of the long-range scouts flying regular recon missions from Fifty Fifty.

The Solarian scout had hastened to get off a robotic message courier, which ought to be able to carry the news back to the atoll faster than the scout ship itself could do so, at least in space relatively heavy with gravitational fields.

After dispatching that first robot courier, the scout ship spent the next few minutes hanging in position to observe the enemy fleet, while its livecrew of two or three Solarians exchanged terse comments among themselves.

Then the spacecraft commander fired a second courier back to base with some details. He could now count upwards of twenty large berserker vessels in the force that had just been discovered, but unless the scout closed to a suicidal range, it seemed impossible to be sure whether any of them were carriers.

Shortly after sending its last message courier, fearing it had been discovered, the scout turned and ran for home.

Each robot courier, on arriving in the vicinity of the atoll, actually materialized in space at a distance of a hundred klicks or so, then darted in to hover in a position several kilometers above the center of the base, and from there sent its burden of information to the ground in a tight beam. This was the usual procedure, a few minutes faster than actually landing the courier, and was virtually just as secure.

Jory watched the latest of these couriers arrive at Fifty Fifty. When its movement flickered to a halt, it was so low that she could see it hovering in the perpetual thin overcast. She knew that the courier was probably transmitting urgent information, saving precious seconds, even as it came darting down to land.

She hurried over to Colonel Shanga's headquarters, moving as fast as possible in her armor, to which she was still struggling to become accustomed. She didn't expect that she would be allowed inside HQ, where no one would be able to take time to talk to her anyway, but she could at least hang around outside.

For the last several days the colonel and his staff had been spending most of their time in the central command bunker. When Jory got there, she tried to find out what the latest news had been. But the people inside were obviously very busy, and the guard at the door had orders to keep out all civilians. Jay Nash wasn't visible.

Everyone on the atoll could tell that a message of importance had just arrived, but this time the colonel and his aides released no information.

But soon any lingering suspicion that this alert might be only practice had been removed; an enemy fleet must have been sighted, for preparations were being made to get all spacecraft up into space.

Jory had already learned that a scout normally carried four or five such robot couriers. She gathered that they were generally of the same type as the little vessel in which Spacer Gift had made his escape; but some couriers were smaller, lacking any compartment in which even one human might ride.

Naturally, the more couriers or other massive cargo that a scout ship carried, the more sluggish it became—though craft of that type were still comparatively agile, in a class with fighters, compared to much larger military vessels. If threatened with pursuit, a scout might fire off or jettison all its couriers in an effort to get away.

Jory returned to her own shelter, then reemerged after fine-tuning her equipment. She came out to watch, as well as actively record, the squadron of farlaunchers as they lifted off and went heading out to try to get in the first blow against the enemy.

These heavy spacecraft, informally named Strongholds, were much bigger than fighter craft, and were heavily armed against berserker fighters. Watching them make ready and get spaceborne was thrilling.

The Strongholds were supposed to be able to do without fighter cover, defending themselves effectively against attack by small berserker fighter machines. Each of the heavy farlaunchers carried a solid array of defensive armament, designed for just that purpose.

Nineteen Strongholds went out as Jory watched, bounding up in sequence from their several launching cradles, then gathering in formation, hovering at low altitude, before heading spaceward. Almost before she could blink her eyes, they were silently out of sight.

The lead ship had been informally christened by its crew as the *Knucklehead*. The name was hand painted on the hull just forward of the main left pinna. The glowing letters disappeared temporarily, along with all other insignia, when the ship powered up and its hull went live just before liftoff.

Each of these heavy bomber types carried a livecrew of at least eight, some as many as ten Solarians. So many people were necessary to provide the brain-computer (officially called *bio-hardware,* more informally *fleshware* or *boneware*) combinations that, for reasons still not fully understood, gave better combat results than could be obtained using either kind of thought/reaction alone.

Jory wished she'd been able to go through the interior of every ship type, but there just hadn't been time.

According to her notes, which she hoped to be able to keep out of the censors' hands, each crew included several people whose duties in flight were usually restricted to gunnery. Each heavy-bomber crew included another specialist who concentrated on aiming, releasing, and guiding the main weapons when the proper moment arrived. One was a flight engineer, whose job was to fine-tune the drive when things were going well, and to keep it going as long as possible when things turned nasty.

An astrogator's mind was melded with the programming of the computer maintaining the ship's course, calculating its position, both in normal space and flightspace, relative to its destination. No object in space ever stood absolutely still, relative to any other object. And yet another member of the crew had the full-time job of bonding with the equipment managing incoming and outgoing communications—frequently, amid the white noise of battle, this became an impossible task.

When at battle stations, the whole crew, like that of any other fighting small ship, rode with virtually immobilized bodies and wired heads, blind and almost deaf to their environment, including the presence of their shipmates' bodies almost packed around them, except as they perceived it through their silver helmets. They could sense the location of their own ship, and could study the immediate environment of space in considerable detail—with emphasis, of course, on any suspicious presence that might represent an enemy.

On every small fighting ship that carried more than one crew member, the helmets also provided a kind of intercom, where subvocalized speech was exchanged among the crew. Normally the crew had no other contact with each other. Even a single-crew ship had an intercom, between human and machine.

Physically all the crew's combat chairs were generally

within the same compartment, arranged in a circle, backs together and facing outward, at the center of the ship. In some cases they were arranged around the inner surface of a sphere, putting all of the crew's securely helmeted heads close together near the middle, saving picoseconds on the intercom time. Yet another alternate configuration was to have them all facing inward toward a central, multifaceted console.

All members of the crew were physically very close to one another, but yet could make contact only through the virtual reality they shared through their helmets.

While the helmets were in use, all physical control consoles and panels had been folded away, out of sight and out of reach. Only the pilot had a set of solid controls permanently before him, for use in emergency. These warriors did their fighting for the most part with folded hands, but little stanchions had been installed in the proper places, just to give their space-armored fists something to grip.

No escorting fighters had been sent out with the heavy bombers, given the Strongholds' self-defense capabilities, and the poor quality of the land-based fighters available. But poor as they were, they were going to be needed here.

After an hour or so of flight, with several C-plus jumps included in that interval, the heavy bomber squadron dispatched a robot courier back to base carrying the report that they had sighted the enemy.

Belatedly the Solarian commanders on land and in space realized that what their successful scout had actually sighted was not the berserker carrier group, but rather an invasion force of transport vessels, twenty-seven machines in all including a modest fighting escort of cruiser- and destroyer-class machines. Some of the berserker transports were loaded with the fighting machines needed to force a landing, while the cargo of others consisted of tools and materials for the construction of a berserker base on the space island.

Aboard the various transports, the Solarian leaders speculated, would be the tools needed to begin the swift and efficient construction of a berserker base, with all the complex heavy machinery that such an operation would entail.

The formation of nineteen Solarian Strongholds released their missiles at long range, targeted on what seemed to them the most important components of the berserker task force.

Tight-beam, short-range radio communicators crackled. "I'll take this one, you take that one—"

At a 100,000 kilometers, the berserkers could intercept radio communications and have a fraction of a second in which to put the information to immediate use.

Practice in peacetime conditions, and on simulators, had led the crews of these machines to believe that launching from this distance promised a high percentage of success.

The actual launching went much too fast for verbal orders and acknowledgements, even among members of the same crew, to be useful or even possible while it was going on. Still, each farlauncher crew kept up an excited chatter among themselves, on intercom.

Launching from long range, and from behind thin screens of interstellar matter, protected the farlaunchers pretty effectively from the berserker carriers' defensive fire. But it also made for poor accuracy, and the Solarian missiles failed to hit any of their moving targets.

Somehow the living crew members of these farlaunchers were fooled, or fooled themselves, into thinking that they had done substantial damage to the enemy. Of course, they and their machines did what they could to record the results of the attack, and it was these recordings, computer enhanced, that later assured them they hadn't hit a thing.

Meanwhile their computer copilots were much less emotional in their assessment.

Almost all of the Strongholds were able to return safely to their base on Fifty Fifty. One was lost to unknown causes.

Enemy fighters were in nearby space but had a hard time getting at them.

Once landed, the heavy farlaunchers were hastily repowered and reloaded, so they could get spaceborne again before the expected berserker raid hit home.

Solarian analysts examining the recordings decided that the berserker fleet undergoing this attack might well have been deliberately deceptive, creating what looked like massive secondary explosions and emissions of radiation. An additional effect of the same kind was owed to a peculiarity of the nebula through which they were moving; the clouds of thin gas and dust in which the shooting and missile-launching took place.

From the start, the Solarian leadership had counted heavily on having a third large carrier in space and ready to fight in defense of Fifty Fifty. Days ago, maybe a little over a week, *Lankvil* had been rushed to the dock at Port Diamond for repairs, after earlier combat damage in the Azlaroc Sector.

A preliminary estimate had stated that three months would be needed to complete repairs, but now maximum effort made by the shipyard workers was paying off. Repairs had been completed inside the three-day deadline, and the vessel, carrying Admiral Bowman's flag, had already left Port Diamond, hoping to catch up with and join her escort of smaller ships.

In fact, everyone agreed, the shipyard people and their machines had worked something of a miracle. *Lankvil* was ready for combat on schedule, loaded with fighters, undersluggers and hardlaunchers, and a full crew. Repairs were being completed while the carrier was under way again, in the center of her own task force, designated *Seventeen*.

A human outlook aboard the *Lankvil,* her eyes intent on the main holostage, confirmed the presence of a berserker scout, which had been reported by a robot scanner only a few seconds earlier.

"Looks like we've been spotted, sir."

"Begin evasive action," Admiral Bowman ordered.

With artificial gravity clamping the interior in a rigid vise of normalcy, the huge ship lurched and spun, stuttering on the verge of departing normal space, then skipping back. Around her other vessels of the fleet zigged and zagged, turned and darted, trying to maintain something like a desirable formation.

Now Bowman, pacing his bridge in armor, had to assume that the berserkers knew the location of at least a portion of his Solarian fleet—that now called Task Force Seventeen. The admiral ordered all hands called to battle stations. People on board his flagship, and the other vessels, did what they could to be ready for an attack.

Swarm merged with opposing swarm at headlong velocity. Solarian fighters fought to defend their carriers against the onrushing berserker attack machines. A complex knot of fire and force, moving more slowly than the enemy had been without opposition, swept in on *Lankvil*. Ten of the small berserker machines had been blasted from space before any of them were close enough to launch against the carrier.

Now it was up to *Lankvil* to defend herself. Automatic cannon, borrowing the synapses of organic Solarian brains to use as oversight circuits, sighted on the incoming enemy and blew most of the hurtling missile launchers into radii of fragments.

But *Lankvil*'s defenses failed to score the necessary clean sweep. A report came to the bridge of a missile exploding on the flight deck. First casualty figures listed seventeen dead and eighteen wounded.

The Solarian carrier's chief damage control officer, in a suit of special armor, followed the path of destruction from deck to deck, directing his crew of robots, which threw themselves—seemingly inspired by his rage—into the job of damping reactions, and fighting chemical fires, of which it seemed a hundred had sprung into existence like blooming flowers.

The center of the flight deck had now been decorated with a hole big enough to drop a fighter through. The same missile, blasting onto the hangar deck below, had started fires in three parked small ships, one of them already loaded with heavy missiles. Quick action by a human officer on duty turned on damper fields and finally a sprinkler system, averting catastrophe for the moment.

And now another wave of berserker launchers was coming in. Again, many did not survive long enough to loose their missiles, but a few did. One scored a very near-miss close astern of the Solarian carriers. Concussion and an inwash of radiation killed half a dozen more livecrew on the carrier, and wounded a greater number.

The carrier turned, unhappily right into a third charge of berserker small ships. One scored a clean hit, with a semi-intelligent weapon, designed to break and burrow its way as deep as possible into a target before exploding. After penetrating the carrier's flight deck, it passed through offices and the ready room of one of the small-ship squadrons. Leaving the latter chamber ankle deep in healthful beverages and snack foods, the intruder finally attained critical mass inside the engine room. All three of the huge hydrogen power lamps were snuffed, and conduits and busbars ruptured. The carrier lost motive power at once.

Having confirmed to their own satisfaction that one Solarian carrier had now been knocked clean out of the flight, the berserker command computers faced a hard decision on the most advantageous sequence of landing and rearming its fighters and bombers.

In addition to those that had just destroyed the carrier, a large number of these machines had recently returned from taking part in the bombardment of the object called Fifty Fifty. All attack machines now needed to be repowered, their weapon systems and defensive fields brought up to full capacity, before they could be sent back into combat. To do otherwise would be simply throwing valuable assets away.

Berserkers were ready to squander their own machines, big or small, with total abandon, as long as the result could be computed as a net gain for their cause. But naturally they preferred to keep their assets intact as long as possible. For a long time it had been computed as virtually certain that, whatever the results of one day's fighting, much more badlife could be counted on to appear upon the next.

In the berserkers' overall battle plan, the destruction of the large Solarian warships, especially the surviving carriers, was assigned a much higher value than merely assaulting—or even occupying—the lump of matter called Fifty Fifty. The atoll, after all, was not going anywhere.

E I G H T E E N

Cedric Traskeluk's first goal, as he turned his back on Port Diamond with his leave orders in his pocket, was to pay a visit to one of his clansmen. This was a member of his extended family whom he had never met, but who, he knew, lived on Uhao. Some time ago Cedric had become acquainted, through a letter from home, with his nearby kinsman's profession—more accurately, his calling.

To fully satisfy the demands of honor, revenge had to be accomplished with one of a traditional group of ritual weapons. Revenge rudely achieved was fully acceptable only in an emergency—though of course, in any case, it was vastly better than no revenge at all.

Compared to Traskeluk's homeworld, Uhao was vast in terms of population. That was why his fellow clansmen who came here tended to settle in the remote, thinly peopled regions. Areas of this world seemed to the visitor insanely crowded. Looking around him, he wondered what the Cradle Planet itself must be like. Bad enough, if all he'd heard and seen on stage was true, to drive a man crazy. He was relieved that he wouldn't have to follow Gift to Earth. But he would have tackled far greater obstacles than that in pursuit of the goal to which he was now committed.

Traskeluk's cousin, a man named Maal, lived with his family approximately a thousand kilometers from the base at Port Diamond, in the midst of a small colony of his and Cedric's compatriots.

Traveling at first by train and then in a rented ground car, Cedric eventually caught up with his kinsman on a grassy, windswept headland overlooking the sea.

There was little physical resemblance between the two men, though Maal was just about as dark. He was also considerably older, taller and not as muscular, with squinting eyes and a wry smile.

The two greeted each other in a language that was not much spoken outside their clan. Cedric had trouble remembering more than a couple of words, when he was called upon to use it in response.

His kinsman, noting his lack of fluency, immediately switched to the more common speech.

Maal and his large family lived in a tent, or rather they shared a collection of tents, with several hangers-on or attendants. The tent fabric was of bright traditional colors, and the housing seemed adequate in this planet's mild climate. Cedric assumed that the tents were part of a harking back to a nomadic, or supposedly nomadic, past. Maal was evidently prospering, and he spoke vaguely of owning flocks, but what kind of animals these were, or where they might be found, were matters on which the visitor remained unclear.

The tents were large, of very modern materials and design, but they were still tents, in keeping with the clan's venerable traditions. At home on their distant planet, Cedric's immediate family lived in a house like everybody else.

As soon as the greetings and ritual hospitality had been concluded, the cousin listened intently to Cedric's story, nodded grimly, and then set to work.

Maal nodded slowly. "It is well that you have come to me."

So far the subject of payment had not come up, and he did not raise it now.

After a moment's thought, he announced that his first task would be to give Cedric his choice among several types of weapons, each thoroughly approved by clan tradition. Or so Maal said; he claimed to be an expert on such matters.

"I," said Cedric, "am certainly no expert on traditional weapons. But I want to do everything connected with this business properly."

"Of course you do. Come with me."

At some distance behind the tents, surrounded by tall grass, was a storage shed, including a workshop, with solid walls. Cedric's cousin unlocked the door and gestured his visitor inside.

A minute later, Maal was holding up a small device for his visitor's inspection. He seemed to have had no trouble at all laying his hand on one. "This little tube fits in between the second and third metacarpal bones—fires a small-shaped charge that I can guarantee you will penetrate ordinary space armor at arm's-length range.

"And this is a somewhat more elaborate system. We combine heat and radiation in the fingertips with enhanced strength in the bones and the polymer muscles."

Traskeluk stared, becoming fascinated despite his original determination to get this over with as quickly as practical. "It sounds complicated. How would I control it?"

"You have the deathdream, right? In your head." Maal raised a long finger, tapping his own skull. "I know they give it to people in certain jobs."

Traskeluk wondered if his cousin had once worked for the Space Force, or for the Templars, but decided not to ask. He shook his head. "I had the deathdream, but no longer. They removed it when I was in the hospital just now. The idea was that from now on I will be working in a safe job, at the base."

"But they did not dig out all the mechanism that was put into your head? No. They usually do not, in cases like yours. So, we adapt what you have left in there, the control system, to working this new tool that will be in your new hand. Don't worry, it won't kill you when you use it. And I have no need to open up your head!" The older man laughed, a fierce sudden bark. "Sit down here, let's have a look at you."

When Cedric was seated, his cousin put a probe into the skullport under his scalp at the back of his head, and in a moment had activated the icon.

Cedric was distracted by the icon of the device that he had thought was permanently erased. But now suddenly it was back, drifting slightly in his visual field. For a little while, he had allowed himself to think that he was done forever with such things. The little glowing shape appeared in both his eyes. And he was distracted even more by the thought that it might be there perpetually.

That question had to be answered right away. "Am I going to be looking at this thing for the rest of my life?"

"Not at all. It will go away as soon as the weapon is used," Maal assured him. "Anyway, you get accustomed to it. You should have as many to look at as I myself have."

Traskeluk didn't care to ask how many icons that might be. His own original icon, now returned, was a skull with blinking eyes. When it was hooked up to the deathdream there had been an intermediate stage, so that the skull had only appeared after a preliminary ritual of thought.

But now it seemed that for the time being, at least, he was stuck with the skull. The little icon stayed where it was, up in the upper left-hand corner of his visual field, however he moved or focused his eyes. You might think that a man would be able to get used to it; it was really so inconspicuous. But . . .

Maal was giving him his preliminary instructions now. To trigger the device, in any of its modes of destruction, he was going to have to look directly at it, and think a certain thought—adapted from the termdream he no longer had.

And through all this Cedric was conscious of no physical discomfort. It seemed that underground technicians could be every bit as skillful as those with official jobs.

Even when Traskeluk closed his eyes, the icon was still

there, though it dimmed in intensity. He knew from experience that it wasn't going to keep him awake at night—at least it never had, when it was wired to his own suicide.

"What if I have to go offworld?" Traskeluk asked. "Is this new hardware going to show up on a detector at a spaceport, or someplace like that?"

"No. No ordinary detector will see a thing. Don't worry about that. I know my business. If anything a little funny does show up, they will attribute it to your old termdream installation."

Cedric tended to accept Maal's word. He knew that some branches of the extended family, the clan, had long experience in these matters.

The weapon's components were soon hidden between the artificial bones of Cedric's left hand, inside the small bones of his fingertips, and amid the large polymer muscles of his forearm.

Now they were coming to what Maal called the really enjoyable part. Cedric's first intention had been to choose whichever variety of lethal hardware that could be installed most quickly, and he still wanted to get this business over with. But he allowed himself to be talked into a somewhat more elaborate array—it was easy to see that Maal really had his heart set on that installation.

Maal waxed enthusiastic, and even poetical, about the death agonies of the miserable victim under attack by the more elaborate weapon system.

His client kept trying to cut him short. "I'm not that much interested in his death agonies. What I mainly want to do is just finish him off."

"Bah. Think about it a little. There is plenty of room for artistry."

Cedric had no need for an anesthetic during the installation, since none of the work would be done on live flesh or live nerves. But his mind was wavering. There were moments when he thought that coming here had been a mistake.

Once this skilled artisan had the work in hand, he was not so humorless. This job put him in chronically high good spirits, never better than when contemplating some plan of serious revenge. As he toiled, he muttered anecdotes regarding his own vengeance upon some merchant he thought had cheated some family member, while his impassive wife, with veiled face and tattooed arms, and their barefoot children looked on curiously from the background.

The two men continued their discussion, in and out of the workshop, while Maal worked steadily at choosing and fitting and calibrating the technology. Meanwhile the women of Maal's household cooked and cleaned, or supervised the labor of their human and mechanical servants, sending clouds of dust blowing through the air, along with appetizing aromas. Most of the clan owned few robots or none, and the only hardware on which they set great value was mainly lethal, or of symbolic value only.

Cousin Maal was deeply interested in the crime for which the man called Gift had now been sentenced to such a deservedly painful death. He kept pressing for more details of Cedric's story, and after hearing them he heartily agreed that Cedric now had only one honorable course open to him.

Once more Maal paused, with tools in hand. "Where is he to be found, this wretched scum of a traitor?"

"I'm not sure."

"Ah! How do you plan to locate him, then?"

The hunter sighed. "It will be difficult." He realized that in the ordinary course of events, it was quite possible—no, even probable—that he and Gift would never see each other again. There weren't going to be any crew reunion parties.

"Will he have summoned his own clan members to his assistance?"

Cedric made a little throat-scraping sound of contempt. "I doubt that lump of pig dropping has any clan. Or that they would do him any good, if they are anything like him." When he thought about Gift, his rage heated up again; there were moments when he wished he had opted for the poison after all.

His relative shook his head, expressing wonder and contempt. "You will denounce him to the authorities? Hey?" Maal's tone implied that he felt confident of a negative answer.

Is this a trick question? Once again Traskeluk was seated in a comfortable chair in his cousin's workshop; the younger man's left sleeve was rolled way up, and the painless fabric of his artificial hand and forearm was partially disassembled.

"I have thought of that, of course. Actually, according to the Space Force rules, it is my duty. And for the most part they are good rules."

"But not in this."

"No, not in a thing like this." Cedric shook his head definitively. "So it seems to me that denouncing him would only make it less likely that I will have the chance I need."

"A man's first duty is to his honor!" Maal began to recite in a singsong voice. "Then to his clan, then to his immediate family. Father first, then . . ."

"Of course." Cedric tuned out, having heard it all before.

The lethal device, as finally installed, provided a mechanical clawing power of deadly capability, as well as pulses of lethal heat and radiation that lay waiting to be unleashed, buried in the fingertips of Traskeluk's innocent-looking left hand. The mechanical clawing, Maal insisted, was perfectly in keeping with tradition, as well as very appropriate for a traitor who had abandoned his comrades to the berserkers. There was also available a one-shot detonation, what Maal called the shotgun blast.

There appeared to be no outward sign that the client was now equipped with a single-blaster, a kind of high velocity shotgun that would fire once, powerfully enough to devastate almost any target, once Traskeluk could get himself within reach. He flexed the fingers.

Maal peered at him as if reading his mind. "I think that even if your man is in armor when you catch him, he will not escape you. If you happen to be in armor at the time, you can slip off your left gauntlet. Hey?"

No medical expertise was required for this operation on

the artificial limb—any more than a blacksmith needed to be a veterinarian to shoe a horse.

In a matter of a couple of hours, Maal, with the help of a specialized robot of his own, and a set of advanced tools, had installed the weaponry of vengeance. The job was skillfully done, the flap of artificial skin invisibly reattached. On the homeworld, the cousin had done this sort of thing frequently.

Spacer Traskeluk stood up and flexed his fingers, examined his hand. The tingling that had bothered him during the operation had subsided almost instantly once the probing was over. The absence of any residual soreness seemed eerie. Just as before the operation, he had faint sensation in the artificial-nerve network running through the polymer skin of his left hand and forearm, as if it were covered by a thick invisible sleeve.

Cedric was startled at how fast the work went, and how easily his cousin accomplished what had sounded like extensive changes. "That's all you're going to have to do? It seems like there should be more."

A startling grin. "What more would you like? What I am doing will be more than enough. Believe me."

Cedric was suddenly struck by the idea that his cousin must have done very similar installations on numerous occasions. The clients couldn't all be family members. Revenge must be a substantial business, and no doubt crime was even more substantial. And without a doubt there were men who just liked the feeling of walking around with a thunderbolt or two concealed up their sleeves.

"Now I think that we must do at least one test, to make sure that the whole installation is properly under your control. Which mode of operation would you like to test first? Not the shotgun, of course; that will rather ruin all the rest of my work if it goes off."

The radiation didn't sound like a good bet for testing, either, to Cedric. "How about the claws?" he offered.

"Very well, good choice." Maal looked about him, right and left, as if hoping his eyes would light on a suitable subject. Then he snapped his fingers. "I know, I have a dog. Penned up.

Vicious beast, and I am thinking of getting rid of it anyway. You will really get the feel of the gear better with a live subject."

"No thanks," said Cedric immediately.

His cousin fixed him with a look. "If you are shy of mangling an animal, what will you do when the man stands before you?"

Something clicked in Cedric's brain. The man is right. He allowed himself to be led around behind the workshop, where a large, dark furry shape snarled and barked ferociously inside a painfully small area behind a fence. The animal was going to be killed anyway. Trask imagined that it was Gift who now stood before him. . . .

Still he momentarily hesitated. Impatiently Maal opened a latch and loosed a furry, snarling whirlwind, and Cedric had to grab for its throat in self-defense. . . .

The dog's throat was closed completely in midsnarl, the artificially powered fingers crushing flesh and bone alike. The weight of the leaping animal threatened for a moment to cost Traskeluk his balance, but with a staggering effort he managed to keep his footing.

He thought he could feel the life go out of the heavy, furry body that dangled in his grip.

Other functions were necessarily left untested. When the icon was properly manipulated, by direct nerve impulse control, the artificial fingers began within two seconds to generate intense heat. It was a searing surge of power that could turn steel red-hot, or burn away a man's flesh in no time at all. Another possibility, controllable through the icon, was an armor-piercing explosive charge.

"But remember, cousin, if you use that, you will have no hand left. No body left, either, unless you are careful to point the fingers all away from you at detonation."

Traskeluk's whole visit to his cousin had taken only part of one day.

When all the details were taken care of, he paid Maal for the work—there was a ritual limit on the amount that a weapons maker could charge a kinsman in such a case.

Traskeluk had his ritual killing machine. Now all he had to do was get close enough to Shifty Gift to put his new tools to good use.

While the Solarian defenders dug in on Fifty Fifty had been cramming in all the battle preparations possible before the expected onslaught, back on Earth the high authorities, up to and including the premier, in their various offices or shelters, were grappling with strategic problems.

A cabinet meeting had been called by the premier, which certain key members of Earth's parliament were also expected to attend. The lawmakers were showing up now in the cabinet room, along with the heads of departments. Some were young, some old, some businesslike, some abstracted; all were worried. One or two, who in the past had talked privately of trying to come to terms with the berserkers, were silent on the subject now. The reception their colleagues had earlier given that suggestion had convinced them that to bring it up again could be dangerous.

There was some discussion of what the Carmpan—one of the few non-Solarian intelligent races known to exist in the Galaxy—might have meant by their recent pronouncements. They had been quite enigmatic, as most of their statements were. This was not the purpose of the cabinet meeting, but it was a question in which everyone was interested.

The Carmpan talk regarding historical parallels seemed particularly hard to interpret.

The premier had instructed one of her most trusted aides to find out, if possible, what historical parallel the non-Solarians had in mind.

"It's something specific they're urging us to do?"

"Well, they are entreating us—if that's the right word—to keep on fighting, even if things look bad. They're always urging us to do that; not that we'd have much choice anyway. Our common enemy is not someone with whom you can negotiate and make a treaty. No, today's statements from the Carmpan strike me as something new. It's more as if they think they've actually succeeded in steering events a certain way."

"Steering? How?"

"I have no clue as to how. Steering the course of history into a kind of track, as it were, that will make it easier for us to push the train of events the way we want them to go."

Blank faces regarded one another from their respective holostages.

"We're tracking some parallel series of historical events."

"That's the idea, yes."

"Well, if it's something out of Carmpan history, forget it. That's always been a closed book to Solarians. Oh, they've let us into their archives. But still . . ."

Admiral Bowman had earlier appeared in person in the cabinet room to confer, and to plead the case for Hypo. But, as the premier reminded someone who asked, by today Bowman was back on his flagship in deep space.

The premier herself, plainly dressed, her silver hair tied simply back, came in to preside.

In recent months she had spent a great deal of time in the underground shelter from which she was conducting today's meeting. It was not her preference to live like this, but what could one do? The cabinet room here was a physical double of the one in her normal aboveground office, except of course the windows were not quite the same. This one, reached by twisting tunnels, was somewhere beneath the Alps—very few people knew exactly where.

A brilliant array of flowers and plants were in view on the full-sized holostage with her, the idea being to lend her image an air of confidence. All these living, growing things were becoming something of a personal trademark. They served now to remind the premier and her audience that not only humanity but all of Galactic life was dependent on her care.

The artistic composition was quite skillful. Some of the flowers were actually elsewhere, and others had no physical existence outside of a data bank of graphic images.

When it came time for speech making, the world was going to see the premier standing, or alternately seated at her ease, upon a balcony, behind her a clear Alpine sky, a sky confidently free of defensive force fields.

On certain days—but not today—she preferred to project a military, besieged look to her fellow Earth-descended humans, on remote worlds, who in a few days or weeks would be watching this recording.

She was in fact about to issue a general plea to Solarians everywhere to rally round and defend the Cradle Planet. That help would be important; but only if the coming battle of Fifty Fifty could be won.

Should it be lost, no help could come from elsewhere in time to save the Earth.

The secretary of war, himself technically a civilian, was on hand to represent the military's point of view.

A number of the other important people who were taking part in the conference had also been trying out the latest in deepsecret shelters. Some might be speaking from those places now. None of them much liked the idea of going deep underground, and none were sure that it would do them any good, if and when the berserkers eventually descended in force on the homeworld.

The premier herself personally disliked the idea, though here she was, under the Alps. "The planet is only thirteen thousand kilometers thick, after all. How deep can you dig? Have you already gone more than halfway through?"

"No, ma'am." The answer was delivered with sober patience.

"If everyone in this room is blown up, won't our successors carry on with at least as much success as we have demonstrated?"

And alternate shelters were proposed, elsewhere in the home solar system.

Within a few days after the berserker attack on Fifty Fifty, word had reached Earth of Hypo's success at predicting the circumstances of that assault.

"Yamanim was right. His crazy genius, Commander R, and her machines were right."

And the premier, fortunately for her political future, was

demonstrated to have been right in deciding to trust the estimates from intelligence; and the enormous expenditure of effort and hardware on the new information-gathering system was apparently justified.

Back on Uhao, deep in Hypo's workroom, people and machines were as busy as ever.

"So the organization must be in your organic brain," a machine was commenting softly to its human controller.

"Never mind my organic brain. What does my brain have to do with our problems?"

And so the work went on.

The cryptanalyst computers, their talent unsurpassed in their comparatively narrow field, were deep in an attempted analysis of the randomizing procedures their berserker counterparts seemed to employ in making their periodic changes of code.

One of the machines, taking a more constructive tack, remarked to its human overseer that theoretically, it might someday be possible to predict what the next version of the berserker code would be before it actually came into being.

" 'Someday' isn't very helpful. Is there anything you can do along that line right now?"

"Right now such an achievement is impossible."

"I know, I know. That's what I thought. Keep working!"

Most people who knew anything about the cryptanalyst computers had great faith in them. It was supposed to have been a Carmpan (not himself allowed inside the Hypo room) who once had said, "Paradoxically, our unliving allies are—"

"We prefer to use the word *inorganic*," Mother R had corrected softly.

"Whatever. Our *inorganic* allies, it would seem, are paradoxically more trustworthy than the living when it comes to fighting those pure machines, berserkers."

But that someone should think that Hypo's computers were alive raised a suspicion of that person's attitude toward berserkers.

"Nonsense. Our human cryptanalysts work continuously

with the machines, they observe individual idiosyncrasies; they
tend to unconsciously equate mere quirks and eccentricities
with life."

"Nonsense, you think? Well, maybe."

Another event had cast another person under some suspicion of berserker sympathies—this time not directed at a
computer program. One of the more timid souls in strategic
headquarters on Earth—in fact one of the premier's personal
advisers—had recently put forward a suggestion that the space
atoll called Fifty Fifty be evacuated. It was a small, exposed
outpost, hard to defend against a superior force. According to
this point of view, all Solarian forces should be pulled back
much nearer Earth, preferably entirely within Sol System, where
they could concentrate on playing a purely defensive role. A logical extension of this strategy—if one can call it a strategy—is
that Port Diamond might as well be written off too.

The timid soul who came up with this proposal was
promptly transferred Earthward, to a different and less important job. At least he had not advocated abandoning Earth herself. No one above him in the chain of command gave his ideas
any serious consideration—except as basis for review of his security clearance.

Meanwhile, out on Fifty Fifty, a voice, impressing Jory
as remarkably calm for that of an organic human, informed
everyone that a wave of enemy bombers and strafers had been
detected no more than a few minutes away.

Jory had just taken off her armor in hopes of getting in a
shower, and now had to scramble back into the suit without
even taking time to put on the coverall first. The inner lining of
the armor itself was soft, and would be kind to her bare body—
she hoped.

Everything that the atoll could put up in the way of fighters had scrambled, long minutes ago, to try to intercept. After
giving the fighters priority to get clear, other spacecraft moved

to their launching pads, and up, simply to escape being sitting targets.

Looking around the empty field, the defenders congratulated themselves on the fact that there would not be a single functional warship on the ramp or in any of the docks when the berserker raiders arrived. The few relics that remained on the ground would be a waste of enemy ammunition.

Some technicians who had finished their assigned jobs ahead of time had then, on their own initiative, fabricated one or more imitation fighters, having no other purpose than to draw enemy fire when the expected attack swarmed in.

Waiting on the ground was suspenseful and difficult. Though not, as she recalled, as difficult as being out in space and getting shot at.

Everyone was in armor now and at a battle station. Nash's people, some of whom were wearing borrowed armor, had all their fine equipment up and running, or ready to go. They were focusing on what they considered would be the prime berserker targets.

Jory marveled at how calm everyone around her seemed to be. Not for the first time she observed how calm, like fear, was contagious.

A few minutes' flight time from the atoll, an extended dogfight between Solarians and berserkers had erupted. Some radio message to that effect came in from an intermediate distance.

The search phase and the dogfight phase combined lasted for several standard hours, though the latter was soon over. It was an unequal contest between the outmoded small livecrew ships sent out to defend the Fifty Fifty outpost, and the incoming raiding force of up-to-date small berserker machines.

On the ground, the minutes passed slowly, with little actual news available. Everyone helped to pass around a slow continuous dribble of rumors. Contact had been made with the main berserker fleet, then lost again. The main battle was going to be elsewhere. People huddled in shelters, or stood in ground armor squinting into space, waiting for the first sight or signal of the returning crews.

It was time for them to be arriving now. But ominously few were coming back, and those who did get back were late, their ships more often than not seriously damaged.

As knowledgeable folk had predicted, the berserker fighter machines generally outclassed the obsolescent ships in which the human pilots defending this sector were forced to ride and fight, and mowed them down ruthlessly.

People grumbled and swore at the sad fact that this level of Earth's defenses, so near the homeworld, had been allowed to deteriorate so greatly. Someday we would have new machines, the best weapons.

"Yeah, someday."

Nash's people fretted. So far they had no action to record. But Nash himself was in good spirits, and if he had any fear for his personal safety, it didn't show.

Within an hour or so of their departure, the first survivors of the dogfight were beginning to limp home. Eventually a count revealed that fourteen out of twenty-six fighter pilots had been lost, along with their ships, in their first sorties against the approaching berserker fleet. Only two of the fighter ships that made it back to the docking facilities on Fifty Fifty could be made fit to fly again; and at the moment there was no chance to repair anything. The enemy the fighters had failed to stop— whose numbers they had not managed to appreciably diminish—were right on their tails. The dogfight protracted itself while the raid was going on.

A few minutes after the enemy departed, a signal was transmitted recalling all defensive fighters, but only six came in to land—these were in addition to the four that had crash-landed back on the atoll while the attack was still in progress.

Admiral Naguance, his helmet off at the moment but carefully within reach, put down his morning cup of coffee on the arm of his combat chair. He was something of a connoisseur, and usually insisted on grinding his own coffee beans.

He was enjoying his morning brew on the bridge in the presence of several members of his staff, with an elaborate holographic display scrolling out before the group.

When he had everyone's attention, Naguance announced that he was now going to open the orders that had been handed him by Yamanim before the *Venture* had lifted off from Uhao. Breaking open the thick paper envelope, closed with a heavy official seal, the admiral extracted a single sheet of paper, and gave it a mere glance: He had already been told by the field marshal, word for word, what the message was going to be.

He now recited it, aloud, to his listening staff of officers, and called for comments.

For several minutes Naguance discussed his orders, and the plan he and Admiral Bowman had agreed on for implementing them, with his assembled staff. Naguance had made sure all these people—making a point of including the majority of his staff who didn't know him very well as yet—knew he wanted them present for this discussion.

"How widely do you plan to separate our two carriers, Admiral?"

Hearing the numbers, when the admiral gave them precisely, the questioner looked doubtful. "Sir, is there a possibility of communication problems, if we're that far apart?"

"In battle there is a virtual certainty of communication problems, even if you're within shouting distance. But if we stay close together, in effect we give the enemy one big target."

Another of his aides spoke up, when asked for comments. "Sir, I must protest against the tactic of dividing our fleet."

Naguance took the criticism in stride. "I've been thinking about this. For an outnumbered force to divide, in the face of the enemy, certainly flies in the face of all classical military doctrine. But in this battle we are not using battleships. Our striking power, you see, lies not in our large ships directly, but in the squadrons of small ships they can launch. And those squadrons can be concentrated even though their bases are separated."

Many people had been surprised when Yamanim chose Naguance to take over for Admiral Yeslah, who had been knocked out of action by a mysterious skin disease. "Not that he isn't competent. But . . ."

The two men were opposites in many ways. Still, Naguance had been chosen by Yamanim, at the hearty recommendation of Yeslah himself.

Early in the game Bowman had realized that his only logical course, given the shaky state of communication between his flagship and Naguance's, was to relinquish effective command of the operation to the junior admiral, who was closer to the enemy, and had two effective carriers under his direct control. Accordingly he had sent a courier to Naguance, authorizing him to take the lead.

The orders Naguance had just opened were from Yamanim, and ran in accord with what was generally known as the Principle of Calculated Risk: "Which you shall interpret to mean avoidance of exposure of your force to attack by superior enemy forces without good prospect of inflicting, by such exposure, greater damage on the enemy."

"That seems to mean we should try to punch them without getting punched in return. A nice plan, if we can bring it off. Well, after Port Diamond, we can't stand to take a great many more punches."

Before being alerted that combat was imminent, the crew of the *Venture,* like those of the other ships in the task force, had been passing the time in various amusements, some gambling, some composing letters home that would, after the censor had seen them, be sent in microform when courier space happened to be available.

Back on Fifty Fifty, Warrant Officer Tadao, the guide who'd given Jory Yokosuka her tour of the parked warships, was now busy getting ready to perform his primary job, that of communications gunner on an underslugger. He was aboard his spacecraft, running through his preflight checklist, making sure he had the equipment he would need, and in good working order. But in the back of Tadao's mind he kept remembering how eagerly the woman journalist had looked inside every type of small ship she could get near. How eager she'd been to get her hands in everything, even wanting to try a helmet on. Cute gal too, but tougher, more aggressive than he would like a woman to be if he was living with her. Take her as a crew member, though, if she had the training.

To her, Tadao thought, he must have sounded like a real expert. But he felt like anything but an expert now. It now seemed to him that his brief training had been just sufficient to let him understand that he wasn't really ready for this. Nor were most of his shipmates, nor most of the people in his squadron, with a couple of exceptions among the leaders.

Not that he would have voiced these complaints and objections to any correspondent, or any other civilian. That would have made him sound like he wanted out of this situation—and he didn't. His place was here, with his crew, all of them driving beside their comrades in the other ships. That was just the simple truth, and it had nothing to do with anyone trying to be heroic.

The raw question still kept coming up in his mind, forcing itself to his attention: How in hell did people, mere human beings of flesh and blood like himself, think they'd ever be able to go into a fight, one on one, against *machines,* machines whose design and manufacture had been perfected over the centuries with only one relentless purpose in the computer minds of the greater machines that made them. And that purpose was to kill Solarians. . . .

One human advantage in fighting against machines, especially when groups of ships and machines are involved, is that members of a human team, whether in the same ship or not, tend to know, even with zero time allotted for overt communication, what other team members are going to do.

He knew, intellectually, that it had been demonstrated over and over, that flesh and blood people could indeed hold their own in such a battle, hold their own and sometimes more than that. With the best machines humanity could devise to help them, they even had some theoretical advantage.

With the best machines humanity could devise—yeah, that was the key. What was actually available to fight with was far from the best.

Too many corners had been cut, in the name of economy. The belief had grown too strong that the homeworlds were simply unassailable. The hardware the human defenders would have to use today was a long way from the best.

She'd been trying to learn what it was like when you strapped your armored body into that combat chair, and pulled the helmet on. And Tadao had tried, and then had given up, and told her that there was really no way to describe it.

She'd asked him wistfully: "I wish I could go out on a patrol."

"Sorry, no chance," he'd answered automatically.

Certainly the world inside the stewpot was quite different

from that perceived by the usual well-defined and separated senses operating in what the world had long considered a normal human skull. In the stewpot, sight and sound and even touch were blended and blurred. Some said the sensations were dreamlike, and others called them indescribable. A fairly large number of people were unable to endure the experience at all, and the dropout rate was high in the early stages of training.

Virtually the same experiences were available to groundbound civilians, in the form of games. *Virtually:* that was the key word. When you knew it was a game, the experience could never be anything like the same as when you knew that the integrity of your own skin depended on the outcome.

Admiral Naguance remained determined to get in the first space-to-space blow against the enemy.

He now found himself in absolute control of the fleet of Solarian ships that had been designated Task Force Sixteen. Nominally he remained under the orders of Admiral Bowman, but Bowman, whose flagship formed the heart of Seventeen, was a goodly distance away, and wisely refrained from trying to manage Sixteen's tactics from afar.

Right now, Naguance's force was maneuvering in flightspace, more or less in formation, escort ships protectively surrounding *Stinger* and *Venture*. His task force, poised to deliver a punch as soon as the target showed itself, was now out a day's travel or so from Fifty Fifty, the outpost he was trying to guard.

Task Force Seventeen, built around the rebuilt carrier *Lankvil,* and under the direct command of Admiral Bowman, was maneuvering at a somewhat greater distance from the oncoming berserker carrier force. *Lankvil* was carrying one squadron of fighters, two of hardlaunchers, and one of undersluggers, some seventy-five small warcraft in all.

Admiral Bowman, in command of the whole operation, wanted to hold *Lankvil*'s striking power in reserve—he had been stung before, during the Azlaroc battle, by committing all his forces and then finding his own force open to counterattack.

Scout ships from both Solarian task forces were kept in

space continually, working in calculated search patterns. The search went on around the clock, except when space "weather," in the form of nebular disturbances on a cosmic scale, made the odds prohibitive against success. The Gulf was known for its calm weather as a rule, but breathtaking storms of matter and energy were not unheard of.

Even when conditions were at their best for search, the problem of finding even a large fleet of ships or machines, in the immensity of space, could easily be compared to that of locating the proverbial needle in the haystack.

But the task was not completely hopeless. Superluminal travel left traces, in flightspace and above, as does any rapid passage through normal space. There were what some called shock waves, disturbances that sometimes propagated faster than the ship or machine that caused them, and traveled in advance of it.

Space here in the Gulf was emptier than most of the volume of the Galaxy; but still this stretch of barrenness between Galactic arms contained enormous amounts of thin gas, along with occasional dust clouds, dark matter in its many forms. These intrusions offered concealment to moving machines, and at the same time tended to retain the trails left by the passage of ships or of machines.

Word came in to Naguance and his staff that *Lankvil*, too far away for them to see her, was being hit with a savage attack.

On the bridge of the flag carrier *Venture*, a dozen Solarian bodies, bulked up with armor, lay strapped into combat chairs with ligatures of polyphase matter.

He was in occasional contact with Fifty Fifty by courier. But a courier needed several days to reach Port Diamond from here, and one coming in the other direction might well take twice as long, if it ever succeeded in finding the fleet at all. Messages of unusual importance were often sent redundantly.

The individual units of Task Force Sixteen were, as on any long cruise, popping back into normal space from time to time to keep in touch with each other, and to make sure of their course, speed, and location.

Naguance's intention, which he'd made plain enough to all hands once they were in space, was to try to strike from the flank at the advancing enemy carrier task force, as soon as he could determine the enemy's exact location. As far as Naguance knew, he might be facing as many as six carriers. But the numbers arrayed against him made no essential difference; he was going to have to hit them anyway.

And then the word that Task Force Sixteen had been waiting for arrived, in the form of a courier from another scout ship.

Deciding what was an acceptable degree of accuracy in scouting reports was simply a judgement call. Of course the target of both task forces was generally the same; but it was hard to be certain, in the heat of battle, just how many enemy fleets there were.

Naguance, given a free hand, decided to believe the reports before him, and to strike with everything he could get off his decks.

Naguance launched his first attack, led by a squadron of undersluggers from *Stinger,* as soon as he felt confident that his scouts had in fact located the berserker carriers. This happened before the berserkers attacking Fifty Fifty had had time to get back to their motherships.

Meanwhile, the berserker leadership had so far observed nothing to make it doubt the accuracy of its earlier strategic computations. It had no reason to expect that a well-organized Solarian force would be waiting to ambush the machine fleet on its way to seize Fifty Fifty. Certainly the berserker computers did not even suspect that their enemy knew when they intended to arrive, and in what strength. Their calculations still called for them to take the Solarians in general, and those on Fifty Fifty in particular, by surprise.

As usual, when two or more squadrons were to be launched in one attack, an attempt was made to achieve coordination.

Undersluggers, the slowest of the three types of attacking spacecraft, lifted off first, expecting to be overtaken en route by friendly hardlaunchers and fighters.

The hardlaunchers were second into space, followed by the fighters that were supposed to protect them as well as the undersluggers on their way to the target and back again. If fighters found no enemy fighters to engage, they could go in and strafe the target with their comparatively light weapons, and draw defensive fire away from the bombers with their deadly important loads.

But circumstances simply delayed some of the fighting spacecraft, and prevented others from finding the enemy at all. Whole squadrons, with surprising frequency, failed to locate the targets they were seeking. Coordination remained a mere ideal, impossible of attainment. Searching for a moving target multiplied a ship's chances of getting entirely lost.

Venture began by launching two squadrons of hardlaunchers and one of undersluggers. These were followed quickly by ten units of Fighter Squadron Six, meant to serve as escorts to keep berserker interceptors away from the hardlaunchers and undersluggers. But the fighters lost contact with the small craft they were supposed to be protecting, cruised in sight of the enemy carriers without seeing a single enemy fighter in space, and then, with combat assets dwindling rapidly, had to come home and repower. A small ship could cruise only a few hours in combat mode, with shields and fields deployed. It would be suicidal to risk encountering the enemy in any other mode.

First to liftoff from *Stinger* was Underslugger Squadron Eight, whose obsolete spacecraft were all demolished by enemy fighters and defensive fire. Only a couple of them even succeeded in getting close enough to a berserker carrier to make a serious attack.

Stinger like its sister carrier launched ten fighters as escorts—but these fared even worse than their unhappy colleagues from *Venture*. *Stinger*'s ten fighters failed to close with the enemy at all, stretched the limit of their combat range, ran out of power completely when their reserves were drained by a dangerous wrinkle in flightspace, and were left drifting helplessly. At least they had regained normal space, and most of the pilots survived until picked up by friendly craft.

Stinger also launched two squadrons of hardlaunchers— and these looked for the enemy in vain. Many landed on Fifty Fifty to repower and then returned to their carrier.

This was the first real experience of combat for the vast majority of the men and women making up these crews.

Underslugger Eight, from the carrier *Stinger,* had no trouble at all in finding the enemy. The squadron commander was named Nordlaw, and his small ship was among the first Solarian craft to disintegrate under fire from a berserker Void. Nordlaw and his two livecrew mates were among the first to die.

Ensign Bright was flying the rearmost ship in the same squadron's formation, an underslugger coming in on the port side of a huge berserker carrier. To launch his missile Bright had to use the manual release, the electrical connections having been shot away.

For one fleeting moment Bright contemplated driving his ship on a suicide crash into the enemy. But some interior voice vetoed that move, and in another instant he was working as hard as ever to stay alive.

Bright launched his torpedo, then drove his small craft skimming breathtakingly close to the black-hulled leviathan at which he'd aimed his missile. He could feel his small ship shudder as the defensive fields of the enemy tried and were just too slow to focus on and crush the speeding intruder.

And then the huge berserker was behind him, and he had done his duty for humanity, and now he could focus on trying to keep himself alive, for his wife and child back on Uhao.

He thought that his heavy missile had found a way through the enemy defense and struck its target, but it was impossible to be sure.

And then the world exploded around him.

. . .

When his craft was hit for the last time, Bright suffered a sharp impact and fiery pain, just above his left elbow. For a moment he thought his chances of survival had fallen to nothing at all. But grimly he kept fighting for his life, doing the things that his survival training had impressed upon him must be done in this situation.

He looked at his arm. Beyond the basic shock and pain he felt an eerie series of burning touches; in a moment Bright realized that he was feeling the loose fragment of enemy ordnance that had hurt him, as it rattled around inside his armor. The piece was still hot enough to inflict superficial burns.

Bright had no choice but to take his helmet off, to learn his own physical situation. If cabin integrity still held, he could still breathe. He was going to have to fly his spacecraft and deal with his immediate environment at the same time. Putting the ship on autopilot gave him a few moments in which he might be able to turn his attention elsewhere without disaster.

Looking around inside the tiny cabin, his own two human eyes now blinking in the dim reddish emergency lights, he saw at once that his two shipmate gunners had been killed. A large globule of blood came drifting toward him in midair, in the near absence of gravity.

He realized that he was bleeding inside his armor, and whatever little medtech devices were still functioning as components of his suit were getting busy. There was nothing else he could do now for his wound. At least the piece of shrapnel had cooled to a bearable temperature.

The helmet had to go on his head again. He dared not leave the situation to the autopilot a moment longer.

Bright's wounded left arm was not totally disabled. And the crablike little medirobot inside his suit was giving him something that hopefully might control the pain, while letting him retain function. And now he was going to have to abandon his spacecraft, before the old ship blew up.

Bright hitched himself around in his combat chair and made sure, before making his own escape from his ruined ship, that both of his gunners were quite dead.

No doubt about it. Bright could see how the personal armor of both had been punctured in several places, the incredibly tough metal bent in like so much skin. One gunner's helmet was turned toward him, and the dead face inside the statglass plate, now that he had a good look at it, was the greatest shock of all. Bright had never seen human death before—as a reservist recently called up, today was his first experience of combat—but the sight was unmistakable.

His mind half-numbed with shock, an arm going numb with his suit's automatic first aid, he got out of his chair, his body unthinkingly running through drilled-in emergency procedures. A moment later he was out of the wreck. Searching the sky around him, orienting himself with some difficulty, he soon realized that he must be drifting somewhere near the middle of the scattered berserker fleet.

The faceplate of his armor could be adjusted to provide mild magnification, and he tried that. With all the pyrotechnics nearby, the residue of violence only slowly fading, he needed a full minute before he believed he had himself oriented.

He was still alive, but far from safe. The trouble was that there were berserker machines in every direction, none of them, thank God, very close. Over *there* was the direction his squadron had come from. Fifteen undersluggers, simply boring in, because their human pilots had mastered no better tactics. Coming straight on, until . . .

Nowhere in all the sky could Bright discover any evidence that anyone else in his squadron had survived. There were the puffy, glowing gas clouds that surely marked the end of several. But it was equally certain, his determination and his hopes assured him, that at least a small handful of them must have come through alive—after doing serious damage to the enemy. They'd be heading back to the *Stinger* now, with a victory to report.

But nothing that Bright could see suggested that the battle was over—or even that any of the enemy carriers had been seriously hit. What a seat he was going to have for the rest of the show!

Staring in the direction in which, if his attempt at orientation was not hopelessly wrong, he thought the biggest berserker machines were cruising, Bright could make out movement, could pick out an individual machine or two in every direction where the background was bright enough to show up a dark machine by contrast.

Gradually, he realized that the scenery, in almost every direction, was spectacular indeed. Faint glowing swirls, and here and there the pitiless black background showing through.

And there was something moving. He recognized a berserker, much smaller than a carrier, probably a scout of some kind. And it was coming in his general direction.

A drifting space suit presented an immediately recognizable shape. The enemy would be sure to spot him, sooner or later.

Fortunately, there was something he could do to change the odds. Bright caught sight of a chunk of wreckage the size of a garage door. The general look of the thing identified it as Solarian hardware. Once it had been part of some hapless ship—very likely his own, though in current circumstances he was unable to recognize it. For a minute or two he maneuvered awkwardly, prodigally spending the energy of his suit's tiny thrusters, to get the object between his suited body and the prowling berserker. The jagged slab of wreckage was full of holes and provided only a partial screen—he could only hope that the enemy's attention would be concentrated on matters it considered far more important than the occasional badlife survivor.

Gradually, as he clung to the metal fragment, his attention became focused on the twisted fragment, which included one side of the pilot's cockpit. Instruments, mostly broken, studded the outer surface. Among the projections Bright recognized the business end of a small optical telescope, meant to bring amplified images into the pilot's helmet.

Bright moved to examine the telescope and discovered that it was still functioning. If he could no longer do anything to affect the outcome of the battle, at least he might be able to see what was going on.

In progress at the moment was yet another farlauncher attack. The heavy spacecraft had to be land-based, and therefore must have come out from Fifty Fifty. After a preamble of maneuvers, which at Bright's distance from the action seemed to be carried out in slow motion, the attack itself was over in a few seconds. Bright clearly saw explosions bracket two berserker carriers. He thought that a third giant machine, barely visible in the background, was getting the same treatment, but it was too far away to be sure.

After the farlaunchers had disappeared again into flight-space, he could discern no evidence of damage to the enemy.

At least, he thought, the Strongholds, unlike Bright's own squadron and some others, seemed to have been able to withdraw without suffering many casualties themselves.

Ensign Bright was willing to bet that not a single Solarian crew had failed to do their best to press an attack home, once they had got within range of the enemy.

But not a single crew had succeeded.

A scout ship that had succeeded, at great peril, in driving in a circle entirely around the enemy fleet, now sent word to Admiral Naguance that the berserker carrier force was strengthened by the presence of one battleship.

Naguance received the message coolly; he didn't really think that one battleship more or less was going to make much difference, the way this battle was developing. A quick study of recon recordings identified this machine as the one which had been assigned by Solarians the code word *Hate*.

The Solarian admiral and his staff, in hasty conference, pretty much decided to ignore the *Hate* if possible, planning no attacks on that machine unless and until it gave some indication of getting them within range of its devastating weapons, including some C-plus cannon.

If that ever happened, they would be forced to concentrate on it in self-defense.

"Meanwhile, we are going to keep after those carriers. As soon as our hardlaunchers and undersluggers get back, we'll get them ready to lift off again."

Each operator of an inflight control system adopted some system, that he or she personally found effective, of assigning image symbols to various objects. The first class of objects to be represented in an operator's system were those comprising his or her own hardware. Then other parts of the ship, and fellow crew members, all of which were less intimately connected to the operator. The subjective universe inside the helmet took on different characteristics for each human who entered it. Your ship itself, your weapons waiting to be taken up and used. Some operators liked to use images of their own two hands, moving faster than human flesh and bone could ever move, grabbing up different objects and smiting or parrying with them.

Moving out further and further from psychological center, one next had to consider the way in which the world of Galactic and Universal distance, one might call it the neutral world, surrounding the ship, was to be presented inside one's helmet. Next choice was of the method of displaying other ships, carrying other crews into the fight beside your own. At best you could perceive the individual images or allied ships quite clearly when you focused on them. Of course in the blur of combat, the fog of war, when space and time themselves were torn and stretched, first the fine details and then everything tended to be lost. More than one small ship and berserker machine had been blasted entirely out of the universe in which it had been built.

Every human crew member saw, heard, and reacted in a slightly different way to the information pouring through helmet and organic senses to the brain. Some individual differences made the operator more effective, and were encouraged. But the many subjective universes all had many elements in common, mostly those that were generated by machines. And another way of perceiving the enemy, when the far-ranging optelectronic senses of your ship teased out a distant presence and then locked on. Many humans chose to tag berserkers with vivid skull, or skull and crossbone, images. One legendary operator had grafted onto the enemy a graphic of the face of a hated superior officer. The stunt had provoked a burst of official condemnation and new regulations.

There was the final preflight checklist to go through, human voices talking back and forth, and the ship's voice prompting, requiring some answers, and answering other questions in turn. Some quality in the optelectronic voice, a kind of metallic twang, rendered it astringently clear, and at the same time unmistakably distinguishable from any of the humans.

Then came the time of greatest tension, waiting for the order to lift off. Commanders at every level agonized over timing at every stage of a mission. Launch too soon, and the enemy might well be unfindable, out of reach. Delay your launch too long, and the berserkers would hit you first, catch your warbirds on the ground or on the deck. And none of the decisions at this level could be left entirely to the combat computers.

So far, everything had followed the routine of one of his training flights—there had been all too few of those. Oh, of course he'd had plenty of simulator time, which was supposed to be the same but never really was, and all too little time in space. Shortage of instructors, shortage of good equipment.

The notice that they were lifting off, when it came, was given in the human voice of the spacecraft commander.

Then rendezvous in nearby space, with the other ships of the squadron; and then cruising out, following the squadron leader. All of course while guided by the presentation inside the helmet. No way, really, to distinguish this from a training exercise in virtual reality. But his gut and his heart understood the difference.

Fame was fleeting. Not many people on Uhao, or on Earth, or anywhere else for that matter, were still following the career of that heroic Spacer Nifty Gift, the so-far-unsuspected betrayer of his comrades. There would be no stories on the news to reveal to the man who sought him where Nifty could be found today. Or at least that was the way the situation looked to Traskeluk. A newer hero with an even wilder story to tell—Traskeluk himself—had taken over first place in the popular mind.

And like Gift before him, Trask soon discovered that when he put on civilian clothes, he tended to disappear.

The truth was—as he had been managing to find out, starting with some well-timed help from good old Mother R—the truth was that Gift had started for Earth as everyone had assumed he would, but for some reason had turned back when he got to a transport hub in low Earth orbit.

From that point, practically on the planet where his family lived, Gift had turned around and come right back to the planet from which he'd started.

He hadn't come back hitching a ride on military transport, though there was plenty of such traffic from Earth to Uhao. Nothing so plebeian as that for Mr. Nifty now—if he'd done so, he couldn't have brought his girlfriend along. The conditions of his return flight had been rather more upscale.

Now why would good old Nifty bounce around in such an unusual fashion? Security hadn't seemed to care what the wounded hero did; no reason for them to be suspicious. Of course, there was no rule saying that Gift, or anyone else, had to go home if he didn't want to spend his leave that way. And it couldn't have been that Nifty was attempting to shake off pursuit; he'd made the turnaround before he could possibly have learned that all his shipmates were not dead after all.

It had already occurred to Traskeluk to wonder if security might have routinely put a tracer on him too. But where and how did they attach such things? Of course they would allow for the fact that a man changed his clothes at fairly frequent intervals. Therefore it ought to be attached right to his body somewhere. . . .

He stopped, looking down at his left hand. Of course, the new arm. That might very well have been the place they picked to plant their little toy. Suppose, before Maal had ever worked on it, security had had the medics install some kind of tracer? They might have built it right in. Traskeluk was envisioning some almost microscopic speck. That would be all the size they needed. If so, possibly Maal had inadvertently dug it out again. But he couldn't be sure of that.

He shot a glance at the icon in the upper left of his field of vision, and looked away again. The problem of a tracer—if it was a problem—was too vague to worry about. Whether it was there or not was not going to make a damn bit of difference to Cedric Traskeluk. Nifty Gift was going to see the man who was about to kill him, and then he was going to die, and that was all there was to that.

Commander R, genius in some matters, seemed to be rapidly getting in over her head in this. She gave the security agent a piercing look and asked: "You put on the tracer without the subject's knowledge?"

"Ma'am, it wouldn't be much good if they knew about it."

One hundred and seven small berserker machines—the defenders could count them quite accurately as they drew near—their numbers about equally divided between bombers and fighters, came sweeping in out of space to attack Fifty Fifty.

The gear Jory was operating from inside her bunker picked up an accurate count from the defensive network. The number was not as large as had been predicted—which probably meant that a sizable force was being held in reserve.

For several hours now, the defenders' early-warning robots had been waiting out at the maximum range of effective radio, and they had been instructed as to where and when to look with special diligence for an attack. The prediction based on Hypo's information was right on the money, and the early-warning system, before the berserker fighters wiped it from the sky, provided its master with a clear, accurate count of bandits.

The attackers had made their approach to the atoll in a series of risky, high-speed C-plus jumps, leaving their carriers still at a distance measured in light-years.

The Vals, the Voids, the Killers, all were coming on now in microjumps, mere tens or units of kilometers as they closed swiftly on their target, their drives burning up space in the vicinity of the atoll. Until they were within a thousand kilometers or so, their slick unmarked bodies had driven forward at an effective velocity not quite outpacing light. There was no sun-sized physical body anywhere nearby, so they could get away with that. Each type of attacking machine was holding a tight formation, making it possible, at least at intervals, for units to communicate with each other.

Down on the ground, several meters under the artificially hardened surface, Jory could see and hear quite well, through the information being fed to the little stage before her by her own robots' eyes and ears. She saw how the berserker fighters, the Voids, moved protectively near the deliverers of death, in a position from which they could rush quickly to intercept any new swarm of Solarian interceptors that might come out to interfere. Ideally, she understood, escort fighters on either side would try to hold friendly bombers encased in a kind of englobement pattern, themselves remaining ready to challenge anything the enemy put up in an effort to knock the bombers out of action.

The swarm of outdated Solarian interceptors had already been pretty well disposed of.

It always amazed Jory, when she thought about the technical difficulties, that either humans or machines could ever find anything as small as a planet or an atoll, when interstellar distances were involved. For returning war machines to find something as small as the carrier they needed was even chancier.

The defenders had been ready, and Jory's recorders had been allowed to tap into the available information. The bomber machines, the equivalent of Solarian farlaunchers, and thirty-six hardlauncher equivalents, were in two formations, each a V of vees.

She had been just beginning to learn how to get comfortable in government-issue body armor, melded with a special helmet owned by her employer, which allowed her to plug in her recorder-operator's headset. Now she was huddled in her sheltered position, which offered a little psychological security at least. Nash, in a burst of something like gallantry, had refused to allow a woman to join him in the most exposed observation post.

She was still sharing her shelter with several other people, and the place was now crowded by the presence of a military damage-control party, ready to rush out with their own distinctive equipment when the need arose.

This shelter was a sanctuary set aside for what the military considered nonessential folk, those who were not commanding gun-laying systems, or maintaining defensive force fields or power flows, only huddling down. From hour to hour the cast of characters tended to change, with different people running in and out.

Meanwhile, Jory's dog-sized recorder robot, and a couple of even smaller machines, were darting about on the surface, focusing their specialized senses on sound and movement.

Her earlier intention of naming her robot Pappy had somehow never got off the ground. There were a couple of reasons, the least important of them being Nash's predictable displeasure. Many people thought it bad luck to assign a "human" name to any kind of a machine. Not that Jory herself was in the least superstitious about anything, of course. But this was war, and war was—different.

Stricter penalties than any Colonel Shanga might enforce were in effect for not wearing a helmet; over the last two hours, atmospheric oxygen had been deliberately drained away from the atoll's surface, in an attempt to minimize fire damage from the blasts of heat that were sure to come.

There was a certain tragic angle to that decision, or at least a lot of people would view it as tragedy, and Jory wasn't sure how the military censors were going to allow her to report it. A few of the awkward, mutant birds, and other breathing life, had been removed first, but most were going to die. A selected remnant of the birds, a breeding stock, were being kept alive in a deep freeze, somewhere underground. The decision to remove the oxygen had been made late in the game, and the safety of wildlife had been well down on the defenders' list of priorities.

As the underground machinery worked at its task of sucking oxygen out of the thin air, there appeared a scattering of weird, dead birds, all across the landing field and the surrounding terrain.

The dish antenna intended to receive urgent information from returning scouts was one of the first objects blown up when the berserker attack came in.

Only the mounded, rounded top of Jory's dugout was higher than the nearby revetments.

Every minute or so she daringly, against orders, stuck her head up on the surface to take one more look around.

Meanwhile, the defensive force fields, powered and energized by generators buried underground, sunk as deep as the roots of the atoll itself went down in normal space, helped to bind together and stabilize the whole atoll. Their fields damped explosions, slowed shock waves, screened out a sleet of radiation, drew the energy from, and lowered the temperature in, flashes of searing heat. Thus tender human flesh might be enabled to endure.

Back in the snugness of her shelter Jory watched, in utter fascination, the first appearance of the enemy, not directly, but on a holostage.

This, at last, was real. She vividly recalled having the same thought during her previous combat experience. Then too she had been aware of the same hard-edged look and feel of reality.

Alternately she knelt or crouched on the hard floor of the shelter, shifting awkwardly from one cramped position to another. When the explosions began in earnest, up above, some of the near-misses pelted her armor with bits of hard material spalled off the interior walls of the shelter.

The little holostage in front of her, on which she watched, melded, and directed what was going on, was as crowded as a three-ring circus, with feed-ins coming from several robots at once; and she fretted that perhaps she ought to be out on the surface. It was essential that she have the most direct view possible of what was happening up there, if the recording she put together was going to be anything more than merely mechanical.

A couple of her shelter-mates were hanging over her armored shoulders, eyes riveted on her stage. The others found other ways to keep busy. Maybe some had left the shelter for some reason, through a connecting tunnel or up the passage leading to the war above.

For most of her life Jory had been subject to a chronic fretting that technology, and other things, conspired to keep her at one remove from reality. The nature of reality chronically concerned her. This was one reason, she supposed, why she had chosen a profession that consisted largely of asking questions.

For days before the berserkers came, the defensive satellites, of which she estimated that ten or twelve were visible at any one time, had already been orbiting at blurring speed around the small, dense atoll. Now they shifted into faster, tighter paths. Their movements suggested to Jory depictions of subatomic particles quantum-jumping, their images taking on almost the aspect of solid celestial rings.

Now Jory, watching intensely from the ground, had barely time to catch a glimpse of these last-second defense adjustments before the first explosions jarred the world. Maybe before the attacking machines were in range of human eyesight. The stentorian mechanical voices that had been calling everyone to battle stations at last fell silent.

No doubt the machines that were fighting on the other side emotionlessly took note of the fact that their onslaught had failed totally to achieve surprise.

Even after the first wave of enemy spacecraft had begun to hit their targets on the ground, the surviving Solarian fighters that were still spaceborne continued to do their best to mix it up with them, and with audacity and determination shot up several bomber machines. Wave fronts of radiation jarred the hurtling fighters, the darting enemy, and on the ground knocked armored running figures sprawling.

Such success as the Solarian livecrew ships enjoyed endured for only a few more seconds. And then the doughnut-shaped Void fighters of the enemy, falling on their prey like raptor birds, had closed with the ground-based Solarian clunkers, taking most of the pressure off the bomber machines.

Quickly most of the inferior Solarian vehicles were being blasted out of space. There went one, lost in a glorious streak of flame; and there went another and another, winking out in explosions of a brightness that was momentarily painful, even through the filtering faceplate of combat armor. Jory winced.

A few of the clunker pilots, protected by their personal armor, survived the ruin of their spacecraft. Some were swept clean away from the atoll in currents of thin nebular material, lost to their friends and to their enemies alike. Several of their suited forms showed up in Jory's images, drifting down with apparent lightness through the mottled irregular gravity of the atoll. And one or two of these, as she discovered later, had actually made survivable landings somewhere on the surface, out of sight of the landing field.

Those less fortunate were subjected to some ground fire, aimed at them in the belief that the armored figures being feathered down to the surface on their own force fields were berserker machines, the first landers of an invasion force.

On top of that, one of the Void fighters diverted itself from fatter targets to strafe the falling humans. A ground observer saw a helpless pilot die, and her voice came over the defense intercom, cursing the enemy. Jory, caught up in her own job, cursed also—she had just missed getting a good recording of the event.

In the next minute, a cheer went up in hundreds of voices, many of them audible in Jory's headset, when ground fire, skillfully directed by computers melded with human minds, brought down another and then yet another of the attacking machines. Colonel Shanga's defensive force fields, reaching out into space for hundreds of kilometers, continued to slow down the incoming bombers, as well as the missiles that they launched, to the point where human eyes could follow their movements with little difficulty. Meanwhile, other enemy units became visible only in the streaking explosions that marked their destruction.

The apprentice journalist so far was coming through without a scratch, and managing to do her job in a satisfactory way.

Whammo! Whammo! Whammo!

Jory cowered down, her ears and teeth, her very bones, aching with sympathetic vibrations. Reflexively she tried to put her hands over her ears, and through the sensors in her armored gloves felt only the smooth, curved sides of her helmet.

Meanwhile, she could gather from snatches of conversation heard on intercom that Nash himself, sticking to his relatively exposed position, had been wounded in the arm or shoulder.

Jory, on the private intercom used by Nash's team, heard him groaning and muttering. She thought he sounded too energetic, too full of pride and anger, to have been badly hurt.

The sky, as modeled on her little stage, was full of streaks and fiery blossoms, of colors and intensities that wanted to hurt the eye, even through a statglass faceplate. Here and there a ghost of airborne flame suggested that the self-replenishing atmosphere still held enough oxygen to support burning.

A moment later, some giant's hammer, underground, came smiting upward against Jory's suited feet, threatening to launch her armor-weighted body into the thinned-out air. Some kind of a near hit. She staggered and swore and got back to her work.

The ground-based Solarian fighters had failed dismally to stop the attack, but they had done their best to blunt its force. Other factors also worked to that end. Many lives were saved by the warning received many days ago. The humans had been given priceless time to dig in, with force fields and hardened emplacements, and this prevented a major disaster.

With the exception of a score of live pilots who had vanished with the wreckage of their doomed, inadequate fighters, Solarian casualties were light. No more than a dozen of the ground defenders had been killed outright.

Some facilities on the atolls, including a repair dock for small spacecraft, and the tight-beam antenna for courier downloadings, were extensively damaged, but other important sites, including most of the deep shelters, were left practically untouched.

The Solarians remained for the most part entrenched, more than half buried in the hardened ground, while they fired back as best they could. On the displays, the antiship fire they put up sometimes looked like an almost continuous sheet of flame. They inflicted serious casualties on the wave of small berserkers.

"We can take satisfaction," the young journalist was now saying into her recorder, (meanwhile feeling pride in the steadiness of her voice) "in the fact that every Solarian spacecraft had already been launched, with a full crew—some of them hours, some only only minutes—before the berserkers swept in. The attackers are going to be absolutely denied one of their important goals, one which the defenders here think they had computed as exceedingly probable: They will catch not a single Solarian fighter or bomber still in its launching cradle. Nor is a single one of the livecrew members still on the ground and vulnerable to this assault. They are all in space, where they have every chance to fight back."

That was what she had been told, and she could at least hope that it was true. How many of the young crew members who had gone to meet the enemy were dead by this time was another question she would have to try to answer.

Death had come out of the sky and snapped its jaws at the Solarian defenders on the ground. But the human volunteers, three thousand of them and more, were still dug in on

Fifty Fifty, with no intention of moving out. They had no intention of dying, either, though they were still defiantly occupying the enemy's chosen target. When the enemy finally came, the dominant emotion of these people was relief that their long wait was over. They fought back with everything they had, even as the world around them erupted with blasts, flames, and murderous vibrations.

A roaring berserker machine, one of the biggest taking part in the attack, hit by fire from a heavy gun, disintegrated in the upper atmosphere, which on this peculiar world lay only a couple of hundred meters above land surface.

Blast followed blast. It seemed to Jory now that she could hear her mother shouting at her, and for a moment her self-possession wavered. Then it settled back. I'm dealing with this, thought Jory Yokosuka, in brief self-congratulation on her own aplomb, and then went back to a selfless concentration on operating her equipment. She was doing this through hand controls under the armored fingers of her suit, as well as giving verbal orders to her robots through a kind of headset, a less compulsive version of the arrangement worn by the live combat fliers-spacers, which plugged into the helmet of her armored suit, and left most of the operator's face covered only by the armor's faceplate.

Ka-slaam, ka-slaam!

The attack went on, minute after minute. The enemy machines were circling at high speed in the sky, diving, retreating, climbing, and coming back. Now some people in the shelters, civilians as well as military, began to react to the ongoing strain of bombardment by rushing wildly out of their shelters for no good reason, firing shoulder weapons into a sky more weirdly streaked and color-stained than any sunset on a volcanic planet. The gesture relieved a need for action, but was ineffective; it hardly seemed possible that any of the many incoming missiles were going to be hit and detonated by small-arms fire.

And then Jory's equipment went totally dead. There must have been a hit nearby, a blow that had hardly registered in her awareness. Maybe the last one of her active robots had been wiped out.

The young woman stared blankly at the dark, lifeless stage for a moment, then ripped off the wire optelectronic fiber connection to her helmet, abandoned her relatively secure position underground, and rushed out, scrambling through the little tunnel, climbing the steep hardened stairway to the surface. This was at least partly because of her ongoing wish to see directly what was happening. Evidently some splinter or splash of energy had penetrated her little shelter and found a vital spot in the equipment.

Once her head rose above the level of the ground, an avalanche of noise, like nothing she had ever heard before, forced its way right inside her helmet and seemed to be lifting it off.

Her dog-sized robot, its hindquarters melted into bubbling slag, stared at her through one lens that was still turning in its immobilized head.

Almost at once her eye fell on a fallen object, lying not ten meters from where she stood. It was a dead man, his armor wrapped on arm and leg with Templar tokens, lying like a bundle of discarded laundry. The body lay half out of a small shelter, which had been ripped open by some kind of blast.

If the small yacht he was riding on had a name, Gift hadn't heard it yet, and didn't want to. Nor did he really want to be told the identity of the Teacher, the ship's owner that Gavrilov, with an air of awe and mystery, mentioned every once in a while. Nifty envisioned some crabbed old patriarch, head of some idiotic peace cult on whatever remote planet they were now bound for. Nifty expected it was going to be unpleasant there, but it wouldn't be nearly as bad as facing Traskeluk—or a court-martial, either, come to that.

Gift's only real problem now was that he still couldn't tell where they were going. He tried talking to the ship several times, when the other man was out of the compartment, but Gavrilov had the controlling codes, and had blocked the vessel's optelectronic brain from discussing any astrogational matters.

Gift was used to ships where the human crew took some active part in every aspect of the voyage. The autopilot and the other machines were generally reliable, of course, more so than humans in many ways. But . . . still it made him uneasy.

They were still in deep space a long way from any solar system, the yacht's autopilot still following whatever course had been punched in by Gavrilov. Gift was wondering whether he should be worried—this was turning out to be a longer trip, involving more C-plus jumps, than he had expected. Possibly that was because they were taking evasive action, against what seemed to Gift the even remoter possibility that they were being followed.

Flower, acting as if it were a matter of course, had moved into the little cabin with her Nifty—it was quite a comedown from the quarters they had enjoyed aboard the luxury liner.

But Flower was no help to him in finding out where they were bound. She seemed perfectly willing to let Gavrilov make all the important decisions.

"He knows what he's doing, Nifty. He's been involved in this kind of thing for a long time."

"What kind of thing?"

"What he's doing for you now. Getting people out of the military, when they don't want to be in it any longer."

"Oh."

Unless Gift could obtain access to the instruments—and Gavrilov was making certain he could not—there was no possible way for him to tell where he was being taken. Unless he was willing to really make an issue of it, there was no way to pressure Gavrilov into telling him.

What the hell, thought Nifty Gift. Once you decide to trust someone, then trust them, until they prove you wrong. If Gavrilov and his mysterious Teacher and whoever else was backing him want to play the cloak-and-dagger business, let them. Maybe they knew what they were doing.

Several times in the course of this voyage Gift felt an urge to confess to Flower the reason why he was so afraid of Traskeluk.

He said to her once, "There's some things I did I'm really sorry for. One thing in particular."

"What was that?"

He didn't answer directly. "When I ran away from the berserker, it was because I was trying to stay alive."

"Why else?"

Gift, when he thought about it, understood that he had deserted long before he met Gavrilov, or even Flower. He'd made that decision many days ago, in deep space and in the face of the enemy. No, it was more like he hadn't made any decision at all. It had just popped into existence, the first time he'd confronted a berserker.

Gavrilov, tired of his continued hints that he wanted to be told which planet they were going to, told Gift at last: "We're headed for a place called Paradise."

Gift thought for a moment. "Never heard of it."

The other was silent.

"Maybe it's called by some other names as well?"

Gavrilov shook his head.

"Paradise."

"That's our name for it."

Now Gift shook his head, in disgust. "You're not just driving me around in a big loop and bringing me back to Uhao? Some really clever maneuver of that type?"

"No. I'm not doing that. When I say Paradise, I'm not talking about the weather." And nothing more could be got out of him.

At first Gift had been convinced that the worst purpose his new companions had in mind was to help him to desert.

Gift said, in announcing his decision to desert, "I've paid my dues—let someone else get shot at for a while."

"You said the Space Force was going to give you a desk job."

"That's what they told me."

She and Gavrilov both understood that he was afraid of berserkers—not that they thought any the less of him for that. They were both afraid of berserkers too—but in their case, it was the way that some people feared God. Well, all the gods of space knew that he was as scared as any of them. Only Flower, who had been with him longer, thought she understood Gift's motives better than he did himself. She wanted to convince herself that he was reluctant to fight those nice machines any longer.

The hours went by, growing into days. The ship continued piloting itself, toward whatever destination Gavrilov had punched in. Days ago the world of Uhao had shrunk to nothing on the holostages (Gift was the only one who had bothered to observe the process), had become a lovely blue Earthlike dot, and presently had disappeared when they dodged into flightspace for a long jump.

Flower dabbled around, day after day, in the yacht's various cabins, playing games much of the time, keeping busy at this and that. She seemed happy and proud to be with Gift the military deserter, and at the same time nervous.

Gift, with little else to do, kept trying, in a friendly way, to gather information. "So, tell me something about this planet we're going to. Even if you can't tell me its real name."

Flower looked uncertain.

He asked her, "Have you been there before?"

"No, but . . . I know about it."

"How do you know?"

A pause. "Well, I really don't know much."

"What about Gavrilov? I assume he's actually been there?"

"Oh, yes."

"And he's told you all about it?"

"No. Actually . . . no."

Gift might as well have saved his breath.

Solarians over the centuries had established hundreds of colonies across their modest morsel of the Galaxy. Gift could not have named them all, and many were no more than names to him. But several had chronically strained relations with the Cradle World, and he thought he could come up with a couple of possibilities when he tried to guess Gavrilov's destination. That the ship was small for an interstellar craft meant nothing;

no ship carried, or could carry, all the power that such a journey required. True interstellar drive units had to tap the resources of the Galaxy itself.

He persisted. "Any reason you can't tell me now?"

"Just that I promised the Teacher I wouldn't."

Gift had gradually become more and more drawn to, entranced by, the idea of getting to some planet, or some continent, or at least some island, where deserters could hide out, where the Space Force and all its allied military organizations weren't very well liked.

It got so he had to keep reminding himself to be a realist. No place was perfect, no matter what its enthusiasts might call it, and he would like a little advance notice regarding what the drawbacks of Paradise were likely to be. These loonies, or their even crazier Teacher and his sponsors, were willing to spend a modest fortune on space travel to get him there. But maybe Gavrilov had been ready to make the trip anyway.

With nothing else going on to catch Gift's interest, he gradually became more insistent about being told their destination. He couldn't see any reason why they shouldn't tell him now.

Traskeluk, somewhat to his own surprise, was beginning to be nagged by a wish that he had volunteered to give up his leave. In that case he might well have been placed aboard one of the carriers going into combat. Of course, the demands of honor had kept him from even thinking about doing such a thing.

Until now.

If he had been allowed to sacrifice his leave, assuming he would also have been judged medically fit, he could now be assigned to one of the jobs he had been trained for. He was qualified both as a gunner and a detection countermeasures operator. In DCM you used specialized equipment in an attempt to neutralize whatever fields the enemy sent out. As with every other livecrew position, you had to rely on your hardware for practical speed, while the organic brain, always a couple of steps slower, set strategy.

Damn Nifty Gift, for keeping him from honorable battle. Now Trask had yet another thing to blame the bastard for.

Traskeluk thought of sending his distant father and grandfather some kind of message, strongly hinting at what he intended, assuring them that he was going to do what must be done; but no, he didn't want to risk alerting security, or Gift. When Dad and Grandfather heard what he had done, after it was all over, that would be time enough for them to have their reassurance.

At first, it seemed important to Traskeluk not to say anything, not to accuse Gift, because it was necessary to be sure, to give the man a chance. A vow of vengeance against anyone was not to be lightly undertaken, not where there remained the least possibility of a misjudgment regarding guilt.

When he had realized the truth about Gift, what the man had really done to him and Ensign Terrin, he, Traskeluk, had been still a little groggy, still lying in his hospital bed, and no one was surprised by his failure to respond cogently when people started talking to him about his heroic shipmate.

"Gift reported your ship lost with all hands but himself."

Traskeluk's eyes had opened fully. But it was a little while before he spoke. "You're telling me that Nifty Gift survived."

"Oh yes. He's quite all right, was sent home on leave, I should imagine. He told us in debriefing how all three of you had abandoned the spy ship and were trying to reach the courier, and there was some kind of weapon blast, and he was the only one to make it. The two of you should have quite a reunion."

"Yes. We should."

The debriefers would certainly have taken notice if Traskeluk and Gift told them two substantially different stories. But maybe not. Different people had handled their respective debriefings, and like as not there had been some administrative foul-up—there usually was. The discrepancy might easily not be noticed until people at the next level up took a look at both stories.

The evidence, when someone finally got around to looking at it closely, suggested that Gift might have run out on his shipmates. But the other survivor had not accused him of anything.

Whenever anyone referred in any way to Gift's role in the disaster, Traskeluk fell back on saying that he had trouble remembering those last minutes of combat. Eventually this provoked a closer examination of his brain, and then a shrug. "Memory is tricky, and we're a long way from fully understanding it."

"Weapon blasts," he murmured. "Yes. There were a lot of those."

"Spacer Gift was certain that you'd been killed."

A thoughtful pause. "I suppose it must have looked that way to him. I guess you checked his brain out too."

"How did it look to you?"

"Oh. My memory of those last minutes is still a little vague. So, Nifty got away after all? That's good, that's real good."

"I shouldn't worry, if I were you. The memories will probably come back, sooner or later. We've given you some stuff that ought to help."

"That's good." Traskeluk closed his eyes, and appeared to be sleeping.

In fact, the memory aid they'd given him worked better than he was willing to admit: It brought back the sequence of betrayal in startling, vivid detail.

He knew enough about Spacer Gift, had exchanged enough stories with him in a long tour of duty, to know where on Earth the man's family lived. Traskeluk thought he could even feel somewhat familiar with the place.

When it came time for a more serious and detailed debriefing, back at Port Diamond, Traskeluk pleaded that his memory of those last long minutes on the spy ship and outside it was still fragmentary and confused. There didn't seem any reason to adopt stronger measures to help him straighten it out; no vital information was at stake.

In his own mind he figured out a satisfactory version of

what had really happened: He really did remember firing at the enemy with the shoulder weapon he'd picked up, and he supposed it was remotely possible that the berserker had succumbed to that fleabite counterattack. More likely, it had belatedly fallen victim to some kind of burrowing bomb that had managed to get in under its skin minutes earlier.

Later, when the debriefing sessions seemed safely over, Traskeluk began to try to develop a scenario in his mind, one in which he stood confronting Gift. Constructing the scenario was not a joyful business but a kind of work. It seemed important that he do as good a job of it as possible.

In this play of the imagination, Traskeluk, when the time finally came, would say to the rotten bastard: "All I had to do was look blank, and listen carefully to what the debriefers told me, what questions they asked. From that it wasn't hard to piece together the story the way you'd told it to them."

What kind of expression would Gift have on his stupid face at this point? Maybe they would be talking at long range, over some kind of communicator, and he, Trask, would have to try to read the look on the face of some tiny image.

"Traskeluk, listen. I know what it must look like to you, the way I just took off and got out of there. I—"

"No, *easy,* shipmate. You all take it easy now. Truth is, here I am, see? Hardly a scratch. Good as new. Certified for active duty."

In this imaginary dialogue it was always Gift who finally brought up the name of their mutual shipmate, the woman who'd died screaming inside her helmet, so close to Trask that he could almost feel the vibration.

Traskeluk raised his eyebrows politely, as if he really hadn't thought about that aspect of the matter yet, but was ready now to be reminded just who she had been.

Gift, as seen in Traskeluk's imagination, looked around wildly, thinking, hoping, that the other person he had betrayed might have also come through alive.

"I thought—I thought that Terrin might be—"

"That she might have made it too? No, Nifty. You know where Terrin is. She's right where you left her."

Or, especially if there were other people present, Traskeluk would pretend to harbor no ill-will toward the man who almost killed him.

"Come, have a drink."

And Nifty would start to feel relieved, though still a little wary. But after the first drink, and some more talk, he would really let down his guard.

And then—

TWENTY · TWO

There were dead people everywhere on the atoll now, Jory supposed, though the one before her was the sole example she had actually seen. So far she had heard no report of casualties. Probably none had been compiled as yet; but such was the pocked, scorched, and blasted appearance of the atoll's surface, as far as she could see, that she assumed the numbers must be high.

The attack was still going on, but she couldn't let that stop her. Running to where she thought she might find spare parts, hoping to restore or replace her damaged equipment, she saw how antispacecraft weapons swiveled and spat fire and distortion from their blunt, solid-looking muzzles. Well underground the breathing, sweating gunners, their heads sheathed in optelectronic helmets as if they played at being robots, manned the active defenses. One skilled human could, when necessary, meld with the optelectronic controller of a whole battery of guns. Meanwhile live humans—medics or members of repair crews Jory supposed—were visible here and there, trotting or walking or sometimes crawling across the surface.

The antispacecraft guns hammered away, unleashing their self-guiding lozenges of plasma, the shock waves of their passage coming almost in one continuous roar. But now even the guns were drowned out by the louder explosions of more missiles incoming.

Jory had almost reached the storage area that was her goal when something, a jolt of force, took her clean off her feet in midstride, sent her protected body rolling, until it was stopped by slamming into a revetment. A surge of heat built swiftly inside her armor, then was damped away by her suit's last inner defense, a fraction of a second before her skin began to burn. The landscape shook and seemed to spin around her armored head. Sometimes the full violence of even nuclear charges could be damped almost to nothing—but "almost" was, ultimately, not going to be quite good enough.

Several holostage flagpoles, and at least one traditionally crafted of real and solid wood, were spotted at various locations around the base. But for some reason no one had thought to raise a flag today—maybe someone on general intercom screamed this sudden discovery in Jory's hearing—and one officer communicated with the commander to ask whether this should be done.

She had her sound and pictures back, at least on some of the equipment, at least for now. Colonel Shanga was startled, and his face on Jory's little monitor looked momentarily dismayed. Then he snapped: "Hell yes! Get to it."

She had her own job to do. Her body was functioning; nothing seemed to be broken or bleeding. But somehow she could not tear herself away from watching the business about the flag.

And then there was some uncertainty as to which flag the officer, armored fingers poised over the controls at his console, would choose to raise.

People all across the settled Galaxy were given to argument about whether there was, or could be, a single Solarian symbol, one that all Earth-descended humans on all their planets might be willing to recognize as deserving of their loyalty. Just get something up there, dammit, Jory prayed, slowly dragging herself back to her feet. Ordinarily she had no feeling on the subject, but this was different. We need something.

What went flickering up the flagpole (the nearest to Jory was a virtual pole—in fact a holographic projection—that could be sliced again and again by blast and shrapnel, and never fall) moments later was the closest approximation: A round sun of red, with blue planet-dots arrayed in a double loop around it, making on a white background the horizontal figure eight of the mathematician's infinity symbol.

The flag and all its symbols appeared in three dimensions, and in several locations around the sphere of peculiar matter making up the atoll. The image was set at a brisk fluttering, as of real cloth in a spanking breeze.

The Templar banner was much different from that of Earth-born humanity that flew above it on the same pole. The former displayed the image of an ancient knight in handmade armor, and the red cross of the original Templars had been adopted as part of the design. Here, the emblem stood crushing a berserker that crouched on crablike legs.

Some anonymous voice, no doubt one of the fanatical Templar Raiders, was shouting, off-key, what Jory assumed must be an ancient battle chant:

> Mine eyes have seen the glory of the coming of the
> Lord
> He is trampling out the vintage where the grapes of
> wrath are stored . . .

Jory Yokosuka could recognize that as a Templar song.

Moments later, the singing was swallowed up, with every other sound, in the renewed roar of the attack.

Jory, having done the best she could in the way of gathering replacement parts, headed back for her battle station, running from one shelter to another, bounding along in the servo-powered armor at a faster pace than she could have managed sprinting across a real beach while stripped for swimming.

All it took, she thought, was a little practice, and a lot of fear.

Here lay another casualty. She staggered, almost falling, to a stop.

The servo motors in her own suit lent her a power lifter's strength as she grappled the mass of a wounded man in armor, and dragged him into a shelter.

Then she had to get back to her own job.

When she got back to her station, there was Nash's face, on the intercom channel.

"What in hell's going on at your end?" he demanded. "Are you all right?" It sounded as if he would consider it the ultimate disloyalty if she got herself killed.

Some of her equipment had been hit, early in the raid, she explained in a breathless voice, and she had needed to obtain a spare part.

Nash's flat little image on the small screen showed one of his arms now splinted in some kind of cast or bandage. But he was still on his feet, barking orders and abuse.

"Shut up," she commented, and turned him off. She knew what job she had to do, so now for God's sake let her do it.

With all her gear up and running again, it struck her as amazing, the number of people who, like herself, were out of their shelters, not actively crewing weapons but simply running this way and that, for no good reason at all that she could see.

Of course it was impossible to take her helmet off, even momentarily, without risking a collapse from anoxia, because of the depleted air—not to mention deafness. One would have to slip into a pressurized chamber somewhere to make such a change.

In the last hours before the attack, another rumor had swept across the atoll, this one to the effect that there would be a goodlife man or woman riding with the raiders. Jory had considered that a perfect example of the type of wild speculation that some people's minds broke out with, like a rash, in time of stress.

Whammo! Whammo! Whammo!

Space itself seemed to ring like a giant gong, mocking the strength of the defensive fields laboring to muffle the explosions.

Inhuman giants were at war here, one with another, and there were moments when it seemed mere humans could do no more than huddle down and pray.

And then, as suddenly as it had begun, the attack was over. The attacking machines, except for the minority brought down on the atoll or vaporized in space, had retreated in the direction of their launching carriers. A ringing silence reigned. The surface of the atoll underfoot was still. People on the surface and in their shelters raised their heads and stared at one another like newborn children.

As abruptly as they had appeared, the raiders were gone, flickering away through a diminished opposition of defensive fields. Then an order to cease-fire, leaving a sudden, startling, aching silence in the unearthly sky. The perpetual, illusory overcast that hovered over Fifty Fifty was now empty of everything but clouds of particles, and the poisonous afterglow of blasts. The bright orbital rings of the defensive satellites—now notably fewer than before—relaxed their protective grip upon the miniature world and slowed once more to a mere blurring speed.

Jay Nash, in what was for him a stroke of good luck ("Good planning invites good fortune") had personally obtained a good recording, sound and sight, smells and vibrations, of the main repair facility going up in a cloud of flame and dust.

That stream of information was so good that it looked like something faked with computer graphics. But every bit of data in the picture was purely authentic.

When they took him away to the base hospital to have the dressing on his arm redone, he shouted and chortled his elation that he had been wounded in combat, that he had survived, that his raw recording was going to be beautiful.

The real flag had been riddled with holes; the real flagpole, of real wood, was badly splintered now. But splintered or not the pole was still standing, holding up the flag.

It crossed the mind of someone, monitoring pollution levels, that the atmosphere of Fifty Fifty was going to need more than a fresh supply of oxygen to set it right again. A complete rebuilding would be in order when the fight was over.

The birds and other breathing life were dying off.

Colonel Shanga's command post had survived the storm with only minimal damage, and the surviving journalists tended to congregate there—probably because the bar had not yet reopened.

Reports of damage and casualties, claims of enemies destroyed, were coming in from every quarter of the miniature world. Human casualties in fact were light, thanks to an early warning and heavy preparation. Early analysis of combat recordings confirmed the number of attacking berserkers at well over a hundred; it would take a while to make sure how many had been shot down.

The garrison commander, coming on line to make a general announcement, was grimly satisfied—for the moment—with the way the people of the garrison had performed. Neither he nor anyone under his command doubted that the enemy would be back, probably soon, and in even greater force. Emergency repairs were started, reserve resources redeployed upon the surface. Thanks to the early warning, casualties had been light.

Once more able to move freely around the surface of the atoll, Jory soon found herself exchanging smiles with Jay Nash, who was in fine spirits, proudly brandishing his bandaged arm.

A couple of little robots bearing the company logo, ignoring the devastation all around, were busy maintaining the equipment Nash had been using personally.

"Any enemy landers reported?" Jory asked him.

"Not yet. But they'll be back. That little skirmish was just to soften us up." He beamed at her happily.

Damage had been inflicted, but there appeared to have been no softening at all. People and machines, thousands of armored figures, the great majority intact, had come pouring out of shelters. All the digging in had really paid off. A stern voice in Jory's helmet reminded everybody to keep their armor on; the oxygen had been drained from the atmosphere, and the enemy had dumped in poisons, or deadly microorganisms. Somewhere, distantly, some kind of an alarm was ringing. Closer at hand, some wounded human's cries for help drifted through the attenuated air.

A quick look at the recordings showed that Jay Nash and his crew had been hard at work. Every member of his crew, including his newest employee, had performed creditably. The capture of live combat scenes had been amply successful. They had focused their equipment on the right places. But under the circumstances no one but themselves was paying much attention to the people from the entertainment world or to their results.

The wounded, several dozen of them in scattered locations around the atoll, were cared for quickly. The handful of dead were respectfully given temporary burial. Defenses were patched up, machines reloaded and rearmed.

No one on the ground doubted that the berserkers would be back, and most expected the second wave of the assault soon.

A new rumor was now rapidly spreading among the defenders, to the effect that a Solarian carrier force was somewhere in the area. Not everyone believed it, but morale went up a notch.

A small handbook appeared, *What To Do If Captured,* but many people swore they were not going to be captured.

Half an hour after the cease-fire, orders came to stand down from full alert.

Nash's yacht, the *Araner,* carrying most of his people and equipment, along with the more seriously wounded, was preparing to make a dash for Port Diamond while the going was good.

The early-warning system reported nothing incoming, at the moment.

Jory observed, with a lightening of her spirits, that the building housing the bar had not been totally destroyed in the berserker raid, though it suffered some picturesque damage.

Large holes in the walls and roof, but fortunately it wasn't going to rain. And now she noticed taut bubbles of plastic, sealing all the holes. Visiting such an establishment would seem rather pointless if one couldn't take one's helmet off when one got there. Fortunately, the interior could still be pressurized.

Jory heard one of the bartenders say, while waiting for the next (never doubting there would be more) berserker onslaught: "It has been said from old times that a battle is a succession of mistakes and that the party that blunders less emerges victorious."

Jory wondered, as she had on her previous visit to the nameless bar, why the place was open. But, feeling ready for a drink herself, she wasn't going to protest the fact.

The place seemed empty, or it would, Jory thought, when Jay Nash and his wild stories were gone, along with his self-consciously macho crew of hard drinkers and swearers. Most, but not all, of that bunch were men.

Now the roaring music changed, suggesting the presence of a striptease dancer. Only in a holostage recording. Doing a strip of some entertainer's idea of space armor, piece by piece, with nothing underneath? That reminded Jory, with a faint shock, of her own actual situation. Well, she'd get back to her quarters, and some privacy, in a few minutes.

As usual, the performance alternated hardbodied young men and women, or at least their computer-generated images, in that role. Some kind of entertainment. Different varieties, at the push of a button. There hadn't been any live musicians on Fifty Fifty for a long, long time.

Jory thought of demanding a male dancer next, but she was too tired. To hell with it.

People were arguing, a couple of tables away. Someone had a theory that no one had ever got around to telling the robot manager of the bar that it had to be shut down. No, the door had really been locked, half an hour ago. Well then, someone had slyly deprogrammed the robot to forget any closure command within an hour after it was issued.

If a high state of alert still obtained, then the bar should have been officially closed. Now that Jory noticed it, a great many of the customers seemed to have been wounded. People were drinking, chewing, and inhaling various substances, some in exotic combinations.

The newest fad, popular among the celebrities of Port Diamond and Earth, and taken up eagerly by their followers, was the subtle effect attained by simply sipping ordinary wine.

"This is what wine was originally like."

The taster frowned judiciously. "Fermented grape juice? Nothing at all added?"

"Nothing."

Whooaop went the music. *Craaash!* God, you would think these people had had more than enough of noise during the last few hours—but evidently not.

People gasped, taking in fumes, and chewed and drank. In dark booths a few couples were rubbing each other's bodies with perfumed ointments, while the bulk of the customers ignored them. Discreet placards on the walls proclaimed the availability of antidote substances that promised to restore the Solarian brain from various kinds of intoxication to full alertness and coordination in a matter of seconds, if some call to duty did not allow one to enjoy the prolonged high otherwise attainable from the various psychoactive party materials.

Here and there, in corners of the large room, serious matters were under discussion: "Or put it this way . . . 'He who makes the next-to-the-last blunder wins.' "

The nearest bartender responded, off-the-wall.

Someone else commented, "A truly Zen reply."

Hours were yet to pass before some military police officer eventually realized that the manager robot had had its senses scrambled; it had started giving irrelevant answers to questions, and sometimes answering queries that had not been asked at all.

A few years ago there had been an adjoining small tourist hotel, but that building had been converted, months ago, to other uses. Putting up some temporary buildings was no problem, nor was anything strong or elaborate needed, in the absence of rain and snow and wind; probably the atolls experienced almost nothing like weather in the usual planetary sense.

The male dancer was long gone. And now again the device switched, in response to a request. Now it was putting up an enhancement of some twentieth-century 2-D movie.

The berserker raid, as Jory realized, listening to the talk around her, teeth-rattling and mind-numbing as it was, had been really of no more than moderate intensity. Obviously it was intended as a mere preliminary to an intended landing and occupation—the berserker plan called for cleansing the atoll of all life without shattering it into bits. In the face of determined Solarian resistance, even that modest objective proved impossible to attain. The land-based defenses, forewarned and forearmed, were still strong when it was over.

Nash, after agonizing briefly over the question, reluctantly confirmed for Jory his decision to get himself, his crew, and his documentary out. He had accomplished what he'd come for. Now the job called for getting the material he'd gathered into shape. Staying here would only endanger what they had so far achieved.

The commander of the garrison was ready to see him go. The colonel had a million other things to tend to that were more important than recordings or public relations.

Nash, prominently displaying his bandaged arm while he sipped a beer, told Jory he had been about to send for her.

"Here I am."

"Okay, girl, I want you to pack up and get ready to move out."

Jory bristled. "What? Who? Just me?"

He grinned evilly, and seemed unconscious of the fact that his opposite hand came over to stroke his bandage. At least today he was keeping his artificial eye in his head where it belonged. "No. Fact is, I'm leaving too, pulling out the whole crew. Got what we came for."

"I'd like to stay."

"No, ma'am. We've got what we came for, enough to make the documentary."

It was a good point. "All right. When?"

Nash looked at his old-fashioned wristwatch. "We're lifting off in about two hours."

"You're the boss."

"Damn right. Don't forget it." Nash grunted some additional comment to the effect that no woman was going to take that kind of risk while he moved on to safety; no, sir, not if he could help it.

Jory sighed. It was as if the hundreds of women who were here in the military, among the volunteer defenders, had escaped his notice entirely. Well, it was a job.

When she left the tavern it was with mixed feelings, including a twinge of disappointment. Now she could wish that she'd made some fuss earlier about her own trivial combat wound; if she'd ever been given a medal to wear, she'd certainly be wearing it now, just to irritate the boss.

TWENTY THREE

Grimly Admiral Naguance considered the first reports of Solarian casualties. A majority of the fighters and bombers sent out in the first waves against the enemy carriers had not returned. Underslugger Eight, from *Stinger*, comprising fifteen hardlaunchers and thirty people, seemed to have been totally wiped out without scoring even a single hit on a berserker. Certainly not one ship of that squadron had made it back to *Stinger*. Hope that some of the missing crews might still be recovered was fading fast.

The losses among Naguance's small ships, including both those who had managed to find the enemy and those who had not, looked so high that he refused to think about them, though part of his mind was keeping an automatic inventory of the people and machines he still had left with which to fight. Pilots from Fighter Six, who had failed to find the enemy in their first attempt, had landed and repowered their ships, and stood by to liftoff from *Venture* again. But overall, the totals were disheartening low. Still, despite the horrifying losses, the admiral had no regrets about his chosen plan of attack. Going all

out to destroy the enemy carriers was the only way this battle
could possibly be won.

There were still two squadrons of hardlaunchers to be
heard from.

As minutes dragged on into hours, Naguance's carrier captains, his surviving flight officers and enlisted crew members, as
well as the humans assigned to maintenance and support jobs,
tried to work as tirelessly as their machines.

Meanwhile, Admiral Bowman and the entire crew of his
flagship had been fighting with all their strength and skill to
keep the heavily damaged *Lankvil* from blowing up. For a time
it seemed that the damage-control people, working heroically
beside their faithful machines, might turn the trick.

Every few minutes Bowman took time-out, mentally, to
congratulate himself for having turned Naguance loose; there
would be one less thing for the commander of Task Force Sixteen to worry about.

Meanwhile, the disaster might not be as complete as he
had originally feared. *Lankvil,* all her hydrogen power lamps
once more fired up, and other essential emergency repairs completed, at first succeeded in throwing the newest wave of attackers off by taking sharp evasive action, turns and
acceleration that strained the artificial gravity.

Eighty thousand metric tons of steel and composites, pep-
pered with vital specks of other materials, including fragile
human flesh, all locked in a domain of gentle subjective acceleration, by one of the finest fields of artificial gravity ever generated.

"We've taken three direct hits, sir, and there's four nuclear
reactions burning." Self-propelled atomic piles held an hon-
ored place in the berserker arsenal of weapons. Other, more sophisticated boarding machines had to be feared also, but so far
today those murderous gadgets had not been used.

"Keep at it." Robots and armored humans were struggling
in hellish conditions to restore the flight deck to some kind of
functional condition, and laboring just as intently belowdecks,
beset by fire and radiation, in getting the wounded to sick bay,

getting the ship's essential systems all working again, and removing the dead.

"Here the sons of bitches come again!"

Only minutes ago, the crew of *Lankvil* had succeeded in clearing the last wreckage from the essential portions of the flight deck. Only seconds ago the operations officer had proclaimed the ship ready to begin launching the ten fighters that had repowered and were standing by.

Bowman issued orders, keeping his voice calm. The launching proceeded, in the teeth of the renewed berserker attack. Eight fighters made liftoff. The last one to get spaceborne was piloted by Ensign Mike Horn, a stranger to combat who only six days ago had come aboard a carrier for the first time.

Propelled into space, almost fired at the enemy like a missile, Horn wrenched his fighter into a tight left turn, and immediately cut loose with all his weaponry at a berserker hardlauncher that appeared seemingly from nowhere directly in his path. He just had time to see the bandit disintegrate into radii of fragments before he was hit himself by a bone-wrenching jolt. Horn had only a moment in which to suspect the truth—his fighter had been struck by antispacecraft fire from his own carrier—before he had to abandon ship. The pilot drifted briefly in space, surrounded by the flares of battle, before being hauled to relative safety by a Solarian ship of the destroyer class. Less than a quarter of a standard hour had passed since he was cleared for liftoff.

But effort could not beat the berserkers back this time.

This time Bowman happened to be caught momentarily out of his combat couch. Superb gravity or not, he had to pick his armored body up off the deck.

The jolt when the first berserker missile struck was terrifying, to veteran and raw newcomer alike. Bowman himself had a vision of his flagship as a small animal in a predator's jaws. The screens of his combat displays cracked with the vibration, and someone on intercom began muttering a prayer. Regular electrical power had gone out, and vital systems were operating on backup.

The deck had now canted steeply beneath the admiral's feet. *Lankvil*'s artificial gravity developed a list, and gradually over the next few minutes it let go altogether, first in pockets of failure, then throughout the ship.

The second missile strike, only seconds after the first, killed everybody who had been trying to get regular power restored. Now communications, and even emergency lighting, were almost gone. Maneuvering the ship had now become practically impossible.

It was just too much. Too damned much. Bowman was forced, reluctantly, to give the order to abandon ship. He was now down to his suit radio as his only means of communication. But it was vital that he remain in close touch with other ships of both task forces. He was still the admiral, still officially in command of all the Solarian forces now engaged in space. With that in mind, his next duty was clearly to switch his flag to the cruiser-class vessel *Jonjay,* which, as he learned with some difficulty, was standing by.

"I don't see any sense in frying two thousand people just to stick with the ship."

From everywhere below decks a horde of men and women in armor drifted and groped through midnight passageways toward the surface of the ship.

The latest wave of attackers had withdrawn, and at least the ruin they had inflicted would not have to be dealt with while still under fire. *Lankvil*'s fighting small ships now in space were, when possible, signaled to try to reach *Stinger* or *Venture* for recovery.

Getting the admiral and his aides off the doomed ship and aboard a smaller one, while everyone else aboard was also trying to abandon ship, was a tricky business, particularly as no one knew at what moment the berserkers might strike again. Just evacuating people from the jerking, vibrating *Lankvil* was a difficult task. Fighters, hardlaunchers, and undersluggers had zero capacity to carry anyone save their own crews. The few other small craft available were promptly overloaded, and space in the vicinity of the carrier's dying bulk was sprinkled with hundreds of inhabited suits of space armor.

At last the transfer was accomplished safely. But the accompanying difficulty in communication had kept Admiral Bowman out of touch with most of his fleet for eleven long suspenseful minutes.

Meanwhile, Task Force Sixteen, comprising *Stinger* and *Venture,* with their two dozen or so supporting and escort craft, had first launched attack ships at 0838, on the standard day on which the fighting began. *Stinger* had begun at 0700, and *Venture* at 0706.

Halfway to their objective, the flight of six undersluggers passed, at great velocity, a single Void headed directly for Fifty Fifty, evidently trying to catch up with the other machines that had gone raiding there. The humans had another enemy in mind, and it seemed that the berserker did too, for neither party changed course.

Soon afterward, the Solarian squadron came in sight of the berserker fleet, and Tadao could identify two carriers.

Then a flight of Voids, materializing out of a background of thin nebular dust, caught up with the six undersluggers from behind. Berserker weapons blazed.

At the second enemy pass, Smith felt the ship vibrate badly. Damage indicators came on in his helmet display, showing which systems had been shot up and how badly.

Turret Gunner Manning was killed, his symbol on intercom freezing into an NFR symbol.

In the pilot's display, Manning's image (when Smith called it up) was frozen. The machinery was quite capable of sensing that Manning's brain had ceased to function.

The pilot could hope that the spacer's helmet had been shot off his head, leaving him still alive. Stranger things had happened in combat. Everything that was possible, and much that seemed impossible had happened to someone at one time or another.

The underslugger carrying Chief Warrant Officer Tadao, his pilot, and his fellow gunner, was hard hit by berserker fire.

The other gunner was killed. Meanwhile, Tadao and the pilot were wounded.

Only with the greatest difficulty did the pilot succeed in getting his damaged spacecraft back to the atoll from which they had lifted off.

Running swiftly through a checklist, the pilot quickly discovered that additional damage had left the underslugger's armament useless—the doors to the missile bay would no longer open to allow the launching of any of the small missiles under his control.

Part of the flight-control system had also been shot away, and only by discovering that another part, a kind of trimmer force field, could do the same job in a pinch—though very slowly and awkwardly—did the pilot manage to maintain any control at all.

Task Force Sixteen, and what was left of Seventeen with its carrier abandoned, remained in sporadic communication with each other by means of message couriers. They had no reason to believe that the enemy intercepted any of these—and as far as any human knew, the berserker enemy still lacked the sophisticated system, invented by the Solarians, of reading information from a moving courier. So far the luck of battle had shielded Sixteen from any onslaught by berserker small ships, whereas the luckless Seventeen had been located not once but twice.

They were within a light-minute of each other, and so were able to use tight-beam radio waves with some practicality. Also, they could observe each other with fair success.

The only immediately apparent results of the fumbling, groping, sporadic attacks launched up till now took the form of disastrous losses among the squadrons of fighters, and especially of undersluggers, that Naguance and the other task force commander had hurled out in their first attempt to hit the enemy.

Hardlaunchers in general were doing better than under-sluggers. Among the former squadrons, only *Venture*'s had been really badly mauled in their first attack, losing sixteen out of twenty ships.

Enemy fighters, and ship-to-ship weapons fired from the big berserker carriers, were wiping the old bombers and their crews out of the sky.

Events so far had demonstrated that even the newest So-larian fighters were not really a match for the crewless Voids. The fact that a live body had to be protected inside each war-craft was not really the cause of the discrepancy; the inertial forces produced by combat maneuvers could be quite satisfac-torily damped down within any volume as small as that of the cabin or cockpit. The advantage of having a living brain in the control loop slightly more than compensated for the mere fact that the enemy's lifeless machines were somewhat more ma-neuverable. Organic neurons were believed to perform some part of their function outside of any version of spacetime that was accessible to mere machines.

The berserker advantage in hardware was not intrinsically impossible to overcome, but was owed rather to superior design and materials. Comparatively few of the attacking Solarians were even able to get close enough to the berserker carriers to launch their heavy weapons before they were blasted out of the sky. And of the heavy weapons actually launched, a majority missed their targets. The few, particularly torpedoes, that might actually have struck their targets had evidently failed to ex-plode.

The only material advantage gained by the Solarians in these early attacks—and at the time this seemed very slight—was that the enemy formation of carriers and escort machines was thrown temporarily into confusion, and their progress to-ward Fifty Fifty temporarily interrupted. Their timetable had been thrown off. Their defensive fighter craft suffered some losses, and their supplies of power and ammunition were depleted.

Radio messages from various ships in both fighter and bomber squadrons arrived tardily at the two carrier flagships, so late as to be practically useless to Solarian command, sometimes long after the ships themselves would have returned—had they survived.

Some of these messages, borne in the living voices of crew members who were dead before their signals reached the carrier, were exultant, claiming substantial hits on big berserkers. For a while these gave some comfort to the admirals—but they had learned to be suspicious of damage claims.

In fact, the undersluggers' attack on the berserker carriers did zero direct damage to the enemy.

And people on the *Stinger* waited, without result, for even one of the ships in Underslugger Eight to return. On the carrier a live cook had to adjust a robotic chef, a service machine, to keep all of their chicken dinners warm.

At last, after many hours, the robot chef, in the absence of further human orders, saw to it that the plates and utensils were scraped clean, the spoiled food thrown into the recycler.

People on the carrier waited in vain. Berserker fighters, and defensive fire from the big machines, had blasted out of space every unit of Underslugger Squadron Eight.

When Ensign Bright, still drifting in space, in the intervals between attacks, looked out in a certain direction, away from the embattled berserker fleet, the idea struck him, almost like evidence of another physical assault, that light quanta that had been traveling unimpeded for two billion years were now entering his faceplate, dying there indifferently as they delivered their sparks of energy, almost immeasurably tiny, to his eyes and brain.

And for the drifting man, even the battle between death was suddenly remote. Without warning, Bright felt himself momentarily overcome by a perception of ultimate power being displayed before him, of unfathomable purpose, to which the struggles between organic brains and rogue computers were sublimely unimportant.

The moment passed, and he began to breathe again, and feel in terror for his life. At least he wasn't dead yet. The balance of fear and hope swung back again, tipping toward life. His armor was still protecting him beautifully, and if his luck continued to hold, it would continue to do so for several days at least. In survival school he'd been told of people who, wearing standard armor no better than what he had on now, had survived shipless in the void for a standard month or even longer.

Bright waited, breathing and listening, searching the field of the disorganized berserker fleet with his telescope, getting an occasional crash of battle static in his ears.

He was looking out over an extensive graveyard of Solarian small ships. He had lost count of explosions, and he could only keep hoping that all his shipmates and all his colleagues from other carriers weren't dead yet, their bodies and all their obsolescent small ships not yet reduced to little red-hot clouds of gas and dust. The enemy was still essentially unhurt, and he could only pray that he might see at least one more attack.

Every now and then the nearest
billows of nebular mist shifted in Bright's view—they were
clouds of emptiness, distinguishable only by contrast with the
almost absolute vacancy in which they were contained. Sometimes the ghostly cloud shapes changed form with amazing
speed. On a scale unimaginably smaller, the transient smoke of
battle drifted toward dispersion. And now the latter change afforded Bright the chance to see one of the prowling enemy machines quite clearly.

It was the most direct look at the enemy he had been afforded yet. Bright realized with a chill that the berserker could
hardly be a hundred kilometers off. Perhaps much less—the
small telescope made the dark and elongated shape certainly
recognizable as that of a berserker carrier, one of the machines
that Underslugger Eight had destroyed itself in an attempt to
reach. The size must be enormous, much bigger than any of the
Solarian warcraft.

With his scavenged telescope, he thought he might be able

to distinguish details as small as a human body—not that there would be any human bodies there.

He had thought that he was being carried slowly away from the battle, from the berserker fleet, but now, to his horror, he observed certain indications that he was drifting closer.

In his enthrallment by the action, the implications of his improved vision had not dawned on him immediately. That he was increasingly able to distinguish undersluggers from hard-launchers from fighters could only mean that he was drifting considerably closer.

Quickly he used the tiny thrusters on his suit in an effort to stop his drift in the direction of the berserker fleet. He measured out brief bursts of energy, not wanting to completely use up his capacity to maneuver.

Then he tried looking through the telescope again. In many cases he could still not make out the actual shapes of individual small ships and machines, but he could follow trails, and try to deduce what they meant.

Large ship-to-ship missiles left trails that were visible under these conditions. And of course the explosions, which at the height of an attack came thick and fast, like rippling fireworks.

At least the monstrous shape that had come very near him was not headed directly in his direction; instead, it held to a smoothly passing course, from left to right. As far as Bright could tell, the enemy was paying him no attention. It was possible that, if those lenses and logic circuits recorded the presence of his suited body at all, they took it for a drifting corpse. If he could see them, certainly they ought to be able to see him too—except that he was much smaller than they were. It was also possible that he had been seen and then ignored. Those automated tools of glass and metal, those information banks, were doubtless busy looking for other things, urgently on guard against yet another Solarian attack.

Bright could distinguish some of the more distant units of the berserker fleet only by the tracks they left behind them, plowing the thin matter of the Gulf in their fitful maneuvers.

The sharp curvature of the tracks showed that they had been taking evasive action. Whatever formation the berserker fleet had been trying to maintain had certainly been scrambled.

Apart from the malignity of the enemy, and his own helplessness, there was something frightening in the sheer perspective and dimensions of the spectacle in front of Bright. It gave him an eerie feeling, it awoke a twinge of sickness deep in his gut, something deeper even than the sight of death, to realize that some of those far-off, blurry footprints in the deep had to be millions of kilometers long, and he was seeing the vast trails as they had been whole minutes earlier. Each track was a string of wide-spaced dots, the long breaks between dots representing the considerable intervals across which the machines making them had carried their flaring energies outside of normal space.

And in comparison with the local nebulae, the trails themselves were nothing, mere insect marks on the side of a mountain . . .

The machine that had alarmed him was diminishing slowly, getting smaller and smaller with distance, until it disappeared.

One moment it was there, and the next it dropped without warning into flightspace, and Bright even through his armor felt the passage of some kind of wake.

Still Bright had seen no indication that his own squadron's self-sacrificing dash into the jaws of death had so much as scratched any of the enemy machines. Certainly that none of their big ones, the carriers, were seriously damaged. Since escaping from his own wrecked craft, he hadn't seen any explosion worthy of a carrier's destruction, nor had he sighted a new star, of a brightness that would suggest a carrier-sized object slowly melting down to incandescent slag.

The timepiece visible as a dim reflection inside Bright's faceplate informed him that approximately an hour had gone by after the carrier's passing, when yet another small berserker, no bigger than a message courier, going about some unknown search or other task, came puttering very near the place where the shivering human lay willing himself to disappear. The Solarian, suddenly afraid even to breathe, tried unconsciously to diminish himself, to shrink inside his armor.

How near was very near? No way to tell without bouncing a signal off the object, and he was certainly not going to try that. He saw only the track, and not the thing itself. He kept trying to tell himself that the murder machine must be at a safely enormous distance. It might be a thousand kilometers away—much, much farther than the one whose shape he'd earlier identified.

For a time he actually closed his eyes, afraid to look. Dear God, if it comes, let it be quick. But then the immediate peril passed. God was still around, however. No face to be seen, but almost palpable.

Bright still kept trying, uselessly, to determine how much damage had been done to the enemy. Actually, as the disturbances in the thin gas cleared, he couldn't see any evidence that any of the berserkers had been damaged at all.

Slowly the whole scene, including all its components, kept shifting around the castaway. What Bright had earlier assumed to be the Galactic Core now gave hints, as the intervening nearby mist changed its configuration, of turning out to be only a globular cluster, its distance and dimensions shrunken to mere hundreds of light-years instead of many thousands.

Some of the berserker tracks remained clear and sharp in outline, and the idea crossed Bright's mind they might do so for the next million years.

Another frightening phrase came drifting into consciousness: *Mere hundreds of light-years . . .*

The universe was dissolving around him, and he was losing the bearings he had thought he had.

Eventually the drifting man came to the conclusion that his suited body, along with the bit of wreckage to which he intermittently clung, was being swept along with the movements of the great enemy machines. He had been helplessly caught up in the trailing wakes of their force fields, so that he had no choice about maintaining his beautiful observation post.

Gradually, he supposed—he could devoutly hope—he would be left behind by the enemy fleet. His mind rebelled at trying to calculate the odds on rescue, but it ought to be far from impossible.

If only he could communicate what he was seeing to the flagship—but that of course was impossible. At least his present movement ought to be carrying him, though at a hopelessly slow pace, back toward his own fleet, toward the ship from which he'd taken off a few hours ago.

It would have been possible, of course, at any time, to switch on his emergency beacon, in an effort to summon help—but this close to the enemy, there was no chance that anything but a berserker would respond. Again Bright scarcely dared to move his arms or legs, or even breathe. The air seemed to move in his lungs and throat with a loud roaring noise, and surely a machine so close could somehow hear it.

As time passed, Bright kept nervously expecting to see yet another Solarian attack fall upon the fleet before him. Sooner or later, he supposed, there would have to be one. Unless the battle had gone the wrong way, in which case he supposed the enemy would be reorganizing its formations and moving on.

In which case the world as he knew it would pretty well have come to a halt. Things would definitely get a little lonely then . . . but he wasn't going to fight that hopeless battle in his own mind. Not yet. People got picked up in space all the time— by other people, that is.

Evidently his use of his suit's thrusters had succeeded in stopping, perhaps actually reversing, his drift in the general direction of the enemy fleet.

When the next attack came sweeping in, the sight of the flaming streaks and explosions did not reach him until minutes after they'd taken place. He was watching a silent light show, very faint.

He wondered if there might be a perceptible blast wave propagating through the deep-space mist of dust and particles, occasional atoms of stray hydrogen. Probably, he thought, that was a mad idea. But had such a wave existed, a drifter in space might try to determine the distance of the action, of an explosion for example, by the time lapse between the arrival of the flash and of the shock. Not that there would really be a shock, of course; no, nothing that would be even perceptible, except with the finest instruments; the medium was far too rarefied. For a little time he tried to distract himself with mathematics.

Again Bright saw nothing in the way of convincing evidence that the human side had scored any major hits.

He looked and listened and waited. He tried to think of his family, the wife and child at home worrying about him, and then he tried not to think of them.

And somehow, painfully, another hour passed.

Everyone on the bridge of Admiral Naguance's flagship looked haggard.

Their instruments showed them, with a delay and in the distance, how *Lankvil* and one or two other craft of Task Force Seventeen were taking a fearful pounding from squadrons of berserker killing machines.

Naguance had already sent what defensive help he could in that direction. But most of his own fighters had gone as escort with his undersluggers and hardlaunchers, resources intensely concentrated on hitting at the enemy. And not many of those escort fighters had come back.

Now a courier, escaping from that melee, brought them word that the *Lankvil* had been heavily hit—again—and her skipper had ordered abandon ship. Bowman had changed his flag to a smaller vessel, or was in the process of doing so. Naguance with his two carriers was more than ever on his own, against a berserker fleet confirmed to have at least four.

Looking directly out over *Venture*'s flight deck, then alternately surveying that impressive expanse on their displays, Naguance and his staff watched as exhausted survivors of one attack or another came straggling back. Sometimes the returning survivors had to delay their landings until the warriors of another wave went out.

· · ·

These attacks, both land-based and ship-based, were not as well coordinated as they might have been—in fact the whole effort had not been at all well orchestrated, with the fog of war frustrating all attempts to plan and execute methodically. The admirals were throwing punches as fast as they could draw back their fleets' remaining arms and gather remaining attack craft into a fist.

The enemy computers, though successfully defending themselves and their fleet against one harassing wave of attackers after another, must by now have begun to calculate that the secrecy of their communications in space had been for a long time seriously compromised. No other explanation could realistically account for the fact that their battle plans seemed to be known to the badlife in elaborate detail.

Though the berserkers did not realize to what extent their combat codes had been compromised, most of them had prudently been changed just before the battle started. As a matter of routine, the security mode of transmission would be changed again, but only after a certain interval. To attempt to switch codes in the midst of battle might actually increase the risk.

But for the time being, calculation revealed no reason for the berserker side to implement any drastic change of strategy or tactics. Damage from the Solarian assaults so far had been improbably light—very improbably indeed. Combat effectiveness of the badlife was even worse than predicted. The waves of livecrewed ships seemed to be randomly timed and directed. In one fumbling effort after another the badlife were demonstrating their incompetence. Certainly there was no reason to withdraw, and every reason to press on expecting victory.

The fact that the Solarian attack force included some spacecraft known to be based upon the atoll, convinced the berserker admirals that a second strike against the Fifty Fifty outpost was going to be necessary.

The computer commanding the entire berserker task force issued silent orders. At once its auxiliary machines began preparations for a second raid on the atoll. The changeover in type of armaments aboard the fighting machines would necessitate some delay in launching; but by the strict demands of logic it remained the best alternative.

From a kind of sheltered alcove, a comparatively flimsy, temporary construction on the flight deck of one berserker carrier, a pair of human eyes were looking back, through a thin transparent roof, toward the piece of wreckage that had so far successfully sheltered Ensign Bright. Yet the distance was so great that the fragment, and the man that it concealed, remained unseen.

The eyes were those of a man named Roy Laval, who of his own free will had chosen to be aboard a berserker carrier. He was dressed in a kind of parody of a military uniform. The tattered jacket fit him well. Around his waist a simple length of metal chain was held in place, like a belt, with a simple padlock.

The slender figure of a woman emerged from an inner recess, and came to stand beside Laval, in the pose of one who had chosen to be where she was. Her age was indeterminate, her clothing as wretched as the man's, though simpler.

Turning his head, the man in the fragmentary uniform spoke, not to the woman, but to another shape, some three or four meters distant behind a grillwork barrier.

"Soon we may see some more prisoners aboard, Templar. What do you say to that?"

"Soon you may be dead yourself, you goodlife bastard! Dead before you ever see another prisoner!" The Templar's answer rang out loudly, with insane cheeriness. He was imprisoned with only his head visible, sticking out of a cubic block of translucent force field.

Laval ignored the insult; he knew from experience that there was no way he could get at the other. The Teacher wanted its prisoner in the best shape possible before beginning serious interrogation.

But there was nothing to prevent the exchange of words. Laval smiled gently, and there was satisfaction in his voice as he said to the Templar: "You can look forward to some serious interrogation, you know. Have you any idea what that will be like?"

Laval, and the woman who had chosen to share his lot, knew as well as anyone that they were going into battle, for their Teacher had more than once told them so. In the last hour or two they had seen signs of the same futile Solarian attacks that had been observed by Ensign Bright; one or two near misses had come close enough to elate the Templar momentarily, and cause a momentary darkening of Laval's countenance.

But now, from the goodlife point of view, everything looked fine again.

Except that for some reason, the Teacher had almost entirely broken off communication with its most faithful worshiper. He could only hope that when the coming battle was over, it would have more time to spare, and would once more treat him as he felt that he deserved.

"Teacher, how soon will the battle be?"

A long pause.

"Soon." The answering voice came from no visible source, but out of some speaker so hard to find that it might as well have been deliberately hidden.

Lately there were frequent pauses in any conversation in which the machine took part—so many pauses and so long that it could hardly be called a conversation at all. It was as if most of the Teacher's attention was concentrated elsewhere.

Laval had more than once put in a request for reports on how the battle was developing. But these were totally ignored.

Laval sighed, and abandoned any thought of pursuing another subject he had recently started to discuss with Teacher: He had been asking the machine to give him a new name. The man was determined that theirs was going to be a long-term relationship.

Once, days ago, when it had had time to think of other things besides the coming battle, the machine had asked him why he wanted a new name (and perhaps the woman had asked him too) and Laval had said: "The man who was called Roy

Laval is dead. Since coming to live with my Teacher, I am a new person."

When the berserker chose to ignore all such requests, he had thought of making up new names for himself, and submitting them for approval.

But then he realized that the Teacher in its wisdom was perhaps more likely to assign him a number than to choose a word in some Solarian language.

No response. Laval had decided that he was being tested, perhaps to see how good he was at enduring nothingness; whether he was indeed a fit subject and even viceroy of the Kingdom of Death.

A few moderate twists of space-
time distant from the long groping and the deadly violence of
battle in deep space, back on the lovely planet of Uhao, the
hunter named Traskeluk had now equipped himself as well as
he was able for his task. And now he had to decide how he was
going to come to grips with the object of his revenge.

Where in hell was Nifty Gift?

Traskeluk knew perfectly well where Nifty Gift lived, or
had lived, on Uhao, and if Gift wasn't home, it ought to be possible to learn where he had gone. But of course if Trask went
there and asked, the neighbors or barracksmates would be more
likely than not to warn the piece of shit that Trask was looking
for him. Others might well wonder why, but Nifty would know.

Without the help he'd fortunately received, the searcher
might have hitched himself a military ride and traveled as far
as Earth, an effort that would have turned out to be entirely
wasted.

Traskeluk tried to picture himself looking around on

Earth, where he had never been, talking to members of Gift's family. That wasn't something that he would look forward to.

As matters actually stood, the only method of finding the son of a bitch that seemed to have even a moderate likelihood of success would be to hang around near the base, to intercept Nifty when he came back from his leave; but people would be sure to notice Traskeluk if he did that, and people would get suspicious.

The code of Traskeluk's clan demanded that he devote the rest of his life, if necessary, to a quest for vengeance. In his childhood he'd slightly known two distant male relatives who'd carried out serious acts of revenge. But, except in the old stories, Trask had never encountered anyone who'd spent his life at it. Those old stories had been tremendously thrilling once—when Trask himself had been twelve or thirteen years old.

Every day now Traskeluk kept expecting to get a message from his father, or grandfather, or maybe one signed by both, intended to stiffen his resolve. He wouldn't have been surprised to hear that the older men feared he might be weakening. Whether they ever got around to sending a communication or not, he could feel their silent waiting, ready to sit in judgment on the way he handled this situation.

The hours of his convalescent leave were passing, relentlessly adding up into days. The constant burden of his thought was finding Gift, and he still had no good idea how to go about it. Intensely conscious of the weapon now installed in his new technoarm, he said a ritual goodbye to his cousin and his family, and set out determined to track down Spacer Gift.

Grim and taciturn, the young man was driving, over winding roads and through beautiful scenery, the same rented ground car he'd used to reach Maal's lands. He headed back in the general direction of Port Diamond, mainly because he didn't know where else to go, but with a vague idea that there he might be able to get a clue to Gift's whereabouts.

As Traskeluk drove, he carefully considered such clues as he had already been able to discover.

He flexed his left arm, unable to decide whether it felt noticeably heavier than it had before Maal did his work. Trask no longer doubted that the technician knew his business. His new weapon would stay peacefully where it was, inside his artificial hand, for days, months, years if necessary. But he found himself developing a habitual blink, trying unconsciously to rid himself of the small glowing icon.

In the live muscles of his upper left arm, he could still feel the weight of the dead dog twitching. He could still smell hot fur, and dirt, and death.

Yes, what was he going to do now?

He came back to the idea of haunting the entrance to the base at Port Diamond, and the depots from which public transport ran in and out of town, watching for his quarry; Gift would have to come back sooner or later. But Traskeluk would prefer to catch up with his enemy somewhere away from the base. Under those conditions he would have his best chance of doing what must be done, without interference—and possibly without his deed ever being discovered, or himself called to account for it.

In the back of his mind the searcher had a couple of additional contacts, names of people Gift had known and had talked about, who, if Traskeluk could find them, might be able to provide him with more clues regarding Nifty's whereabouts. Trask knew it might well take him a day or so to run through those, and they might well get him nowhere. If only he had the full capabilities of security at his command . . . but of course that was not going to be.

Unless, he thought, he could somehow get Commander R to provide him with additional help. Maybe just a word from her . . . it wouldn't be easy to just phone her, from anywhere outside her own system of secure communications.

The seeker of vengeance looked at himself in a mirror, and pondered what he saw.

He had at first logically assumed that Gift, setting out on his leave, had gone straight to Earth, his place of enlistment and home of record. But there was the evidence from security that the traitor had immediately looped back to Uhao—and Traskeluk had the impression that people in the Hypo security office generally knew what they were doing.

According to the information he'd obtained through security, thanks to a few words from Mother R, Gift had actually started for Earth, as everyone had expected. Had been given a ride on Admiral Bowman's cruiser. But Nifty'd got no farther than a transport hub in low Earth orbit before doubling back.

That, like any other unexplained behavior, had caused at least a twinge of interest in the professionally suspicious minds of security.

But so far that was as far as it had gone. Security thought it reassuring that Nifty had made no secret of his whereabouts. Since coming back to Uhao, might he even have called in to the office, to try to straighten out something about his orders? Maybe apply for an extension on his leave? You needed a good reason for that. And Nifty wouldn't have done it if he had known that Traskeluk had been rescued. In that case he, Gift, would fear being arrested.

And if Gift had called in he'd probably have given Hypo some address or com number on Uhao, someplace where he could be reached with information or amended orders.

You'd think that being on the same planet with your quarry would make a search much easier, but Traskeluk had the feeling it wasn't going to be that way. The bastard might as well be at the other end of the Galaxy. It could very well be a devil of a job, he thought, to locate a man who seemed to have dropped out of sight again. . . .

How did journalists do it? Take that Jory Yokosuka, for instance. How would she go about finding Gift, if she decided she wanted to talk to him again?

She'd given Traskeluk her personal number earlier, when she'd interviewed him in the hospital.

What the hell, it might be worth a try.

On the first attempt Traskeluk made contact with Jory's robot secretary, identified himself and left a message, trying to hint that he had a new story to talk about. Then he sat in his car waiting, hoping, for her to call back.

Damn it all, if he'd only been able somehow to catch up with the Nifty one on the first day of his search, or even the second day; he'd have tried out all the new power in his artificial fingers, and then some. He'd not have fretted about having or not having the correct ritual weapons. He'd simply have strangled the yellow son of a bitch on sight. A kick in the balls would be too good for him.

But now . . .

He wondered what Gift was going to say to him when they first came face-to-face. He still had not figured out the ideal scenario for that encounter.

And there was something else that Traskeluk was trying not to think about. Some things that the traditions of his clan and family ignored as matters too trivial to worry about, were not really trivial. Not in the modern interstellar world. A citizen of the Galaxy couldn't, except maybe in a few places where civilization was at an ebb, strangle a man or blow his head off and then just calmly walk away. Cedric had been out in the big world long enough to realize that the law on Uhao, and elsewhere, took no very liberal view of the demands of honor, whatever the elders of the clan might say or do. The few millions of people who took those elders' word for law counted for very little in the great world. If you killed a man for revenge, and you were found out, such behavior was going to put quite a dent in the rest of your own life too. Cedric felt sure that his grandfather, and probably his father, would love him for it. But most of the rest of the world, including the Space Force, would think he had gone crazy. Probably he'd be able to plead combat stress. Still, the best he could hope for if he was caught would be to be locked away for a long, long time.

His car phone chimed: Jory Yokosuka, returning his call.

"What's up, spacer?" The journalist sounded brisk and cheery.

"I was wondering how you are at finding people."

"Usually pretty good. Who are you trying to find?"

He told her, and there was no surprise in her voice; she made no comment, only asked, "Where are you now?"

She explained that she was on her way to her boss's house. Jay Nash had rented a big, antique-style home, about an hour's drive from Port Diamond. Nash had given her a key to a locked room in the house, where he kept some of his most valuable tools and materials.

"He wants me to bring him back some things he needs, for this job—have you heard anything about this documentary we're making? We just got back from Fifty Fifty—that was quite a show."

"I bet it was."

"Anyway, we're down to the cutting and editing, putting in an introduction and the touch-ups, and we're trying to get the damn thing finished. Also he was wounded, in the shoulder, and some nerves were damaged, and now that's giving him more trouble than he thought it would at first. He has to stay where he can get treatment."

Traskeluk and Jory made arrangements to meet, at a point only a few kilometers from Nash's house. Trask parked his car and got into hers; her errand was quite important, she said, and couldn't be delayed. "But meanwhile we can talk about finding Spacer Gift for you."

On seeing the glum-looking spacer, now in civilian clothes, Jory remembered more details of their brief previous encounter.

Trask hadn't been wearing his uniform since he'd started out on leave. This was private business, not a Space Force matter.

"And what will you do with Spacer Gift when you find him?" she asked, as friend to friend, as she got the car moving again.

The lady didn't seem at all surprised.

"Say hello to an old shipmate." Trask went on. "Shake hands with him. Left hands."

"You once told me you were going to give him some kind of a present."

Traskeluk appeared not to have heard that.

Jory pressed on: "Come on. You don't track someone halfway across the homeworlds just to say hello."

Traskeluk hesitated, then replied: "There's something I want to—talk to him about."

"Something to do with the way your ship was wrecked?" No reply.

"That's odd, I am too. Looking for him, I mean. But maybe it's not so odd. From the first time I met him, I've had the feeling that he could tell me more of a story than he did."

The journalist was intrigued; there seemed to be a bigger story here, concerning these people from the lost scout ship, than anyone else in her profession had yet realized. And she found herself being personally intrigued by this strong, intelligent man with the smoldering anger he was trying to keep hidden.

Anger, certainly. And something else, less easy to identify.

Jory remembered the coincidence of the two shipmates having suffered almost the same injury. "How's your arm?"

"Fine." Traskeluk admitted he sometimes brooded on the fact that Gift too had been fitted with a prosthesis, also a left hand and forearm. Trying to extract some deeper meaning from what could hardly be anything more than a coincidence.

Traskeluk, like many billions of other people on many worlds, had heard of Jay Nash, and had enjoyed some of the producer's shows. So had Gift, Traskeluk supposed. But he couldn't remember the rotten apple of the crew ever mentioning Nash's name in conversation, or claiming any relationship with celebrities. "And I think he would have done so, if he could. He would have made a big thing of it. He's that type."

"What type is that, exactly?"

"Basically selfish."

Jory said to him: "I get the impression that you don't much like your shipmate."

Traskeluk didn't say anything.

"Did he do something he shouldn't have done? When you two were aboard ship together?"

The tough-looking man looked at her for a while. Then he asked, "You want a good story? A big story?"

"Of course I do."

"Then help me find him."

Jory, with a lot of other things to keep her busy, had still been wondering what Traskeluk was going to do when he got out of the hospital, whether he was really going to look up Nifty Gift. Maybe she'd even heard that Trask was somewhere on Uhao, and that he'd been asking after his old shipmate, asking with an air of urgency. Her journalist's curiosity, never satisfied with the story of the mysterious scout ship or whatever it had been, had been tweaked anew.

Jory had no security tracers available to help her locate people when she wanted them, but she had her own methods, and she was good at using them. Some of them worked on the people who did have physical tracers to employ. And Traskeluk was not making any effort to conceal his own whereabouts.

Jory and Trask talked about Nash's injuries too.

"So," she concluded, "you're all three in pretty good shape, then. Lucky none of you wound up in a marcus box." That was the fate of folk whose organic bodies were so severely damaged as to lose the ability to effectively support an organic brain. More often than not, near-total regrowth and reconstruction was possible, but such a project took years. Meanwhile, the surrogate of metal and composites, or marcus box, was never made in anthropomorphic form. A few people who had them came to prefer them over nature's way.

"Yeah," said Traskeluk. "There are worse things than marcus boxes too. Like being dead, or being goodlife."

"Mmm-hmm." She nodded at him thoughtfully. "You know, it always strikes me as just a little odd that folk I've known with real heavy handicaps usually aren't that bitter. In my experience, most people who have such very real practical problems don't take up the game of playing goodlife. And that's what it is for most of those who do—a game. Many start to play it as a way of getting back at their parents—for God knows what—for whatever bad things, as they see it, their parents once did to them."

"Yeah. I guess it must work that way."

Continuing her efforts to draw him out, Jory told Traskeluk she had heard of his home planet. And she had always wanted to talk to a member of his kind of clan or family, or simply to someone from his planet.

"It's a great long way from here."

"It certainly is. A great many of your fellow clansmen join the Templars, I've heard."

"A lot of our young men do, yes."

"Why did you join the Space Force?"

For one thing, I wanted to get away from home. He didn't speak those words aloud, but as he thought them he knew that they were true.

"But no Templars for you, hey?"

"No. They seem too . . . " He made a vague gesture.

"Fanatical?"

"That's about it." Traskeluk nodded.

Jory said: "Let me tell you something I've heard. I'd like your reaction."

"Shoot."

"It has to do with your people, and it says that among them, certain weapons and methods are traditionally specified for the settlement of personal grievances. I wonder how much truth there is in that."

The car was driving itself, and she could take her eyes from the road to give him a long inquiring look.

"There's some truth in it. But of course the main idea is not to let any serious wrong go unavenged—whatever kind of weapons you have to use. The one-shot firearm is a favorite. Has been, for centuries, I guess."

"Very interesting. Say, hypothetically, you were engaged in one of these feuds, or—what would be your weapon of choice?"

"That would all depend," said Traskeluk. He was thinking that he could give this woman a good story, all right. See, lady, what I've got hidden in my new arm here is not a gun in the usual sense. Rather a whole set of hardware, including some things that turn my hand into a motorized claw or meat grinder. A tiny battery for power supply that will give my fingers a berserker's strength, and maybe enough heat to melt through steel, for just a handful of seconds. And then there is what my cousin, who knows all about this stuff, calls the shotgun.

See, by turning my gaze to the proper section of my icon, which is a little glowing skull that I can always see, and controlling my thought-images, I can activate any or all of these destructive powers. Not too hard a trick for a spacer to learn, not for someone who's had some years of practice in controlling ships' systems in much the same way.

It also seems appropriate, don't you think, that the limb I lost by Nifty's treachery is the same one I'm going to use to pull his guts out?

In response to Jory's questions, Trask tried to explain the world in which his family lived. Even the most traditional clan members admitted that in special situations, including wartime, almost any kind of weapon would do. The code was flexible enough to allow for that. In a real emergency, any means, however untraditional, could be used to punish treachery. The worst thing would be simply to allow it to go unpunished.

The journalist in Jory wanted to ask him if he had ever been involved personally in any such death feud. But the expression on the young man's face suggested that the answer might not be one she wanted to hear, and she moved on to say something else.

Traskeluk and Jory reached Nash's house around noon, within a few hours of their first phone conversation.

Approaching the front door down a curving walk, they could hear from around back the waterfall sound of what was doubtless a very fancy swimming pool.

The house sensed their approach to the front door, and the butler met them there. Only a machine. Two machines, because in the nearest room an active holostage was playing, showing a news program.

"Mr. Nash sent me," Jory informed the butler.

There was a noticeable pause before it said: "Yes, madam."

Sometimes, thought Traskeluk, the fancier they make these machines, the less reliably they work.

In its right hand the metal butler supported a tray, near shoulder level, as if it might be about to serve a round of drinks. But at the moment there was no burden at all upon the tray that was being held in such a perfectly level plane. Trask assumed that somewhere in the thing's programming a fairly high priority must have been assigned to the act of carrying a tray about.

Why, Trask wondered, would a robot watch news programs on a holostage?

One reason might be that someone had commissioned it to find out something that was going to be mentioned on the news. But as a rule it was perfectly easy to call up any kind of news program for yourself, wherever you were.

He let the mystery drop for the moment.

On impulse, Trask took a chance and asked the robot if a man called Spacer Sebastian Gift had been here.

Burymore protested demurely that his programming did not allow him to record personal conversations unless instructed. Therefore, he had no record of the names of people who had been here in the past.

"Could you give me their personal descriptions, then?"

"I regret, sir, that is not possible in the absence of my employer, whose approval would be necessary."

The gist of what the robot was willing to admit on the subject appeared to be that three people, one of whom might have been Nifty Gift, had indeed departed this house days ago—or possibly only hours ago. It seemed impossible to learn from Burymore whether Gift was expected back, or when.

"Then whenever this recent departure was, exactly," Jory summarized, "it involved three people. A fourth stayed behind." This was not a question, and so it was not answered. She pursued. "Where is this person who stayed behind?"

The robot seemed to be thinking the question over.

Traskeluk prodded it. "You're not counting yourself as a person, I hope."

For once the reply was prompt and definite. "No, I am not."

Jory's turn again. "Well then, where is he, or she? Is there anyone here or not?"

"Now you are here, ma'am. And you, sir. Otherwise not."

The two humans exchanged looks, signaling their mutual willingness to give up.

The butler stood back and with a sweeping gesture admitted the pair of visitors to the house. Well, a household robot wearing human clothing. Trask had lately been developing some definite feelings about machinery, and in his opinion it was just too much to dress up a machine like some kind of goddamned doll. The robot had, of course, a human shape to fit those clothes, and it also walked on two legs like a Solarian human. Slightly taller than the average man, so that the dark lens-eyes were noticeably angled downward at Traskeluk when he stood before it. The facial features were only suggested by curved metal of a neutral color. They were immobile, except for the eyes, where recessed lenses could be seen to move. Straight nose, gently smiling lips that did not change their position when the well-modulated voice came out.

After it had allowed the couple in, and had seen to it that the front door was closed again, it turned and walked away down a broad and sunny hall, leaving the visitors uncertain as to whether they were presently going to be welcomed by a human being or not. From the back, and from a distance, you might easily be fooled into thinking the thing in human garments was a man.

Except that it had no hair; the top of its head had been sculpted into a smooth curve of dark brown, suggesting hair of medium length combed neatly back.

But the most immediately noticeable thing about the almost humanoid machine, when viewed from the back, was that it wore an enigmatic, hand-lettered placard: MY NAME IS BURYMORE

Traskeluk stared. *Burymore?*

Jory frowned in concentration, ferocious but brief. Evidently as intrigued as Trask was, she called after the machine. "Wait a moment. Shouldn't your name be spelled 'B-a-r-r-y-m-o-r-e'? With an *a* and two *r's*? At least I seem to recall that there was once a famous fictional butler of that name."

And Jory was trying to remember if her boss had said anything about having acquired a robot butler.

The tall shape stopped walking and turned back when it was called, but then stood silent and motionless. Jory had to repeat her question about its name.

In its mellow voice the robot said: "My name was given me by my owner, madam, during his last period of residence here . . . some days ago. I had no part in its selection. Will there be anything else?"

It sounded to Jory like the butler, or maybe the whole house, was having some kind of system trouble. Nash had told her that sometimes he had trouble getting a message through to the house. After exchanging a glance with Traskeluk she turned back to the machine and repeated an earlier question. "Are there any people here now? Besides this gentleman and me?" She spoke slowly and distinctly, as if to a child.

"Not at the moment, madam." And Burymore turned away, as if to go about some household business.

Jory shrugged, exchanged a glance with Traskeluk, and said: "Well. Why don't you wait here? Or in the next room; it looks like a library. I don't want to have to report to my boss that I brought a stranger into his inner sanctum. It shouldn't take me more than a minute to pick up the items he sent me for."

Traskeluk nodded. Feeling ready to be distracted, he went wandering into the next room, hearing behind him Jory's steps go crisply down the hall. This house indeed looked like an interesting place to wander in. From time to time he shot a glance into the adjoining rooms. The butler was hovering vaguely in the background, dusting and rearranging things, but meanwhile giving the impression that it was keeping an eye on him. Well, that would have been natural behavior for a human attendant, with a stranger in the house.

Jory had no trouble locating the room Nash had described to her as his inner sanctuary, and the key he had given her promptly let her in. It was a sunny chamber, whose comfortable furnishings included a narrow bed, now neatly made up, various tables and chairs and three holostages, two of which seemed to be intended for technical work, such as graphics editing. Against one wall stood a small, manually operated stove, cabinets, a sink, and a refrigerator, the latter about half the size of the usual kitchen appliance. Everything was neatly in order, except for one or two minor oddities. First, a set of small plastic grillwork shelves that looked like they would probably fit inside the refrigerator were neatly arranged on the little stove's flat cook top. That would seem like one place you wouldn't want to store them. Also a faint, unpleasant odor hung in the air, as if the refrigerator might not be working properly, and something inside had begun to spoil.

Willing to do what she could to be helpful, Jory reached for the handle of the refrigerator door and pulled it open. The bad smell gushed out powerfully, but she hardly noticed.

The woman Jory was looking at, whoever she might be, had obviously been dead for days.

What kind of household robot concealed the presence of a human body, violently done to death? Either an extremely, incredibly defective robot. Or else . . .

Even with the shelves all taken out, the woman's corpse, clad in a simple brown dress, was a tight fit. It looked like a good many of her bones had probably been broken to get her in there. Arms and legs were folded into improbable positions. Startled-looking brown eyes stared dully somewhere past Jory's waist. In life she had been young, and probably attractive. Now . . .

Letting go of the open door, Jory backed up a step. She could hear herself making little whining noises, as if experimenting to see how a full-throated scream would go over . . . then she mastered the impulse, and pushed the door shut silently. Gagging from the smell, she turned away.

Certainly Jay Nash hadn't killed a woman and put her there. Certainly Nash wouldn't have then gone off and forgotten all about it. So, either the man who had been engaged as caretaker was a murderer, or . . .

The thought occurred to Jory that maybe the male human caretaker had been mangled too, his lifeless body crammed into some other improvised hiding place. In the face of that second possibility, it wasn't going to do to run out of the room screaming, mindlessly raising a general alarm.

She had to remind herself forcibly to actually find and pick up the material Nash had sent her to find. Then, struck by a thought, she looked at the wall opposite that where the refrigerator stood holding its ghastly burden.

A pair of handguns were mounted as a decoration on that wall. Maybe they were fakes, props from some holostage drama, and in any case their power charges had probably been removed. But she could think of nothing else to try.

Acting almost without conscious thought, she took one of the pistols down from its support, and slid it into her briefcase along with the things Nash had sent her to get.

Then she walked firmly to the door, and stepped out into the hall, knowing that she was going to scream uncontrollably if the robot should be waiting for her there.

But there was only the peaceful-looking, almost silent house. Somewhere in the background an antique clock, or its simulacrum, was ticking audibly. Jory remembered to lock the door of the private room behind her.

She was thinking that if Burymore was some kind of a berserker, as he evidently was, he couldn't be a normal one. Not the kind of machine people went out into space to fight. Because he was certainly also capable of functioning as a butler. A kind of specialized device, then, an infiltrator and observer, rather than an all-out killer; physically stronger than almost any human, but almost certainly lacking the physical power, and the sharpness of senses that you would expect from one of *them*.

Now it was vitally important that she somehow let Trask know what was going on, or at least convey to him that they had to get out of here as quickly as they could, without letting the robot know what she had found.

"**T**rask. Let's get out of here."

He turned to see her standing in the doorway of the library, clutching her briefcase, looking pale and strange.

He put the book he had been looking at—all paper, no electronics—back into its place on the shelf. "What's up? You look like you've seen a ghost."

"I want to show you this," she said in a tight voice, and reached into her briefcase. Trask had barely time to register that the object she pulled out was a gun, and that it was aimed at Burymore, before the butler, moving with the lethal speed of a sprung trap, struck out at Jory's hand holding the weapon.

The robot had been watching Jory since she came out of the locked room—it hadn't realized that she might have a key, and it couldn't compute with certainty whether she had discovered the dead body or not.

Thus the brawl began, with a crash and a scream, right near the middle of the house.

The pistol fired when the robot struck and grabbed at it. The sharply focused blast damaged one of Burymore's legs, so that it went down on one knee, and had to hobble when it regained its footing.

But despite that, Burymore could move with frightening speed. Jory was knocked down and slightly dazed, the pistol pulled from her grip before she could try to fire it again.

Trask stood for a long moment paralyzed with astonishment, a delay that was almost fatal, since it gave his enemy a chance to regain its footing. Then Traskeluk and the robot both went scrambling after the pistol, which had gone skittering across the floor and under an overstuffed chair. The machine hurled the chair aside and came up with the weapon, and fired it at Traskeluk from three meters away. But the old charge was now almost exhausted. The blast seared Trask's shirt, and scorched his skin beneath, but left him standing.

He turned and ran for the outside, working on a half-formed plan of distracting the thing, drawing away from Jory so she could call for help. He leapt for an open window, his flying body tearing and splintering its way through one of the antique insect-repelling screens.

He could hear the thing coming after him, crabbing on three limbs, then hobbling erect on its damaged leg. Surely it must be moving almost as fast as it could have moved before being shot. Trask threw a look back over his shoulder and saw the smile, then dashed on faster than ever, instinctively dodging around bushes and rolling under lawn furniture, trying to get away from it.

There beyond the rear of the house was the swimming pool, complete with a roaring, gushing water slide, and his mind seized on the possibility that getting there would offer him some kind of chance. The robot, especially in its damaged condition, might not cope at all well with deep water.

Feet skidding on short mutant poolside turf, Trask dodged halfway around the kidney-shaped pool, then dove into deep water when he saw that he was still not going to be able to outrun the disabled killer. The smiling thing kept coming, and it was gaining ground.

The poolside area, with its high surrounding wall, formed a pretty effective trap for Solarian humans.

And even while it chased him, it was calling up reserves.

Trask surfaced in the middle of the pool, treading deep water, looking to see what was going to happen next. Burymore stood beside the water slide and smiled at him; it wasn't going to plunge in and try to swim.

Here came three automated serving machines, short flat-topped legless things on rollers, too innately stupid to know or care whether they were being commanded to hurt humans or not. But they were all under control of the berserker, in a system that must work great when you were giving a huge party. The servers, moving briskly and silently, took up their positions at poolside, spreading out along the water's edge on the side away from Burymore. What they would endeavor to do to Trask when he came out he didn't know—maybe try their armless best to push him back and drown him. At the very least it seemed certain they could delay him until the hobbling killer could make way around the edge of the pool and catch up with him again.

And there were other possibilities—as if it had read Trask's mind, the butler abruptly sent one of the servers rolling smoothly forward, splashing deliberately into the pool. If the idea was to short out the machine internally and electrocute the swimming man, it failed miserably. If Burymore's hope had been to get at Trask from under water, that succeeded no better. Looking down, the man could see it sitting inertly on the blue bottom.

The servers' anthropomorphic leader, its butler's livery now somewhat torn and in disarray, stood smiling at him from beside the water slide, and thought things over. The two remaining servers would be adequate to keep him in the pool.

Now Burymore, while evidently trying to decide on a next move, produced a small round metal tray from somewhere, and stood once more with tray in hand, balancing it at a perfect level.

Optelectronic insanity, thought Trask, treading water. When sophisticated software breaks down, the results are likely to be bizarre.

Some twenty-five meters to Traskeluk's right, and Burymore's left, one of the side doors of the house opened, and Jory came tottering out. His heart rose at the sight; at least she wasn't dead or crippled. The butler tried hurling his tray at her, from clear across the pool, but the metal disk sailed in an airfoil curve and only smashed a window.

The woman, battered and still somewhat dazed, her hair in disarray, was leaning against a table on the terrace, and hardly bothered to dodge the missile.

In a loud voice she called out: "Trask, the phones are all dead! I can't get a message out!"

"Get out yourself." Traskeluk was very much aware of the maximum effective range of the weapon he had built into his artificial limb. And also aware of the fact that he had only one shot, plus a few seconds each of the weapon's other capabilities. He dared not squander his only chance.

Jory ignored his order. "Trask, there's a dead woman in the house. Her body's jammed into a cooler. That's how I knew."

He nodded his head in answer, saving breath while he continued to tread water. All right. He knew that he had to actually come to grips with the robot to be effective—but he had no way to communicate that necessity to Jory.

Was time on the robot's side, or on the side of the living? For all Trask knew, days might pass before another human showed up at the front door.

Jory's head had turned. Something eastward along the side of the house had caught her attention. Trask followed her gaze. There, under a little canopy to keep off rain, was a woodpile, of real wood for the real fireplaces inside. And there . . .

She pushed her bruised body away from the table. She was hobbling her way over to the woodpile, going to get the ax, whose handle Trask could barely see, sticking up on the far side of the pile.

And the robot had now seen what human eyes had seen, and was scuttling quickly to cut her off from the weapon.

Now or never, thought Traskeluk, and splashed to the pool's edge at the right spot to intercept Burymore. The butler was having to come the long way around.

Jory, keeping an eye on action around the pool, naturally thought that what he was doing would be suicidal, and screamed warnings to him to get back.

Now the fight had really started, and pulling himself up out of the pool was easy. This was the encounter Trask had been spoiling for, and he was going to stay and see it through. He had no breath for singing left, but he could hear the words of an old battle song come roaring through his mind.

One of the serving machines darted forward at him, fast as it could dart, and Traskeluk faked one way and dodged another. The robot on its party-serving wheels shot past him and went splashing into the pool to join its colleague.

The remaining simple server was hovering in the background, and he couldn't wait to see what tactic it might try. Instead, he went right for the butler in a football tackle, and caught the hard repulsive body squarely. Its bad leg failed and man and machine went down together, both of its arms pounding on his back like logs.

The remaining serving machine rolled closer, spraying something hot. Not quite boiling liquid, or soup or coffee, scorched and spattered at the back of its live opponent, heat steaming through his clothes to strike at skin already burnt by the spent pistol. That seemed to be the best, or the worst, that a simple server had. In a minute, thought Trask, as he tried to get his own hidden weapon into position, in a minute, if I live that long, it will be spitting knives at me, and trying to generate poison gas.

Then he heard a scream, an unpracticed battle cry in a high feminine voice, and from the corner of his eye he caught a glimpse of Jory, assailing the server with her ax.

Meanwhile Trask was still being clubbed with baseball bats, or so it felt. He tried to roll back poolward, thinking that if he could get Burymore into the water the berserker might drown him, but once it was on the bottom it would not be getting out. Burymore must have been calculating the same thing, for its resistless mechanical power rolled Trask the other way instead.

Traskeluk's mind was racing even as his body struggled. The machine was physically stronger than he, in every part but the left arm, and maybe even there. But not as strong as, for example, one of their boarding machines, like maybe the one he'd rifled down in space. Some functions of the device were only moderately powered, as they would have been in an ordinary robot butler.

That gave him the idea that he might be able to break one of Burymore's arms if he could get the proper grip. A hold that would let him use the super power in his left fingers and forearm. But while he was breaking one arm, what might it be doing to him with the other? It would not feel pain.

And now, of all the goddamned luck, his left arm was pinned down, under the weight of both their bodies; and the robot, with the one hand it had free, was knotting up the collar of his shirt. And that was how it was going to strangle him— he fought its left arm with his fleshly right, but he might as well have tried to lift the nearby house and throw it at his foe . . . the world was turning red and fading on him . . .

The ax must have hit squarely on Burymore's back, for Trask, his senses failing, could feel the jar of impact through the robot's body. He heard a little sobbing breath that was not quite his own and must have come from Jory.

Her blow with the ax against the metal torso had not quite carried crippling force, but maybe it had made a hole—anyway, it was more than Burymore wanted to experience again. The robot twisted half away from Traskeluk, and shot out one hand to seize the woman by an ankle. Jory let out a scream and fell.

And the berserker chose this moment to begin babbling sweet words, in a leisurely voice, through speakers that had never been inconvenienced by the need to draw breath. Philosophical-sounding arguments culled from overheard human conversations. Words, no doubt, that had proven effective in arguments with certain other humans.

Jory, in desperation, somehow broke free, leaving one shoe and patches of ankle skin in the robot's grasp.

Between great panting breaths she yelled to Trask, "Another pistol—in the house—I'll get it!"

And even as she yelled, she scrambled and staggered to her feet and ran.

Burymore, scuttling like a giant crab, pursued her back into the house.

Trask, lungs gulping air in a desperate effort to make up a deficit, grabbed up the ax and came after the killer.

· · ·

The berserker still had a few more serving machines that it could call into action and hurl at its badlife enemies. Trask met them, fortunately one at a time, on his way to the house, and beat them off with the ax.

Then he dashed into the house, through the French windows where Jory had gone in—and paused to see what she and the robot were doing.

In front of Traskeluk as he looked about him lay available a whole range of tools or other objects related to Nash's success as a fabricator of dreams and fiction—awards, recorders, trophies, cartridges, a broken chair used in a famous fight scene, images of actors frozen in crystal cubes. Nothing in all of this a damned bit of use just now.

The man took two steps forward—

—and the robot shot out, in a blindsiding ambush, to grapple with him again. The ax went flying, somewhere out of reach.

When Jory appeared again, a frantic figure in the background, Trask could see that her clothes, like his own and Burymore's, were torn in several places. So were the humans' skins.

The fight swirled into a large room laid out as a theater.

The entry of moving bodies made the lights spring on, and a curtain roll across the windows, screening away the outside world.

An elegant male voice came booming into life; the house had sensed that people had entered the theater.

"Welcome, ladies and gentlemen. I have something special for you this Thursday evening." And the holostage lit up, with the illusion of curtains of fine shimmering fabric.

And now, down on the wood floor at the foot of the stage, the butler had Traskeluk once again in a death grip, though the butler was by now down to one usable arm; one of Burymore's arms was never going to kill anyone anymore, because the ax, antique-styled and double-bitted, was back in Jory's hands, and the arm had been left dangling by a savage blow.

The heavy blade came crashing back. Now a good part of Burymore's smiling, deader-than-a-corpse face had been wiped from the front of its steel skull. But the mouth still smiled, one lens-eye still beamed at the butler's current victim.

The butler's good arm released Trask momentarily, lashed out with machine-tool speed and precision, parrying the wooden ax handle as that weapon swung again. And now the ax lay broken, and Jory staggered back.

The expression on the remaining portion of Burymore's face had not altered in the slightest.

Jory's head was reeling, her arms and legs unsteady, and she tottered around the theater, under the loud voices and the music from the stage, trying to get in position to use the ax again. The handle, broken short, made a great handicap. She tried once more to bury its keen edge in the robot's back, but the heavy blade only scraped ineffectively off steel and slid away, tearing expensive black fabric.

Now she was afraid of hitting the struggling man if she swung again.

But she could see that Trask was getting killed, and in desperation she tried, and came very close to hitting her partner, and did the robot only minor damage. But yet once more the robot's grip was jarred a trifle loose.

Traskeluk could hear only the roaring of the blood in his own head. The sound of his own breath had stopped while the world once more turned red before him. Jory was somewhere nearby, groaning. It was the point of the butler's shoulder, or the butler's knee, that now crushed Trask's throat and was cutting off his breath. Both of his arms were now pinned behind his own back. Both wrists caught in the crushing grip of the butler's remaining hand.

It was eerie that stress produced no sound at all within the robot body.

Burymore meanwhile was groping with his half-dangling, erratically jerking hand, trying to find some other weapon with which to finish its male badlife opponent off more quickly. The robot had not forgotten Jory, either.

She wouldn't let it. She dragged at Burymore, then beat on the side of the butler's head with the heavy end of the now broken-handled ax, imperiling its remaining eye, so that the machine had to shift again to get rid of the distraction.

Traskeluk's left arm came free at last. His eyes and mind sought out his built-in icon and the practiced sequence of mental images.

Cedric still had no certainty of where the butler's brain was housed, but he could wait no longer to find out. This game wasn't going to last till the next hand.

Looking at the icon in the upper-left corner of his visual field . . . hooking it with his gaze, or with a blink, and dragging it into place. Thinking the proper thought. . . .

The fingers of his left hand abruptly twitched and jerked with monstrous power. Each fingertip became a lance of heat and radiation. The thin steel casing of the butler's belly and chest caved in under the assault; the unbreathing optelectronic vitals were coming into Traskeluk's grasp.

He used his icon for the last time.

Burymore convulsed with deadly violence. It seemed that the ghost of a mad dog leaped at Trask. . . .

Old Space Force training with the icon had taken over. Traskeluk used the various powers of his arm in sequence, as best he could. Miniature accumulators exhausted themselves in detonating surges. Tiny sparks and molten droplets splashed and flew, raising puffs of smoke from what was left of the man's clothing, and the machine's. . . .

With the blast of a small destructor charge, meant to wipe out whatever secrets its brain still held, the berserker died. The artificial hand and wrist that were now buried in the enemy's torso took the brunt of the explosion's force. . . .

The man's body was flung back, by the front plate of the butler's chest, striking him with stunning force. Trask's left forearm was a jagged stump, composite surrogates of metal bone and bloodless flesh.

Jory had slumped down, crying and gasping but totally alive, in front of the first semicircle of comfortable seats.

The butler was right up on stage. It lay there smiling at its conqueror, as if offering hearty, sportsmanlike congratulations

. . . but its body was ripped open, and not even Burymore's eye-lenses were moving now.

Lights and action. Towering above the fallen robot came an image of Morrison Duke, the most famous of the heroic stars in Nash's dramas, striding broad-shouldered and costumed, glaring at some invisible offstage opponent, and muttering threatening words.

Gavrilov, crouching stoop-shouldered in the small ship's single pilot's chair, had been closely watching the controls for the past two hours. And for most of that time Gift, standing a couple of strides away, had been curiously watching him. Flower, meanwhile, had consciously lost herself in some kind of computer game, at the other end of the compartment.

While Gift was watching the yacht had slowed, popped into normal space, minijumped again, then gone through the process once or twice more. And all with no kind of solar system anywhere in shouting distance. Some kind of rendezvous, then. . . .

Gift even looked out several times through a cleared port, during one of their long intervals in normal space. Hopeless. Like getting a glimpse of ocean, and trying to tell from that where you were on a planet's surface.

A rendezvous, all right, because the signals indicated that a docking was coming up.

Gift didn't get this at all, but by now he had just about given up asking questions.

There came a muffled thud, and the faint sounds of machinery.

Nifty looked forward to meeting whoever was about to come aboard; they could be as crazy as Gavrilov if they wanted to, just so they were a little more willing to pass out information. He was going to demand to be told. . . .

And then the airlock opened, and he knew that for the rest of his life he was never going to demand anything again.

Because he had just seen that his life was over. Because the new pilot had come aboard. A figure stepping out of the worst of Nifty's nightmares came walking out of the airlock, focusing on him with its lenses, taking little notice of the other two people who had frozen in their positions. It was the size of a man and very roughly, the same shape. Two metal arms, ending in five-digit metal grippers. Two metal legs supported a body that had never known either blood or breath.

There was a long moment in which Gift would have used his deathdream—if he'd still had one. Involuntarily his gaze turned away from the shape in the hatchway, turned upward and inward, looking for the deathdream icon, which was no longer there.

Flower was startled at first, when the berserker entered, then joyfully excited. She came quickly to Gift's side where he stood quivering against a bulkhead, and clung to his arm, murmuring. He understood she was trying to reassure him, though his terror would not let him understand a word of what she said.

Gavrilov was not surprised at all by what had come into his ship. It was what he had been expecting, no better and no worse.

Fear and pride together showed in his voice and manner, as he spoke to it.

"I am here," he told the thing. "As I promised my Teacher. And I have brought you an important prisoner."

The invader ignored the remark. "Move quickly," it told

them all, speaking in the standard language, sounding the deadly, squeaking berserker voice tones. "Discussion later. A battle is impending."

Meanwhile, at no great distance from the newly boarded ship, the man who wanted to be called the Viceroy, and the quiet woman who had chosen to humor him, still huddled in their odd shambles of quarters aboard a berserker carrier. They too had been told by their Teacher that a battle was impending. The man's eager requests for more information had been ignored.

In recent days Laval had been trying his best to garb himself in an impressive uniform, but very little in the way of spare clothing was available. The Teacher had offered no help, or even encouragement, and without help not much could be done. Part of his uniform was a length of chain he wore looped beltlike around his waist, and padlocked.

The Templar prisoner was still present—his unrepentant head just visible above the top surface of a force-field cube, with the appearance of shimmering gray gelatin. Now and then a machine came by, to spoon-feed the helpless man with food or water.

Roy Laval had been aboard this machine for a long time now. So long that his dark hair and beard had grown long, and he had lost track of the duration of his stay.

Laval was gaunt and hollow-eyed, of indeterminate age. He bore a vague physical resemblance to Nifty Gift, whom he had never met.

Laval and his companion had just taken notice of the approach of a small ship, but they had no idea whether any life units, either goodlife or prisoners, might be on it.

While the two of them were talking about this, the Templar prisoner, visible only as a talking head atop his force-field block at a little distance from the others, kept rudely interrupting. "Hey, clowns! What makes you think that any berserker has any reason to tell you anything, except maybe sit down and shut up, and follow orders. Why should it tell you about the way it's going to do business?"

Laval cast over a scornful, almost pitying glance, but said nothing to the Templar. The woman turned her head and looked at him sadly, as she looked at everything.

Then Laval resumed a kind of lecture he had been delivering, to his only disciple. "If the Teachers in their wisdom chose to create machines that could pass, in casual inspection, for Solarian slime units, we would have no role to play at all. But the truth is that they wish us to share with them, in the creation of a new universe." Laval's face took on an exalted expression as he spoke.

The nameless woman nodded silently. From her blank expression it was hard to tell whether she had really understood a word or not.

"I'd like to see your new universe," the Templar said, and cackled.

"You never will, life slime. You will be dead before it comes about."

"Lucky me! Hey, how do you know," the Templar cried, from his impregnable sanctuary, his perfect prison, "that I am not just such a machine, sent here to test your loyalty?"

"You are only a crazy man, and the only reason our Teacher allows you to live is to test our sanity," Laval muttered over his shoulder. "Shut up."

"Shut me up, if you can. Maybe one of your own group, your precious goodlife, is just such a machine. Have you thought of that?"

Reflexively, Laval and his woman looked suspiciously at each other. But neither of them could believe that.

And then distraction came, not totally unexpected. The ship they had so recently noticed making its approach was now docking—or landing, rather, coming down gently to rest in the standard generated gravity, at a spot right next to this fenced-off portion of the flight deck.

Laval and the woman who had abandoned her name got to their feet. Presently they could see that someone was indeed approaching. A man and an experienced goodlife, judging by the calm way he moved in this environment. Then he walked out of shadow and into a place where the light of distant starclouds fell through the transparent overhead to reveal his face.

"Gavrilov," said the one who meant someday to be the berserker viceroy of Earth.

The dark man, casually clad, walking in his distinctive stooped fashion, approached and acknowledged the greeting with a cool nod. He did not appear much surprised to find Laval and his woman here; possibly he had even been expecting them.

Flower was following Gavrilov slowly, keeping in the background and looking about her with a stunned expression.

It was obvious from the way these two men faced each other that they had met before, and that they were not particularly pleased to be meeting again.

And all the while, on the deck in the background, the spasmodic dance of berserker fighting machines went on, as they prepared to accomplish the next step in their dual plan, of occupying the atoll called Fifty Fifty, and annihilating any Solarian fleet that might attempt to challenge them.

It was also soon obvious that the newcomer considered the "viceroy" his rival, and was not disposed to tell him anything.

The feeling was mutual.

"What news from the slime worlds?" Laval inquired. "Are the Solarians still holding any planets?"

"Quite a few, as a matter of fact."

The Templar, from his privileged position in the background, laughed at that.

Gavrilov only now became aware of the presence of the prisoner. He looked through the shadowy grillwork barrier at the man's head, sticking up out of a block of dim, shimmering force field.

"What have we here?" the newcomer inquired.

Laval, still not minded to provide his rival with any useful information, remained silent; but the Templar himself offered a kind of twisted explanation.

He had not got far before Laval interrupted. "Never mind that slime. I think his slimy badlife masters have drugged him so that he feels no fear. But the Teacher will be interrogating him soon." Now his eyes widened as he suddenly caught sight of Flower, who had come to a stop in the background, her attention raptly on her new surroundings. "Here, you! Who are you?"

Flower was plainly not impressed by his uniform, or indeed anything about him. She continued to look around her as she gave him her name. The excitement and anticipation with which she had come aboard the enormous machine were fading visibly.

"Where are we going to stay?" she asked at last, addressing the world in general.

By now Laval's nameless woman had emerged from the little shelter, a kennel-like and improvised structure at one side of the enclosed space reserved for life, to confront Flower. The two women began a halting conversation. Meanwhile Gavrilov and Laval were continuing the argument they had begun on first seeing each other.

There were certain things the two goodlife men agreed on: All, or most, of the evils of the universe could be blamed upon the stubbornness of Solarian humans—and perhaps a few other life forms that in their own ways, all relatively ineffective, tried to resist the machines.

Gavrilov believed that once the berserkers had perfected an imitation human, then there would be no further need for goodlife like themselves. Machines could do an infinitely better job of infiltrating the remnants of the human resistance and preparing its final downfall.

And in halting speech the nameless woman was explaining to Flower that for the time being all right-thinking goodlife were going to have to rough it. The worldly paradise, when living machines and life-hating people would exist together in perfect harmony, still lay in the future.

Flower was staring at the shabby kennel, at the ragged, haggard woman who had just crawled out of it, and the look on Flower's face indicated that she was waiting to be told that this was all a joke, an initiation of some kind. At any moment now the secret door would open somewhere, and the laughing, kindly people would pour forth, well-fed and well-dressed. And with them would come their friends, the wise, harmonious machines. All along she had believed, really and truly, that Gavrilov was taking them to a paradise world.

And Nifty Gift was a witness to most of it. He had been escorted by two machines out through the small ship's airlock, emerging after Gavrilov and Flower. His captors marched him into an area that was out of the other humans' sight, but still part of the walled-off portion of the flight deck of the giant berserker carrier.

When the two berserker robots had abruptly closed in on Gift, one on either side, he prayed that they would kill him quickly. But no such luck.

He could hear human voices at a little distance, but was not taken to join the others. Rather he was put into a closet-sized cage, or holding cell.

Obviously, this was a prepared place of confinement. A spigot on one wall gurgled with cold running water, and right below it a hole in the deck was ready to serve as a crude latrine.

The two man-shaped machines locked him in, closing a force-field door, and left him. He scarcely had time to look around before one of them was back, carrying an odd-shaped bundle that Gift automatically assumed must be some instrument of torture. But the bundle opened turned out to be a suit of space armor—one that appeared to have undergone some peculiar alterations.

His inanimate jailer gestured at him, then watched while he put on the suit, over his frayed and dirty civilian clothes that had remained unchanged during the voyage from Uhao. Then it tossed him a matching helmet, and stood by until he had tried that too, and made sure it mated with his suit.

Then the thing that had brought the suit turned on its two legs and went wordlessly on its way, once more closing the force-field door of his little cell behind it.

Gift heard a murmur of voices. Looking through the grill-work of one side of his cell, he discovered that he could see and hear most of the conversation among the other Solarians, though they could not see him from where they were. They had no suits of armor.

As soon as Gift began to move around inside his special little cell, he realized that the suit they had given him had been altered. The servos were weakened, so that the wearer would have no chance to resist berserkers—the suit felt heavy and slow-moving. But Gift supposed it would still offer substantial protection against injury.

Still the purpose of the special treatment he had received eluded him. Why would a berserker protect an enemy prisoner, but not its goodlife friends? What threatened him, except the berserker itself? The chance of running into any Solarian patrol in this vastness ought to be really almost infinitesimal.

It was after Gift had begun to listen to the strange conversation taking place among his fellow Solarians, that there dawned on him a likely reason for all this concern over his welfare. He closed his eyes and leaned his head against the bars.

He, like the Templar in his block, was being saved for interrogation. The Teacher really wanted to talk to him; but it just had to fight a battle first.

The goodlife living quarters on this machine seemed to be all above decks, consisting of a few walls and inflated balloons, improvised under a thin transparent canopy. A few rags of padding on a hard surface. Water pipes and holes in the deck were the extent of plumbing, and food provision was decidedly sporadic.

Judging from the maneuvers of berserker small ships that he was able to observe on the adjoining flight deck, artificial gravity seemed to be in operation across the whole deck, perhaps throughout the whole machine, not laid on only in the life-unit pens. He supposed this offered some advantage. Gift as part of standard military training had been taught something about how large berserkers were usually organized, designed, and put together. Trouble was that his teachers had been notably short of firsthand experience in their subject. He'd be able to teach the course now.

Listening to Gavrilov's argument with the other goodlife man, whoever he might be, Gift felt the numbness of terror giving way slowly to sullen hate. Somehow these idiots had convinced themselves that berserkers really wanted to be benevolent rulers—hell, if the berserkers ever won the war, it would be because humanity was too stupid to be allowed to live.

As far as he could tell from what he overheard, Laval's plan, or maybe Gavrilov's, or the plan of both, had been to teach their mechanical Teachers what the best (read: the least human) of humanity was really like. Then the Teacher machines in turn would come to love and trust him—and see that when the time came, they would see to it that he was recorded, thus becoming as much like the superior life form as it was possible for him to become.

But Laval and the others who had chosen to be goodlife were quite right about one thing: Their metal masters wanted to learn from them what humanity was like. Great optelectronic brains always gathering data, bits and pieces of information that would form a great mosaic, from all their prisoners. Eventually the vast structure of information thus created would enable the berserkers to understand the phenomenon of Solarian humanity sufficiently well to crush it out of existence.

And while his fellow Solarians—slime units was the name that some of them preferred for their own kind—haggled with one another, Nifty Gift stood voiceless in his cell, ignored except for an occasional look-in by one of the machines that had given him the suit.

He wasn't really thinking anymore, but he was starting to take stock of his surroundings.

To begin with, this was an enormous berserker, vastly bigger than the one that in some bygone age had crushed his spy ship. From what he could see on the expanse of deck stretching away beyond the little area fitted with life support, it had to be a carrier.

Nifty was gradually coming to grips with the realization that his worst fear had now been realized. This was just what he had been willing to kill his shipmates to prevent: He was a berserker's helpless captive, in deep space, beyond any hope of rescue.

And then another thought suggested itself to his stunned mind: At least Traskeluk would never be able to find him here.

The more he considered that idea, how terribly successful his flight from Traskeluk had been, the funnier it began to seem. Gift started laughing, gradually sliding into a helpless hysteria.

In a minute or so Flower, coming back evidently to see what had happened to him, stopped at the door of his little cell and looked in at him curiously. It was as if she were looking everywhere for an explanation, but he had none to give.

The man-sized berserker units, Gift noticed, seemed indifferent to Flower's presence. They were allowing her to wander back and forth at will, within the boundaries of the small region where life was temporarily tolerated. This, then, was Paradise. Her eyes roamed restlessly about. Gift could see that she was looking sadder and sadder.

When Flower left Gift's door and wandered back in sight of Laval, the would-be viceroy barked more questions at her, trying to satisfy himself as to whether she was goodlife or a prisoner. Evidently to him the distinction was of tremendous importance.

He assumed that he had now met everyone who had just arrived on the ship.

Under this interrogation Flower's growing shock and horror turned into fright.

Meanwhile, Gavrilov had looked back toward the yacht once or twice, with a faintly puzzled expression. He might be wondering what had happened to Gift; but he kept to himself whatever thoughts he might have on the subject. Laval was not going to be given any information free.

Except for Gift and the separated Templar, the humans making up the strange little group were standing, now and then sitting or reclining, in what looked like an arena ringed with fire;

along with what felt like normal artificial gravity, their unliving host had provided air, and presumably food and water, at least the minimal life support that goodlife and badlife alike required if they were going to answer questions and demonstrate for the machine the almost unfathomable complexities of Solarian psychology.

And the Solarians' talk returned to the subject of possible berserker imitations of humanity. Why is it the machines, with all their computing capacity and technical skills, have never accomplished that successfully? They seem to have some built-in block against doing it.

"The berserkers have never been able to build an imitation of a Solarian human, or any other complex life form, that would convince passersby who saw it in a good light. It seems, in a way, that they've never wanted to try—or have never been *able* to make a good attempt."

"Why is that?"

"I think that no organic being in the Galaxy knows why."

Laval once more expressed his great contempt for all organic beings. The way he looked at his own hands as he spoke seemed to indicate that he was including himself.

Then one of the three goodlife advanced an explanation. The machines wouldn't lower themselves to the apparent duplication of dirty life.

And from the background the voice of the captive Templar, who had been almost forgotten, came, saying: "Berserkers have them, it seems. Or at least these do. Like a dog has fleas. Or is it lice?"

One of the goodlife men jumped up and tried in vain to punish the Templar. The man in the force-field block laughed, maniacally, and then began to sing.

And the machine, in its untiring examination of human motives, only wanted to hear more of the Templar song:

The prisoner was ready to oblige:

He has sounded forth the trumpet that shall never call retreat
He is sifting out the hearts of men before his judgment-seat;

Oh, be swift my soul to answer him, be jubilant, my feet!
Our God is marching on!

There was a momentary silence.

And still Gift continued listening, in a curiously detached way, from behind the bars of his prison cell. He thought that hundreds of berserkers over the centuries of conflict must have had the concept of God explained to them a thousand times— as many different explanations as there were explainers—in contradictory theologies: By cool goodlife cynics, by devout prisoners almost frightened to death, by fanatical preachers who had come to preach to their unliving hardware. How the idea of a divine creator, or a first cause, figured in the calculations of the death machines, if at all, seemed impossible to guess.

Now this particular berserker, a computer or program evidently in command of the task force that was about to complete the devastation of the Solarian Gulf Fleet, wanted to know what a trumpet was, and how feet could possibly be jubilant.

And the berserker, as before, wanted an explanation of the Templar song, and what it meant to the life units who seemed to draw strength from what they perceived as the presence and leadership of this mysterious *God.*

"Where," it inquired of the prisoner, "do you believe that this entity called God is to be found?"

An answer came immediately from the human head that seemed to rest bodiless atop the force-field cube: "Everywhere."

"I do not perceive him," the berserker answered.

"You are not fit to do that."

Gavrilov jumped up and made motions at the barrier, trying to get at and punish the prisoner; then subsided in frustration when he was unable to reach him.

And presumably the berserker continued to watch it all, dispassionately. At least the Teacher made no further comment upon the behavior of life units good or bad.

Or perhaps, Gift thought, the Teacher had been distracted

by something the humans could not perceive, and was no longer bothering to watch.

Gift could only marvel that the captive Templar had been able to maintain his defiant attitude under these conditions. It must be a kind of madness. But probably there were drugs that would have that effect. From time to time the helpless captive again broke into song, the same song that Gift remembered Traskeluk singing:

> I have seen Him in the watchfires of a hundred circling
>   camps
> They have builded Him an altar in the evening dews and
>   damps
> I can read his righteous sentence by the dim and flaring
>   lamps;
> His day is marching on.
>
> I have read a fiery gospel, writ in burnished rows of
>   steel . . .

Once more the song succeeded in arousing the berserker's curiosity. The machine broke in, turning up the volume of its squeaky voice, wanting to know what certain of the words meant.

"You will tell me now, or later, under interrogation."

But the Templar only sang some more.

Laval had now turned his attention more fully to questioning Flower. His voice was smooth and quiet, but his manner had turned sadistic, talking to her about the horrible things that usually happened to prisoners, and assuring her that her safe status as a goodlife unit had not yet been confirmed.

Gift thought of shouting at the man, but that wasn't going to make Flower's life any easier.

Laval also managed to imply that Gavrilov had not entirely established his goodlife credentials.

Gavrilov naturally contested this, and both men tried to get some confirmation of their status from the machine.

It was possible to believe that the fate of prisoners in general was not necessarily the worst imaginable. After they had given the machine what seemed all their useful information, they were quickly killed. After all, death, not pain, was what a berserker was programmed to achieve. Pain was a part of life.

The crushing of organic bodies—like every other activity involving them—was always messy, and always entailed extra effort on the killers' part to make sure that all the microorganisms that were inevitably associated with Solarian bodies were expunged from existence too. Microbes were after all also alive, and therefore required to be killed. Viruses too seemed to fall into the banned category, as the berserkers computed it.

Among supposed experts on the subject who had never been caught by one, it was widely supposed that, in return for cooperation, the machines were willing to grant prisoners the boon of a quick termination, by being popped naked out into space. Or cast into some equivalent of a roaring furnace, where the matter in their bodies will furnish fuel for the berserker engines, and where there would be no possibility of even the microorganisms in badlife bodies surviving for any substantial period of time.

Laval had let Flower go—for the moment. From the way he looked at her, Gift could deduce a certain sadistic refinement. She wasn't going anywhere.

Given the chance, as the men resumed their dispute, she drew apart from the others again, while the nameless woman crawled back into the kennel. Once again Flower's wanderings carried her out of their sight, brought her back to see what had happened to Gift.

Nifty felt sorry for Flower, and said as much when she came wandering back to him again, but there was nothing he could do for her. Having come as far as he had come, he knew that he was already dead.

He could look at that fact and think about it now. The worst had happened, and here he was.

Gift experienced a curious relief.

Now in his exhaustion, his strange and newfound peace, he actually dozed; it was only for a few minutes, and he dreamed of Traskeluk and Terrin.

He awakened to see Flower looking in at him through the force door of his cell. When she saw he was awake, she whispered: "I was afraid you were dead."

"I am," he told her after a while.

She looked at him, not understanding. It was funny, damned funny, but Gift understood that she was now more frightened than he was.

Gift said: "Actually, I've been dead now for about a standard month. One of your machines killed me over on the other side of the Gulf . . . no, I take that back. Out there I killed myself."

"I don't understand."

He reached out and tried to hold her hand, but the glassy, repellent force of the door, almost invisible, prevented contact. "Never mind."

Presently Flower drifted away once more. Climbing slowly to his feet in the awkward suit, going back to his observation post, Gift saw how the goodlife, including Laval, were still pining away for lack of a kind word from their supposed Teacher—well, at least Gift himself had not yet been physically mishandled by the machines. Considering only physical comfort, he'd undergone treatment almost as bad aboard regular coach-class transport, in his limited experience of civilian travel.

Drifty Gift, he thought. And a terrible, detached clarity seemed to be growing in his thoughts. It was as if he had been drugged, ever since the spy-ship skirmish, but he was coming out of it now. Not by chemicals, no, by something else.

Hell itself would hold no terrors for a man in his condition. Hell itself. . . .

When Laval grew curious about current events, he liked to climb up a couple of steps, to a slightly elevated spot giving a slightly better view of the flight deck of the berserker carrier, that the Templar said was code-named *Pestilence*.

Roy Laval often preferred to watch from the elevated spot, as if this gave him some claim to prominence. Or enabled him to understand what was going on, when he was given no explanation. When he talked to the berserker now, as often as not it did not answer him.

It seemed to Laval that his great Teacher had now completely given up talking to him, or to anyone—as if it had forgotten there were any life units at all on board. But Laval kept trying to read some great philosophical purpose into the neglect.

From time to time the berserker launched a small machine into space from the flight deck, what looked to Gift like a fighter or hardlauncher popping straight up like a round cork from a bottle. No mass launching yet, though from the look of the preparations, something like that certainly impended. Or some fighter or scout came in, straggling back to its mothership at last, and docked. Sometimes when this happened Laval caught himself unconsciously waiting for a human figure in armor to climb out and walk across the deck.

Everything that Gift could see out on the flight deck confirmed that the berserker carrier was preparing for battle, getting ready to launch a swarm of smaller killer machines, analogs of Solarian fighters, hardlaunchers, and undersluggers.

Laval had gone into a kindly goodlife phase, had stopped being overtly sadistic, and was now trying to recruit Flower—it seemed a minimal achievement to sign up at least one more person to join the goodlife cadre he imagined he was forming.

The more Gift studied the construction and the life support that was keeping everyone alive, the flimsier it looked. Obviously, the berserker wanted to protect a lot of other things more than it wanted to protect even the most devout goodlife.

The modest space reserved for the housing of life units looked out into a much vaster domain. This was covered by a glassy overhead of crystalline matter or maybe purely of force, curved like a visual sky.

On the berserker carrier, the doomed Templar and the one or two goodlife—observed and overheard by Spacer Gift, who was present largely as a result of human cross-purposes, and berserker miscalculations—were standing or sitting half exposed to the raging sky.

It tended to get very cold here, standing on the face of Death, whose jaws were open if not quite visible. Very cold, with occasional waves of almost searing heat, sufficient to keep all the slime units from actually freezing. What air there was tended to move about in gusty drafts, and there were abrupt pressure changes. The concept of physical comfort did not seem to enter into berserker calculations.

"There's some very effective artificial gravity in effect here. It's making a considerable effort to keep us alive—or some of us."

"It has to do that, if it's going to bother with having us here at all. We are objects of study."

Gift, suddenly feeling starved, bit into the food cake when a machine brought it around. Ordinarily it would have seemed little better than just edible, but right now his hunger made it intensely satisfying. His body was eager to nourish itself. Right now life—what little he had left of it—seemed infinitely precious. He thought that he was not going to try to kill himself again, the way he had during his first encounter with the shape of Death.

Flower kept on telling Nifty that she was sorry she had got him into this.

He murmured something inane, to the effect that it didn't matter. The two of them were still separated by the door of Nifty's cell.

Suddenly she asked, innocently: "Why's it got you locked up in there, by yourself?"

"I guess maybe it's saving me."

"For what?" After thinking over her own question for a few seconds, she suddenly cried out: "Oh, Nifty. I'm sorry!" She looked over her shoulder, toward the sound of human voices. "I didn't mean to do this to you. I didn't know . . . I haven't told any of the others that you're here. . . ."

"Never mind, not your fault." The situation had a curious feeling of inevitability about it. He put his hands to his head.

"I'm so sorry . . . I wanted to go back on the ship, but now there's a gate and it wouldn't let me."

And the small Solarian ship that had brought three people out here remained beached on the flight deck, tantalizingly almost within reach. It had not been moved from where it had come down. Gift was able to reach a position, on the opposite side of his cell from where he watched his fellow captives, from which it became visible. Gift hadn't been able to get a good look at it when he went aboard on Uhao, because most of the hull had been under water. Now he could see, through the transparent wall of the life pen, a smooth hull, house-sized, unremarkable as small civilian spacecraft went. Near at hand, but it might as well have been a million klicks away.

The yacht, as far as he could tell by looking from this angle, was just resting lightly secured out on the open deck—no fancy landing docks here—and looked as if it would be perfectly easy to drift away in if one got the chance. Fat chance. It would be scheduled for decontamination in the berserker sense; all the live microorganisms it might contain to be incinerated.

The Solarians, goodlife and bad, gasping and shivering alike in the violent changes of temperature, argued tersely with one another, over everything, as it seemed to the listening Gift, and nothing. Now and then Laval or Gavrilov or the Templar snarled their mutual hatred, while machines recorded everything for later evaluation.

Roy Laval, droning on in his endless argument with Gavrilov, remained deeply immersed in his plans to be the quisling ruler of Earth. He plans to be the viceroy set on a throne, or the equivalent, by what he imagined would be a berserker hegemony over life units that would be allowed in some sense to live.

Before the others arrived, and the time for battle drew near, the berserker had been letting Laval play with visual displays, planning what he imagined his palace on conquered Earth was going to be like. But now the machine seemed to have no energy or interest left for such games, and the display was dead and dark.

The lighting in the area of confinement was uncomfortable for human eyes, some areas in shadow and some in harsh glare, and the noise of nearby mechanism was occasionally deafening. The air was first hot and then icy cold, and stank sharply of some chemicals, so that someone imagined it might be a berserker's breath. That would be a good idea for Flower to have.

Now and then a machine came by, rolling or treading through the fringes of the area on some unexplained errand, sometimes moving faster than a man could run, and the people had to stay out of its way—at least the most experienced goodlife took good care to stay out of the way. And they always answered obsequiously on the rare occasions when a machine had anything to say to them.

Flower, when she came back to see him again, had some kind of extra fabric wrapped around her now in an effort to keep warm, but Gift could see that she was still shivering. Under this extra wrapping, he noticed, she was wearing the dress she'd had on when they first met.

She was hungry too, but still she brought Gift a share of the miserable food one of the man-sized machines had given her; a pink-and-green cake from some rudimentary robotic life-support kitchen.

She was relieved to discover that the machines had already fed him, on stuff that looked and tasted better than her rations; evidently they considered him more important than her, and he wound up sharing his nicer meal with her.

"That does look better." She sniffed. "Smells better too." They threw hers away.

This time, when Flower went back to join the others, Laval renewed his interest. He grabbed her, and after he had enjoyed twisting her arm for a while, confined her, chaining her to a thick pipe of unknown purpose, that came up out of the deck and curved away to vanish in shadows far overhead. He used the chain he had been wearing as a belt, and secured it with the same padlock.

Goodlife and machines alike stood by and watched without interfering.

And Gift, watching unseen, could taste blood, where he had bitten his lower lip. He knew that any protest on his part would only make things worse for her.

TWENTY-EIGHT

A typical preflight briefing, on any Solarian carrier, began in the ready room, where two dozen men and women, already in partial armor, crowded in, filling the specially wide chairs built to accommodate armored bottoms.

A human officer stood live before them, telling them the most recent plots on the enemy's supposed location and strength. The plan of attack, and the point in spacetime where the carriers were to be found after the strike. Small ships in combat expended their power prodigally; miss rendezvous and you were likely to become a drifting speck a light-year from the nearest friend.

Then standing and sitting around, killing time, waiting on a knife edge.

Once more, for what seemed the hundredth time, the order came: "Crews to your ships!"

And feet pounded in a running scramble. The ground crew of humans and machines had everything ready.

Spaceborne again, and again the Voids came on, always

the Voids. Accelerating faster than any Solarian small ship could, and turning faster. Intensive coordination between organic brain and Solarian machine was necessary to win a dogfight with one of them. The lifeless optelectronic brains of the berserkers never blundered, but sometimes they were forced to make decisions based on inadequate information. And again, sometimes they randomized their tactics, making moves that though unpredictable turned out to be as bad as blunders.

Wondering, grumbling to himself, Jay Nash came driving up to his rented house in a suburb of Port Diamond. It was months—he'd lost track of exactly how long—since he'd been here. At first he'd thought his house sitter was reliable. But lately, things had been happening that made him wonder.

Nash's shoulder, deeply punctured by berserker shrapnel on Fifty Fifty, still felt numb, and spasms of pain now and then marched up and down his arm. He'd had to spend a couple of days in the hospital. Not as young as he once was, and he'd been wounded.

Remembering that he'd now been through a real battle made him smile yet once more with satisfaction.

It was also in the back of Nash's mind that before leaving Uhao he probably would stop in once more to see his current girlfriend in Port Diamond. But he wasn't completely sure about that; it always bothered him when he failed to be faithful to his wife. He considered his family, who were back on Earth, vitally important components of his life; it was just that he didn't choose to spend much time with them.

Wondering, all through his drive out here to the house, what the hell had happened to Yokosuka. He really needed the stuff he'd sent her to get or he wouldn't have bothered sending for it. And again, when he'd tried to phone the house, he'd got signals that indicated something was wrong with the equipment. For all he knew, the damned house had burned to the ground, and no one had bothered to let him know.

If you really wanted something done right, there was no substitute for doing it yourself.

Maybe the gal had tried fooling around with some of his

special recording gear, and had popped the circuit breakers somewhere. Thinking about it, he grumbled to himself.

As he turned his ground car into the drive, he was frowning at the lightless grounds and windows. The closer he got to the main building, the funnier things looked. Whatever had gone wrong seemed to have brought on a total blackout. The house had been unoccupied until Yokosuka got here—or at least he'd thought it had. Of course, he'd left that damned funny robot in charge. . . .

When he got to the front door, the house at first refused to recognize that anyone was standing there, let alone the lawful occupant. Damn it, he knew he was paid up on the rent. Next the emergency lights, powered by a backup supply, came on—even if this was daytime—and Nash discovered that something also seemed to be wrong with the house's comsystem. This was not entirely a surprise. He'd tried a couple of times to call ahead, but once he hadn't been able to get through, and the other time he got only weird, unsettling answers. Speaking into his wrist phone now, he tried again, with no better luck than before.

His memory for practical housekeeping matters had always been lousy. But there was no chance of his forgetting the current butler's name—not with all the joking that had gone on about it.

"Burymore? Where the hell are you?"

No answer.

"Anybody there?"

Damn. And he'd been expecting to find a lot of important messages waiting for him too. The way his luck was running today, they were probably all wiped out.

The press of other business had delayed his getting back here. But now he was ready, and more than ready, to settle in somewhere for a while. He had work to do, and things to think about. Especially he wanted to savor having been right in the middle of the first—and almost the only—berserker raid on Fifty Fifty.

He was doubly disconcerted, after experiencing all these oddities, to find that the front door of the house was unlocked. He pushed it open, stepped in, turned on a light when he had advanced into the next room, where for some reason the window shades were all completely closed—and swore eloquently, in two ancient languages, at the scene of ruin by which he was confronted.

He was still standing there when more lights came on, and Jory and Trask confronted him.

"Yokosuka, what in hell has happened to you?" The young man with her looked like he'd been in some kind of major wreck. "And who the hell is this?"

"This is Cedric Traskeluk," she told her boss. "Security is on its way."

"What—?" Nash made a helpless gesture. Then he looked at Traskeluk again. "My God, young man, what's happened to your arm?" Even after what he'd seen on Fifty Fifty, even after what he'd felt—*especially* after what he'd felt in his own shoulder—Jay Nash fainted.

They helped him to a chair, and soon his mind was reasonably clear again. It wasn't fair, he was thinking, even as he listened, sitting down, to the first horrifying rough outline of an explanation. Ever since he'd come back to Uhao he'd heard a hundred rumors about the war. The most common was that the real action was now going to take place somewhere far away from Fifty Fifty. One variation on this had the berserkers going straight for Earth—to people with any real understanding of the forces involved, that last was strategically very unlikely, with all the active Solarian bases the enemy would have to leave in their rear to do so.

And there had been rumors also about infiltrating berserker machines.

Over the years he'd learned a few things about rumors. Generally it was safer to dismiss any one that came along than to take it seriously. And anyway, military strategy wasn't Nash's strong point, and he knew it. Right now he just wanted to rest his wounded shoulder, catch up on the therapy that he was supposed to be getting so maybe it would stop aching, put his feet up and relax. And catch up on his sleep; he wasn't a young man anymore. And after that, set himself up a real office and studio

in his rented house, so he could do the production work required on his new documentary. The Space Force expected a
good job from him, and they were pushing the project all they
could.

And then, when he had satisfied himself that he had done
his duty—and only then—he would settle in, perhaps with a
trusted old friend or two, maybe by himself, to do some serious
drinking. The world might not see him for a standard week.

Security of various ages and sizes, some of them in neat
uniforms and some in civilian clothes, were on the scene a few
minutes after Nash's own arrival. They had, of course, a thousand questions.

"What about this robot that was supposedly on duty?"

"What about it?"

"It was your machine, Mr. Nash. Your robot butler."

"Burymore," Traskeluk put in, from the other side of the
room, where he was getting his injuries looked at. When the others looked at him, he reminded them. "There was a sign on its
back that said 'Burymore.' The sign isn't there anymore."

Nodding his head, the director fell into a chair, bemused,
trying to remember. The name he remembered perfectly, but
where it came from . . .

"Yes, I suppose I did put that on. The sign. Before I went
out to Fifty Fifty, we were having a party . . . drinking . . . something to do with an old story."

"But where did the machine come from?" a security
woman asked.

Where *had* the butler come from? "People just give me
things, sometimes."

"Try to remember."

"Oh, I will. I will."

Even before the experts arrived, Jory and Trask between
them, while helping each other patch up their wounds, had
come up with a satisfying scenario: The machine that had killed
the woman had been basically only an intelligence-gathering device, not capable of making policy decisions on the level of, say,

a berserker admiral. It existed primarily for the gathering and transmission of information. When forced to make decisions for which it knew itself to be unqualified, it experienced some opt-electronic analog of anxiety.

A few similarly disguised machines, on other planets, had been recognized by their Solarian enemies, rendered inactive before they could self-destruct, and taken apart.

Careful examination of the programming in each of those cases had revealed firm evidence that each disguised berserker was still basically a killer.

Some of these machines (called *Trojan horses,* "horses" or "Trojans" for short, in the jargon of Solarian counterintelligence) might even be programmed to be sincere in their offers of peace and cooperation—while their unliving creators of course were not. A few people, ready and willing to believe, had been taken in.

Somewhere, Jory was telling Traskeluk when she had a chance, she had read of Solarian philosophers (or had they been Carmpan? She couldn't remember) or cosmologists, who had stated a certain law. As nearly as she could remember, it ran something like this: *Complex programming, when passed on from one generation to another of inorganic machines, without the intervention of organic thought, tends to drift away from its original purpose.* Berserkers, the experts agreed, were aware of this law—as much as they could be aware of anything—and allowed for it in their manufacturing programs, by imposing redundant layers of quality control.

Maybe if too many intelligent machines were produced, by whatever creator, and for whatever purpose, would they tend to drift away from their original programming? Would berserkers tend to become indifferent to the cause of death?

Someone, obviously pleased with his own wit, had called it an analog of Original Sin—whatever that might have been.

All through their history, berserkers must have imposed a rigid quality-control program at their factories and bases, just as humans must. To achieve this, would one of the original, first-generation berserkers be present at every factory? Or some inspector approved by a panel of first-generation machines?

The tendency of succeeding generations to drift away from an original purpose is some kind of natural law, and must be continually opposed. The Antiteleological Principle, that was it. Theory held that it inexorably affected organic as well as nonorganic computation, from one generation to the next.

The universe for some reason is sharply antagonistic to the concept of universal death.

In the same vein, Solarians, or any other branch of humanity, would never be able to simply populate the Galaxy with their own loyal servants, by sending out Von Neumann machines. Any such devices tended to drift away into random and purposeless (from the human point of view) behavior, mining lifeless chunks of rock to obtain the materials with which to build sometimes elaborate and usually harmless gadgets. In practice, at the necessary level of complexity, all serious efforts at replication of the original machines invariably stopped within four generations at the most.

Obviously, the berserker record, over an enormous volume of time and space, was much better than that; hundreds of generations of machines must have been produced, all still true to the basic command. But the inevitable trade-off was that the numbers of machines successfully built had to remain comparatively low.

Was it possible that even if all Solarians were wiped out, natural forces would in time defeat the berserker effort? That something in the nature of the Galaxy, and of the universe itself, required the presence of life?

The berserkers had endured for more than fifty thousand standard years, but on the Galactic scale that was a mere flicker of time, an aberration that might be corrected in the next heartbeat.

One of the security officers said, turning away from Burymore's enigmatic smile: "This unit here, what we are probably going to start calling the Port Diamond machine, seems to have suffered the computer equivalent of a nervous breakdown."

More unpredictable, and deadlier, than a live tiger in the house. Tigers as a rule killed only when they had to eat. Some quirk of programming, tipping a hidden balance, told the machine it had to kill this human being in front of it, destroy him before he could reveal its identity, or take some other step that would be seriously damaging to the overall berserker cause.

Jay Nash, soon entirely recovered from his fainting spell and grown loquacious once again, did his best to take over the investigation, trying to make sense of death and ruin, to figure out how a berserker had come to be installed in his rented house. The more he thought about it, the more it angered him. Of course, in general a berserker would prefer to be inconspicuous, to look just like a thousand or a million other serving machines. And to behave like them—most of the time.

"I wonder—I wonder if the people who put it here were hoping I'd take it with me to Fifty Fifty. Out there it could have got a firsthand look at our defenses. But how would a machine know about the planned attack there? It must have had some goodlife help even to get as far as it did. How would a machine get itself crated for shipment?"

No one knew.

Nash still couldn't recall the exact circumstances of the butler's arrival at his house. He might well have been absent somewhere at the time. Silently he gave thanks that he had been somewhat wary of the thing. There had been no question of his taking it with him to the front. Even if someone thought it was quite capable of handling business, he wasn't going to trust anything as important as the recording of a combat documentary to this goddamned toy that looked like Jeeves in a tin can.

Burymore's modestly capable optelectronic brain had classified everything that hung on the walls as decoration. Only when the pistol had appeared in Jory's hand, held and pointed like a weapon, had the machine classified it as a functional firearm, and behaved accordingly.

"But how did the damned thing get in here in the first place?"

Some scheming goodlife had chosen Nash's house, or had gladly accepted the chance to use it, as a base for the disguised berserker for two reasons. One, getting the machine installed here was achievable; and two, Nash was known to have intimate contact with the military. He held a reserve commission, and for all the goodlife knew, had knowledge—maybe extensive knowledge—of military secrets. Nash was, after all, going to Fifty Fifty to make a documentary—that in itself was not a secret.

Therefore, Berserker Burymore's goodlife handlers had managed to get their disguised monster installed, a month or two back, in the house they knew Nash had rented.

Investigators now had examined carefully the body in the refrigerator. The unit had thoughtfully been removed from Nash's kitchen.

"Her name is Tanya something."

Tanya had at least been identified as an acquaintance of Martin Gavrilov, and at least some indirect connection had been established between Gavrilov and a known goodlife group.

Investigation soon revealed that the dead woman, Tanya, had once worked for a domestic catering service.

"And the butler killed her—the way her bones were broken took more than ordinary human force."

Getting access to the house was relatively easy, and such neighbors that took any notice would not have been concerned, because all kinds of civilians as well as some military people were in the habit of showing up at any place where Nash happened to be living.

The place was usually tenanted by a couple of human aides or servants who worked for Nash full time. But with the war on, and heating up, those people had enlisted, or were otherwise occupied, in new jobs that suddenly seemed more important than any entertainer's comfort and convenience.

And now those interested in the case of the Port Diamond machine were also starting to wonder what had happened to

Spacer Gift, who was known to have been in or around the house a few days earlier. The tracer put on Gift by security demonstrated that.

Traskeluk was wondering whether he would have to brace himself for a confrontation with the man he had been hunting. But the question now did not seem nearly as urgent as it had only a few hours ago.

He and others still wondered if some connection could be established between the missing Gift and a ring of goodlife agents. At first look, Gift's record had nothing in it to suggest such a thing.

Of course, his record really had nothing in it to suggest otherwise. He'd passed the usual security check that everyone in Hypo was subject to. Pretty dull and routine, up until his first experience of combat.

Eventually, a holographic recording of Gift was extracted from the house's own security system, which Burymore had otherwise rendered just about totally moribund. It showed Gift coming in the front door, the figure of a young woman with braided metallic hair hazily visible at his side.

"Who's this character?" asked a late-arriving officer.

Traskeluk, having declined an immediate ride to the hospital, was still on hand to make the identification, and Jory backed him up.

Of course, it would be hard to be sure that any image left in berserker-controlled hardware, despite its verisimilitude, wasn't some artifact.

But not this one, it looked too natural. The unexplained fact was still that berserkers had never been able to successfully fake human images or human bodies. It was obvious that this device, except for the murderous optelectronic brain, had been assembled in some Solarian factory. There were a few truly human-shaped machines sold as sex dolls; but as a rule they had no more brains than can openers.

Jory Yokosuka found herself pondering whether she was going to have to take a vacation from journalism for a while.

Maybe it would be wise. Her instincts urged her to keep working, but now maybe other instincts were urging her to hold back.

Traskeluk naturally had already admitted to having a certain amount of extra hardware in his arm. The way things were working out, he could see that he wouldn't necessarily have to own up to carrying around an explosive charge—the final blast could be accounted for by an internal destructor package built into the berserker. Security only wondered that it had not been larger.

And Traskeluk, exchanging glances with Jory, wasn't going to have to admit to being loaded with weaponry for the benefit of Nifty Gift.

When Nash looked at his former butler, he saw the torso a blackened ruin, the smiling robot face still partly undamaged. One hand and arm was still intact, and one leg still in good shape. The man's clothes it had been wearing were more than half shredded and burned away. Two puny humans had quite thoroughly murdered the damned thing.

"Well," she said to Trask when they were alone again, "you told me you were going to lead me to a story."

From the start it struck security as odd that Nash's robot butler, contrary to all common usage and standards of Solarian propriety, had been constructed in a very anthropomorphic form. People made machines like that only for very special purposes, or with deliberate intent to shock. Berserker units of that shape were not uncommon, perhaps in expectation of being able to operate captured equipment made to fit Solarian (or Builder) bodies.

How did it happen to have this shape?

"We may not have a good answer to that one for a while. There are ID numbers on the robot, of course, and we'll have to look at the place where it was manufactured. I understand they turn out a lot of custom units."

This untypical berserker had of course been obedient to

its special programming, and had refrained from killing on many occasions when it had previously had the chance. (Security's thorough examination of the house revealed that the butler must have been routinely sterilizing large areas of the house and grounds, eliminating all microorganisms, as part of a regular cleaning routine. This was a form of life-destruction it could carry on without arousing suspicion.)

Jory was helping Trask prepare for his coming interview with security—maybe they would, after all, have discovered how much lethal hardware he'd been carrying concealed in his artificial arm. Inspiration sprang up where it was needed: "And so your cousin told you that the next time you ran into a berserker, you had better be ready for it. Of course neither he nor you had any idea it was going to be this soon."

Traskeluk was looking at her gratefully. It *was* a good story, she realized, even if—as she felt sure—it was not the real one. And, by Jay Nash and all the gods, she was going to write it up.

Jay Nash was looking, or had planned to look, at a preliminary staging of the material he'd brought back with him for the documentary. People's images were coming and going, in lifelike three dimensions, on the several holostages in this chamber that served him as a conference room.

One of Nash's lesser concerns over the past month had been to think up a good title for his latest holographic production, the Fifty Fifty documentary.

He had enlisted his friends in this task, and a few of the fragmentary recorded messages that had come in during his absence had a bearing on the subject.

"How about *Berserker Fury*?" suggested his chief programmer, Nodrog Brag, stroking his neat gray mustache with one finger. No, he hadn't the faintest clue as to where the strange machine had come from, but he remembered seeing it at the party. "Damned unusual to have an efficient butler that's so man-shaped."

"Berserker Fury, hey?" Nash considered the suggestion, running fingers through his reddish hair, talking back to Brag's

unresponsive image. "Could be. Could be. But I think not quite specific enough. Doesn't really *kick* me, you know?"

A couple of other producers, Adnilem and Egroeg, also were on stage, conference calling from Port Diamond—and each had a different title to suggest.

The ground car in which the house sitter and two others had departed was now back in the garage, and from examination of equipment on board it was possible to deduce where it had been driven.

Later, evidence was found that a small spaceship, having interstellar drive, had been kept in the lagoon.

Security came to the conclusion that Nifty Gift was probably no longer within a hundred light-years of Uhao.

Jory Yokosuka, in exchange for the guarantee of certain exclusive interviews, went along with security in hushing up, for a time, the fact of the death machine's presence in Nash's house. The intention was to prevent a local panic.

"Not really my house, of course," Nash muttered.

Whatever else happened, he knew that he would have to submit to a rigorous investigation, try to prove that he hadn't known about the damned thing. His highly placed connections were likely to spare him the worst of any such investigation, but still it must take place.

That even a shadow of suspicion could fall upon his loyalty scared and outraged him.

Examination of the damaged communications system of the house showed that the disguised berserker must have been listening in on all the occupants' messages for more than a standard month. Most likely ever since the goodlife had smuggled it in. Fortunately, it seemed highly unlikely that anything of value to the berserker cause, relating to Nash's military activities, could have been learned and passed along. Almost all the messages consisted of jargon from the world of entertainment, all but unintelligible to the security agent who ran through them the first time.

· · ·

A twist of spacetime away, out in deep space on the day of the battle, Ensign Bright continued to watch the show. Long minutes went by when he would have much preferred to turn his gaze away, but that was not a realistic option.

He saw a third and fourth, and then a fifth and sixth, attack hurled by the Solarian task forces against the berserker carrier armada, and he had seen them all blunted and broken, against formations of ravening Voids, against the tough inner defenses thrown up by the carriers themselves—and against the less-easily seen, but very formidable, deficiencies of outdated technology.

The fourth attack fell on *Death,* and Bright on his suit radio was able to hear enough jabber between spacecraft to know that it was being made by planes from *Stinger.*

And he could see and hear that again the attackers failed to inflict any serious damage, and sustained heavy losses.

The fifth attack was carried out against *Death* by far-launchers, operating at extreme range, and they were therefore totally ineffective.

One minute later, *War* and *Pestilence* were both under attack. Yet again their auxiliary machines managed to defend them successfully.

But here they came again, and Bright's spirits, as tough as those of any other pilot, surged up loyally once more.

He saw two squadrons of hardlaunchers, winking into existence in normal space not far from the nearest carriers, then rapidly closing in.

And this time, when the hardlaunchers came *pop pop popping* out of flightspace, for once everything going perfectly for the Solarian side, just as in a flawless practice session, the berserker fighters were way out of position. It reminded Bright of the way a good boxer, or a karate fighter, used up three or four good serious punches, assuming they would be blocked, just to get the opponent wide open for the one that really mattered.

On the bridges and in the plotting rooms of each Solarian flagship, in the territory where the admirals held forth, stress and strain continued to mount.

In the sick bay aboard each remaining Solarian carrier, casualties were slowly accumulating, mostly wounded flight crew who had been lucky enough to make it home.

Now each successive wave of attacking Solarians had a slightly easier task in locating the berserker carrier fleet. Those livecrewed fighters and bombers who managed to make it back to their motherships were able to give pretty accurate coordinates of where they had left the enemy; and the enemy fleet was now pretty much immobilized.

During a period of two or three hours following the raid on Fifty Fifty, the berserker task force, compelled to defend itself against one inadequate attack after another, had become virtually stalled. Whatever plans those optelectronic admirals might have had when the battle began had now been seriously disrupted. The huge carrier machines had been unable to maneuver in pursuit of any offensive goal, their engines silently churning space while they concentrated on evasive action, dodging wave after wave of outclassed livecrewed ships.

The fact that the enemy was thus kept off balance meant that still only one Solarian carrier had come under direct attack.

But the cost of keeping the enemy off balance seemed prohibitively high. Solarian fighting strength was being used up at a fearful rate.

Ensign Bright, who had no choice, continued to watch the show, and to listen to those small parts of it that he could hear on his suit radio.

Today he'd seen a lot of his fellow spacers vaporized, along with their ships, but he still wasn't sure that he'd seen even one solid hit against the enemy. He kept telling himself that here were two fresh hardlauncher squadrons, maybe delayed en route somehow, but here they were. And humanity had at least one more chance.

Remaining in normal space afforded the enemy one definite benefit, making it easier for berserker scouts to locate the Solarian carriers. From the beginning the berserker computers had assumed that two or three more such vessels, besides the one they'd already sighted, were probably somewhere in the area.

The berserkers, though so far forced to remain largely on the defensive, were not about to retreat from what they considered an inferior force. Especially not when their own carriers had so far escaped unscathed.

Solarian crew members who had come back alive from the earlier hopeless efforts—and with skill and luck had achieved survivable landings on carrier or atoll—tended to have shattered nerves, and a great many of them were physically wounded. Some had to be carried out of the burning or imploding wreckage of their crash-landed ships.

One or more of the little ships coming home to the atoll exploded on the ramp at Fifty Fifty, and at least a couple of more on the flight deck of a carrier.

At least one came home and then blew up, its damaged drive gone wild, before the still-living crew members could all be extracted from it by the rescue robots.

The best chance of snatching a life from the disaster came when a live rescuer went in. Studies suggested that this was because the robots could not be depended upon to be sufficiently ruthless—there were times, fortunately rare, when it was necessary to handle a victim roughly, even to chop off an arm or leg to save a spacer's life. A robot plunged first into the small inferno, and then backed out, quivering with the optelectronic equivalent of a nervous breakdown.

Chief Warrant Officer Tadao was pulled, still alive, out of one of these rough landings. All the survivors reported seeing and hearing evidence of great carnage among their mates.

Through the optimized senses provided them by their silver helmets, they had caught sanitized but still savage glimpses— usually no more than one quick image—of Solarian spacecraft and human bodies crumpling, burning, vanishing in the white heat of explosions. Often disaster struck so swiftly that it was impossible to trace its progress in real time; that would some- day be a job for the debriefers, working with whatever record- ings had survived.

Today there was no time for any postmortems. There was only time to make tactical decisions and carry them out; and Naguance, who was now effectively in command (because Bow- man was less immediately engaged) decided to keep pressing the enemy.

"Right now I'm throwing into action everything that hu- manity has in place to throw. If it should turn out not to be enough . . ." The admiral left the sentence unfinished.

The sporadic but relentless onslaught of livecrewed Solarian ships against inanimate machines continued over a period of about one standard day.

But the decisive action—the Solarian attacks leading up to the destruction of the first three berserker carriers—had been concentrated within about three hours, starting about six hours after the battle's opening shots.

The earlier attacks, gallant and futile in themselves, had forced the berserker fighters to stay close to the carriers they were trying to protect, and depleted the fighters' energy reserves. The successive waves of Solarian small ships were not detected by the carrier machines' defenses until they were almost within attacking range. The berserker command computers received only scant warning of each successive attack. With each carrier forced into a random pattern of evasive action, it was impossible for them to proceed with any coherent plan.

The hardlaunchers, each crewed by two humans, were designed to multiply the force of their attacks by bursting out of flightspace while hurtling toward their targets. The hardlauncher pilot located the target on instruments while it and his ship were both in normal space, then jinked his ship in a mini-jump toward it, a maneuver that ideally added a special energy to the weapon. The gunner's attention remained concentrated in the search for attacking enemy fighter machines.

A perfect launch, seldom if ever attained in combat conditions, occurred with the missile no more than microseconds away from its last emergence from flightspace.

Sometimes the hardlauncher in its attack doesn't *quite* come out of flightspace, doesn't emerge all the way into the version of spacetime that most of the human race regards as normal. Just close enough to perfection to launch a missile that will break through. Or comes out completely for an interval measured only in picoseconds. Ten to the minus twelve, or one million millionth. This is the narrow gap of time in which the fields binding missile to ship must be cut loose.

In the battle for Fifty Fifty, the successful attacks on the four berserker carriers were delivered in classic style. It was always extremely dangerous for any ship or machine to enter or exit normal space in close proximity to a large mass, or a nuclear explosion. Such a desperate maneuver only increased the likelihood of fatal damage, and made it unlikely that jumping ship would reach the spot that it was aiming for.

Ideally, before releasing its weapon, the small attacker first closed to a short range, within perilously few kilometers of its target, sometimes well inside the target's defensive force fields. "Diving" into flightspace, then popping back from flightspace to normal space, under such trying conditions was a tricky maneuver, calling for thorough pilot training and razor-sharp execution.

Some gunners were also schooled in effective mind-melding with the communications equipment—which like other optelectronic hardware could perform most efficiently when working in direct connection with the human brain.

Other gunners had been trained to perform as capable backups for everything a pilot had to do—and other crew positions as well. Similarly many pilots had received the necessary cross-training to allow them to handle a gunner's job on the defensive armament.

Meanwhile, the defending fighters, those unsurpassed Voids, were throwing deadly obstacles into flightspace right in the path, or on the tail, of the onrushing bombers or undersluggers. Hails of small missiles, some fragmenting, bits no bigger than rifle bullets.

And the big berserker target, with nerveless mechanical efficiency, was throwing up a screen of antispacecraft fire. Its huge guns, if they could not precisely hit small targets, still generated buffeting field-vortexes, knocking off the Solarians' aim.

Of the several hardlauncher squadrons taking part in the final strike against the enemy, each small Solarian ship that got in range of its target carried and released one to three heavy missiles.

Almost each and every hardlauncher did so. A few of them had accidentally fired their heavy missiles prematurely, because something unforeseen had gone wrong with the latest mind-machine interface. But these hardlauncher pilots flew the remainder of the mission anyway, putting themselves at risk to distract the defenses.

Each missile successfully released from a hardlauncher massed three to eight times as much as a normal adult human body. On impact it released nuclear energies, but as a rule these were *almost* completely damped by the defensive fields with which any military target was almost certain to be permeated.

In that "almost" lay the attacker's prospects for success.

A gunner, on a hardlauncher, whooping with joy. Gunners on those ships tended to have a better view of the target than the pilot did, once the missile had been released. They could more easily afford to concentrate on it, assuming there were no fighters to be beaten off at the moment.

Even one direct hit with this type of weapon would almost certainly do serious damage to a mothership/carrier-type large berserker; minor to moderate damage to a battlewagon. The truly serious destruction in either case was done by secondary explosions, and runaway surges of nuclear and other energies, released when the vulnerable weapons and power systems of the loading fighter machines were struck by an incoming missile.

In many ways, as Space Force recruits were patiently taught when they showed signs of being overawed, a berserker was like any other machine. No matter how large it was, or how well designed, it could carry, manipulate, and release only finite stores of force and energy. If a machine is concentrating all its energies on one task, such as launching an offensive strike, others must perforce be neglected.

Defensive force fields protecting the huge machines had been partially, marginally lowered or tuned down, owing to the exigencies of reloading and refueling the small machines as rapidly as possible. Or the defensive fields had been deployed against the most recent attack, by undersluggers.

This meant that those fields now had to be redeployed in normal space, a procedure that took no more than a few seconds; but it turned out that those few seconds represented just a little more time than the berserkers now had available.

The accidentally perfect timing, and the fortunate composition of this final, winning strike were as unexpected as all of the earlier futile onslaughts, seemingly randomized, had been.

The combat computers in the Solarian fighting ships, when presenting the ship's livecrew with the image of a confirmed berserker, generally adorned the image with the blazoned insignia of skull and crossbones—a symbol of death and danger almost universally accepted on worlds occupied by Earth-descended humanity.

The members of the little human gathering aboard the berserker flagmachine had scarcely moved since Laval had chained Flower to the curving pipe, but their environment had changed around them. Some of the changes they could not per-

ceive directly. The priority assigned by the machine to their survival, never very high, had been downgraded further. Now the
people were surrounded by what appeared to be a vast colon-
nade of gilded arches, more than tall enough to support the
Gothic roof of a great cathedral, marking out a space floored
by dark slabs that were glassy hard, and more like rock than
metal. Dimly the local portion of the deck reflected the images
of people's bodies.

Roy Laval, confident that these badlife would never have
a chance to take any supposed secrets away with them, had
brought up the idea of berserkers imitating humans, as an advance that would inevitably be made in the near future. This was
of course purely a goodlife idea, but he had convinced himself
that it was a berserker secret.

He was still arguing with Gavrilov. "Once that is done, the
badlife resistance will swiftly crumble. It would be ridiculous for
them to oppose us, when we are moving among them, striking
them down at will." His eyes glowed as they focused on some
inner, private vision.

The voice of the untouchable Templar still drifted past the
barrier, hectoring. " 'Us'? You're not a machine, Laval. You're
flesh and blood; have you forgotten?"

Stung, the would-be viceroy turned around. "That state of
affairs may not persist for long. The Teachers have promised
me—" And he fell abruptly silent.

"Promised you what? That you will be recorded, and then
provided with a robotic body?"

Laval drew himself up. "It will be so," he said with dignity.

"You delude yourself. Why should they let you in on any
real secrets? Why should they do anything at all for you? Because you are alive, you are loathsome scum to them—as you
are to us."

Immediately on receiving the report of a Solarian carrier's
presence, berserker command assigned new priorities to all its
fighting units. The livecrewed, badlife carriers were now judged
to be by far the most important target, and the process was

begun of changing the arming and loading on the small space-going attack machines.

Looking up, the Solarians could actually see a few of the attacking small ships, popping out of flightspace, very near, with sudden violence. They could see the brighter, even dazzling, flares and streaks of belated antispacecraft fire, lashing out from turrets on the carrier.

The banal argument among the goodlife continued, with the machine still silent. Then the Teacher's voice, booming and squeaking from hidden speakers, started to say something. But it broke off again, before a single word had been completed.

Utter silence held, while seconds ticked by.

And then people were looking up, and someone cried out that the hardlaunchers were on their way.

"Helldivers!" Gavrilov screamed, and dove for cover where there was none to be found.

Gift, in his private cage, was unable to see the missiles coming, but he could see how the whole group standing at a little distance from his cell snapped their heads back, looking almost straight overhead.

In a reflex action he grabbed up the helmet of his prison suit. Then he looked up again.

The berserker did not waste time or energy in commenting on the tactical situation. It had abruptly fallen silent shortly before the newest attack, before any of the people on the deck had any means of knowing what was about to happen.

Gaping skyward, badlife and goodlife alike were transfixed by the sight, somewhere above the transparent roof, of the three hurtling, swelling small dots that could be nothing but Solarian missiles. Unstoppable, inside the last of the carrier's defenses. This time Gift could see, he could feel in his gut, that they were not going to miss.

Incoming missiles that were slow enough to be seen in flight by human eyes had been deliberately slowed down by their internal mechanism. High velocity, bullet speeds and more, did not give maximum efficiency in the penetration of force-field defenses. Such a weight of kinetic energy only made the repelling force fields more effective.

Gift could see plainly how the first incoming round to reach its target hit squarely on the flight deck's forward elevator. Not with the speed of a bullet; more like a runaway ground truck. The blast picked up the whole platform, sailing it like a chip right against what passed for a control island on this carrier, pinning a fold of the transparent wall of the life compound beneath it.

Gift in his armor was thrown across his little cell, and slammed into a bulkhead. He picked himself up, as quickly as he could in the slow and clumsy suit. Reflexively, he reached for his helmet, then changed his mind and threw the pot aside.

Laval, who had been in the act of mounting to his favorite observation post, was hurled to the deck. A moment later he bounced up, looking around him wildly.

The first blast had torn the roof right off Gift's cell, and for the second time in a few hours he thought that he was dead.

The transparent roof above, which he had judged to be some thirty meters overhead, had broken like a cheap window. Shards were falling, swirling, in the makeshift gravity. One struck him on the shoulder of his suit.

There came another dazzling blast, hurling people off their feet and causing minor damage. That was only another near miss, Gift told himself, in the threatened privacy of his own skull.

But there was no doubt, no thinking at all required, about the next one. The only question was whether anyone at all had survived; somehow they all did.

And when that roar had faded, the Templar bellowed, before yet another explosion cut him off:

Mine eyes have seen the glory of the coming of the Lord;
He is trampling out the vintage where—

Another bomb penetrated the glassy deck, and for a measurable fraction of a second longer it was possible to think that not much was going to happen. Then the detonation came. Knocking a large structure, what Gift thought must be some kind of launching cradle, into a massive superstructure that towered over the flight deck at one side, forming one solid supporting wall for the flimsy-looking cover that had been improvised to shelter life units.

Drifting Ensign Bright was now watching the most spectacular show that he had ever seen, or ever hoped to see. And now, with all the attacking spacers in this wave still alive, he was able for the first time to pick up a great deal of their talk on his suit radio. Pilots abandoning their usual controlled voices, exchanging directions, and yelling their triumph, in the clear.

Solarian scout ships brought back word to their admirals that the enemy carrier machines indeed were burning, parts of them melting down like furious fission piles. Clouds of gas and fine debris were dribbling and bursting into space.

About half of these smart bombs, even those launched in the last, successful Solarian strikes, missed their targets, were deflected, or failed to detonate.

But enough of them, and more than enough, hit home to get the job done.

Some people returning from the day's earlier missions had reported hits, but never in such glowing, detailed terms. When these latest reports reached the Solarian carriers, and were confirmed by unemotional machines, triumphant rejoicing reigned among the admirals and their staffs.

But in the next minute, even as the holostage still held before them the evidence of triumph, they were once more grimly cautious and alert. The battle wasn't over yet.

Naguance said: "The enemy is going to attack our carriers too, as soon as he—it—they—can find us. We don't know how many attack machines they may have already put in space."

Someone in the company of one of the Solarian admirals was wondering aloud about those eleven enemy battleships whose presence in the region could be deduced from broken codes. Only one of those murderous machines, the *Hate,* had been accounted for so far—fortunately it was too distant from either Solarian task force to be able to bring its heavy weapons to bear on any of humanity's large ships; and those weapons were too ponderous to work well against the darting small-ship onslaughts.

But no one on the human side knew where the other ten berserker dreadnoughts might have got to. Since the raid on Point Diamond, humanity in the Gulf had nothing that could stand up toe-to-toe and match them in open battle. Even one of those huge berserkers, getting in range of Fifty Fifty, could raise holy hell with all the installations on the ground.

People at every level of command kept fretting about these matters, though most people did so silently. It would be hell to see those monsters come bursting out of a nebula within missile range. Or C-plus cannon. Intelligence had given its opinion that the remaining battleships would be safely out of the way for another day or two, and intelligence had been proven right so far. But still . . .

One of the berserker carriers, because of the need to make defensive maneuvers in the first hour of fighting, had become considerably separated from the other three, making fighter-machine coverage of them all a problem.

And the movement of what Solarians were calling the Main Body toward Fifty Fifty had been temporarily stopped, with the big units of the berserker fleet kept busy making defensive maneuvers.

Of course, thought someone on the flagship *Venture,* finely coordinated attacks were the goal of every military planner. If you had to take on a fleet much larger than your own, that kind of operation offered the only reasonable chance of success. But there was no possibility of the Solarian commander's waiting until his crews and machines should get themselves into some ideal state of readiness.

· · ·

Back on Uhao, a suspicion that Nash was goodlife had briefly worried both Traskeluk and Jory. In Jory's case the doubt was promptly dismissed. She had met her boss only briefly, and could not say that she liked him, but she had been through a battle with him, and would have a hard time believing such an accusation.

And any remaining doubt the journalist might have felt was completely laid to rest the moment Nash walked in the door and discovered the damage. The dumbfounded look on his face was utterly convincing.

Commander R, when at last she was interviewed by security officials (even they had had a hard time getting to her in this busy time), told her questioners that she had noticed nothing strange about Traskeluk's behavior, or Gift's, during her last brief meetings with them at Hypo HQ. "After all they had been through, one would expect the dear boys to be still a little upset, no?"

Traskeluk and Jory were now both somewhat receptive to the idea that Gift had possibly joined some goodlife cell, maybe had belonged to one for a long time, instead of being, as Trask put it, just a damned yellow-bellied coward. But Jory was not so sure about the coward part. And neither she nor Trask could really be sure about the goodlife.

Of course the authorities were now at least formally suspicious of everyone who had recently been in the house where the berserker had been hidden.

Traskeluk, as a war hero, was the least likely subject of further investigation. Gift shared pretty much the same status. But there seemed a good chance that the missing man had been the victim of foul play. A full-scale search was now launched for Nifty, whether he proved to be victim or perpetrator.

The idea that a goodlife agent might have infiltrated Hypo as deeply as either of those two men was a frightening one indeed. It implied that there might be another agent in some position that was even more sensitive.

An alternate theory was that the heroic Gift had been kidnapped or done away with by some goodlife cult or cell.

Traskeluk, belatedly accepting the ride to the hospital, thought things over as he watched the scenery go by.

The record indicated Gift had really been here in Nash's house. It suggested that Nifty had been willingly or unwillingly involved with goodlife . . . it was looking less and less likely that he, Trask, would ever be in a position to carry out his vow of vengeance.

Which, Traskeluk decided, trying to find a comfortable position for his burned back, was just as well.

Maybe tomorrow or the next day he would send his father and grandfather that letter after all. But it would be a different letter from the one he had first planned.

If Gift ever turned up, he would very likely be court-martialed, some day, on Traskeluk's evidence. And maybe he, Cedric Traskeluk, would stand in the dock too, for not telling the truth about the spy-ship incident. Well, if that time ever came, Traskeluk meant to tell the truth as well as he was able. If Gift never did show up, that was another matter.

Nifty had made his own choice, dug his own grave; let him lie in it.

Jory in the next seat had been watching him. "Trask."

"What?"

"You know, you're a hell of a fighter."

"Thanks. So are you."

"Thanks—a hell of a fighter, but it's my opinion that as an implacable avenger, you wouldn't have been all that effective."

Traskeluk nodded slowly. He didn't pretend not to know what she was talking about. "I'm not going to break my neck chasing the son of a bitch any further. If I ever run into him . . . "

"What'll you do?"

Traskeluk thought about it. When they reached the hospital, Jory was still waiting for her answer.

Solarian planners assigned
berserker computers ranks comparable to those in the human
forces, just as they would have done with human opponents. According to the number of units each seemed to command, and
their relative importance.

There was one berserker computer involved of even higher
"rank" than the one aboard the *War,* but that superior admiral
had remained too far away: Perhaps a thousand light-years distant from the carrier battle, aboard the largest unit in the force
of battleships that it was holding in reserve.

The plan called for a heavy attack on Fifty Fifty, in the expectation that this would lure the Solarian fleet, or whatever remained of it after the Port Diamond raid, out into battle. Then
the berserkers would shift the weight of their onslaught against
the human fleet, and crush that force decisively.

Fifty Fifty would then fall like ripe fruit—not that the
communications exchanged between enemy units used any symbol so vivid with life. Once a berserker base had been firmly established on the newly sterilized atoll, another strong raid on

Uhao, and the badlife would soon find that planet and system indefensible.

The way to the homeworlds would then lie open to the berserker hordes, and mere planetary defenses would soon fail without a fleet to support them. Before massive human reinforcements could be brought into place from other sectors, all of those worlds, including Earth itself, could be thoroughly cleansed of their great pollution, the disease of infected matter that called itself life.

But as the battle actually progressed, the battleships, with their crushing field generators, their well-nigh irresistible C-plus cannon, had been laying back too far from the carrier strike force to have any effect whatsoever on the outcome of the fight. Communication proved even more difficult than was to be expected over such distances, and the battle was effectively over before the dreadnoughts could be brought into action. To have held this force so far back now appeared as a major strategic blunder.

One of the premier's cabinet members asked: "Did you say 'human opponents'? In a war?"

"I know." She nodded her noble head of silver hair. "We strain our imaginations trying to envision even ourselves, let alone any other branch of Galactic humanity, fighting a full-scale war against other intelligent life forms. But we constantly have evidence before us that violent human conflict is possible, even common. And we know that such war can happen on the largest possible scale; the Builders engaged in at least one, of which the berserkers are our legacy. And the pre-Expansion history of Earth is full of dark passages; in fact there are long stretches in which the story seems more darkness than light."

"Yet here we are," said the secretary of war, after a thoughtful pause.

It would seem that a computer of the rank of the berserker admiral, given complete information, could produce a foolproof battle plan. But of course no military commander in history had ever been granted complete information, in the sense that a chess player surveying the board could have it. Certainly, the computers in question were getting only sporadic and misleading robot courier reports on the progress of the battle.

The controlling computer of the fourth berserker carrier, code-named *Pestilence,* found itself cruising at some distance from the first three, after all four had spent some minutes taking evasive action, which perhaps involved microjumping in and out of normal space. *Pestilence* did not succumb to the Solarian hardlauncher attacks until several hours after the first three, and managed to get off its own attack wave before it was hit. These were the machines that fatally damaged the *Lankvil.*

That Solarian ship was hit hard by the first berserker wave, but survived the assault. Heroic efforts by damage-control people and their robots made great strides in overcoming the damage inflicted.

After today's first pummeling by berserkers, *Lankvil* might well have been able to make it back to Port Diamond, either in tow or under its own power, there to undergo a second resurrection. But before it could leave the theater of operations, the wounded carrier was hit again, and heavily, in a second attack by berserker undersluggers. Soon after that, *Lankvil* had to be abandoned.

A great effort was made to evacuate all of the wounded from the dying carrier, transferring men and women to smaller, destroyer-class vessels. The effort had only partial success. In the confusion, no one passed the word to abandon ship to the medics working in the operating room.

One or two injured people struggled above decks on their own, and were eventually saved.

Hours later *Lankvil,* hopelessly battered by enemy bombs and torpedoes, gutted by fire and more exotic reactions, blew up in a maelstrom of fragments and radiation, almost two days after the last berserker carrier. One Solarian warship of the destroyer class had also been totally blasted in the same attack. The majority of the crews of both these vessels abandoned ship successfully, were picked up by other smaller Solarian craft, and survived the battle. Many hundreds more, on those two ships and others, were wounded, and the loss in fighting machines and other material was considerable. But here in the homeworlds sector, that loss could be made up in a year or so with new production. But berserkers trying to replace losses in this sector were at the end of a long, long supply line. There were reasons why they could not simply fill the Galaxy with berserker factories.

A volunteer salvage party had reboarded the carrier, a day after the official order to abandon, and were still trying to save the ship when the finally fatal attack hit home. Some died, and some survived in spectacular and unlikely ways.

One factor greatly contributing to the Solarian victory was that each of the four berserker carriers was caught loaded with numbers of small attack machines—in two cases whole squadrons—crammed together on deck below deck, all in the very process of being serviced, rearmed, and repowered for offensive missions when Solarian missiles set off secondary explosions and chain reactions among them. The energies that both sides crammed into their small craft were devastating, however and whenever they broke loose. The string of firecrackers effect, with nuclear and other exotic reactions taking the place of simple quick oxidation.

Berserker command, after the Main Force was targeted by land-based bombers and torpedo ships, had decided that a second strike on Fifty Fifty was necessary. Preparations for that strike were under way when scout machines sent word that they had discovered the Solarian carrier force, or part of it.

The defenders of the atoll remained dug in and waiting for another blow that never came.

The impact of Solarian missiles had shaken the berserker carrier, taken the damping defensive fields beyond the limit of their resistance, and bringing them down in invisible rubble that melted instantly back into the fabric of spacetime from whence it had been drawn. Nifty Gift, fighting to clear his mind after the dazing impacts, felt he had attained important insight. He decided that life, like death, had a long history of predation too. There had been living killers long before there were berserkers. The damned machines were still far behind; maybe by a billion years or so, when it came to a determination to destroy.

The artificial gravity tilted the floor of the captive humans' little compound at a sharp angle, then slowly came back again. Gift, who had fallen to hands and knees, slid over against one wall of his cell, and when he looked up, his gaze drawn by a sudden alteration in the light, he saw that the roof of his cell had been blown away.

The vital machinery below decks must have been hit hard on several levels. The force-field door of his cell had dissolved like the substance of a dream when its power supply failed. So had the gate that had earlier blocked the way to the airlock of the little ship.

Looking the other way, Gift saw that the Templar had now been freed as well; the force fields forming the almost-gelatinous cube that had confined him had vanished in the general epidemic of computer forgetfulness. But the man was evidently weak from long imprisonment, or had been stunned by the concussion; he too was down on hands and knees, and for once he did not seem about to burst into song.

The indications were that every berserker brain aboard, or at least any which had been concerned with the management of prisoners and goodlife, had been knocked silly by the string of hits.

Laval, tumbled from his observation post, lay at least momentarily stunned. For the moment, at least, the artificial gravity was holding.

Gift had hated him at first sight, before he had even put his dirty hands on Flower.

Before the blasts struck home, Gavrilov and Laval had been arguing about many things, several of which had sounded quite insane to Gift. These topics had included the likelihood of berserkers being able someday to counterfeit humanity successfully with machines, and the chance that faithful goodlife would be granted bodies of well-nigh imperishable mechanism.

And now Nifty had an inspiration. What Laval and Gavrilov yearned to be given, the gift of true berserkerhood, he would take for himself. Many days ago he had, in a sense, become one with the enemy.

And the war had already made a start at purging his body of flesh and blood.

Gift was already moving as fast as his unwelcome armor would allow. He quickly got out of his cell, before the power should decide to come back on, and his force-field door be reinstated. As soon as he was out he began to unfasten the segments of the useless suit. Section by section he cast it from him, to lie on the deck beside the helmet, which in itself would be useless without the suit.

He had got that far when a fierce rumble of new blasts below decks, secondary explosions, delayed results of the Solarian missiles, toppled him momentarily from his feet again.

But it was all right now, Gift thought, standing erect in his ragged and filthy civilian clothes. The garments he'd put on—how many days ago?—when he had wanted to look like he was going to a picnic. Sooner or later the big berserker got its rippers into everyone, and he was now about to do all that he could do. . . .

And Gift stalked around the corner to confront the goodlife.

Even though Gift fully realized what Flower and her friends had done to him, he still felt somehow responsible for Flower. He was inclined to forgive her, though not the others, for dragging him out here, to an astronomical distance from the rest of humanity, to face certain death.

He almost expected to discover the shadowy forms of Terrin and Traskeluk standing with the odd little Solarian group.

He felt at least a passing impulse to punish Flower, if he could, along with all the rest.

Flower from her confinement stared at him in utter blank astonishment.

Laval looked at him with pure incomprehension. "Who're you?" The viceroy got out at last.

"I am your Teacher." Nifty had cleared his throat before he started, and now he made his voice higher than usual, close to a monotone. The little quaver that came into it unbidden would not sound strange to anyone who'd ever heard the squeaking and squawking of berserker speech.

People on the bridge of Naguance's flagship were listening to the radio reports coming in, the actual cross talk of the battle, which increased dramatically in volume once the shooting had actually started. Little need for comsilence then. Recon ships had gone out to survey the blasted berserker fleet, having succeeded in getting close enough to confirm the damage, and sent robot couriers back to the Solarian fleet with recordings to be viewed on holostage.

No doubt about it, a glorious victory. Three of the Four Horsemen had already vanished, disappeared from sight in the flames and smoke of their own destruction.

The fourth enemy carrier was wrecked a couple of hours later, by flights of small ships from *Venture* and *Lankvil.*

In a closely related action, the berserker analog of a heavy cruiser was destroyed. Two such machines, their mechanical brains scrambled by combat or Solarian mindbeams, crashed into each other while retreating, and one was seriously damaged in the collision.

Days later, the logbook of Naguance's flagship showed that three berserker spacecraft carriers, code-named by humans *Death, Famine,* and *War,* had been destroyed in six minutes of intense attack by a few squadrons of livecrewed Solarian hardlaunchers.

Losses in the wave that was finally successful totaled fourteen, out of fifty-four ships. The Voids had been too far out of position to stop the Solarian small ships from attacking, but did manage to blast some of them after they had released their missiles.

None of those shot out of space in this phase of the action were from *Lankvil*. All had been launched from *Venture*, and many of these ditched when they were damaged or ran out of fuel. Even when not directly hit, they had exhausted their last reserves of power in the fight, shooting at the enemy and shielding themselves, and had nothing left to get home on.

The survivors among those who forced home the winning attack—and this time the great majority survived—realized that somehow the door to success had been opened for them by a greater number of other squadrons, who had sacrificed their lives in what for many hours had seemed to be a hopeless effort.

One option for berserker control at that point had been to take fighters still below decks and scheduled for escort service and switch them to defense—but that of course would have lessened the probability of the berserker attack succeeding, when it could finally be launched.

Computers were every bit as vulnerable as organic brains to the fog of war—perhaps more so. With communications blurred by distance and by combat, even as were those of the badlife enemy, berserker control opted to use the bulk of its fighters for offensive purposes. So far the Solarian attacks had proven ineffective. The probability mounted that any assaults still to come would be just as inept.

The decision was to endure whatever attacks might come, meanwhile preparing a decisive counterstrike against the Solarian carriers.

Taking stock of the battle overall, after the last shot was fired, some 332 small berserker fighting machines, tactical spacecraft, had been permanently ruined, the majority of these while nestled in the storage decks of their carriers.

Comparable Solarian loss was 147. Almost all of these (except for whatever was on *Lankvil*) were lost in space. Almost none were destroyed on the ground or on a carrier.

The objective of this berserker task force had never been to blast the space islands of Fifty Fifty to atoms—which could have been an almost impossible task, even if the place had been undefended. Rather they intended to preserve at least the basic structure of the islands, so that the berserkers in turn would be able to use them as a base.

A Solarian critique of the battle conducted shortly after it was over attributed the human victory to the series of eight successive attacks by Solarian small ships of as many different squadrons. Each attack in itself, except the last, had been no more than a gallant and costly failure. Their overall effect had been to leave the four heavy berserker fighter transports almost undamaged—but the fighting and maneuvering necessary to preserve the four and their supporting and protecting machines had left them just sufficiently disorganized and out of position to be vulnerable—amateurishly, almost ludicrously so—when the last Solarian assault, in the form of two squadrons of hard-launchers, came in.

The fact that the four heavy carriers had been forced out of their chosen formation, had become strung-out through a considerably greater volume of space, meant that more fighters would have been required to give them adequate protection.

THIRTY ONE

The optelectronic brain called fleet admiral by its living opponents was aware, emotionlessly but thoroughly, of the disaster that had overtaken it, and the magnitude of the setback suffered by the whole berserker cause.

The flag machine that carried the chief berserker computer was now burning and melting on every side. Explosions wracked it, the drive had failed, and the hydrogen power lamps were out.

In the midst of chaos and destruction, the unit that Solarians called a berserker admiral paused very briefly, emotionless as always, to dispatch a message to another carrier in its task force, intending to make sure of the condition of all the life units on board: All experiments with viable life forms to cease immediately, on all machines of the task force. All life aboard to be eliminated, by the most efficient method locally available. Good- and badlife alike would be reduced to jelly under the first pressure of combat acceleration, once the artificial gravity in the life-support areas had been turned off. Of course a follow-up sterilization of the jelly would then be required, to obliterate all microorganisms.

Having taken care of that last bit of business, the fleet admiral arranged to shift its flag, to have itself physically transferred to a smaller machine. It was now obvious that the big one it had been riding on was doomed.

The solid-state components housing the admiral's programming, its intelligence, were no bigger than a Solarian armful of Solarian human heads. Whether at rest or being moved about, they were always encased in a bulk of armor, and closely connected to a power supply, that made the total package considerably larger.

A new strategic plan would be required. New pathways must be conceived and developed, leading to the inevitable goal of the destruction of all Galactic life.

But aboard the single other carrier that indeed had life units aboard, the order for their disposal was never acknowledged. The first or second Solarian hit on this carrier—all four carriers were now being hit—knocked out or at least fragmented the great machine's memory, as well as almost paralyzing its ability to act.

With the possible destruction of the small berserker brain in charge of handling goodlife, the computer net aboard this particular carrier had for the time being totally forgotten that it had any life units on board at all.

Gift, confronting the two goodlife men, was keenly aware of Flower screaming at him, rattling her locked chain, pleading to be released, but he kept himself from turning his gaze in her direction. On his own face he was able to hold a smile.

Laval and Gavrilov, recovering from the first shock of the missile strike, stared at each other, and there was a moment in which it seemed that they might try to kill each other—for no better reason than that each wished to demonstrate for the Teacher a homicidal goodlife enthusiasm.

Gavrilov had not objected to Flower's being chained for punishment, and he was indifferent to her situation now. Laval had been actively intending to use her in a very nonmachine way. But for the moment both men had practically forgotten her existence.

The other woman, she whose name Gift had never heard, was already dead, killed with merciful speed by one of the missile strikes. Her body lay caught under the edge of the elevator platform, which when blasted loose from the ruined flight deck had caved in one side of the small area set aside for life support.

The Templar, though temporarily stunned, had been released from his bonds, as a result of some secondary explosion or power failure below decks. His inert form, now fully visible clad in a spacer's shipboard coverall, sat slumped against a bulkhead, partway between where Gift was standing and the open hatch of the little yacht.

The world lurched beneath them. Secondary explosions, somewhere below, continued beating out such life as the great carrier of death possessed, right under the humans' feet.

Gavrilov was also particularly aware of the yacht as a possible means of escape, and was arguing that they should use the small ship as a means of transport to one of the other large berserkers, and there continue to serve the Teachers, keeping up the fight against humanity—while of course preserving their own miserable lives.

But Laval was not going anywhere. He babbled that their loyalty was being tested—only minutes ago, if Gift had heard them right, both goodlife men had been asking their Teacher to give them some test of loyalty.

Laval and Gavrilov turned simultaneously to confront Gift. They were surprised at the appearance of this stranger, but he could tell from their faces that the meaning of his presence hadn't fully registered with them as yet. Gift could see that subtlety on his part wasn't going to work. This pair of donkeys had not really caught the idea that should have been so obvious to them: That Gift was a berserker, the latest in secret weapons, the long-awaited android that was able to move among Solarians undetected, accepted as one of them.

Ignoring the two damned fools, he strode forward, and was standing at the side of Flower and trying to get her loose, when Laval woke up at last. The would-be viceroy simply barked at Gift as if he thought this newcomer a mere human.

Gift reminded himself again to control his voice, to make it sometimes jerky and uneven, as if the damned machines had not yet quite been able to achieve such a seemingly simple effect.

"Badlife," he said, doing his best to transfix Laval with an icy glare. "Badlife, stand back."

But Laval only glared back at him for a moment, then demanded: "Who the hell are you?"

Gift could think of nothing better to do than maintain his gaze in frozen silence. The "viceroy" abruptly spun away. Two strides on the sloping deck carried Laval to the side of a damage-control machine that had gone dead right in the compound. The last blast had tipped it over, like many other objects on the now-slanting deck. From a kind of caddy on the back of the machine, Laval seized up a cutting torch.

Gift saw Flower out of the corner of his eye, and heard her, still screaming and pleading to be released. But he ignored her and took a forward step, straight toward the bright, needlesharp flame that was suddenly being thrust in his direction.

It was as if, after all, the universe might have suddenly repented all the nasty things that it had ever done to Nifty Gift.

He knew that waiting behind him, not fifty steps away, was the very ship that had brought him and Flower out to the berserker. For all he knew, the small yacht's drive and autopilot were all ready to go—there was no reason they could not be. The ship lay with its passenger hatch opened directly into breathing space. The atmosphere was starting to go, but yet there remained a little space and time.

The opening in the transparent wall that had given access to the ship's hatch had automatically sealed itself; there had been some kind of lock there to allow the ship to come in without prematurely killing all of the berserker's prisoners. But he was sure that there were holes, only little holes so far, in the transparent barriers that kept in air. He could hear his life and everyone else's whining out through those holes into the deep.

When Laval came right at Nifty with the torch, Gift deliberately thrust his left hand in the weapon's way. This tactic enabled him to grab the tool right by the nozzle. He felt no more than a stinging vibration up his arm as the flame took off most of his artificial hand. Meanwhile, he brought his right hand around to seized the torch by its handle and pull it free of the other's suddenly paralyzed grasp.

"Slime unit Laval," he said on impulse, in his slightly quavering berserker voice, "if you are still determined to be recorded, one step in the process is now available. We'll get rid of that messy organic body right now."

Keeping his face as blank as possible, Gift held the arm up where his audience would get the best possible view, displaying the injury; the shocking absence of blood. In the breathless silence, he made his voice as flat and machinelike as he could. "Badlife, after all. The Teacher will punish both of you."

What remained of his mechanical hand was dangling, and he seized it with his own good hand, burning his live fingers in the process, and with a wrench tore the useless thing away from the mechanical wrist, which still held firm.

Laval groaned. His eyes were fixed on the ruin of the artificial hand, with the look of a man beholding his own death. He made no effort to defend himself as Gift reversed the torch and cut him down with it. Flesh and clothing steamed and burned.

Gavrilov, unable to tear his gaze from the shattered machinery of Gift's left hand and arm, had been totally convinced in an instant that Gift was indeed a machine.

"Teacher, forgive me! . . . I am so utterly stupid. . . . I—I thought you were only a slime unit, like me." He stared at Gift with a strange mixture of pleading and reproach.

But a moment later this surviving opponent had taken a step backward and was staring at Gift's forehead. Suddenly leveling a pointing forefinger on a trembling hand, Gavrilov charged: "Blood."

Something must have scratched him, one of those times when he was knocked down; he hadn't even noticed it till now. "Of course," said Nifty Gift. "I'm very realistic. They made me quite convincing. I look just like a badlife spacer. Goddamn heroic badlife spacer." And he advanced, thrusting forward with the torch again. It was a very effective weapon, but not an instant killer, and Gavrilov tried to dodge out of the way, and Gift had to keep at it for a while. What was left of the atmosphere now smelled like a giant barbecue.

"Just goes to show you," Gift said in his robotic voice, looking carefully at what was left of his two late opponents, for any signs of life.

And then he turned away and struggled one-handed, using the awkward and unfamiliar cutting torch, to release Flower from her bonds.

As he stepped close to her again, she recoiled from him in horror.

Gift said: "I am one of the good machines you always wanted to meet. Come, we are leaving." The torch had taken care of the chain quite nicely.

She kept staring at him with as much astonishment as either of the men had shown. She seemed incapable of moving, until Gift with his one still functional and fleshly hand grabbed her by the arm and started dragging her away.

Abruptly she started screaming again. What now? Maybe, he thought, it was just the impact of the discovery that her lover was no more than a machine.

He didn't try to hold her. And Flower, suddenly released, tore away from him and went running for the open hatch of the little ship.

Gift tried to follow. His first awareness of the Templar's presence came when he heard a hoarse cry of triumph from behind him, and saw from the corner of his eye a figure darting forward. Before Gift could fully turn, a smashing impact on the back of his head threw up a Galactic panoply of stars across his eyes and brain, then plunged him into darkness.

Some time later—it couldn't have been very long—he regained consciousness, and got back on his feet, too late. The air was going quickly now through all the leaks, and his life would soon be going with it.

Turning around shakily, Gift stood staring at the spot where the little spaceship had been sitting. The wall had closed over the empty spot where its hatch had been, preserving a remnant of atmosphere a little longer.

Neither Flower nor the Templar were anywhere to be seen. There were still only dead bodies and frozen machinery.

"Victory. Somebody ought to sing," said a voice very close to Nifty Gift. It took him a moment to realize that he himself had spoken. The air was going out faster now, and everywhere he looked there were only dead human bodies and frozen machines.

Something moved, flashing past at high speed outside the barrier, and Gift in solemn greeting and salute, raised an arm to the last wave of attacking Solarian small ships. None of them were going to see him now. But with image enhancement of their recordings later, who could say what might be possible? He'd seen some pretty amazing tricks pulled off.

No more missiles came. They would be wasted on this ruined target.

And then he could no longer stand. Oh yes. Singing. It was hard to draw a good breath in this lousy air, but Nifty remembered what lines came next, and he whispered them through bloody lips:

> . . . the grapes of wrath are stored
> He hath loosed the fateful lightning of his terrible swift
> sword . . .

The hardlauncher crews who unleashed the finally successful missiles, saw, and were quick to report, that they had delivered a succession of fatal blows on three of the four berserker carriers.

The livecrews in the Solarian fighting ships yelled and screamed their elation inside their silver helmets. Mailed fists, helpless to strike the enemy directly, pounded joyfully on console ledges. The virtual worlds through which these men and women saw the world erupted in glory, in the symbols of their chosen languages.

None of the attackers ever realized that there were some goodlife people, and also at least one badlife prisoner, on one of the big berserkers when it went smash.

It would have been quite impossible for any living crew member on an attacker to distinguish human bodies, living or dead, on or near the great berserker, as the hardlauncher swept

376 · · · · F R E D   S A B E R H A G E N

by in its curve of flight; a path that would take it back into flightspace the instant that became practical.

A military analyst reviewing the battle of Fifty Fifty, after it was safely over, reported thoughtfully:

"Out of all that chaos, out of all that confused heroism that seemed so futile—somehow came tactical beauty, victory, perfection. As if some superhuman genius had planned it all. . . ."

A Solarian colleague disagreed. "We can claim no genius. Not in this case, at least. Not except for the code breakers. We just had damned good luck."

"There's more to it than that. We had to be there, fighting, ready for the good luck when it came."

At the crucial moment, not only were the great majority of the small berserker interceptor machines low on power. With all the berserker carriers' energies devoted to arming and armoring their small machines for the next offensive strike, the defensive force fields were weak all around the great launching platforms. Shifting power back to them could not be accomplished instantly.

In some cases too, the small machines' computers were no longer functioning at peak efficiency because of an overload of combat information. Trying to formulate a plan that would account for the apparent craziness of Solarian tactics and weapons sent them reaching too far. Very few of their problems were really owed to the direct action of Solarian weapons.

But most importantly, in meeting the series of previous attacks, which had followed one after another in rapid succession, the berserker fighters now found themselves hopelessly out of position to defend against the climactic one. Their position was analogous to that of airborne fighters caught at low altitude while an attack screamed in from on high. Meaning they had to go around a large cloud of gas or dust to get back to their own motherships and the attackers.

· · ·

Do you know karate? someone asked. A descriptive phrase, long used to describe that art, floated up from somewhere: Empty hands, and a mind like the Moon.

Well, our hands were damn near empty. That was a little too true for comfort.

The overall effect, something the Solarian command would have loved to achieve, but which no planner on their side could take credit for, was that of an exquisite combination of kicks and punches, none of which really got home except the last. But that last blow was quite enough. It hit with catastrophic effect. Unplanned; and yet, in a sense, the Solarians had forced the winning combination by their planning, by determining on an unremitting attack.

At last, after a long run of bad luck, the determination of leaders and fighters alike had them in a position where they were ready to take advantage of superb good luck when it came. The enemy lay for the moment exposed to a barrage of deadly punches.

Early journalistic reports credited the heavier land-based Solarian ships, the Stronghold farlaunchers coming out from Fifty Fifty, with doing most of the damage to the enemy—in fact, they had inflicted no real damage at all.

Ensign Bright, still alive, still strong enough to wave vigorously with his good arm, was picked up by a Solarian patrol craft, a long-range ship coming out from Fifty Fifty, on the day after the big battle, after spending approximately one full day in space. What remained of the enemy fleet had withdrawn hours ago—they were heading back across the Gulf, with Solarian task forces in cautious, tentative pursuit. Fortunately, he hadn't been *too* close—just near enough to have a ringside seat at a comparatively safe distance from the doomed machine, as *Pestilence,* code name for the fourth berserker carrier, burned and finally exploded.

One never knew whether a given big berserker was carrying human prisoners or not—logic suggested that the chances were very small, because such a situation was really rare—

berserkers were single-mindedly devoted to killing people, not making them uncomfortable. But legend thought otherwise, and the situation did come up from time to time. Well, if *Pestilence* had had any live victims in its grip, they certainly hadn't come through all that alive.

Some berserker fighters, Voids, getting back into defensive position a few minutes too late to save their last carrier, observed the little spaceship's liftoff from the flight deck. Most of these orphaned killers, all of them doomed themselves, assumed that a small craft lifting from a berserker must be under berserker control, while a substantial minority of the Voids' computer brains were quite as confused as organic pilots in their place would have been, so that they found it impossible to compute any decision regarding the small ship. It got away unscathed.

"I never saw the like before," the escaping Templar told his new shipmate, in one of his more lucid moments. "It looked almost exactly like a man—might have convinced me—except where its arm was broken, I could see the hardware spilling out."

Flower was hardly listening. She was punching commands into the autopilot, not knowing or caring where she was telling the yacht to carry her, as long as it got her away—somewhere.

The fourth berserker carrier blew up, its fragments vanishing irrecoverably into a tricky local fold of spacetime, some four standard hours after the other three, and seventeen hours after being first hit by Solarian missiles.

And with that the Battle of Fifty Fifty was effectively concluded.

The Four Horsemen of the Apocalypse had been beaten back yet again—the heart of Solarian humanity was still beating, and home could still be defended at something of a distance.

Compared to other great, decisive battles of Solarian history, the casualties in the battle of Fifty Fifty were very small, almost trivial—except of course when considered from the viewpoint of the individuals and the units directly concerned. In this sense too it must be counted as a defeat for the berserkers. The Solarians officially lost 307 people killed, and 147 small ships, in addition to one carrier and one vessel of the destroyer class.

Some experts described the site of the battle, the environment out in the middle of the Gulf, as being subject to cyclical changes analogous to those of day and night upon a planetary surface. Certain great thin gas clouds tended to go through regular phases. This under the right conditions afforded ship captains and admirals certain opportunities to maneuver free from all but the unluckiest chance of enemy observation.

Pulsations from variable stars washed through nebulae of varying density, and synchronized pulsars played a part in creating cyclic changes with a period of hours. Those stellar objects produced heavy microwave transmissions, but almost all of their radiation was absorbed inside the gas.

Thus heavy disturbances in the interstellar medium could propagate in a periodic way, driven by pulsar beams. Mere humans and machines remained to some extent at the mercy of forces that reduced to insignificance anything that they might do.

Both sides naturally tried hard to predict how this

"weather" was going to be days in advance. But chaotic behavior in the gasses and dust clouds made it impossible to tell more than a couple of standard days ahead.

In one of these periods of diminished visibility, causing confusion in the radar wavelengths as well as visual, an interregnum that was expected to last for several hours, the Solarian fleet retreated toward Galactic east (i.e., roughly toward Port Diamond and Earth), rather than risk a direct encounter, at comparatively close range, with the berserker battleships that were still believed to be somewhere in the region. Those battlewagons were probably faster, in either kind of space, than any of the big carriers on either side.

Still, all of the human recon efforts during the course of the battle of Fifty Fifty turned up no more than a single battleship, the *Hate*, though several times cruiser-class machines were mistakenly identified as dreadnoughts.

Intelligence intercepts—those that had been made before the enemy's last code change, or else as soon as the new code was broken—confirmed that berserker command had made a strategic decision to keep those ships of the line—little more than spacegoing gun platforms—well in the rear. In fact no battleship on either side ever saw action during the entire battle.

The berserker units that had been so fortunately (from the point of view of Life) kept in reserve could, if brought forward in time, have done a superb job in reducing the land-based defenses of Fifty Fifty, pounding the place into a lifeless, steamy fog bank of little particles. But before they would have been able to get in range to do that, they would have been vulnerable to attack by small fighters and bombers coming out from the islands. To the enemy, this did not seem to be the time or place to gamble heavy assets.

And admirals on both sides pondered a large question: Was it possible that the day of the battleship was truly over?

Some people aboard the ships of the task force grumbled angrily when the admiral, having at last stunned and staggered the enemy, ordered a retreat. The protesters swore that

Naguance was making a blunder, wasting all the good fortune that had brought success to the task force; he should now be going after the crippled enemy with all the force that he could muster.

Naguance listened to the arguments from some of his staff, and though some were impassioned, they did not sway him. When he thought he had heard enough on the subject, he told the arguers so, in no uncertain terms.

After setting a course that would take his fleet away from the berserkers for several hours, perhaps keeping in normal space all the while, or maybe making a few routine jumps, the Solarian fleet, relishing success but wary—and after a prudent hesitation perhaps dictated by the uncertainties in Galactic "weather"—turned back toward the enemy again.

The admiral's aides who had complained about his sudden lack of enthusiasm for battle began to understand. Naguance was hanging in the area, ready to fight again as soon as conditions turned favorable for the Solarian side—but he was doing his best to avoid running into a fleet of battleships at close range and head-on.

Long-range visibility was pretty good again. Now, if the berserkers were still intent on trying to take Fifty Fifty, the livecrewed ships were ready to resume the task of defending it.

A journalist aboard the flagship took note of the fact that Admiral Naguance had turned east, away from the enemy, then north (toward the Galactic Core) for three quarters of an hour, then south, then back west again a couple of hours later.

Wise maneuvering, but, as it proved unnecessary. The enemy was in full retreat.

The berserker fleet had now lost all four of the carriers that formed its heart, and which had provided the reason for its existence. Before the battle, the linked computers forming the berserker general staff had calculated that any setback of that magnitude was so wildly improbable as not to deserve serious consideration.

But now they remembered that one simulation, in which

the lifeless computers prepared themselves for battle, had ended similarly. But that result had been discarded—it computed as too unlikely.

However, now that the disaster had happened, berserker command decided to withdraw rather than risk the rest of their fleet in what looked like a losing fight.

After finally deciding to commit their battleships, but then being unable to locate the main Solarian fleet, they determined to return instead to their distant base and stronghold, where the plan had been made for the ultimate assault on Earth. The vast computers ran test programs on themselves, and on each other; the results were inconclusive. Something had gone severely wrong, and it was hard to determine what.

Solarian scoutships located the enemy again, and kept it in sight for a long time, as the shattered berserker task force headed back across the Gulf. Robot couriers came in with reports from the network of automated spies. The retreat was genuine. The war would go on, as fiercely as ever, but for the time being, and for some number of years to come, Earth was saved.

Back on Uhao, Cedric Traskeluk, at the landing field to watch part of the fleet come home, from time to time still braced himself for an uglier confrontation that would never come.

And now, only a few meters from Cedric Traskeluk, here came Ensign Bright, moving briskly among a small crowd of other walking wounded, stepping on the ramp of a landed shuttle, into clean air and sunlight, being welcomed home by weeping relatives. Music performed by live musicians stumbled and glittered in the fragrant air.

A young woman and a child came rushing in the forefront of the waiting crowd, their arms open to enfold their man, as he ran the last few steps to meet them.

Down on them all shone the brilliant sun of Uhao, where Bright had been stationed and his ship had been based. The planet was his carrier's home port.

And was still his.